STREET
SONGS 1

STREET SONGS 1

New Voices in Fiction

Edited by Jane Hill

LONGSTREET PRESS
Atlanta, Georgia

Published by
LONGSTREET PRESS, INC.
2150 Newmarket Parkway
Suite 102
Marietta, Georgia 30067

Printed in the United States of America
94 93 92 91 90   5 4 3 2 1

Library of Congress Catalog Card Number: 89-63788

ISBN 0-929264-27-4 pbk.
ISBN 0-929264-36-3

Design by Laura Ellis. Cover painting by Susan Sisk.

"The Hua Guofeng Memorial Warehouse," by Glen Allen, was first published in *Quarry*, Vol. 38, No. 1 (Winter 1989); PO Box 1061, Kingston, ON, Canada K7L 4Y5. "Crow Man," by Tom Bailey, was first published in *Greensboro Review*, No. 45 (Winter 1988-89). "News of the World," by Louis Berney, first appeared in *The New Yorker*, April 3, 1989. Copyright © 1989 by Louis Berney. Reprinted by permission. "The Bear Head," by Will Evans, first appeared in *New England Review and Bread Loaf Quarterly*, Vol. XII, No. 1 (Autumn 1989). "Square Dance," by Elizabeth Graver, was first published in *Story*, Vol. 7, No. 1 (Autumn 1989). "Quickening," by Terry Griggs, first appeared in *Malahat Review*, No. 87 (June 1989). "What I Wanted Most of All," by Daniel Hayes (Vol. XXX, No. 1 [Spring 1989]), and "The Whale," by Philip Simmons (Vol. XXX, No. 2 [Summer 1989]), reprinted from *Massachusetts Review*, copyright © 1989 by The Massachusetts Review, Inc. "Wheat Fields Under Threatening Skies with Crows," by Paula Horowitz, first appeared in *Pennsylvania Review*, Vol. 4, No. 1. "Twenty Clicks," by Ivor Irwin, was first published in *Indiana Review*, Vol. 12, No. 2 (Spring 1989). "We Gather Together," by Eugene Kraft, was first published in *New Mexico Humanities Review*, No. 31. "Astronauts," by Wally Lamb, was first published in *Missouri Review*, Vol. XII, No. 2. "The Minor Leagues," by Scott Lasser, first appeared in *Wind*, Vol. 19, No. 65. "The Nature of Some Things," by Karen Latuchie, was first published in *Paris Review*, No. 112 (Winter 1989). "Kenosha," by Joseph W. Mockus, first appeared in *STORIES*, No. 22. "Family," by Lance Olsen, was first published in *Iowa Review*, Vol. 19, No. 1 (Winter 1989). Copyright © 1989 by the University of Iowa. "The Girl from the Red Cross," by Sharon Sakson, was first published in *Nimrod*, International Literary Journal, Vol. 33, No. 1 (Fall/Winter 1989), published by the Arts and Humanities Council of Tulsa, Oklahoma. "Kerby Dick Launches His Wife onto the International Art Sea," by Rose Scollard, was first published in *The Fiddlehead*, No. 160 (Summer 1989). "Obstetrics," by Michael Lee West, first appeared in *Kennesaw Review*, Vol. 2, No. 1. "Up," by Gary D. Wilson, originally appeared in the Baltimore *City Paper*, October 20, 1989.

CONTENTS

PREFACE

The stories included in *Street Songs 1* were chosen from
those published in the magazines listed in the appendix
at the end of this book and from those nominated by
teachers, writers, and agents. The only requirements for
consideration were that the story had appeared in a
serial publication copyrighted in 1989 and that the
author had not, as of December 31, 1989, published a
book of fiction, either a novel or a collection of short
stories.

The writers included in the anthology could have,
and some have, published a book of nonfiction or poetry.
They could have been included in another anthology.
They could have published any number of individual
stories. Translations and excerpts from novels were not
knowingly considered.

The magazines, both commercial and literary, listed
in the appendix were generous enough to respond to our
request for a complimentary subscription so that their
fiction could be part of the selection process. It is our
hope that additional magazines will choose to participate
in future years. For it is our plan to make *Street Songs*
an annual event, a fixture of our spring list, and to make
it as comprehensive a representation of the American
and Canadian literary scenes as possible.

Because little magazines and journals often find
themselves behind in production and printing schedules
for various reasons, we have chosen to consider copyright dates rather than the dates given on title pages and
spines in order to let a story compete with the other
stories that were made available to readers in a given
calendar year.

The response from magazine editors in the United
States and Canada has been overwhelming in its generosity and its enthusiasm. At a time when many literary

and little magazines are facing serious budget crises, these men and women did not hesitate to support our efforts on behalf of new writers. They sent their magazines, paid postage, and often took the time to write a note of support and encouragement as well. The project would never have gotten off the ground without them, and their contribution to its success is immeasurable.

In a similar way, teachers and directors of writing programs across the country took time from their already overcrowded schedules to nominate work by their students — to send copies of stories and to provide biographical information on the writers, many of whom had already completed the writing programs and moved on. These teachers and others who responded by calling our attention to work of merit are also responsible for the successful launching of *Street Songs*, and their contribution is greatly appreciated.

In a very real way, the twenty stories presented in this book stand for the energy and enthusiasm with which the project itself was greeted, represent all the new writers — young and old, in writing programs or not — who are working, day in and day out, to keep writing alive, to tell the necessary stories. The twenty stories in *Street Songs 1* and the magazines in which they appear have been chosen to honor the accomplishment of their authors, the contribution of their original publishers. But the honor also extends to the other stories and other magazines that were part of the process. The larger honor is bestowed upon the raising of new voices and the providing of outlets for those voices.

Invaluable editorial assistance with this project was provided by Allison Adams, Bob Hill, Betsy Martin, and Joycelyn Woolfolk, and my students, past and present, in the creative writing program of the Continuing Education division at Kennesaw State College. They have made and continue to make me rethink and reevaluate my sense of fiction, week in and week out, make me per-petually clarify, for them and for myself, what makes a story work.

And, finally, Chuck Perry made the project pos-sible by making a commitment when it was nothing more than an idea in my mind and by sticking to that commit-ment when the complexity and the demands of that idea revealed themselves.

To all of these people, my lasting thanks.

—Jane Hill
Atlanta, Georgia
January 1990

MARIO PASCO, THE WOW PRINCIPLE, AND THE GOOD FIGHT: AN INTRODUCTION

It is the spring of 1966, or maybe it is the fall of 1965, and Mario Pasco is sitting on a bench in the breezeway of Florida High in Tallahassee, playing guitar and singing "You Were on My Mind," a song made popular by a group called We Five. I still hear that song now and then on the all-oldies station I listen to on the way to work because I liked the woman who did the show two sets of morning drive-time personnel ago. But when I hear it on the radio, it is not the We Five I hear so much as it is Mario Pasco. I hear him and see him and remember the tiny pieces of his story that I know.

His mother, Mrs. Pasco, had been my Latin teacher in eighth grade. She was one of those myths of a teacher. Tall and strong, with her graying hair done up in a style that was French, or at the very least foreign, to us, she wore clothes that seemed quite bohemian when we compared them to what our mothers were wearing to the supermarket and to drive the carpool—long, flowing skirts and soft, loose blouses that she wore belted outside the skirts. They tended toward purples and blacks and complex patterns that reinforced the foreign feel of her. She spoke in a wonderfully strange and perfectly accented English (and Latin, too, I suppose, although she told us Latin was no longer a spoken language). She taught sitting in a rattan stool that was really a chair with a back and arms, elevated as if her lectern were a bar at which she were sipping a cool drink and conversing intelligently with her peers, unless she was at the blackboard conjugating or declining. She was our best teacher and also our favorite, a rare combination. We both admired and loved her.

On the Friday of President Kennedy's assassination, someone — another teacher, a secretary, the principal, I don't remember who — came to the door of our classroom, fifth period, and told Mrs. Pasco that the President had been shot. She returned to her stool and went on with the lesson, whatever it was. She didn't tell us what had happened, but we knew something was wrong. The liveliness that made her our favorite was gone. She was pale and stumbled over her words. She was not herself. Later, in sixth period, when the President had died and the principal made an announcement over the intercom and we all prayed, for this was 1963 and in the South at least we still prayed at school, we all knew what the messenger at the door had told Mrs. Pasco. An ardent Democrat and a model of a citizen, she felt the tragedy in a personal way that all of us could sense, ignorant though we were of what being an ardent Democrat meant, arrogant though we were about death itself.

The next year Mrs. Pasco was gone from Elizabeth Cobb Junior High, replaced by a Mrs. Murphy, whom we all mistreated terribly, for we had expected Mrs. Pasco to teach us not only ninth-grade Latin but also ninth-grade English. Through no fault of her own, the decidedly inferior Mrs. Murphy found herself trapped in a classroom with a gravely disappointed bunch for not one but two periods a day.

We all knew why Mrs. Pasco was gone. The spring before, the spring after the President's death, her husband had been killed as he crossed the street after a school board meeting. They had what seemed like lots of children, five or maybe six, I think, and a public school teacher didn't make enough money in those days (or these) to take care of such a large family alone. So Mrs. Pasco had left the public schools to take a job at Florida High, the laboratory school of Florida State University, where pay and benefits were better than in the public schools. Or at least this is the story we all accepted as true from listening to our mothers discuss it. The change also meant that all of Mrs. Pasco's children would get to go to Florida High as well, and usually there was a long waiting list for the limited student positions at the school.

My parents had put my brothers and me on that waiting list when we moved from South Carolina to Florida in the fall of 1962. It took three years, but just as I finished Cobb, positions for me and for one of my brothers opened up. I was all set to go on to Leon High, the school Mr. Pasco was leaving when he was killed, with the friends I, a shy and unaggressive adolescent, had finally made. But I had no say in the matter, no vote. We went to Florida High. It turned out not to be such a bad place. My brother, in fact, found himself with Mrs. Pasco for an English teacher. He was not as interested in school or English as I was, and it didn't mean as much to him. But he did have Mrs. Pasco, who sat in the familiar chair, elevated and regal still.

I clung to the vision of her walking the breezeways, in the cafeteria and the library because she was familiar and I was feeling, yet again, like a displaced person. That was the year I first read *The Old Man and the Sea* and understood symbolism, which I explained to my best friend, who was happily ensconced at Leon, when we went to see the movie *A Thousand Clowns*. When Jason Robards feels that he's a piece of meat being thrown to the lions as he sets off to find a job, I said to her, "That's symbolism." It was also the year I had to take a class called Americanism vs. Communism, the year I began to study Spanish, the year I first went to school with blacks because Florida High desegregated before anybody forced them to.

I made some friends, went to ballgames, won a tennis tournament. But I never felt that I belonged. The following summer we moved back to South Carolina for good, and, more than any other year of my school life,

3

that year at Florida High seems like a dream, an aberration in the pattern of my growing up. Maybe that is why I remember Mario Pasco in the breezeway with his guitar, singing away during the lunch break and each afternoon after school. For he too seemed an aberration, there because of his parents and events beyond his control.

I never spoke to him, can't say I knew him. The girls who stood close around while he sang, the girls who were his friends, I suppose, smoked cigarettes and wore eye make-up and dark hose. They drove themselves to school. One rode a scooter. Their mothers didn't pick them up. That's for sure. Perhaps he was singing for them, to attract them. But in my mind there is an inviolate circle of space between him and these girls, a mystical preservation of his identity, his suffering, his art, like the circle that surrounds Hester Prynne. I focus on what's inside that circle: Mario and his song, that one simple, quiet song that I remember (though surely he sang others as well), the scene colored as it was and is for me by the bits and pieces of his family's story that I had access to.

Back in South Carolina there would not be anybody like Mario Pasco at the school where I finished my last two years and graduated. I would be two years into college before such people became common on my campus. "A hippie," the jocks and cheerleaders and student council presidents and good old boys and girls I hung out with would have called him, "a dirty hippie," maybe. After a while I wasn't such an outsider anymore. I was back home, and the ways of home are hard to shake. My protests weren't loud or long enough when my friends tried to make excuses for Kent State and the Cambodian bombings and all the other things that were to happen. But I held on to that image of a boy who'd known loss and suffering making music, singing his song, on sweet, innocent high-school afternoons, as a quietly gutsy thing to do in the midst of all the ordinary straining to be what everybody wanted you to be. I held on to the notion that people stronger than I were about large things in the world. I remembered Mario Pasco, or what I had made of Mario Pasco. A symbol.

In the months since the idea for *Street Songs* emerged, I have thought, every so often, of Mario Pasco. He has been my totem for the project. As I've opened hundreds of issues of magazines and read the eligible stories, I have tried to think of each writer as Mario Pasco. I have seen them sitting in the bright Florida sun, partly obscured by the late fifties architecture of a Florida building, but bathed nonetheless in a magical yellow haze. I have envisioned each writer as reaching out, through words, art, to a small circle of admirers. And from the dizzying swirl of what came to seem a million Marios, I have chosen twenty in hopes of widening their circle of admirers, of saying to them that there are those of us who listen and admire, people they'll never know, never suspect that they have touched.

Street Songs was born on a wet, chilly afternoon in early April 1989, as my husband and I drove home to Atlanta from a literary festival in Chattanooga. There had been much to praise and celebrate in the gathering: fine talks and readings by Gail Godwin, William Styron, Josephine Humphreys; the startling discovery of a talent as fresh and genuine as Larry Brown; the palpable interest of Chattanooga's non-academic community in serious literature; the beautiful restoration of an historic downtown theater. But there was also the overwhelming feeling of despair and depression that overtakes me each time I sit through a panel on the future of literature, the health of serious writing in my region, my country. No matter how much I promise beforehand that they won't, such discussions leave me feeling as paralyzed and silent as I was when my high-school and college friends shouted down my feeble efforts to join the protests against our government's actions in My Lai or Selma or Kent.

I couldn't change the essential nature of how books are published and sold in this country. I couldn't reverse the trend away from solid mid-list titles toward blockbuster-only list-making. I couldn't stop takeovers and mergers and loss of personal identity in publishing houses. I couldn't restore funding to the hundreds of little magazines and journals that Reagan-era cuts in budgets for the arts had crippled or destroyed. I couldn't counter the dominance of bookstores that lure even the most devoted purchaser with convenience and deep discounts, while their no-surprises cookie-cutter predictability in the selections they offer fatally wounds many worthy books before they have a fighting chance.

I think of Thoreau and his insistence that no enterprise can succeed unless it pays heed to the sacred minority, but the sad truth is that what Thoreau thinks hardly matters to bookselling and publishing these dark, dismal days of short attention spans and MTV mindsets.

OK. OK. We've all heard it all before, as my husband is too kind to point out on trips permeated by my litany of injustices and inequities for right-minded people everywhere. At least it's a short drive from Chattanooga to Atlanta.

Then, seized by an uncharacteristic urge to think positively, I decided to stop enumerating what I couldn't do and speculate on what I might be able to accomplish. My New-Age friends would probably say that I stopped blocking the flow of positive vibrations, or some such. Left-brained creature that I am, I prefer to think I became logical instead of emotional. Either way, *Street Songs* is what I can do, what Longstreet Press can do.

Here, then, are twenty stories, the twenty best stories I read, by writers who haven't yet published a book of fiction.

Yes, there are other best-of anthologies each year, most of them quite good. But most are dominated by established writers; many of the best stories are written by people who are household names. When's the last time such a collection didn't feature a Joyce Carol Oates story, for example, have one or more Updike stories listed as finalists or outstanding or something else superlative? This is not to say that the stories aren't superlative. It is to say that the new kids on the block don't have much chance against such competition. It would be like expecting Mario Pasco to have drawn any audience at all if Joan Baez had been singing from the next bench down on the breezeway.

And, yes, there have been other efforts to give new voices a chance, the old *Intro* series, now to be revived under the auspices of the AWP, for example. But most upstart projects that succeed slowly begin to look a lot like the establishment they started up against. When Arsenio Hall first began his late-night talk show, it was rumored that nobody who appeared on his show would appear on Carson's. And certainly *The Arsenio Hall Show* remains a real-party party, compared to the *Tonight Show*, which is these days more like a stale dinner party most nights. But haven't we started to see crossover guests? Aren't the same films being hyped and clipped on both? Isn't Arsenio's bandleader getting essentially the same press Doc gets, or did? How do you capitalize on success and stay young and hungry at the same time?

I don't know. This is only *Street Songs 1*. But the idea is that by limiting the contributors to those writers who have not yet published their first book of fiction — whether they are associated with a writing program or writing in total isolation from any and all communities of writers — we can keep ourselves true to the spirit of the project. We also hope we can further the careers of promising writers who will go on to become the stand-bys of other best-of collections, who will be the Oates of *Best American Short Stories of 1997*, the Carver of the O. Henrys of 2003. We'd like for some of those future household names to find a home at Longstreet. We'll be happy for serious readers everywhere if others find other publishing homes.

So how do you decide what's best? There's an inherent arrogance in the process. For a while I tried to pretend to myself that I was using logical criteria — originality of plot and language, significance of theme, coherent blend of form and content, impeccable structure, memorable voice. But along about November I started to panic. There was so little time left, so many stories. How could I read, apply the logical and necessary criteria, go back and do comparative analyses among possible finalists? Was this such a good idea after all? Who was I to judge? In short, negative thought crept in, established a foothold, and wouldn't budge.

Then my family came for Thanksgiving. They are from rural South Carolina, a place where there is no cable TV. Thus, their main pleasure in our home is, apparently, to lie inert before our set, remote control in hand, and flip through our thirty-plus channels for seventy-two uninterrupted hours. From this ocean of sound and images, I seized upon one, drawn from a commercial, and have clung to it like a drowning woman, substituting one mediocre advertiser's phrasing for all my high-blown critical criteria. I have adopted the wow theory as my one selection principle. The Wow Store is a new commercial enterprise, opened just in time for the holiday shopping bonanza. Their ads feature "normal" folks exclaiming "Wow!" every time they hear the price of an item for sale in the store. These are truly bad ads, the way lots of locally produced commercials are, the kind you suspect of starring the closest relations of the person who owns the business. But they made me realize that I was choosing stories that made me feel the way this store's prices allegedly made these normal folks feel. I was picking stories that made me say "Wow!" for whatever reason.

I know this is not the sort of admission you make in these days of deconstruction and semiotics and new historicism. But there is literary precedent. Emily Dickinson said you knew it was poetry if it took the top of your head off. I knew it was a winner if it made me say "Wow!" After all, it's pretty hard to make somebody who reads "slush pile" manuscripts say "Wow!" We tend to be a pretty jaded and hard-to-impress bunch, we slush-pile readers. So there it is, an honest statement of my editorial criterion: the wow principle.

A person says "Wow!" in different tones, for different reasons, of course. Some of the wows that found their way into the final version of *Street Songs* surprised me. I don't like baseball. I usually think of it as a lot of impolite spitting and scratching in public. But Scott Lasser's image of the coach in his lawn chair, watching boys play ball in a midwestern field, wouldn't leave my mind. Likewise Eugene Kraft's Mennonite narrator's deconstruction of *Uncle Tom's Cabin* and the nineteenth-century American press. I couldn't forget them. Just as I couldn't explain what exactly it was that drew me to the young woman in Sharon Sakson's story "The Girl from the Red Cross." Then I realized that she is a twentieth-century Daisy Miller: young, beautiful, innocent, American, caught up in the complexities of a foreign setting with the power both to appreciate and destroy her. Once I figured that out, I was wowed.

Others I knew from the moment I first read the story that they'd be there in the end. How could Louis Berney's opera singer's panties not be included? Those perch rising to the surface in praise of golden Kenosha in Joseph Mockus's story? Tom Bailey's description of the aviation derring-do of Mississippi crop dusters in the thirties? The wet tights and panties left by the Brownie in Elizabeth Graver's "Square Dance"?

I'm a sucker for certain kinds of stories. As soon as I realized Wally Lamb knows, truly knows, what it is to be an English teacher in a public high school, he had me. I was wowed. But other kinds of stories I tend to resist. I like realism. Yet Lance Olsen made his ghostly visitors as real to me as any family reunion I've ever heard about. The same for Mattie Dick's dead children in Rose Scollard's story. They are as alive for me as they are for Mattie and her husband. I see them there, playing with their animals, lying in fields awash with flowers blooming in concert despite seasonal differences, different requirements of soil and light.

That's an important advantage of the wow principle. It allows you to stick to your preconceived, logically developed standards when you want to and permits otherwise inexplicable and contradictory deviations when you need them. The wow principle also makes it possible to honor equally a story that makes you rejoice at the good humor of a character's triumph, as I did when I read Michael Lee West's "Obstetrics" and Glen Allen's "The Hua Guofeng Memorial Warehouse," and a story that disturbs certain fundamental assumptions in ways that are, finally, unresolvable, as is the case in "Twenty Clicks," "The Nature of Some Things," "Quickening," "What I Wanted Most of All." Then there are those stories that do both of these in a single tale: Philip Simmons's "The Whale" was, for me, a regular roller coaster of wows. I was laughing one minute, profoundly disturbed the next.

Sometimes a surprising moment appears in a story of ordinary family life, as in Will Evans's "The Bear Head." Other times, as in Gary Wilson's "Up," ordinary life seems altogether suspended, the whole story a freeze-frame moment of surprise. Either way, I was wowed. Or, again, there are those stories that are magical combinations of both these approaches. In Paula Horowitz's "Wheat Field Under Threatening Skies with Crows," ordinary life for the characters has been suspended by impending death. Yet they create, through the force of imagination, a series of surprising moments to carry them through their odd suspension. Wow!

All in all, the wow principle has served me well, I think, and the writers and their stories, I hope. For the most arrogant thing of all is to assume that good writing, well-told stories have no place in commercial publishing. The magazines in which these stories first appeared — mostly small, non-commercial publications fighting every issue for their lives, economically and editorially — are in the trenches, fighting the good fight year in and year out, giving new voices their own breezeways with just-right light and a devoted band of listeners. They are doing the hardest work. The greatest glory is theirs. *Street Songs* is an effort at reinforcement. It calls attention to those magazines, their editors, and their sponsoring institutions, as well as to the authors of the chosen stories and to all the fine stories there is not room enough or time enough to include, in hopes of calling a broader attention to their solid efforts, in hopes of giving new life, new voice, to some necessary story too long unspoken and unheard.

The importance of this mission — of telling the necessary stories against commercial odds and popular sensibility — was brought home to me when I took a night off from finishing *Street Songs* and went to see the film *Glory*, which tells the story of the 54th regiment of the Army of Massachusetts, the first black regiment in the U.S. Army, and of their courageous assault on an impregnable Confederate fort during the Civil War. *Glory* is a wonderful movie, a fine piece of art, and should be seen for that reason alone. But, as someone who grew up and was educated in the state where the historic battle took place and who was eventually certified to teach in that state, I grew increasingly ashamed of my arrogance about my own knowledge as I watched the story that the film has to tell.

I began to think that my students would have been better off if I had been able to tell them the story of these men who had marched through their very town instead of telling them how to make their verbs and subjects agree, instead of telling them about a mythic Scottish king who was seized by ambition and listened too much to his wife and a bunch of witches. What if no one had had the courage to risk millions of dollars on a serious film about a black Civil War regiment? What if everyone had said Who'll buy a ticket to see that? Who cares?

Suddenly, I'm back to those overwhelming, unsolvable problems that filled the air on my drive home from Chattanooga. I'm facing a brick wall so wide and so high nobody, least of all me, will ever get over it. So what to do?

Remember Mario Pasco and how he's lived a life of almost twenty-five years in the mind of a woman he'll never even know he touched with his breezeway singing.

Find that space in the wall where a brick or two is missing. Squeeze through.

Remember that there are a million ways to make a reader say "Wow!" Remember that space you've found, pass through it twenty of them now, another twenty later, and so on.

Thus, *Street Songs*, the beginning of a tradition that we hope will someday take its place in the larger tradition of the good fight, the struggle to keep the necessary stories alive, again and again. The writers, the characters, the stories here will continue to be on my mind, just as Mario Pasco and his mother and their stories, or my versions of their stories, are still on my mind after all these years. May some of them find their way into your mind, too.

May you say "Wow!" at least twice.

GLEN ALLEN

The Hua Guofeng Memorial Warehouse

from Quarry

If there had been one thing in Chicken Man Wang's life that never seemed to end, that came back and back again like a meal of spoiled tofu on a hot day, it was loss itself.

He had lost his sturdy mother and angelic father to one of Chiang Kai Shek's hangmen three years before Liberation. He had lost his only brother, drowned swimming to Hong Kong. He had lost his wife, when, on the day of their wedding sixteen years before, a jealous cadre had assigned her to "northern duty" thirty-two hundred kilometres away (she left within the hour, waving madly from the back of an army truck, so he had not, at least, lost his innocence).

He had lost a year of his life during the Great Leap Forward when he was locked in a windowless barn with thirty-five other comrades, all, like him, English teachers at the Fukien Institute of Foreign Languages. He had lost another seven years during the Cultural Revolution (it was then that he lost his hair) digging yams in the countryside with other banished intellectuals.

He had lost his chance to go to an American university when a colleague, reading a page of a diary he had lost, noticed a politically dubious quotation from John Donne and reported him to the Leadership.

In the heady days following the Downfall of the Gang of Four he had lost his bicycle and most of his teeth in the first fight he had ever had in his life (he lost) with a deeply aggrieved Maoist cousin.

Yet it seemed to his comrades that Wang wanted nothing, that he loved his aloneness, the bareness of his room perched out above the nursery where he could hear the happy cries and songs of the commune's children. Everyone saw that he managed to live contentedly without a radio or TV set (he had lost all his consumer points when one afternoon, deep in Byron, he had failed to present himself at the airport for the arrival of the institute's first foreign expert, a fat man from Canada accompanied by his fat family). Indeed he had no appliance beyond a splendid pencil sharpener sent to him by an uncle in Kuala Lumpur (it had stopped working years before).

And Wang had not lost the respect and affection of his neighbors. Everyone, workers and intellectuals alike, loved him for his generosity and resourcefulness. He always had cooking oil left over from his monthly ration and gave it to the most deserving. He was called "Chicken Man" because every Spring Festival he slaughtered the dozen chickens he raised every year, leaving their bald and headless bodies on the doorsteps of the lame, the halt, the blind, the mentally ill, the politically discouraged and the two hapless teachers of Russian on the campus. He was only sorry there were never enough to go around.

Wang was "correct," they all said, a scholar in his field and a sympathetic teacher who, even when volunteer labor was not compulsory, soon began to spend his Friday afternoons collecting the night soil from behind the Canadian family's apartment, a job no one else would do, for the Canadians, as everyone had remarked, smelled grotesquely of milk and butter.

They also called him "Chicken Man" because, with his uncanny skinniness, the loose wattles that gathered at his scrawny fifty-year-old throat and the way his long chicken limbs flailed at the soggy tropical air when at 4:30 every morning, long before the loudspeakers brayed the morning message, he jogged through the ragged jungles of mimosa and hibiscus all the way to the filthy commune fish pond and back, he looked like nothing so much as some underfed and demented cockerel.

"There goes the Chicken Man," said Old Chen each morning through the baffles of the mosquito net which separated her from her snoring husband. Old Chen, alert all night to the sounds of domestic discord coming from her neighbors on either side, never slept and spent the night hours reliving her memories of the Long March to Yenan, so that when she heard the pad-pad-pad of Wang's light feet passing by she knew that sunrise was near and that the past was again about to become the tedious present.

"There goes a real socialist," she shrilled at her companion, the disgraced son of a Manchurian general who had never worked in his life, who spent his empty days reading bad erotic verse into his giant bootlegged tape recorder and who had disappointed her many times.

But Wang had a dark and terrible secret. His faith in socialism had gone the way of everything else, though fear and endless practice had given him the colors of a true believer. When every morning and evening he scattered crumbs and purloined grain for his fowl, calling out in his chicken man's voice that cut across the searing heat like some antique piccolo —"here Shakespeare, here Hemingway, here Dickens and Dreiser" — to his hungry

17

little flock, he often dreamed of a future full of forbidden comforts: American bathrooms, steam heat, cheeseburgers, long sleek cars, profit and loss. Sometimes in his mind's eye he saw a chicken factory as grand as the East Wind Hotel in nearby Anwei, with tons of glistening chicken flesh, mountains of eggs, riches beyond counting.

"With my money I would buy an office, a position, just as they do in America," he told Grand-Uncle Yu, an unregenerate opium smoker so ancient that the Revolution had passed him by without leaving a trace on his old capitalist heart. "Something modest but useful," said Wang, recalling a classmate who had become deputy director of the Sixth Ministry of Waxes, Soaps, Foodstuffs and Footwear in the capital and a man who every year sent him cards showing himself displayed against the yawning door of a Red Flag limousine.

"Just once," he told Yu, coloring with embarrassment at the great gulf of his greed, "I would like to eat lean pork, see foreign films, wear real leather on my feet."

Yu yawned widely, showing a gobful of black and snaggled teeth. He was not only Wang's only living relative but his only confidant, the keeper of his clandestine ambitions. But Wang's enormous guilt bored him.

"My son," he said, idly stirring a pot of ugly green broth on the charcoal stove in the corner of the little hut from which he dispensed herbal medicines to those who had given up on pills, doctors and hospitals, "we are all imperfect. We all have dreams. In the old days I had money in seven Shanghai banks, a concubine, a home three floors high and a leather chair stuffed with the hair of wild Mongolian ponies.

"It will all happen again, just like the turning of the seasons," said Yu, who saw China's recent history, the many years he had lived, as simply a series of circles returning on themselves.

"This," he said, waving out his tiny doorway at the exhausted Chinese earth, the crumbling piss-yellow buildings and a water buffalo, its impossibly thin body covered with elaborate designs of blue blowflies, that was relieving itself on the front steps of the students' dining room, "this will not last forever. Your moment will come and when it does you will know."

And so it happened that late one night word sped from door to door that China's leader and Party chairman, Hua Guofeng, the man put in office by the great Helmsman himself, had been dismissed. So it had been reported on the public television set that flickered to life from time to time outside the junior teachers' quarters. The camera had shown Hua's bulbous squirrel's face and the announcer had proclaimed that he was "indisposed" and would be replaced in all his functions.

Like priests reading a particularly complicated set of entrails, all members of the community set to analysing the wording of the announcement, its position and duration on the national news and the conjunctions of the moment. Alone and together they concluded that there was a new order in Beijing, and they were not wrong.

Wang could not get to bed that night and sat for hours in his only chair staring absent-eyed at the comings and goings of a lizard that skated jerkily over the fractured walls of his room.

It was two in the morning when the idea flowered in him. He jammed his feet into his cloth slippers, bounded out of his chair and hurried off to Yu's hut. Yu that day had got his monthly prescription for opium, a right reserved for all aged and confirmed addicts, and was deep in revery, his mind illumined with visions of the rich past, his youth, restaurant meals, fine silks on his back, the downy skin of his mistress. He felt himself a tree in early spring, sweet sap rising from trunk to branch to twig to bloom.

"Uncle," cried Wang to his all but unconscious elder. "The time you talked of has come. My mind is full of plans." Wang then told the old man of his scheme, so far-fetched and perilous that he spoke in a whisper, so daring and pregnant with promise that he could hardly catch his breath.

Yu, when he heard what Wang had to say, returned to reality, laid his pipe aside, and said "Yes, it is right. Wait until tomorrow night when I am rested and I will help."

Then the old man groped among the galaxy of vials and bottles beside his sleeping mat for the decanter of Szechuanese green bamboo liquor with which he celebrated all great occasions, and the two drank, both sealing and legitimizing their singular enterprise.

The next day at nightfall Wang and his great-uncle rode out on Yu's bicycle, Wang's gaunt legs dragging in the dust, Yu's rachitic body driven by an energy he hadn't felt for years. They headed for the nearest village where, one by one, they entered the school, the party headquarters and the office of the village tea corporation, all of them unlocked and empty. From each public room they stripped one of the large grinning portraits of Hua that decorated every civic wall in China. Night after night they visited all the communes and hamlets around, returning in the early morning with thick rolls of posters of the fallen leader.

After two weeks they had hundreds, but it was not enough. They ventured into the city, this time in daylight, telling the cadres of the government buildings they called on that they had been sent by the provincial Party office to remove the offending portraits. And they were believed, for as all knew Hua's face and name both were being expunged from national life. It would soon be as if he had never existed at all: texts would be rewritten, newspapers removed from files, official films would be destroyed.

When Yu's tiny quarters were teeming with rolls of Hua posters, so many of them that he had to cover them with blankets to hide them from his clients, he told Wang that until their work was realized — until Mao's line was restored, until Hua returned to power and the posters could be resold before they could be reprinted (for this was their design) — they would have to be kept elsewhere. They agreed there was only one safe repository for their contraband, a neglected but weatherproof shack, perhaps the only building in the whole country that was not in use, that had variously served as a rough jail, a depot for outdated political tracts and a millet silo. "This will be our warehouse," said Yu, drunk with his own cleverness. "This will be the Hua Guofeng Memorial Warehouse," he said, cackling wildly at this small deception of the State that had so cruelly and resolutely impoverished their lives.

Wang often wondered in the awful weeks ahead why things went wrong and decided he should have known it all along — in China there was always someone watching, always someone there to see, always a fellow citizen to open the door of a vacant building for no other reason than to be alone. There was no patch of ground, no hill, no valley, no paddy, no vantage point, not even a single tree that could be climbed that ever remained long untenanted.

Why such alarm then that an idle peasant came to the stone shed where the portraits lay in stacks and saw Wang bent over counting them, reckoning the riches they promised? The man, doing no more than his duty, told his brigade chairman, who told the security police, who told the administrators of Wang's institute.

Days later Wang was summoned to a meeting of the Leadership — Director Liu, his thirty-six vice-directors, the chairman of the local Party committee and six of his colleagues in the English department.

Even before he was asked he confessed all: his infatuation with free enterprise, the theft of the posters and, worst of all, his conviction that Hua Guofeng (and so the followers of Mao) would lead the country again one day. He was long used to making confessions of all kinds. It came easily to him.

When he had finished speaking there was wide surmise in his inquisitors' eyes. Even Director Liu, who had forgone his nap to chair the meeting, awakened briefly to glare at him. Wang heard a roaring of blood, a train going through his head, and pondered the punishments they could prescribe. Death? Imprisonment? Banishment again to the dead countryside? Most terrible of all, the confiscation of his books? His precious Shakespeare, the illicit compendium of Joyce given him by a visiting tourist, his Byron, Keats and Shelley, his tattered copy of *Middlemarch*?

"Comrade, we are at a loss for words," said Chang, a fat panda of a man who had never been speechless in his life and who had been named as Wang's accuser. Chang had always hated Wang since a loud and very public discussion in the faculty years before about the uses of the preposition *from*, during which he had demonstrated his truly astonishing ignorance of the language he was supposed to teach.

Chang felt moved to bellow at him. "We must think of the students," he said, "of the example you have set them. To them and to us this is no less than treason. News of this will get to Beijing. We will all be disgraced."

Wang stood there in silence, feeling that his dry mouth was full of feathers. He wished they would allow him to sit and thought of the straight-backed chair in his room, its stern integrity and rigorous angles. He yearned for a chair.

Then his mind raced away from the assembly of his judges and betters to Hsiao Fen, the woman he had married, and settled on the one day in their short and furtive courtship when she had allowed him to lead her into a thicket of bamboo on White Cloud Mountain to hold her doll-like hand, trembling in his like a captured bird.

"You have betrayed us all," shouted Chang, chopping at the long table with his obese paw.

Then there were coughs and much shuffling of feet. A typewriter broke out in a distant room. All heads turned to Director Liu at the end of the long table, who had once again slid open his little red eyes. The verdict would be his. But like so many cadres of his rank he had reached a position of power by never speaking in terms of facts and numbers and issues and things that must be done. Rather he delivered himself of elaborate and ambiguous epigrams in rendering decisions, windy maxims that could almost always be open to any interpretation. When he spoke at a meeting there was always a second or even third caucus of his underlings to decide what it was he had said. Only the week before, examining the case of a newly arrived Peruvian expert who had illegally acquired a dog, Liu said after five hours of wrangling by his juniors that "a black hen can lay white eggs" and left the room. All present nodded their heads at the man's wisdom and at further meetings ruled that Liu had meant that the animal should be commandeered and later serve as the main dish at an institute banquet held to honor the thirty-second anniversary of Liberation.

This day Liu's theme was maritime: as his eyes bore into Wang's he said "He who rows the boat seldom rocks it." There was little confusion in his message and the words fell on Wang like a rain of stones. He had been condemned.

Two weeks later while Wang was putting out water for his flock, a small grey panel truck carrying two sick-looking men wearing dirty, much-patched beige smocks and plastic sandals drove up to his door.

"We are doctors Ma and Tang from Public Hospital No. 14," one of them told him, "and you are to come with us."

Though not a word had been said about Wang's fate, he had been expecting them. "They certainly won't put you in jail," said Uncle Yu after the haunting meeting with the Leadership. "Too many people have been to too many jails. They'll send you for a rest somewhere till all is forgotten. You are too valuable to all of us."

Wang knew that Hospital No. 14 was one of two psychiatric hospitals in the provincial capital, and a place children feared in their dreams. But he had to go somewhere. His job had been taken from him, his students and neighbors both would no longer look him in the eye, and only the day before he had found the neatly severed body of a rat resting against his door. He had been put outside the others, he was as much a stranger as he had been when he came to the place years before.

"We must hurry," said the doctors. "We have many more calls to make today." They pored over a long and filthy piece of paper and said "Our instructions are that you may bring one book with you and, if you insist, one of your chickens."

Wang climbed up above the nursery one last time and entered his room, quickly surveying the pitiful inventory of his life — the enamel tea pot, the coal brazier he used to fight the chill of winter, the crude framed portrait of his murdered mother, an old calendar with its dates clipped off, the lizard frozen on the wall and the tiny frog hopping about the far and perpetually damp corner by his tumbledown bed.

From his shelf of books he took his copy of the Christian Bible for no reason other than that he had never had time to read it before. And from his chickens he selected his favorite, a black bantam rooster named Byron, a gluttonous and bad-tempered bird for which he had the special affection one feels for all rogues and runts. With the holy book in one hand, he scooped Byron into the other and settled into the doctors' vehicle. It occurred to him that he had not been in an automobile for a full decade, and he carefully watched the changing of gears, veers in direction and applying of brakes as they passed the commune's pig-killing pen and the miniscule barbershop where those who had hair lined up for the clumsy attentions of Wei the barber, a lunatic ex-farmer who babbled endlessly of the limits of outer space to his customers. Then they drove by the graveyard of perfectly good heavy machinery, rusting away as it awaited replacement parts that never came, then over the black and viscous Lotus River, so full of oil and chemical contaminants that now and then it caught fire.

The hospital was a comely old building that had once been the clubhouse of a polo league for the Europeans who had owned and run all the businesses in the city. It had a rambling open courtyard with two immense banyan trees whose penumbras seemed to fill the sky.

Within a week Wang had blended with his fellow patients, only two or three of whom seemed mentally disturbed. The others, like him, had taken a wrong turn somewhere. There was a prominent mathematician from Hangzhou who had unwisely found himself courting and then proposing to three different women in three different cities using three different names. There was a teacher of Vietnamese so taken with his subject that he had begun an enthusiastic correspondence with the government of the new, unified Vietnam, China's latest enemy. There was a master bricklayer who had made a sumptuous life for himself by casting the I Ching for lonely widows. Another was a professor of Western music, under perpetual suspicion as it was, who had been caught playing the music of Stevie Wonder to his class. A fifth was a plump Christian, born in Macao, who had led a protest against the unseemly racket caused by the firing squads that abutted his house. Yet one more, a choleric Szechuanese doctor, had refused direct orders from his hospital's directors to put unlicensed newborn babies in the delivery room refrigerator. These and the others were joined by the two weary psychiatrists, Ma and Tang, doomed to tending the perfectly well.

The hospital inmates spent their days together sitting on the burls of the huge trees and hovering over their plain meals of lentils and rice—learning from one another until all were English scholars, speakers of Vietnamese, aficionados of Elvis Presley, experts in masonry, mathematicians and lay psychiatrists themselves.

Wang felt a great ease among his new friends and never once thought of the life he had left behind. Late at night he read his Bible, memorizing the books of Job and Genesis, his busy mind filled with the possibilities of human existence and the good cheer of brotherhood.

When one summer day a year later, the sun beating on the gong of the flat, hard hospital yard, Old Yu wheezed through the gates on his bicycle Wang felt almost troubled at being reminded, even by so true a friend, of the far-off institute.

Yu, who, as always, had escaped all punishment for his role in Wang's calamitous adventure, bore a letter from Director Liu saying that he was forgiven and needed again.

Wang fingered the letter as if it were something both unwanted and even hateful, gingerly setting it on the scarred table in his room. Then he introduced his old uncle to his friends and offered him a cup of tea from the thermos put outside his door every morning.

Yu was won over by what he saw and said, "I think you'd be insane to leave here. I have never seen you looking so well. America could not be better than this place."

He advised Wang to return Liu's letter with a reply saying he was not well yet. So Wang did, writing "I am still unworthy of your confidence. My terrible error is still much with me," and gave the letter to Yu to take back to the Leadership.

"And it is true, my uncle," he told Yu. "I can never go back. A man alone lives like a wolf. I am no longer alone."

That night came the first of the season's typhoons. Byron, wandering about in the dark and lashing rain, his small chicken brain intent on finding shards of nuts and candy sent to the hospital by well-wishing relatives, was hit by a falling branch and died.

When Wang and the others found him the next morning they dressed his body in fine gauze and buried him deep in the muck by the quickening stream that ran by the hospital's far fence. Before the tiny grave was closed, Wang dropped into it a small scroll bearing a quotation from the bird's namesake.

After the others had left, Wang lingered there, the still angry sky above tinted different shades of grey, his wandering mind brimming with a whole constellation of ideas and memories: the theory of numbers, the raging seas he had never seen, Switzerland and a photograph of the Alps he had once owned, the beauty and economy of English pronouns, the perfect, hurting greenness of young rice, the roundness of buttons and wheels.

Even Byron's death brought him as much relief as pain for it meant the end of a lifetime of loss. There could only be gains from now on. On and on and on.

TOM BAILEY

Crow Man

from The Greensboro Review

nominated by John Vema

And Rarden then whining down over the border oaks, swooping down that stick, flapping rudders, to hop, skip jump down over those trees and trailing poison out of his wings, six long thin streams over twelve rows of cotton, and him so low his wheels go to brushing the bolls, a *thup-thup-thup* sound like the queen of hearts stuck in the spokes of my now grandson's bike, and his great double-winged eagle shadow bunched down so small underneath or to either side depending on the time of the summer sun. Straight up and down noon when he would spray out the last of his load, shoot his wad, as he used to say, and buzz back to Legion Field and land and then throw me his goggles and leather helmet, which he wore but of course didn't have to, and jump in his truck and head for Nadine's.

Nadine's where Naomi was, who he called Felicity Jane, and him being from the North and her some breed of Chickasaw, Choctaw, probably Negro, mixed-up kind of blood, cheekbones high and silent, but with a strong questionable nose, and wider lips than maybe she had a right to as just an Indian, and a kink to her hair which was unexplainable any other way.

The truth of the whole thing being he, Rarden, scared the shit out of people whether he was looping and swoop-diving almost crash in that plane, an old barn-storming Jenny, or at Nadine's, drinking Dixie beer or any whiskey they had, and just after twelve noon too, or before even it didn't matter to him. There to see Naomi, saying *Good afternoon, Miss Felicity Jane*, like he was a cowboy or something and this in Mississippi, and, of course, her never saying nothing, and not even hardly raising her eyes.

But it was her that shot him. Nobody else had to do it. Killed him, I believe, like you would stomp the head off a wing-crippled mockingbird. And everybody always used to say there wasn't no need to shoot him even if there was a need to because the way he piloted that plane he was quick on his way to hell anyway. If you ever heard a boom of lightning-flash thunder, first you thought it was old Rarden done bought his ticket, done gone home, but then it never was, and he became a kind of legend like some nine-foot Jesus, gained a reputation, see, for being crazy and so for the most part people left him alone, just shook their heads and waited for him to die, which of course, he did, just not like they expected.

The water tower stood up like a silver head, wink-ing in the sunlight, and as I yanked back the stick and bellied by it the ground dropped and became blue way up sky and away and then spinning under and back rotating blue, green, brown where it should be, and I could read where he'd painted her name, red, candy-apple red, FELICITY JANE, over the kid signs OLD MISS REBELS, CLASS OF '25, JOEY C. LOVES S.M., and older rain-streaked and year-faded loves and cheers. There for anybody who wanted to see. FELIC-ITY JANE. Rolling that old Jenny over and spraying back through Mr. Sutton's fields close by my last tissue marker, and then empty-light and streaking straight back to Legion Field where Rarden would be looped and feeling high, ready to fly, *to be up*, after his whiskey lunch and beer and seeing Naomi. He'd tell me how fine she was. *Something.* And already wearing his leather helmet and goggles and the quick choke snort as the prop died and the dust by our shack at the airfield rose and fell in the different same place, not mattering, and him, Rarden, strolling out with that big smile on his face. *And Jasper*, he'd say to me, *she is so fine. I never met a woman like that before.* Me thinking that he probably had, but that because I was thinking of what kind of Mary Magdalin woman I thought she was and not what he thought she was. Fueling, and him up again, in love and flying, which is what he did, like some men walk or run, or go into business. He fell in love and flew. He just drank on the side.

It was Rarden taught me to fly. Nobody could see a nigger in the air. But me. I could see it and wanted it so bad I could chew it like gristle and toted gas and loaded chemicals for it and don't think nobody would never have let me up but crazy Rarden. *Hey, Jasper*, those low-ground niggers at the cafe say, *Hey, Crow man. Crow. You want to fly*, he said, grinning, ear to ear, those goggles on and dusted so he had to clear them with his finger. *Sho'*, I said. And him being from the North, Ohio or some such place, laughed, and then was a cowboy again from someplace else again, misplaced again, like he always was, a square peg in a round hole, laughing, and talking like me, saying *sho' nuf?* Put me in a cockpit and took me up. *Born with wings*, he yelled over the hum rush buzz of air, me already with the stick. And it was true. After leaving that old ground, there wasn't nothing else I ever wanted to do. Like an angel. Couldn't go back to just being some low-count field nigger no more. 'Cause I been to heaven. I seen that light. *A goddamned natural*, he said and made me his partner right on the spot, even though I told him I didn't have no money and couldn't afford to buy no stock, and he just looked at me. It was true he didn't have no idea what I was talking about and didn't want a dime.

Of course, De La Palma owned her and there never was a chance for them. Owned her not like a slave and like a slave, like a rich man owns a Chocktaw Chickasaw probably nigger that nobody else does and maybe can't get a job but that she's good-looking and quiet and was willing or didn't think enough of it not to go down on her back. But you couldn't tell that to Rarden. He'd just snort and take a drink and offer me the bottle and I'd take a swig and pass it back and him not bothering to even swipe the lip with his sleeve. That was the kind of man he was. This after work, fourteen hours of spraying, flying, and flying the thing between us, air, sky, blue, and we both could have used more, and us both sitting in our shack, with our partner name, R & J, for Rarden and Jasper, fresh-painted on the door. Crop dusters just plain too long and so we left it off.

Fine, he'd say about her, *fine*. Dreamy-like.

And me thinking there wasn't no chance in hell and saying that she was Mr. De La Palma's girl like everybody knew and nobody said or wanted to know just how, like the devil owns souls. He even owned Nadine's though everybody said it was Nadine's. But it was his jack that kept the place going. But saying to Rarden, *She's just a plain girl. Just a girl. Ain't got no people, ain't got no home.*

Felicity Jane? You talking about Felicity Jane. And this frowning, whiskey-thinking look at me. This kind a crazy look. He was crazy. And he was sane too.

And I'd say, *Well*. And leave it at that.

Now she lives down over by the Hushpuckashaw River, in a little cabin there, the trestle bridge rising

over and above her, still on De La Palma's land, though
De La Palma dead and been dead twenty years and
never touched her after she turned thirty no ways. I see
her sometimes snapping beans into a bright Indian-
looking apron. Her gray hair long down her back, like a
cape down her back, earned these fifty years since. But
we don't talk about him. Though maybe we should, both
of us being so old now, over for us, and Rarden being the
best and worst thing that ever happened to either one of
us. The only real free man, white or black or Indian,
crazy or sane, that I ever seen. And for her too. I'm sure
of that. Not De La Palma.

It was both of them that climbed the water tower.
Together. Arm over arm, hand over hand, up that
Jacob's ladder. To the top. And him toting that candy-
apple red red paint and a brush. It was the same brush
he used to paint our partner name, R & J. Up and up.
Until they were up there standing and laughing and no
doubt drinking, because there was that between them
too, or not between but *with* them — and still all that way
to go back down — but Rarden I know didn't care
because he, like any bird, was totally disregardless of
heights, and she too, like me, was more natural and alive
in the air, and so had no fear of dying that way. Wings.
Angels. Crows. Eagles. And I wonder how he saw that in
us? What he saw in us? A nigger and a Chickasaw
Choctaw half-breed nigger too? What was it about us
that he picked out? And how did we fall back to this man
and woman's ground again? 'Cept that we were out of
place as him. And him from a kind of place like Ohio?
But he did pick us. But maybe too it was us picked him.
And he took that brush out, and I can see them now, up
there, kissing, her breasts filling up that beaded shirt,
and her long lightish colt legs under her one skirt, and
swiping that brush across that tower in huge arm-
sweeping candy-apple red letters, big, FELICITY JANE.

The town unable to escape it, obvious now, even to De La Palma.

De La Palma was not one of these Southern sheriffs you see on TV and Rarden didn't hate him, not really, and he, De La Palma, got us more business, more fields — maybe just to increase the odds, more air time, more time for crashing. Give him time. Let God take care of it. He will, you know. But he got the fields for us, and we were thankful. Us flying from dusk 'til dawn to dusk again. Until it was even too much for us, much as I liked to take my turns. So Naomi quit Nadine's and her too now, up. Rotating in and out. That old Jenny whining, humming, thrumming up and up, swooping down, raining pellets to fight that old red vine, that nasty bo' weevil, all them things which creep up on man's cotton. And she was good. More than I. Both of us flying. All three of us flying high. Money. We had more money than what we knew to do with 'cause Rarden didn't want it, see. He just didn't want it. Or if he took some and used it, it wasn't like he cared about it or was hoarding it. And that was the pure thing or what made it the purest thing, flying. And at night one oil lantern and the shadows playing happy with his face and he was good and the best doing what it was he did and maybe touching Naomi's leg, playing with the fringe of her Indian kind of jacket, beads, and laughing. Drinking. And going up tomorrow. Seven days a week. Asking, *Why should you rest when you're doing what you want to do? Why should anything keep you out of the air? Nothing, man,* I'd say, I'm saying. *Nothing.*

From there, the water tower, God's perch, the whole town laid out like something you could read, like something you could understand, like a map maybe: FELICITY JANE and the silver rail tracks north-pulsing glints of sunshine, and the little block town, and then two-lane 46 highway, and quilt fields like red, brown, green, greener, greenest swatches of cloth and pieced together with the stitching border of trees. And the trestle bridge which was an old one, in fact used to swivel to let steamboats through but not any more, crossing the Hushpuckashaw River and just high enough. Just. Barely just. And like a final test of knowing your craft coming down up humping the reaching oaks and then slick slide like a fair ride and scooting down close to the water, taking the slow curve bend and then there suddenly the bridge and just enough to clear the wheels, *sppppppiiiittttzzzzz*, dragging the current, the sound of zipping fishing line trawled by a fast boat, and the wings on either side inches from the bricks and your legs warm weak and weary wonderful like after loving and hand gentle fine and squeaking out and another curve, and a kind of hop back on the stick, ballsy barnstorming, and up over leaning back and the fingers of that gravity tickling you out, upside down, rolling all the way over and loop once sliding long back over the field and out, safe and screaming the best thing you ever done. I seen him do it a hundred times. I done it three. Naomi done it every time she got the chance. And him in the back sometimes too, just riding, drinking, both hands in the air, trusting her.

Free. That's all any of us can hope for. And Rarden was. No strings. Flying. Making love. Drinking. Up and up. The only free man, white or black or anything, that I ever made the acquaintance of. Knew the real value of time and money — which is nothing unless it's to buy and have the afternoon and evening to drink whiskey — and was willing to pass on the gift of flight, or let you know if you had it, to touch you with the chance, which was enough and all anybody can ask for, didn't want to hang on to it for himself. Because Rarden was what he was. No explanations for that. And I can't explain why, because that would be like saying why

something fly and something else don't. When it flies it's
good enough. Fly it.

But Naomi. FELICITY JANE. Choctaw. Chickasaw.
Nigger. Probably white. But she grew up black, or as
good or bad as black. Outside of town. On De La
Palma's place, and that's where De La Palma found her.
Raised her really when, I'm sure, he saw her potential
for beauty. And she was beautiful in that way of mixing
which had come out somehow right and the good strong
features of four separate peoples, giving her something
nobody else — something nobody else woulda even
chosen given the choice — but she had it. Silent as an
Indian and as thoughtful. She would laugh, those nights
spent in our shack drinking and talking flying which
was the only thing to talk, R & J & FJ now on the
door — he couldn't call her just Felicity or just Jane and
never Naomi and she didn't even seem to mind or even
care what he called her, not in a bad way, but like an
Indian, as if she was who she was and a name didn't
catch her no ways, like naming the "wind" — but her
laugh was just a smile, thin-lipped, real, but reserved,
and it was only when flying that I saw her really break it
out, sparkling, beautiful.

But I'm thinking something about the end, why she
killed him. Because De La Palma owned her? Owned her
as much as the land, the soil and earth what made her
and so could never be free from that? Or that she was
free enough for a moment to free him, the best and
kindest way, and a hell of a thing too? And so I am
thinking about being free. What is it about being set
free? What is it about setting someone free? Making me
think, again, now and all these past fifty years, *And
what does free mean?*

She was up, her turn, out spraying, and we were
sitting in our partner shack, the smell of gasoline, and

Poast 316, and lime too, and the radio going on K96, playing, feet up, whiskey between us, the hot taste of fertilizer and dust still in my mouth from my own flight, almost lunchtime. When then a choke and gurgle spit sputter and out the door us already scanning the sky for the Jenny and then saw her worbling in too low to clear the power and telephone wires and then *No!* and the wheels snagged, caught, growl and snatched out of the air like swiping a fly, yanked out of the air, swung down around it, wrapped in the wire, buzzing, crackle, *BANG!* of the transformer and sizzling electricity, popping, and us both running, the plane hung from the wires by its tail like a condemned man from the rope, like a giant trophy fish, engine dead, and Naomi there slung down, arms out, and Rarden saved her, chinned up onto the propellor, shimmied up to the cockpit and pulled her out, unconscious, and lowered her down, and no sooner all of us on the ground when the wires snapped and the Jenny crumpled, nose first, into the ground.

That was the end of R & J & FJ. We had money but not enough for another plane. Rarden even went to De La Palma. De La Palma said he wished he could help us. He *wished* he could.

An angel on the ground, though maybe still an angel, is lacking. She no longer has that something which makes her special. An eagle on the ground ain't no longer no eagle. A crow even less a crow. The water tower now as high as Rarden could go in the flat delta and he went there all the time. He was drunk and he was there all the time, and if people had been afraid of him when he was flying, they were downright terrified of him now. He was gone, they'd say at the barbershop and at the hardware store and on the sidewalks and say *I told you so, I told you,* and shake their heads. Everyone just waiting for part two to see what he would do. *I'll bet he'll go back north*, they'd say, and *I'll bet he'll blow his head off*, some would laugh, and some just, *Goddamn*, and maybe chuckle that De La Palma had Naomi back, which was, like I said, a thing no one knew for sure but knew too. Because even during the day you could see him up there, tiny as a dot at the top of that ladder, and his feets dangling over the side. His FELICITY JANE painted behind him in candy-apple red. And at night he slept there, and I would climb up hand over hand up that ladder and would sit and drink with him. He wouldn't say nothing, and I wouldn't say nothing back neither. Just sitting up there and swiping the Old Crow back and forth. The bridge you could see from there where we sat, but it wasn't nothing no more. It was just a bridge. No longer a test. *The* test of his art. Our craft. I had done it only three times, but those three times were the best three things I had ever done or have done, or I feel safe to say, will ever do in this life. There was still the swatches of land. But it wasn't the same. We were squirrels high up in a single tree where once we had been birds. So drunk I can't even say, so that I woke with the sun kicking my head, Rarden sitting on the edge, the empty bottle caught between his knees. I picked up my aching noggin and said, *Shit, man. Shit.* Shaking. And he turned and looked at me up and down like he didn't have no idea who I was and I had just got there anyhow.

But me imagining those nights her with him, in the air again, her on his lap on a Saturday night with her pretty buckskin skirt hiked up to her waist, I can imagine, flying, her handling the stick, him the rudders, together like that, together, and the other way too, and taking the bridge, like that, right like that, fitted, heads back, yelling all they worth. Just sitting there and

imagining that. Always imagining them like that. Still.
Her. This kind of love. After everything.

Naomi went back to Nadine's and Nadine took
her back because De La Palma asked her to, and I went
back into the fields — stalled long as I could, drinking on
the water tower and pleading we get out of that place, go
someplace else, work up the stake for another Jenny —
but then had to climb back down, put my feet on solid
ground and hitch up into that tractor, snatching
glimpses of the blue from under my cowshed, slow
crawling down them long rows. And that was the first
time I ever saw Rarden angry — though I seen him drunk
and shouting or into a silence plenty of times — when
Naomi took back that job. He busted up our partner
shack. Trashed it. Made kinlin of the chairs, hatched the
table. Smashed the lantern, and then he set it all afire.
We were just sitting there and drinking and talking
nothing back and forth when he just stood up and
swung down that first chair, and I said *Goddamn!* splin-
ters going everywhere. But his eyes was wild with whiskey, and I don't think he even heard me. He grabbed up
the lantern and crashed it to the floor. Me just sitting
there in the almost dark and thinking *what the fuck?*
and watching and not even really believing what was
happening yet. Until he went for the ax and buried it
into the table, so that I had to jump back to get missed
and yelled, *God-damn-it, Man! You crazy!* But he
wasn't listening. Rarden wasn't even there. I grabbed
him by the shoulders to stop him, and that's when he
turned on me, didn't say nothing, just rushed me backwards screaming into the wall. We hit and fell and then
he had me against the stove and his fists and teeths
coming from every which where so that it felt like there
was a whole gang of him. And me throwing one or two,
but bigger and heavier and somehow coming out rolling
up on top and punching him good so that I couldn't stop
until I stopped him and he was just laying there gasping

like a bellied fish and I got up off him and his blood and mine too on my hands wiping my bloody nose and left saying, *Goddamnit, Rarden. Just goddamnit man.* And shaking my head.

And that was the same night she killed him. In self-defense, the *Herald* said. Rape attempt was understood, because they wrote it so you couldn't understand it in no other way. So while that fire was eating our partner shack, me laying on the cool dirt between two rows of waist-high cotton, thinking about what I had just done and touching my ribs and licking at the gash of my knuckles and watching them flames lick up that night, that fire breathing our shack all the way down to the smoldering hell ground, he, Rarden, had dragged himself up, busted lip and nose and blackening eye that I imagine and all, thinking how I hit him and couldn't stop hitting him, and was at Nadine's drinking. And I hear that he called her a whore, and gnashing my teeth to think of it, for *him*, Rarden, to say that about her — hanging at the end of his own rope. People sitting in the booths there heard that and the fact that he was at Nadine's was in the *Herald*. And her working there and sure nobody going to stop anyone from calling her a whore or anything else for that matter. Him the only one, and it was him calling her that. I imagine that he even grabbed her between her slim thighs, treating her like what she was and what he had spent hisself proving she wasn't. This while the flames ate our shack and I lay hidden between the cotton, nursing my ribs, my busted jaw, the jags of light catching the crowd of people's mouths who had come out to watch in *ooohs* and *aaaahs*. Naomi working back at Nadine's and me back on the spring seat of that tractor, up under that cowshed. And I can see Naomi's face too when he called her that, *whore*, bashed, imagine, coming from the only person she would've taken offense to it from, but him saying it, and her doing it all for him too, though she should've known he couldn't never see it that way, *whore*, so that in the end she had to take his hand from out under her skirt and lay down her apron on the counter and lead him like that out the door.

They were found naked, on the trestle, in the middle, where underneath there was the ancient turnstile to raise the sides. Rarden was naked and shot dead nine times. And I can't help but shudder at that quiet awful time she had taken to reload the revolver and start again — the six slow smacked shots and that silence as she emptied the chambers and reloaded shell by shell and started in again, pulling the trigger three more times, waiting for the slap of each bullet to ricochet away between the riverbanks before she shot him again. Found her naked, her feet dangling over the side, staring into the moon-wrinkled water which she had skimmed so wildly, carefully, screaming, on Rarden's lap, the pistol, one of De La Palma's, which it was said, he had given to her to protect herself when he had gotten her back her job at Nadine's, still caught in her two hands. There was also whiskey involved. And from there, I've since checked, you can see the water tower, even at night, with a good moon, bright.

Now, after fifty years, she sits on the front porch of her cabin, under the trestle, and snaps beans. Her hair gray and long down her back. The children, my grandchildren — I have grandchildren now and a wife of forty-five years — think she's crazy, the Old Indian Lady they call her, a witch, and race by, as good as any graveyard. We never really talk. We have never talked about him since. I don't think we ever talked much even before, but then we didn't have to. There was the sky, the air, flying, joining us all three. People still talk about that crazy Yankee and his Jenny from Ohio. But we don't. There was a time when I was in the air. I could fly. I got farther than most people, white or black. But not

any more. On the ground again, I am any nigger, any
joe, bob, harry, frank. Any man. Any woman. Any slave.
Slave to the small things I know and have never let
myself escape. And even my own kids, my grandkids,
don't believe I was once free. And my one witness,
Naomi, who could tell them it was true, is grounded
under the old trestle. And when I bounce by her on my
tractor every morning or every evening on my way back
to the shop, she looks up from her snapping beans and
our eyes meet and we nod or I stop and ask her about
her gardenias or say how humid it is out, but we don't
talk about him. We never talk about him or that night,
and I never want to. Me, I just want to remember him
the way things was. The best thing I ever done. But
maybe still asking myself as I swing the big 3640 into a
day of cotton, *What is free?* It being maybe easier to say
what's not free. That after fifty years.

S eventeen kilometres east of Nachlingen, a tiny farm-
ing community scalloped along the woolly green skirt
of the Black Forest, where this morning the head of
another chicken has popped like a blister from the
heat — "BAVARIAN BIRDS LOSING HEADS OVER
SUMMER HEAT WAVE," he considers as a possible
headline — Frank realizes Raoul Duke must be dying.
"And the Duke, he's fine, too. He's been a little tired
lately, but the vet says that's natural. He's had a long,
long, rich, full life, Frank. The Duke, you know, not Dr.
Vernon. If he was a person he'd be a hundred and twelve
years old." Such news of Frank's past life comes to him
in regular airmail installments: postcards from Univer-
sal Studios and Knott's Berry Farm (his son); concerned
notes from the city desk of the Washington *Post*
(Sandra, his former editor); manila envelopes thick with
documents — sign where indicated — from the D.C. law
firm of Martin, Martin & Sullivan (Anne, his ex-wife,
indirectly); and audio cassettes wrapped in brown
butcher paper and return-addressed 3434 Silver Maple
Way, Landover, Maryland. As Frank pursues and

reports the sensational stories of Europe, these dispatches from home follow him, hotel to hotel (he no longer has a permanent address), across the Continent. It is a tape that speaks to him now, from the Blaupunkt of the rented BMW, in the voice of his ex-mother-in-law. Her hands are crippled with arthritis, and she must use a tape recorder to update Frank on her persistent hemorrhoids, encroaching suburban blacks, and the Duke, whom she accepted into her fenced backyard two months ago, following the sudden splintering of the Frank Borden clan. "So you don't worry about the Duke—he's doing just fine." There is a pause on the tape and a clump of white wooden houses, windows shuttered against the heat, drifts silently past. Out there, Frank knows, beyond the rows of corn, ears drying and curling on the stalk like tiny brown fingers—out there an uncontainable pressure of steam and brain fluids is brewing in chicken heads across the land. More than two dozen have exploded since Monday in this area alone. "And, Frank, I just loved that article you wrote about the little baby Dutch girl with the two heads."

It takes several minutes for Frank's call to roam the thousands of miles of cable between the Federal Republic of Germany and Landover, Maryland; in the meantime he browses through that morning's edition of the *Süddeutsche Zeitung*, left unattended on the counter of the Nachlingen post office. The mail clerk, phone clamped between his hunched shoulder and cheek, fans himself with a sheaf of letters and sighs. When he sees that Frank has come to the right page, he leans across the counter and raps the day's weather report with a knuckle. "Horrible, eh?"

"Horrible," agrees Frank, reading. A cool front is supposed to move up out of the mountains by the weekend, but today the air is as intractable as hot cement.

It turns out that Raoul Duke is, as Frank suspected, dead — dead even before Anne's mother made her latest tape. "I didn't want to worry you, Frank," she tells him, her voice bobbing in a wash of transatlantic static. "With everything you have on your mind and all. I know how you loved old Duke."

"For heaven's sake, Dot," he says. She makes the situation sound much grimmer than it is. Raoul Duke was an old dog, rescued from the gas chambers of the Humane Society when Frank was still in college, more than fifteen years ago. As Dot herself said, Raoul Duke's was a long, rich, full life, and now he has gone to a deserved rest. Pity, Frank has come to believe these past two months in Europe, should be reserved for the truly bizarre tragedies of life — the bi-headed babies and noggin-popping poultry — not the everyday glitches of dog death and divorce.

Listening absent-mindedly to Dot's heartfelt condolences — a solid, stable professional, he has always been her favorite, her other daughters having gone through long strings of sometimes violent U.S. Marines and body-and-fender men — Frank comes to a short article that shows promise: a soprano in an Italian opera company, distraught over uncontrollable weight gain, has fled her company at the summer Music Festival in Salzburg. Authorities say she is believed to be suicidal. Now *that*, Frank thinks — that is something to get excited about; that is *News of the World*.

"He went in his sleep, Frank. There was no pain. Dr. Vernon said it was like a feather floating away in a breeze."

When the conversation is over, Frank hands the phone back to the mail clerk and pays for the call. He cannot imagine Raoul Duke *floating* anywhere. More likely, Anne's mother recruited the Carver boys from next door to lug the huge corpse through the backyard minefield of dog dung and into the bed of their pickup.

45

"Funny, eh?" the clerk asks. He raps a knuckle on the suicidal-soprano story, puffs his cheeks out, and sings a snatch of Wagner in a hoarse, creaky falsetto.

Frank smiles and consults a yellow train schedule taped to one of the post office's imitation-marble pillars. It should be no problem, he decides. He is not due in Berlin until Friday. If his afternoon interviews today go off without hitch or delay, he can (a) speed back to Stuttgart, (b) pick up his luggage from the hotel, and (c) make it to the station by eleven o'clock. He will be able to compose the chicken piece on the overnight train and be in Salzburg ("BEEFY DIVA DIVES TO DEATH," he considers; "THIS FAT LADY WON'T SING ANYMORE") by dawn.

"Thank you," Frank tells the mail clerk. He folds the newspaper into a tight, expert rectangle and tucks it beneath his arm.

Between sips of warm Hacker-Pschorr, the chicken rancher, a friendly old man with corrugated brown skin, motions out the window and claps his hands together. "You are in the barn the work doing and—bang!—out of the hounds the devil it scares." He chuckles and refills Frank's glass.

Frank writes this information in his notebook. "It's horrible," he says. Really, though, not all that horrible. It would have been better if this barnyard blitzkrieg (good, Frank says to himself; he writes the phrase down) were spiked with an element of *human* tragedy; animals, no matter how weird or wacky their demise, generated less interest than would, say, a buxom blond farmer's daughter killed or even blinded by an errant beak or skull bone.

Frank remembers his first big story with the *News*, a story that had it all. It was back in May, not long after he left the *Post* and took the job as a stringer in Europe. Four young nuns drowned themselves in the Seine, just below where the Pont Neuf connects the Left Bank with the Île de la Cité. He and Anne had strolled to the center of that very bridge on their honeymoon, eleven years earlier, perhaps on the same afternoon their son was conceived. Frank plans to take Tony to the Pont Neuf when he comes to visit in August—it's a good view of Notre Dame. *The Hunchback of Notre Dame* with Charles Laughton is one of Tony's favorites. They used to act it out, Tony and Frank taking turns as Quasimodo, with Raoul Duke as the angry mob of Parisians. When the hunchback rang the bells of the cathedral (the bass keys of the old Steinway Anne's grandmother had left them in her will), Raoul Duke would race, barking, around the living room, slipping across the worn parquet floor, his movement more lateral than forward. Eventually he would bounce off a wall, causing the family photos and Impressionist prints to rattle and shimmy on their hooks, and collide with Tony. Down they would go in a giggling, panting heap, thin white arms hugging thick black neck.

Frank smiles to himself without losing the look of rapt and respectful attention he has refined over so many years of interviewing Pentagon officials and Senate subcommittee chairmen. Ignoring the old farmer's amiable chattering, he pushes his family from his mind and brings the daydreams back into a proper organizational framework. Paris: what a story. A suicide pact, rumors of rampant lesbianism at the convent, the possibility of an illegitimate infant child, its throat cut and its tiny body buried beneath a great stone in the catacombs of St. Julien l'Hospitalier. The last part was mostly conjecture, of course, and Frank's new editors in Los Angeles had loved him for it. They—and he—had been uncertain how he would adapt to the nature of his new position, to the nature of the tabloid medium, but the Paris story dispelled all doubt. They gave it a double-truck spread with two banners, five kickers, and, inch for inch, more headline than copy. The Diva idea has that kind of potential, Frank thinks, particularly if she leaps from the heights of Nonnberg Abbey and flattens a tourist or two on the cobblestones below. "Photos of the chickens?" he asks the farmer.

The old man shrugs and smiles. He cups his hand to his ear, and for the first time Frank notices, in the distance, the throaty barking of weimaraners. "The hounds, you understand. It is for them a big feast."

Even if he had the time or the desire, Frank would still find it impossible to sleep on the D-train from Stuttgart to Salzburg — a midnight local that clatters to a stop every ten minutes and never picks up enough speed to blow a cooling breeze through the windows. "The weather is horrible," an old woman in a Bavarian peasant dress tells him. She watches with curiosity as he secures his briefcase to the seat next to him, using two long strips of double-sided tape he carries for such a purpose. He props open the lid of the briefcase and takes from it a ballpoint pen, a legal pad, and a blue plastic box of index cards (blue is for Central Europe, red for Western, green for Southern). He copies information from the index cards — coded "CHIX" in the upper-left-hand corner — onto the legal pad. When he finishes with a card he pins it to a cork board fastened to the inside of the briefcase lid.

The chicken story is completed just as the train crosses over into Austria, a little before three o'clock in the morning. Before shutting the briefcase, Frank retrieves last week's postcard from Tony, realizing that the photo, an aerial view of Chavez Ravine inset with an action shot of Fernando Valenzuela, is reversed — Fernando appears a righty. He taps the postcard against his knee. At least his son will grow up watching a team that plays on real grass. It should comfort him, Frank supposes, that Anne did not choose to pursue her new life (her New Life, as she put it to him in a letter) in Minneapolis or Houston. "Dear Dad, Everything O.K. here," the back of the card reads, as short and sweet as always. "Gramma told me R.D. was sick, and I was sad."

There in the rocking and swaying train car, the backs of his slacks wet against the red vinyl seat, Frank himself does not feel sad. He would have, of course, before taking up his new job. After all, this was a dog so tangled in the weave of his life that Frank can honestly say that he is unable to drum up any image of the past fifteen years without that big black block head eventually pushing and snuffling under the fingers of memory. Frank remembers Anne standing in the kitchen of the little house under the sycamores of T Street, dicing Spanish onions for the potato salad, her blond hair twisted into a ponytail and plugged through the slot of an Orioles cap. It is '79 or '80, because Tony is still in his high chair, hollering and pumping the air with his tiny, no-knuckle fists. Anne is weeping and laughing as she stumbles over Raoul Duke's broad back to pull a box of graham crackers from the shelf. Frank laughs to himself—the Duke always staked out the kitchen when there was the chance of food being dropped. Still, no sadness; Frank is proud of his self-control.

"Apple?" asks the old woman sitting across from Frank, who smiles and shakes his head. She sighs and waves a hand in front of her face as if to brush the stew of hot night air away. It is the hottest summer she can remember, she says, and she was reared in the flatlands near Mainz, where summers are notorious. Before she can extract the pictures of her seven grandchildren (all "big, strapping boys") from the leather rucksack at her feet, Frank reopens his briefcase and busies himself with the task of coding index cards. This new set he marks "FAT" in the upper-left-hand corner.

■

In Salzburg Frank phones in the chicken saga, twelve tight but lurid paragraphs heavy on the adjectives, to the Western Hemisphere editor of the *News*. Cecil, a friend of Frank's since college, now his boss, spends most of his time rewriting clips from the London tabs — gruesome murders, freak accidents, giant lizards on Mars — and punching them into a derelict Compugraphic typesetter that chugs noisily in one corner of his office. Frank can understand, then (even if he does not always appreciate), Cecil's need to chat when one of the regional stringers rings a story in.

"Good stuff," Cecil says when Frank has finished dictating. "Reminds me of that lady from Toronto who put her parakeet in the Waring to spin it dry. 'BYE BYE BIRDIE,' May of '88, mug of the guilty appliance on the jump page. Talk to me, Frank: how's it going? How you doing with the Anne situation?"

Frank works the shoes from his feet and wiggles his toes. From the window of his hotel room he can see the peak of the Untersberg beginning to glow with dawn. The international travel alarm clock he has set on the nightstand says that it is almost nine P.M. in Los Angeles.

"You're working late, Cecil."

"As always. Listen, Frank, Carol and I had Anne over to dinner a couple of weeks ago. She said Tony will be flying over next month."

"Yes," Frank says, brightening. "I thought we'd go to Paris, Munich, the mountains, maybe Rome. He's a big fan of gladiators, chariots, things like that. I want to take him skiing, but that'll have to wait until winter. I think this will really be something for him. I can't wait to take him up to Ludwig's castles."

"I want you to know they're doing O.K.," Cecil says. "Anne has a show on the thirty-first. Just a little place down in Malibu, but it's a start. Some guy from San Francisco bought the one called *Forest*. The one with the things of garden hose? She's doing good."

Frank positions a stack of newspapers on the edge of the bed. Frankfurt, Berlin, Paris, Zurich, Brussels — fresh from the all-night newsstand at the train station. He squares the stack with the palm of his hand and takes out a fluorescent highlighter. Sources in Salzburg won't be up for another couple of hours; he has a chance to get some work done.

"No one I talked to seems to know why chickens, exactly." Frank retrieves an index card from the blue box and glances at it. "Try and get in touch with a Dr. Harold Melton, N.Y.U. He's an animal pathologist. His number is —"

"Don't sweat it, Frank," Cecil says. "If we can't get in touch with a science guy over at the college we'll just jam a 'DOCS BAFFLED BY' on it and run it as is."

With a few calls to Festival officials, Frank tracks the Milanese opera company to one of the hotels just off the Mozartplatz. There the impresario of the troupe, a morose-looking man with an impeccable silver mustache, tells Frank much that was not in the initial news story. This is not the first time his principal soprano, scheduled to sing Susanna, has fled the stage because of an unshakable weight problem. There was London in '85, Bayreuth in '86, and, less than six months ago, Vienna, where she accidentally pulverized a delicate wrought-iron chair at a sidewalk café on the Kärntnerstrasse. She dashed shrieking into St. Stephen's and barricaded herself in a confessional booth. Her husband was sent for to calm her down, which he did, but in her haste and hysteria she had become jammed; carpenters had to be called in to pry her from the small wooden box.

"I see," Frank says, scribbling in his notebook. The story is getting better by the minute. "And they finally got her out with crowbars?"

"So it has happened before," the impresario says, looking at Frank with gloomy eyes. "But this time, we believe, is the worst. Her dilemma, you must understand, causes her the greatest anguish. We believe that this time it may have reached its crescendo. Her husband is searching for her, but we do not have much hope."

"You have no idea where she might be?" Frank wonders how difficult it could be to find a three-hundred-pound woman on the narrow, crooked streets of Old Salzburg.

The impresario shrugs. "Yes, we are all very worried. You should have heard her sing! What a power, what an agility of voice! Not since Ponselle."

"I have to find her," Frank says, standing. There is no time to lose.

"God bless you," the impresario calls to him, touched by Frank's concern. But Frank has already closed his notebook and hurried from the room.

Below the Casino, at the foot of the sheer slate precipice that rises above the Equestrian Fountain, there is no body and no sign of a desperate plunge. Likewise, there is no prima donna clinging to the battlement of Fortress Hohensalzburg, wailing an aria and nibbling a Ritter Sport bar. The sluggish but powerful Salzach would probably sweep away anything that might fall from its bridges, but still Frank picks his way down the steep bank, through the weeds and rocks, past the midday sunbathers, to search along the river's loamy fringe.

His biggest fears now are (a) that the Diva might decide on a private death, opening her veins in the tepid sink water of some secluded pension, (b) that she will delay and delay, until finally Frank must give up the chase in favor of the story waiting for him in Berlin (neo-Nazis who claim to have unearthed the real skeleton of Martin Bormann), or, worst, (c) that, as before, she'll end up returning to her company. A depressed but alive opera singer, three hundred pounds or not, isn't *News of the World.*

A copper-colored, long-haired dachshund falls into step behind Frank, shyly sniffing along the path beside the river but keeping suspicious eyes upturned. Frank stops, squats, and holds his hands out. "Hey, boy, hey boy," he clucks in German to the dog, which lifts its ears but does not advance. "Pretty puppy, good dog, come here, come here." Frank takes a slow, careful duck step forward. The dog scrambles into panicked action, its four stubby legs churning with such ferocity that it backs up onto its hindquarters and topples over.

Frank, laughing, takes another step. "The way to get dogs to like you," he has told his son, "is to show them you're friendly and that you're not afraid of them. Then they'll know they don't have to be afraid of *you.*"

This time the dog remembers to turn before fleeing and manages to dart away, a leash fastened to its collar sizzling through the grass. When it sees that Frank is trotting after it, whistling and clapping his hands against his thighs, it wheels, stops, and begins to growl.

Frank stops also as the dog's growl takes on a higher-pitched, more threatening timbre. "Good dog." Frank backs up and turns to run as the dog lunges at him, its clicking jaws just missing the back of his ankle. Adrenaline, longer legs, and an acute sense of embarrassment (he does not want to become himself a two-paragraph filler) allow Frank to outsprint the dachshund and leap halfway up the riverbank, ripping the inseam of his slacks in the process. The dog struts beneath him, grinning, one long ear flopped up onto its head. Soon a young boy runs up and regains the leash, pulling the dog along in the direction of the Ostbrücke.

Frank glances at his watch — in Los Angeles (in Malibu) it is only six o'clock in the morning — and throws a broken piece of shell limestone onto the flat stomach of the river. A few sunbathers farther down lift their heads off balled towels and contemplate with mild interest the splash and the noodles of heat rising from the water. Frank removes his suit coat, unfastens the top button of his shirt, and begins the climb up to the street.

Frank stops by his hotel to change pants, reaching his room just as the phone rings. The voice on the other end of the line is husky, brusque: Sandra, his editor from the *Post*.

"I'm worried about you, Frank," she says. "Have you talked with Anne lately?"

"Hello, Sandra," he says, his voice flat. "Anne who?"

"It's a cliché, Frank, I know, but sooner or later you're going to have to start thinking about getting back to your life, your career. You're a helluva reporter, Frank, you're a young man."

"I like my life," Frank says. "I like my career."

The downstairs hallway is empty, but the door to the soprano's room (No. 8, as revealed by a covert glance at the company roster this morning) is locked. Frank tries the old credit-card trick with his American Express but manages only to whittle a layer of rust from the heavy bolt. Circling the outside of the hotel, he discovers that the windows of all the ground-floor rooms open on a back alley. He paces off the distance from the corner of the building and then, with the help of a warped plastic milk crate, peers into the window of No. 8. The room is empty except for a small table, two chairs, a large trunk, and a single bed, much too frail-looking for the huge creature Frank pictures as having occupied it.

The window is unlocked and wide enough for Frank to crawl through. He goes directly to the trunk and examines it. At first he finds nothing that could be of use—no diaries, no family photos, no horned Viking helmet—just an assortment of toiletries, several towels, an umbrella. Digging deeper into the trunk, though, Frank finds an enormous pair of pale-blue panties.

"For heaven's sake," he whispers, holding the panties up with both hands. He can picture the photo now: the Diva's Drawers snapped next to a normal-sized pair. Her panties are the size of a large pillowcase.

A cart rolls past in the hallway and someone unlocks a nearby door. Frank wads up the panties and stuffs them into his pocket. Waiting until he is sure the alley is deserted, he crawls back through the window, landing with one foot sunk deep into a box of spoiled strawberries, from the hotel restaurant, left moldering in the heat.

The desk clerk hands Frank a message when he stops by his hotel for dinner. A representative from the opera company called earlier with the good news: the Diva is still alive. Police say that a woman fitting her description boarded an afternoon train to Munich. Her husband has been dispatched by car.

"Damn it," Frank says. He collects his mail — a letter that has found him early; he is due here in Salzburg late next week for a warlock convention — and returns to his room. The gloomy impresario with the silver mustache answers the phone on the first ring.

"No, not even her husband is certain," he tells Frank. "She adores Munich — the English Garden, the Leopoldstrasse, the galleries. She could be perhaps anywhere." Then, after a thoughtful pause: "The glockenspiel is her favorite. Whenever we are in Munich she visits the top of the Old Peter bell tower."

"The Old Peter bell tower," Frank repeats, spreading a Michelin map of Munich onto his lap.

"It is the best view."

The next train to Munich does not depart for another hour, so Frank can no longer ignore the letter. In her loose, fluttering script Anne informs him that everything is going well in California. She is sorry to hear about Raoul Duke. And she is sorry to say that Tony won't be able to come to Europe in August after all. Orientation at his new school starts earlier than expected, and she wants him to have enough time to get adjusted. She guesses Frank would want that, too.

Frank crumples the letter up and tosses it to the floor. His head hurts and the small room is suffocating. The worst part of the day is over, but he sees from the window that the blue of the sky is still tinged with white, as if it had been bled pale by the heat.

Frank lies on his bed and tries to concentrate on the options at hand. Friday, as originally planned, is Berlin: if he takes an evening express to Munich today, there is no way he will be able to reach Berlin until late Saturday. And even that schedule leaves him less than twenty-four hours to find the Diva. Not enough time, if things go as they've gone today. And hers is the kind of story — rich with human pathos and broad comedy — that Frank cannot pass up.

"Won't work, Frank," Cecil tells him when he finally gets through to L.A. "René called from Mexico City yesterday and said she can't send the vampire stuff until she can line up some sort of victim-pic. We have to roll with the Bones of Bormann thing. If we're lucky, the Skinhead Rally at the Olympic Stadium will escalate into a riot Saturday, and then we've got a good, strong Nazi package for the fold on three."

"For heaven's sake," Frank says. "Forget the Nazis. This opera story is a real one. I could *be* there if I hustle, Cecil."

"Be *where*, Frank? Suppose she is at this tower place — what if she decides not to ice herself yet? Are you going to tail her around Europe until she does, *if* she does? Tell me, have you gone out of your mind?" Cecil clears his throat and pauses. Frank knows he is considering the circumstances and already regretting his choice of words. "What I mean, Frank," Cecil continues, in a more reasonable, more artificial tone, "is that you can cover this soprano thing *after* it happens. The other thing you can't. Skinhead Nazi riots wait for no man, Frank. You'll have to forget Munich. We need you in Berlin this weekend."

In Munich Frank rides the U-Bahn from the train station to the Marienplatz. Emerging from the subway, he shivers and pushes his hands into his pockets. In the sky a mass of oyster-gray clouds, coughed up by the Alps to the south, roils overhead, responsible for the slight, sudden chill in the air. Despite the clouds a large crowd is gathering on the square between the St. Peter bell tower and the Neue Rathaus. It must be approaching the hour when the knights and coopers of the glockenspiel spin through their ringing dance for the battery of tourist cameras below.

"Another one not afraid of a few stairs!" The old woman sitting in the tower entrance accepts Frank's five-mark piece and pushes his change across the countertop with the back of her hand. "A crowd today," she says, with a smile and a bob of her hairy chin, as Frank moves quickly past her into the socket of moist gloom.

He takes the steep stone steps of the Old St. Peter Church tower three at a time. By the time he reaches the grid of dusty wooden beams that support the bells, three-quarters of the way up, his legs are burning and beginning to go numb.

In the well beneath the last flight of stairs, just below the door leading outside to the balcony, he comes upon a fellow-climber. The way the man sits, hunched up against the wall, his knees tucked to his chin, causes Frank to hesitate. "Are you all right?" he asks, first in German, then in English. He is about to try French, the only other language he knows, when the man lifts his head and shows Frank a small face red and shiny with sweat or tears.

"Her voice," the man says in slow, broken English. "A voice from the angels! What has her flesh to do with beauty? What is the flesh when she has a voice from the angels?"

When he hears the man's thick Italian accent, Frank feels his chest tighten. The Diva's husband throws up his hands and leans to the side so Frank can leap up the stairs past him. "She does not come down," he sings after Frank. "She does not come down this way."

Frank sees her at once, on the other side of the bulbiform copper pinnacle of the tower. She balances on a sagging balustrade, white and trembling, like an enormous rosebud dollop of whipped cream. The silk dress snaps against her in the rising wind, and Frank notices that the iron railing circling the platform is pearled with moisture from the descending clouds. "Wait," he says, unable to move either toward her or away. They are alone. He has no idea what he should say to her — if he should say anything at all. He stands and stares and tries, at least, to organize his thoughts and alternatives in a rational manner. He can (a) continue to stand and observe; that is why he is here, after all; he has his briefcase and his camera with him. He can (b) run for help — but, really, how effectual, one way or another, would that be? Frank's mental structure begins to wobble, and he forces himself to concentrate. He can (c) try to comfort her, tell her that her problems are no big deal, that being fat is just not, in the end, *News of the World.*

She glances blankly at Frank and then looks away again. In many ways she is how he pictured her — except for her face. Instead of an obese, pallid mask twisted by lunatic despair, her face appears only quietly unhappy. It is just an ordinary face, the kind that Frank sees every day, a face with pretty, dark eyes. Still, for some reason, Frank feels his heart sink with sadness.

"*Qual'occhio al mondo può star di paro*," he calls to her, "*all'ardente occhio tuo nero?*" It is the only Italian he can remember, a snatch of some opera he once reviewed for his college newspaper. Puccini? He isn't sure what the line means, only that it has something to do with pretty, dark eyes. He used to sing that line to Anne (who has pretty, pale-green eyes) back in the days when he still did things like that, when he wanted to be romantic and take her to bed. She always laughed and clubbed him on the nose with a rolled-up magazine. "*Qual'occhio al mondo può star di paro*," he repeats, softly, "*all'ardente occhio tuo nero?*"

For a moment Frank thinks that she will burst into tears. She lifts her thin black eyebrows and blinks. For the first time she seems to notice Frank and the wind, sodden with drizzle, that blows against her. Then she drops her chin onto her collarbone and begins to laugh.

Across the square the bells of the glockenspiel ring, and the appreciative murmur of the crowd below rises to fill out the lower register of the song. Through it all comes the Diva's beautiful, musical laughter, each note perfectly rounded, as articulate and melancholy as her face.

"Oh, damn," Frank says, at a loss for a way to stanch this flow of grief. The balcony is small, and he knows he is close enough to reach out for her, grab her soft quaking shoulder and pull her down to safety. As before, though, he can't marshal the energy to move. He sighs and manages to back up to the support of the tower's copper-plated onion dome, then slides down onto his haunches. Before he realizes it he is weeping, gently but with persistence. It is more a slow leak than a blowout, he guesses, but it is beyond his ability to control.

The copper figurines of the glockenspiel clank to a halt, the mechanical rooster in its cubbyhole gives a final crow, and the last peals of the bells fray and dwindle into the clouds. Frank continues to weep, even after the Diva stops her lovely staccato laughter and slips from the bannister. "Raoul Duke is dead," Frank explains to her in a whisper when she kneels down to touch his arm.

WILL EVANS

The Bear Head

from New England Review and Bread Loaf Quarterly

The head of my father's bear always hung above the fireplace. His armchair stood beneath it, and as a boy I liked to sit in the chair, enclosed within its high back and arms and deeply hollowed seat, lost in the powerful smell of him, of the leather and of gun grease. I would sit and study the bear with its white-shaded muzzle, and I would imagine my father telling the story of how he had killed the bear, would see him bend forward, eyes lit, his face growing flushed.

He had driven up to Errol for deer. It was a Saturday in November over thirty years ago, the sky scratched with yellow before the New England winter. My father sat near a creek bed, his rifle propped on a fallen spruce. The trees stood around him, gray. He got up to walk out the cold. Stepping, standing, stepping again, he followed the slope of a ridge, when a mile along, the wind stiff in his face, he came upon the bear.

"An old bear," my father used to say. "Would've been hell to fight with dogs" (my mother, looking to the sewing on her lap, would silently shake her head).

It was suddenly just there: an enormous, ancient

thing. The thick and shaggy shape of it stood dark against the gray wall of woods, frozen, canting its great flat head, nose high, breath steaming the air.

Then it moved. It crossed the top of the ridge, without hurry, low to the ground, and it stopped and turned to look back at him across one shoulder. My father, breathing slowly, had settled his weight over both of his legs. He had carefully raised the gun — his father's old .30/30 Winchester — and he had sighted the bear, patient, down along the barrel. The double report of the rifle echoed through pine and spruce. The bear collapsed inward, shuddered, and sat back onto its hind legs, then crashed away in the woods, through brush and over blowdown. My father walked silently forward and followed the trail sprayed red, now and then stopping to kneel and roll the blood on his fingertips. At the base of a tall spruce on the ridge, a quarter mile away, the bear lay breathing rapidly, the sharp curves of its nostrils caving in, then widening, its strength dissipating in bleeding. My father shot it again. The bear surged up on its hind legs, rose taller and taller, looming — or so I've always imagined it — and took two or three steps as a man would have walked, red-eyed, swiping and biting the air with a flash of glistening yellow teeth, before its legs buckled, and it crumpled under its weight.

I was five then, the youngest. But I remember the blare of the horn as my father drove up the driveway, the stones and gravel popping beneath the tires of his pickup. He came banging into the kitchen, yelling for my brothers, "Bob! Roy!" Together they drove back to the spot on the ridge, where they dressed out the bear and dragged it from the woods. At home they chained one of its hind legs, then hoisted it onto the bough of a pine, and that night the neighbor men gathered in the yard around the dark mass hung as if caught in a snare. In pajamas, feet cold on the floorboards, I watched through the dining room window. Clouds of breath rose over the men — they hunched their shoulders, stamped their boots — and the sound of their voices rang in the night, my father's loudest of all.

It was late last spring when he died. My mother called to tell me. I was living alone in Chicago, teaching English at a high school there, and I hadn't gone home to New England in almost five years. I answered the phone in the dark near the sink and stood by the kitchen window. The line hummed with static. My throat ached as I listened. My eyes followed the telephone wires away from the lighted apartment house, out over the cars in the lot, to the place where the wires merged with blackness high above the street. That night, I packed and started the drive across country to his funeral. The land beyond the headlights lay wide and silent and deep.

■

I grew up in a sprawling, wood-frame house with ells connecting the barn, on a road outside of Somersworth, a town in southern New Hampshire. It comes back, at first, as a quiet place full of bright, clear light, by a river. The streets, I remember, were tree-lined with small houses set off from them. Our house, which stood about a mile and a half from the southern edge of town, was clapboard and painted white, with dark green trim and shutters.

My father had framed and finished the side porch himself. He was broad-backed and solid, a big, square man with a muscular jaw and a deeply cleft chin. He worked as a mill mechanic at Whitcher's Lumber in Salmon Falls. People in town called him handy — he was good at building and fixing things — and he often spent hours shining his pickup the bright, hard red of an apple, or cleaning and oiling his rifles. He took his hunting trips on Saturdays, by himself, or with one of my brothers. I remember them packing the guns in the truck as I watched with my sister, Ann. Hunting was a family tradition then, traced back as far as medieval times when one of my great-great ancestors had been knighted for spearing a boar. An entire wall in our living room was filled with family photographs, some of them brittle with age, of stern-eyed, grim-faced men wearing hats and cradling shotguns. If I touched them I got spanked. There was one I recall of my father and his brother, Harry, as boys, each holding the rack of a deer, posed in front of the four-room house where they'd lived outside of Asheville, in western North Carolina. Another, the oldest of these, was a wet-plate taken by a traveling photographer of my father's grandfather, R. Q. Lauder, with his dog, his gun, and a bear he'd just killed. R. Q. Lauder, a Scotsman, had settled near Cullowhee, North Carolina, where he'd raised his family on wild meat and vegetables from a kitchen garden.

Uncle Harry remained in Asheville but drove to New Hampshire to visit us about every two or three years. I still have a vivid memory, though I must have been seven at the time, of Harry roaring up to the house in a blue flatbed so pocked with rust it reminded me of abandoned cars I'd sometimes find way out in the woods, burdocks grown up through the flooring. He was a strange and wonderful man, but scary, or anyway, scary at first. He claimed to have killed six bears himself and liked to brag about his father. Back then, I thought he was magical. It seemed to me he could actually conjure up the people in his stories, could make them move and breathe — people who were dead, most of them, long before I was born.

"Your granddad killed a *hundred* bears," he told us that summer, years ago. We were sitting outside on the porch, burning punks to repel the mosquitoes. I sat on the glider with Ann and my older sister, Sharon. (Later that summer, Sharon married and moved away.) Bob, the older of my brothers, sat on the concrete, propped on his arms, while Roy hunched over on a fruit basket.

My uncle ritched back on a straight chair. He worked around the tobacco lumped in the side of his jaw and, occasionally, tipping his head, spit over his shoulder, past my mother's rhododendrons, and out into the night. His left arm, pruned at the wrist, was a smooth button of flesh. When Harry was twelve he shot off his hand. He was hunting, climbing a fence. The rails flew out from under him, he fell on his shotgun, and it fired.

"Your granddad had a shotgun that laid the bears out. Bear looked like a sifter bottom. First time I ever went was with him and Guy and Wesley Griffin. Me and your daddy did." He eyed us one at a time, and when he came to me he stopped. "How old are you now, Billy?"

As I've said, I must have been seven. My birthday was the following month. "Eight," I said, and caught a glance from Ann who had just turned nine.

My uncle nodded, squinting. "I guess that's about what I was." When he coughed to clear his throat, I felt suddenly important.

"We killed one below Sorrel Creek," he said. "Big old bear about five hundred pounds. Was in ivy thick as your fingers, and we couldn't see ten feet ahead, just heard the bear snarling and popping his teeth and the dogs in there yelling . . ."

Harry paused for my father. He'd come from the cellar with a paint can. Hands on his knees, he sat on the can. I remember thinking it would burst.

". . . Daddy told us, 'Don't you go in there. Wes and Guy'll shoot you.' Said, 'They're going to work on that bear.'" My uncle grinned at my father, who smiled to himself and ran a hand through his hair, his crewcut brush-heavy and stiff. Harry spit over his shoulder. "Daddy had that Wirebarrel Riverside."

"Single-shot," my father said.

"God, I love that gun. Still shoot it," Harry said.

The night grew cooler and damp. Harry told us how mornings their mother checked the hearth to see what their father had killed; how sometimes he sent her down Sorrel Creek to pull out the ducks he shot upstream. Then, to my brothers' delight, my father told his story: how he'd happened on the bear while hunting for deer and had shot it on the ridge with the Winchester, how Bob and Roy had helped dress it out, and how they'd all dragged it from the woods.

"Just to drag it was everything the three of us could do," Roy said, and Bob nodded.

It was late when my mother called Ann and me to bed. The two of us whined and stalled but, finally, said good night. Harry shook my hand and tried to kiss Ann. When she wouldn't have it, he shook her hand too.

"You're not eight," she said from her bed in our room, and that done she fell asleep.

Later, in the dark, I lay awake. Sharon walked down the hallway. Then I heard my uncle's gravelly voice — I could almost feel it on my skin. I slipped out of bed, crept through the hall, and knelt beside the banister. My father sat in his armchair. My uncle had lit a cigar. My brothers sat beside him, their forearms on their knees.

Harry talked about things I didn't understand — tools, guns, family matters. He never liked that my father moved north; the family, he said, was spreading thin. He said something about hunting with radios.

"*Used* to be a system of signal shots. I've shot a box of shells to get to Daddy and them."

I lay on my stomach, drifting, trying hard to imagine it.

The next morning I came awake and saw I was in my bed. I wondered how I'd got there and, with panic, thought of Ann. Wearing only yellow pajama-bottoms, her eyes puffed with sleep, she glanced at me as she sat and slid her legs from her bed, then padded out to the bathroom. If she had seen someone carry me to bed in the night, I knew she would have said so.

When she came back rubbing a fist in her eye, I was dressed, waiting for her. I watched her pull on a T-shirt and shorts, and then I told her what I'd seen from the banister. More than anything else in the world, I wanted to tell a story — not that I had much to tell. Ann sat on her bed until I finished, sat still, as if picturing what I said.

"And Uncle Harry had a cigar?" She was holding her pillow against her chest.

I nodded quick as I could.

"I don't believe it," she said.

That morning we raced to make our beds and raced to set the table. After breakfast we rushed through our chores, and then, as we often did, pretended to hunt the bear head. Silent, on our stomachs and elbows, we stalked around the piano stool to the back of my father's chair. From there we sprang shouting gun noise, each trying to be first to shoot, and we "laid the bear out" with our imaginary rifles. The bear, unmoved, stared down at us, far over our heads and out of reach.

The piano was an upright Bush and Gerts my father had bought second-hand, coal-black and carved with bluebirds and laurel sprigs and pears. Sometimes, while Ann or my mother played, my father would sing along, his voice cavernous, dark, like the cold, deep water in a mountain lake, or like the Great Bay at night. Framed portraits and a stack of sheet music stood on the piano top, together with my mother's hymnal — two or three hymns and Christmas carols were all she knew how to play. My sister took lessons from Mrs. Stewart, a tedious, gray woman who lived down the road. Every Saturday after lunch, Ann would lie on her bed, pale, her chin on the edge of the mattress. Then precisely at two, a rap on the door, like the beat of a metronome.

One Saturday after my uncle's visit, I sat watching the lesson from the bottom of the stairs. My sister was playing scales; Mrs. Stewart counted time. I stared at the toes of my sneakers and began to feel sorry for myself. Early that morning my father and brothers had left in the pickup for Errol—I'd wakened at the rumbling of the engine. I leaped from my bed to the window, where my breath clouded the glass, and knelt looking into the thin, blue light until the sound had faded down the road.

I listened to the lesson for a while, and then I went to my mother in the kitchen. She had dark red hair and was overweight (she was always cooking something), though I thought she was amazingly beautiful, if frequently distracted. For a time, I watched her from the stepstool; she was making crabapple jelly. Then I raised the metal steps with my feet and let them thump to the floor.

"What's the trouble," she said, "itchy?" She was holding up a steamy spoonful of syrup.

I nodded as glumly as I could.

"Ann's with Mrs. Stewart, and you're stuck with me."

"Everyone else is . . . out."

She watched the clear, green syrup drip from the side of the spoon. "When it starts to clump," she said, "that's when you know it's ready." She set down the spoon and, licking a finger, stepped to face the sink. "Want to watch it for me?"

I shook my head, throat tight. She stepped back to the stove with a colander of apples and laid them, quartered, into the kettle. With the toe of my shoe I lifted the steps and let them fall to the floor.

"Uncle Harry said I'm old enough," I said, after a while.

"Uh-huh." She thumbed a knob on the stove. "Old enough for what?"

"*You* know," I said, as angrily as I dared.

My mother tested the syrup again. "And what did your father say?"

"Said to wait!" I said, and burst into tears. My mother laid the spoon on the counter, and as I slid from the stool, she hugged me. She rocked me and smoothed my hair.

"Your father's your father," she said.

In the fall, the week before bear season opened, the lumber mill shut down. Everywhere the leaves were in color, the woods bright with saffron and scarlet and gold. Ann and I raced from school that day and rushed in the front door, banging it. My father lay on the sofa, his arms crossed on his chest. His boots stood unlaced on the floor. My mother appeared, finger pressed to her lips, and shooed us into the kitchen. She filled our hands with cookies, and then she sent us outside to play.

At supper that night, though my mother disapproved, there would have been talk of hunting. My father would have told us of the bear pot at work — sometimes as much as a thousand dollars — and my brothers would have hinted for the old family stories, dormant since our uncle's summer visit. Instead, my mother said long grace. My father and brothers, their faces like stone, could only stare into their plates. My sister and I were put early to bed, our mother saying "Night, night." I could hear the murmur of voices downstairs, when Ann began to cry, quietly.

"Ann?" I said, frightened.

She coughed but didn't answer.

After a while: "Ann?"

"Shut up, Billy," she said.

That fall there were no trips to Errol. My brothers pumped gas after school, and my mother took in what sewing she could. Ann gave up her piano lessons — she was glad enough. Though my father looked and looked for work, he found only a job taking census. To save the expense of gasoline, he left in the mornings on foot.

He was out of work again before the first snow. At supper my mother would talk of the choir, or of church dinners or sales, always taking, as was her habit, the brightest possible view of things. Evenings, my father retired to the living room where he'd sit for hours with the local ads or with the ads from Haverhill and Lawrence. When Ann and I went to kiss him good night, we'd step over the newspaper spread by his chair, over ramrods and a can of gun grease. My mother kidded him, saying, "They must be the cleanest guns in the state!" She did her best to keep us playing in our room, and she read to us or found quiet chores out from under our father's feet. To keep busy, he did odd jobs around the house. He would shovel snow, repair my mother's iron or the latch on the cellar door. From an old broom handle he built a coat rack of pegs. Sometimes while I helped my mother, peeling carrots or drying a pan, he'd sort through a jar of nails and bolts or straighten a hinge with pliers. He would ask her about some sewing to return or an errand to run at the store. She'd say, "We have plenty of potatoes," or "I haven't got to it, John," and as she worked would step around him. "Well, all right then," he'd say, as if he'd only meant to remind her. Then turning, he would hitch up his pants and go back again to his business.

I remember one day after school, while Ann and I were playing either Fish or Old Maid, we heard him starting the pickup and we jumped to the window beside my bed. That winter, he barely ran the truck, but whenever he did we were ready. It idled roughly beneath us, where he'd left it warming up. We watched him open the back door and stamp the snow from his boots, and then we hurried downstairs. In the mudroom, we stood in the doorway; he played his usual game with us, pretending not to notice. He buttoned his coat and reached for the door, then paused, scratching the top of his head.

"I thought you were busy upstairs in your room . . ."

Together, Ann and I groaned.

We backed down the driveway in the pickup and swung out onto the road. Ann knelt on the seat by the window, grasping the armrest and peering out, while I sat beside my father, on my hands so I wouldn't slip down. A basket of sewing lay on my lap, and our empty milk bottles clinked on the floor in a box we used for shopping. My father shifted gears, worked pedals with his feet, adjusted a knob on the dashboard — and all of this while he steered.

Whenever we stopped in front of a house, his hands and feet came to rest. Ann would throw open the truck door, and the two of us would scramble out. Carrying pants my mother had cuffed or a dress she had taken in, we'd make our way up the frozen walk, knock on the storm door, and wait. Old people usually answered, people my mother knew from church, or friends who couldn't afford a tailor (not that there was one, in those days, within twenty miles). They would take the bundled clothes from us and pull the storm door shut. A little later the door would crack open, and they'd hand out my mother's charge for her work, never more than three or four coins. Then Ann and I, yelling thank you, would skate back to the pickup, where my father took the coins from us and placed them into his pocket.

When we had finished making deliveries, we stopped at Camire's store. Inside on the sloping floorboards, there were aisles of boxed and canned goods, a meat counter way in the back, and — along an entire wall — a cooler stocked with tonic, beer and, during the summer, Popsicles. George Camire, a slightly built man with a moustache the color of straw, leaned on his hip by the register, his eyes on a local paper and a dead cigar in his teeth. Behind him were racks of sunglasses, fat jars of penny candy, a tray of sugar doughnuts. George gave us each a pretzel stick and a bottle of tonic to split. Then he walked up and down the aisles, my father huge beside him, and together they filled the shopping box with the things on my mother's list.

When they finished, they sat on round-back chairs held together with fence wire. Ann and I stood by the magazine rack, paging through comic books. George talked about taxes, farms for sale, who had been laid off where.

"Pretty soon," he said, and waved the cigar, a backward motion with his wrist, "I won't be in business myself."

My father sat forward, his forehead creased. The cleft of his chin was in shadow. He stared at the wooden floor by his feet and, nodding his head, said nothing.

Neighbors brought soups and casseroles and picked up my mother for church. My brothers worked extra hours at the Esso. My father had to ration our coal.

Two weeks or so before Christmas, Mrs. Stewart called. She offered piano lessons if Ann would walk to her house. That Saturday, Ann and I lay on our rug, drawing Christmas trees and Santa Clauses. My brothers had left for work in their grease-spotted blue-and-white coveralls. My father sat in his armchair, re-reading the morning paper, while my mother sewed in the kitchen and listened to radio hymns. It was almost two o'clock.

"Maybe she'll forget." Ann had begun to look pale.

"Maybe . . ." I lifted my crayon, considering. Then I knew it wasn't possible.

We walked down the road packed solid with snow, throwing snowballs at trees and each other. Our leggings were thick between our legs, and heavy, and running in them was like running in a dream. Mrs. Stewart's old clapboard farmhouse looked gray as the sky that day, the color of chimney smoke. I walked with Ann to the mailbox — a sapping pail, really, hung on a post — and I watched her edge between banks of snow to Mrs. Stewart's front porch.

With nothing to do, I headed back home. The cold sat hard, like iron. I pushed into snow on the shoulder of the road and trudged along, head down. I imagined myself a trapper or an old-time explorer, and I shouted to men who followed me, warning them of Indians and avalanches. I told them stories of the animals I'd killed—deer and elk and bears.

Along one side of the house, the dark green shutters were closed. A light shone yellow from the living room window. The pickup stood drifted in snow. I took off my coat in the mudroom, listening to my mother sing the words to a hymn—"*How glorious must the mansions be where Thy redeemed shall dwell with Thee . . .*" In the kitchen, a plate of gingersnaps was set out on the counter.

"Just two," she said, and twirled a thread in her mouth. I ate both cookies, watching her. A large pot of split-pea soup sat simmering on the stove.

After a while, without looking up: "Where did you and Ann leave your crayons?"

"All right . . ." I said. We had left our crayons on the rug.

Some pants my mother had patched lay folded on the dining room table. Beside them stood the ironing board and a basket of pressed clothes. I stretched to feel the heat of the iron, inching my fingers towards it. Then behind me, just for a second, the lamplight seemed to dim. I noticed the sharp smell of gun grease. I don't remember turning, or why I turned, to look in the living room.

The lamp fanned light on my father's chair, around it and over the newspaper. Two long, cloth-tipped ramrods lay next to the can of gun grease, a few flannel patches, a rag, and—something which didn't belong—a red and white box of cartridges. My father, staring beyond me as though at something not in that room, was standing in front of his chair with the rifle, the .30/30 Winchester. He threw open the lever and snapped it closed. The back of my neck prickled. He stood for a moment, frowning, with a look half enraged, half confused, and then all at once he shouldered the gun and aimed it at the bear neck.

The explosion rocked me backward, the sound drumming my chest. The bear, as if coming to life, sprang from the wall, over the mantle and hearth, and fell to the floor near my father's feet, where the crash seemed almost silent, lost in the echo of the shot. The bear lay propped on its nose, fur raised on the back of its neck. I had never seen the back of its head. I had always looked up at it.

My mother was suddenly there, her hands clenched at her throat. My father stood still, the gun at his shoulder. Sweat gleamed on his forehead. Through a haze of smoke and plaster dust, he stared at the wall, at the hole there, and then he lowered the gun. Slowly, as if he were conscious of each separate movement, he turned and sat on the edge of his chair. He laid the gun at his feet and put his hands on his knees.

I watched my mother kneel and place her hands on his. She whispered something, whispered again, and as she stood with the gun, saw the cartridge box. She began to stoop, thought better, or else got confused. One hand on her knee, she stopped, then turned to me, biting her lip.

"Better go upstairs now."

My father lifted his head. He half faced me, blinking.

"Go on," she said.

I took a step. Then I ran for the stairs.

Outside my window, the sky grew dark. The curtains stirred with a draft. I drew my knees to my chest, suddenly aware I was cold. There were footsteps in the hall. The floorboards creaked with my father's weight, and I heard my mother whisper. Their door latch clicked.

The door swung open into my room, and I could feel her standing in the doorway. She sat beside me on the bed, her hand in the hollow of my neck.

"All right?"

I rolled to my back. In the window light, her eyes were gray.

After a moment: "He's fine now."

I wasn't sure what to say.

She sat for a while, then slid aside, leaned over and kissed my forehead. She shut the door, quietly, and as she went down the stairs, I counted her steps.

A little later, I heard the vacuum cleaner and the clatter of the metal stepstool. Then the back door slammed — Ann, from Mrs. Stewart's.

"You sick?" she asked, in our room. In socks, her cheeks bright red, she stepped around the crayons and sat on the rug near her bed. She placed two gingersnaps down on her lap, broke one, and put a piece in her mouth.

"Well, why are you in bed then?" She grinned, chewing the cookie.

I could only stare at her.

"Mrs. Stewart gave me some candy," she said.

Neither of us spoke that afternoon. I lay on my side; Ann drew. When we were called to set the table, she ran down the hallway ahead of me.

The hall was filled with darkness, light glowing up from the stairwell. My parents' door was closed. Standing beside the banister, I heard the rattle of silverware, and my mother: "Where's your brother?" I started down, my eyes on my feet, and near the bottom of the stairs looked up. The bear head hung on the wall. The living room stood as always. Later, after we started our supper, just my mother and Ann and I, my brothers

came home from the service station, the backs of their
hands shiny, leathered from the cold.

"Your father feels like resting," my mother said,
when they asked. She glanced at me, uneasily. Then she
looked at the soup in her bowl.

■

My mother didn't tell anyone, or at least so far as I
know, and she never brought it up again with me. I didn't
tell anyone either, though I thought about telling Ann,
and I would sometimes secretly stare at the bear, trying
to find the bullet hole, although I never could.

Later that winter, desperate for money, my father
sold his guns. A ruddy-faced man paid him quickly in
cash without waiting for any receipt, then hurried to his
car with the rifles, each as black as a river at night. In
the spring my father found a job with G. E., where he
worked for twenty-three years. In all that time, we never
shared the comradery he'd so easily shared with my
brothers. He never did take me hunting, though even now
I occasionally dream of it, my father beside me out in the
woods, the day oversharp and bright, while everything —
each thread in his Mackinaw, his eyes when he grins and
looks down at me — seems somehow polished, dazzling,
not at all the world as I know it, but a sunlit world in
which we will live forever without a care.

Though the bear head remained above the fireplace, my father seldom spoke of it. He died while he sat
in this chair one night, died quietly, fallen asleep. "God's
grace," said my mother at his funeral. His friends were
all there, from town and work. His children and eighteen
grandchildren traveled from New York, Connecticut,
Massachusetts, and Maine. Uncle Harry, nearly eighty,
now a stooped and trollish man, rode up on a bus from
Asheville.

"Spreading thin," he said, and shook his head. To keep cool in the sun by the grave, he wore burdock leaves in his hat.

When the services had ended, I drove around for a while. The shell of a 7-Eleven stood where Camire's store had been, and most of the houses in town were in need of a coat of paint. The June afternoon was as humid as summer, and by the time I got back to the house, everyone else was gathered in the shade of the open porch. Every chair they could find they put out there—the glider, chairs from the dining room, a stained fruit basket or two. An unsettling awkwardness hung still and hot as the air. The children played out back in the woods while the rest of them stood and talked in low voices, in groups of three or four. A handful of women worked in the kitchen, preparing the chicken and ham, and my sisters served iced tea and biscuits. Some of the men had brought pints.

When at last the food was set out, they all sat and began to eat quietly, the only sounds the clink of the silver on plates and the hushed murmur of voices. Towards evening, as the shadows spread and thickened and chased the children from the woods, Roy lit some punks to repel the mosquitoes. My father's friends traded shop talk, talk of the weather and of politics. Their wives spoke about grandchildren. A few teenage cousins sat off by themselves. Some of the children, growing restless, began to whine and hang on their mothers' skirts. My mother and two of the other women had gone to wash dishes in the kitchen, when Uncle Harry, white-haired, in a string tie and yellowed shirt, leaned back on the glider, lit a cigar, and casually— though no doubt he'd waited for just this moment— began in his gravelly voice to tell an old family story about his grandfather, the Scotsman, R. Q. Lauder.

Tentatively, then more boldly, the children surrounded him. They sat by his feet or on their mothers' legs, their eyes round, bodies still. Harry told them of his mother who'd waded Sorrel Creek for the ducks his father shot upstream. He told them of his father and the Wirebarrel Riverside, stories like ancient songs to me. The older people, in their shirt sleeves and dark cotton dresses, gathered around him too, nodded to themselves and smiled. The teenagers stood behind them in the deepening shadows. A girl asked Harry what had happened to his hand. He winked, and cuffing the shirt from his wrist, he told of the day he fell on the fence. I sat by myself on a straight chair, watching, smoking a cigarette.

Harry talked of the hunter my father had been. Bob and Roy, for their parts, added how he'd shot the bear on the ridge and how they'd helped him drag it from the woods. One of the old men, Ty Wattson, remembered how they'd hung the bear in the tree and had stood beneath it in the November chill, hearing my father boast. Now others — my sister Sharon, even Ann — were telling stories about him. I was leaning in, listening. My mother had come to the doorway, a dishtowel in her hand, and for a moment it seemed as if all of them — my father, his mother, my great-grandfather, all the Lauders dead and unborn — were standing around us in the shadows, beyond where the porch light reached.

ELIZABETH GRAVER

Square Dance

from Story

nominated by Eric Pankey

The radio says bad cold spell, so I go about the house and dress myself for warmth and company. First my own long underwear top, whose pink weave fits me like a skin. Then the brace, Kyra's flannel shirt, my mother's sweater, Kyra's woolen tights, and on top of those, Robin's baggy jeans held up with a purple sash. Most of the clothes I put on have been left out, draped over chairs or tossed in the corner of someone's room. A few I rummage for in closets, knowing they'll be there. Finally, I wrap a scarf around my neck, zip myself into my father's blue down jacket and go out to the creaking front porch to sit for a few minutes before work. At first as I ease myself onto the porch steps, I smell only the wood stacked there, the bunched frozen air, but then as I bring my knees up to my chest, the smells of my layers come to me in their varying shades of clean and dirty, my family on my back. "Stay in, Hannah," I imagine my father saying, but I welcome the cold air seeping through the boards to my behind and remember a fever I had when I was twelve, how my parents sat me down in a cold tub and sang me off-key rounds until my fever broke.

I could, if I needed to, stay here forever. This is what I tell myself, that they would never kick me out; they have plenty of room and adequate money, big hearts. They love me, yes, because I am theirs and came out with the right number of toes and fingers, and a head of amazing orange hair. And grew up the oldest and tallest, the best cook, fastest runner and only fiddle player, and then in eleventh-grade gym Ian Nisbet asked me to square dance, and we do-si-do'd and joined hands and went around the world, and in half a second he had ripped something so hard from my neck down to my elbow that the whole gym twitched like ganglia, and I felt it in my eyes, my back, liquid for an instant, searing, and then the pain hardened, settled, and became solid and determined, lodged like a family of chiggers beneath my skin.

Since then I have shifted my expectations, or rather every time I try to read, a thread of pain runs from my eyes down to my back, and each time I lift my left hand, my wrist tightens like hot, braided wire and my fingers splay. I am, if nothing else, the mystery of East Coast neurologists, with my untraceable dislodged nerve. Angry? How can you blame someone for dancing you too hard, though I never liked him, and when I hear he has graduated from college now, lived in Seattle, San Francisco, New York, I wonder what it was about that spin that sent him whirling in his Southern Comfort T-shirt and left me crouching on the varnished floor.

And around now, my family must be slinging their shoes over their shoulders and walking barefoot toward an empty patch of beach, and my nearsighted father is counting heads and reciting landmarks: "Remember, guys, we're right near the red umbrella. Look for the stripes when you get out." Go on, kiddo, be brave; show them your swimsuit, I think to Robin, who is more confident in cold weather, where he comes off vaguely cute and padded, like a bear. Kyra has crocheted herself a bikini, tiny and ready to unravel on her happy flesh.

She must be belly down on her towel now, glistening with coconut oil, the best vacationer. "Do you want a T-shirt or a tacky plastic something?" she asked before they left.

And now the dog is bounding toward me with a dead rabbit in his mouth, so I say, "Ugh, Utah, get away, you foul thing," and he shakes his head and wheels around, back into the brush. I would like to stay and listen to him plow through the dry sticks, but it's time for my vitamins and pills, and Jacob, the new custodian, will be over soon to drive me to work.

"Utah!" I shout, my voice shrill in the wide yard. "Utah!!"

Then he is back, stretching toward me across the snow, his jaws empty this time, eyes on me. "Come here," I say. "Let's go in." He comes to where I sit on the porch steps, puts his head against my knees, and slowly I lower my cheek to his bony forehead and hold him against me until he shakes himself free.

"Yes, I'm going to feed you," I tell him. "Yes. Then you're on your own because I've got to go."

Once, I had no patience with people who talked to animals. I disliked teenagers who stayed home for the summer, kids who didn't go to college, especially the smart ones who failed their high-school courses because they'd rather get stoned and drive around in souped-up cars. I looked down on many things: prefabricated houses, lawn ornaments, loud make-up, bad grammar, the inability to get off your ass and look for anything better than what you had. The fall I should have gone to college, I sat in my room and memorized anatomy books, and when my eyes and nerves drove me from the page, I quizzed my sister on her times tables, bit my nails until the sides were pink like raw meat, got my mother to take me on long car rides into Vermont and scowled at the bright, unfolding mountains, all that fall.

Still, there were friends I saw now and then, people left over from high school, the un-college bound. A girl named Kelly who lived on a farm near the mountain and raised goats. Paula Canadish, who got pregnant in ninth grade and dropped out of school to have her baby. Darrell, with his long New England face and stubborn chin, who did electrical work and kissed me one morning in our basement where he was rewiring. Slow and careful, that kiss, his arms held flat against his sides, and he drew back in the middle and said to tell him if it hurt. I found myself digging my fingernails into my palms, almost crying, and I said, "For Christ's sake, how could it hurt—it's only my goddamn mouth." Then we kissed once more against the damp concrete, and as he started to undo things, my shirt, my brace, I remembered times before the dance with other guys, how much I had needed to feel skin against me, anything.

"No," I said, because I couldn't go back to that.

And he told me he'd been watching me for years. My track meets, my hair, everything.

"Leave me alone," I told him, "or I'll call the police."

"Shit," he said, in a quiet voice. "You probably really would."

I laughed then and said it was a joke, that I was sorry, but I was not sorry, and then winter came, and spring, and that summer I was more tired than I'd ever been, sleeping all day under a sheet with the fan going high speed, or on a foam mat in the side yard with the pain prodding me like a stick. Mostly it was my left arm that gave me trouble, and my eyes. Sometimes I felt small explosions like bubbles popping in my back and feet; when I tried to bend, my neck and back brace held my torso upright as a porcelain doll's. And there were my younger brothers and sisters growing taller every day: Kyra so pretty you wanted to stop things before they turned sour; Jessie a ringleader, followed about by the neighbor's three little kids. Robin building his model boats in the cool basement, and once when I caught him by surprise he was just in his underwear down there, hunched over the skeleton of his wooden ship.

By the end of the summer, the world seemed wrapped in sleep, and something had moved through me like a sigh. My parents had connections in town, people anxious to help. When I was offered a job as a part-time monitor in the children's room of the library, I took it graciously and performed it cheerfully, and later, when I started getting headaches from the fluorescent lights, I was offered a job working at the local college taking care of the tiny zoological museum and told them yes.

"If we approach it right," said the neurologists, "limited exercise of this sort could be just the thing," and most of the time it was all right, although I never knew when the pain would sneak up from behind. It has turned into four years, feeding the scorpions, dusting the stuffed kangaroo, organizing exhibits on the sounds of dolphins and habitats of bats. Have I compromised myself? My parents tell me not to worry, I'm still young. "Get your health back," they say, "then we'll see." The museum is one big room attached to the biology building—panes of glass and tanks of animals, waxed wooden floors and my desk in the corner next to a stuffed moose mottled from the hands of students and the wear of time.

I am ready for work at nine, but Jacob pulls up ten minutes late—the snow, he says, combing his hair with his fingers, but I am skeptical and think of Mr. Carol, the steady old custodian who used to call me Mrs. Zoo and accepted the extra duty of picking me up with good grace. Slouched over the wheel in his green pickup truck, Jacob mutters something about how wiped out he is. "Played late last night," he says, and I make a non-committal noise.

When I get to work, I unlock the doors and hang the monkey-shaped Open sign on its hook. The museum is small, but visited frequently by college students and kids from the public schools, and people in town look out for the collection. Many of the dead animals are locals: the owl crashed into a Greek professor's window and was brought in to be stuffed; the groundhog was found frozen but intact in a mound of snow. The other animals, the live ones, come from farther off, and I have repainted the backdrops of their cages to mimic tundra, jungle, desert, forest floor. In the far corner is the bones section and the glass cupboard full of jars — a heart in formaldehyde, a floating frog, a tiny human fetus, white and curled as a hand in pain.

And because it is their school vacation, the children stop by to see the sights or warm up between sledding trips on the steep hill behind the quad. Some of them know me, some don't, but I do not intimidate, though the top of my brace pokes out of my sweater like an extra limb. I feed the animals from the narrow hallway around back, which runs the length of the tanks. Peering through, I can also survey my tiny kingdom from behind the scenes. The menu does not vary much from day to day, although in summer I bring in garden vegetables as treats. Most days, I put the same quantity of food in the same corner of each cage, and they nose over, open their pink or black, sharp or toothless mouths, take what is offered, and go on.

The only exception, the only bit of razzmatazz, is the boa, christened Trance because when she arrived at the museum, she lay for days in a tight coil, her long head swaying slightly as if following a slow invisible pendulum back and forth. Each morning, the Head of Biology deposited a mouse in the snake's cage and hovered over her, and each morning, as the mouse hugged corners and ran circles, Trance simply sat. Until the tenth day, when a particularly sensitive mouse's legs gave out, and the snake flicked her tongue, unwound, and killed the animal with a professional squeeze, settling on the floor of her cage to digest. She was the only live animal in the museum who all the visitors swore was dead. Children could bang on her glass cage with their dirty fists, ignoring the Don't Touch signs, and she would lie still as the clay coil pots they made in school. The professors could flash lights in her eyes, adjust the levels on her heat lamp, play the radio at top volume above her cage, and Trance wouldn't twitch. Except when she saw the mouse, and then some muscle-moving, blood-quickening reaction tripped down her thick trunk, and the snake's dull body eased into motion, uncurling on her branch — sliding, sometimes, down the backdrop of fronds and sky, and she squeezed for her supper, and swallowed whole, and returned to her sluggish state.

I am choosing the mouse of the day when the Brownies come in. The mice are kept in the back corridor with the other food, their cages dank and cramped. I pick a mouse with about as much interest as I pick one blueberry from a bowlful; this has been going on a long time. The one I choose is as small, white and quick as the others, and I scoop it into a coffee can with a one-handed motion and turn to give Trance her fix.

But there on the other side, flat against the glass, are six beating hands belonging to three small Brownies, doing their best to pound Trance from her dreams. From my angle up above, I can see only the girls' palms and their brown berets, but I hear their shrill voices: "Ooooh, lookit; I told you he was big. How come he doesn't move? How come it's just lying there? I bet he's dead, huh? Yoohoo Mr. Snakey! Hey!"

I could go out, I think, and scold them for touching, then give them my standard talk about the snake. They are younger than Jessie, around eight, probably. They must just have gotten out of their meeting, cutting across campus to go home. I am tipping the coffee can in my hand, and then the mouse is skidding up the side, trying to bite my fingers with its frantic teeth, and I whisper, "Shit, you little bastard," and fling it in.

Which is when one of the Brownies screams so loud that every creature in every cage seems to stop for a moment to listen.

"Ahhh!" she shrieks. "He's gonna kill it he's gonna kill it!"

And, indeed, Trance lifts her head, swings round her thick body and begins to curve toward the mouse.

"No!" hollers the girl, and by this time I have left my hallway and am there to grab her from behind as she throws herself at the glass front of the cage.

In spirit I am there to pull her back, in intention, but as I tell my arm to reach for her, the tensing up begins within my veins, the freezing up like pistons out of oil. The tunnelling in, so that when it happens, my body becomes the entire feeling world, and although I can see the girl's face, the room, the animals, the glare of snow outside, essentially they are not there. In the beginning, the first few times, I thought it would last forever, this narrowing—my fingers curling toward my palms, my tongue toward my throat, my abdomen and stomach pulled back, reaching like a heated magnet for my spine. Gradually, I learned; it always went away. Like a developing photograph, the room would gain color and ease into focus. My body would lose its grip on itself, and there I'd be, and there would be the world in its prior state, impassive and clear.

"Listen to me," I say calmly to the girl, though my arms hang limp at my sides. "Please stop. You'll scare her."

But she is beating her hands against the glass, pounding her head as her friends look on.

"I told you to get away from that cage," I say. "You're going to break the glass."

The child flails an arm in my direction as if to push me away, but when I step back, she changes tactics, turning now to me.

"Get him out! Get the mouse! Please get him out!"

She throws herself against me, tugs on my sweater, and I turn my good side toward her, put my hand over her eyes and hold her there, thinking of Robin and Jessie the time our father caught his hand in the garage door and lost half a finger, how the two of them hid behind the stacked lawn furniture ducking their heads into their arms; how terribly calm I'd been. When I uncover the girl's eyes and let her go, she is still sobbing, her mouth slack. She puts one arm around me for a second as if I am a logical comforter, then pulls back with a whining noise.

"Shhh," I say to her, the room, myself. "Okay? Calm down."

On the beach, my family must be eating lunch, sandy hot dogs and chips, and my father is making sure everyone gets a fair share, and Robin is saying he is not hungry and throwing flirtatious sidelong glances at the food. We eat chicken, I want to tell the girl. We eat hot dogs. If this mouse did not die here, it would be injected with some chemical, or fastened to wires, or given ungodly amounts of artificial sweeteners, and even if it ran free in a big, wheat-filled, mice-filled field, even then, one day this mouse would die, perhaps in the jaws of a snake.

But the girl has turned toward the fish tank, her arms wrapped around her middle, her cotton Brownie uniform hiked up at the waist. She brushes at her nose with the back of her hand.

"Is she okay?" I ask her friends, who refuse to look at me. "She has to eat," I inform the room. "Snakes eat mice. It is Nature."

Under the high ceiling, my voice sounds like a loud recording, but not even the animals look up. The girl sniffles and then, as we all stand watching, a dark stream appears on her wrinkled brown tights and forms a puddle on the floor. She turns and looks down, then over at me, and something like a willed half-smile appears on her face—forgiveness or revenge. She leans over, steps

out of her rubber boots, takes off her tights and underpants and puts her boots back on. Then she turns to go,
leaving the soiled garments on the floor.

"You need those. It's freezing cold outside," I call.
"Hang on!"

But she has grabbed her red parka from the corner,
put on her mittens, and the others are following behind,
out to the cold blast which I feel as if it were circling my
legs. It will burn her bare skin, but there is nothing I can
do. Although Trance is busy digesting, there are still the
scorpions to deal with, the tarantula and hamsters, the
ailing bat.

Once, I think, as I maneuver her wet tights and
underwear into a plastic bag, once I was a Brownie in
this town and won badges for building fires and weaving
baskets, for jumping on the trampoline and helping at
the Old People's Home, where I did cartwheels for the
men between their beds. What I want to tell the girl, what
the realist in me wants to say is: toughen up. Trance has
her problems, and so do all white mice, and so do you
and I. It is what I would say, if she were to come back, but
she is gone. Probably she is home now, getting new
panties, changing into her snow pants, and then they will
go sledding on the hill, stretching their necks, screaming
and tumbling like badgers in the snow.

More than anything, I want to cry. Not because it is
so sad — God knows, there are worse things than a dead
white mouse or the spirited anger of a Brownie. But at
first, I couldn't do it either. I would feed the other
animals their grains, pellets and bits of green, then Mr.
Carol would come on his cleaning rounds and I'd say,
"Hey, I hate to ask again, Mr. Carol," and while I sat at
my desk pretending not to watch, he would go around
back, grab a mouse by the tail, and drop it in.

"All set, Mrs. Zoo," he would say, pulling his cart of
cleaning supplies past my desk. "Everybody's got to
eat."

And those were the days when I memorized books, trooped off to doctor after doctor, took test after test, and when that didn't work, read up on acupuncture and herb healing. And touched myself at night, alone in bed, experimenting with what hurt too much, circling my good hand up and down like the most expert lover.

In front of my family, I cried. All the time, so often that they learned to keep the conversation going when the streams began, as if it had simply started raining or someone had turned on the faucet at the kitchen sink. There I was, so tired after a while, wiped out, and then Mr. Carol died of a stroke, leaving me little choice, because the new custodian was young and sullen and told me he planned to become famous in a rock band, and I was nothing if not proud.

On the way home from work, I mention the girl, and Jacob says, "Jesus Christ, only a kid from this town could get so riled up about a goddamn mouse."

"What do you mean?" I ask, and he turns halfway toward me and makes a whistling noise through his teeth.

"Fucking Never-Never Land," he says. "Doesn't she have anything better to think about?"

"She's a kid. Everything is relative, I guess."

But Jacob is busy complaining about his green janitor's uniform, and the way a chemistry professor spoke to him today, and how nobody cares about anything in this stupid town, in this stupid country for that matter.

"You get your little house," he says, "and you get your little wife, tra la la, and then you go zooming around in your car and isn't life the greatest?"

"Aw, shit," he says then, and stops abruptly at a stop sign, so that we jerk forward and my hand flies to my neck. I suck in my breath.

"For God's sake," I say. "Could you drive a little more carefully?"

He stops talking and slows down drastically, so that the car behind us honks and tries to pass.

"Go ahead," says Jacob, glancing in the rearview mirror. "Pass me, old fellow. Go wild!"

He swerves the truck over onto the shoulder, and the station wagon moves ahead.

"Hold on tight," he says, pulling slowly back into the road. "We're off!"

Then we are at my driveway, in front of my door, and I get out without a goodbye, thinking it serves him right, almost forgetting my yellow knapsack, but he picks it up from the seat and hands it to me.

"If you're planning to be late again tomorrow," I say, "please call."

"Planning to be late," he says. "Ha."

Then the departure: slamming door, spinning tires on the icy drive, three short honks, and he has grazed a snowbank and skidded back into the road. When he rounds the corner, nothing is left but the aftermath of the honk in my ears and Utah sending staccato sounds out over the front porch, barking as if there were something to protect.

Inside, I play a record, put on water for tea and run a bath. Usually, around now, I am helping with dinner, but with them gone, I wander the house in my sock feet, trailing my hand on countertops and walls. When I was little, accumulation seemed the norm to me, but now, as I catalogue, I am amazed—how they managed it, not only buying the shell of the house but filling it with furniture and children, and kitchen drawers full of years' worth of recipes, bread ties, rubber bands. All this from two people who were not even related once, who met at a Walkathon for charity, both of them well-intentioned but cursed with blisters, lagging behind. My family does not take pictures; just as well—we are an odd-looking bunch, disparate in size, shape and color. But in the bathroom is a family portrait I drew when I was twelve:

we are standing in a line — Robin thinner than life, Kyra plainer, Utah's mother Limerick and I blazing with red hair. I hold my lacrosse stick like a scepter.

I cannot say I haven't learned some things since then. Because of its slow metabolism, the Red Legs Tarantula can survive in the desert without food for over two-and-a-half years, waiting for insects and lizards to wander within reach. Other creatures are more aggressive: a locust will eat its own weight in a day. Half the game involves hiding, the other half, knowing how to ruffle the plumage or flash the orange dot. Slowly, I undress before the family portrait. From its place on the wall, it has seen a long parade of bathers over the years, a baring of our various untidy skins. I grip the steel bar alongside the tub and lower myself through the steam. My limp white limbs are perfect underwater, there where every edge is muted, movement slowed.

At work the next day, I pick-type an index card, arrange a file, wipe down a pane of glass. We have arrived early; I am prey to Jacob's schedule, and he had to move equipment into a chemistry lab before the first class. At feeding time, I move down the back corridor. I am halfway through when I hear the approaching roar of the vacuum cleaner and look through the hamster tank to see Jacob pushing his way across the floor.

And I am not sure why I do it, because it's not as if I can't deal with these things myself, but I wipe my hand on my jeans and go out.

I yell. "Hey, could you do me a favor?"

"Huh?" he shouts back.

"A *favor*! Can you help me with something?"

Jacob turns off the machine. In the abrupt silence, I remember Mr. Carol — his slow, wide face, his head too big for his body, the neat haircut, the sideburns trimmed in a gray line. His uniform was always ironed, his name embroidered in red script above the breast pocket. Jacob wears his uniform rumpled and unclean, the way teen-agers wear army surplus, as a look.

"Sorry," I say. "I mean, I know you're working, but I was wondering—after yesterday, this mouse thing is just bugging me. If the kid comes back or something, and I'm in the middle of feeding Trance . . ."

He squints, tucks his chin toward his neck. I look away.

"What the hell is Trance?"

I turn to her cage.

Jacob swivels to see her immobile on her branch. "It eats one of those things a day?" he says. "Some appetite."

"One a day for two days, then two weeks with nothing."

"Well," he says, "the kid's not gonna come back. Not two days in a row."

I shrug and force myself to look at him, not at his chin, or his chest, or the exhibit over his left shoulder, but at his eyes which are slightly almond-shaped as if he has some Asian blood. Who knows how he came out that way, his skin darker than mine, his hair bordering on blond, a funny mix from staying too many generations in this town. I remember him from high school, his acne, his group of laughing, slouching friends. He stares back an instant, more than an instant, confrontational, and I feel my nerves tensing up, my hand freezing, but I win, because he looks away and asks me, "What?"

Again I shrug. "I know it's ridiculous, but I just don't want to do it."

Jacob drops the vacuum cleaner tube with a clatter.

'They might as well make me a professor. Yesterday I had to hand out tests. Today I get to feed the snake."

"You don't *have* to," I tell him, but he walks into the back hall where the mice are caged, so I follow and hand him the can.

"Okay," says Jacob, and because I see he doesn't

know how to go about it, I take the can, scoop up a mouse, and give it back.

"Here. Now you just drop it in."

We turn to the back of Trance's cage. Jacob is holding the coffee can away from him as if it contained something explosive; I can hear the mouse skittering inside. I watch his hand, the knuckles tightening, the branching veins. He looks into the can, then wobbles and stretches his free arm out to the wall. I am afraid he will either faint, or feign fainting.

"Never mind, just give it to me," I say, but as I reach out, he jerks his arm away and steps back.

"Forget it," he says, and then he has dropped the mouse into the tank and is leaning over it, watching, while I stand looking at the opposite wall. After a minute, he claps his hands together and turns to leave.

"Thanks," I say, but he shrugs. The hallway is narrow; to get by he must shimmy past me and the feed barrels as I press against the wall.

"Does it hurt?" he asks after he's made it past me.

"What do you think?" I say. "It would hurt you to get swallowed by a snake, but anyhow she's got to eat."

"No, the work. It's not like you're sitting down all day or anything. It doesn't, I don't know, strain your arm, or whatever?"

"I'm careful."

Jacob looks at the floor and tells me the day-care center needs a worker, just in case I'm looking for a change. His sister-in-law was there, but now she's eight months pregnant. "Everybody's pregnant," he says. "My sister, my sister-in-law, her friend Kay."

"I'm fine here," I tell him. "I don't mind."

For a moment I imagine he is about to reach out and touch my arm; I'm not sure why. I will it, even, wish his hand against me, but he only examines his palm, runs his fingers through his hair.

"So when are you leaving with your rock band?" I ask, getting back at him.

"We've got to make a demo tape. Once we make that, we send it to this place in Boston that's interested, and then they deal with the bigger places. We figure California in a year or two."

"What do you play?" I ask, and he says, "Everything. Guitar, bass, drums, vocals."

"Everything," I say, my voice sour with disbelief, and Jacob glances through the tanks to the room outside.

"I hate to break up the party," he says, tapping on the glass, "but I've got to finish up that floor."

So there I am, alone in the hall again, and the noise of the vacuum is rising over the tanks, and the mice are nosing each other, scurrying and cramped. Sometimes in high school when I was kissing some boy, I would get the extraordinary feeling of departing from my body and hovering above like a chaperone aunt or Peeping Tom, or narrating like a sports announcer, first and second base. Now I do not lose myself in movement. I turn to the right and feel a flash of heat, clench my jaw and feel a tightness. I lace my hands together as if they belonged to two different bodies, but I get nowhere, each hand a twin which knows the other's old routine inside and out.

Then I wonder, what if it all just went away? If I woke one morning, turned my neck and felt nothing, and touched my toes and felt only toes, and swung round sharply, testing, and saw the other side of the room before me, etched and clear? It is hard to remember how I felt before, but mostly it was a question of not noticing — the body no more than a convenient capsule, a pleasant vehicle, simply there, and I loved to run fast, and bend over my fiddle, and swim underwater until the pressure sent a buzzing through my head.

Here is what I might do, all in a day, in a morning: buy a car, pack a duffel bag, find a guide to the American Northwest or Southwest, Canada or Mexico. I would

move quickly, telling no one of my plans, and while I
might buy a tent to keep off rain and bugs, I would not
bring a floor mat, the curves of the earth negligible to
me — hard angles my pleasure, dissonance nothing to my
liquid nerves. Then I would drive, swinging the wheel in
wide turns, shifting gears, not on straight highways but
on the curving back roads, and it would be summer so
I'd be wearing almost nothing, my freckles crowding
each other out, each one so anxious to appear.

A square dance begins like a piece of geometry, and
you must bow and curtsy and keep the distance right.
Then it speeds up, and the caller's voice begins to dip
and turn, and the dancers skip a little, leap a little, and if
they are agile, the speed keeps building, until it is not
your partner you are dancing with, but the whole
square, the whole room even — part of a generous, sliding
pattern, like the bees who do this for their life.

At night without my pain, I would pitch a tent in a
field and sleep over the grass and ants, and some of the
ants would crawl on my stomach like streams of water or
trailing fingers. Or no, there would be real fingers, ten
besides my own, novel and articulate, and the smell of
skin and his knee flung over mine, and something familiar, anything — Kyra's old blue sweatshirt, my mother's
earring, a lacing from my brace. It is not that I want
them there, these things; they just appear.

The way I will begin is slow, and I'll tell no one but
myself, but waking each day, I'll force myself elsewhere:
India on a camel's back; the Bronx, just for five minutes,
playing basketball with local kids. College, or Kansas
City, or some suburb, pedaling on a bike. The power of
suggestion, said my neurologist, is enormous, and so for a
while I watched ballets on television and stared at the
hamsters as they ran their wheels. Jacob is tall and
brawny, and when I am thinking of nothing else, his
body comes to me like a possibility that could rub off, a
bit of borrowed ease. He will go to California and play in

a rock band; his voice will soften when he likes what he is doing. In his happiness, he will allow himself to love this historic, well-intentioned town, but he'll buy himself a house over there, by the sea.

How painful to see people fooling themselves. In my farthest reaches I go where I have no weight, where weight means nothing — underwater, or on the moon, and I am not alone, but touching fingers with a ring of bundled astronauts, and we are collecting things in sterile containers to bring to solid ground. If we can understand this barrenness, we can understand anything. If we can return from this weightlessness, we will never be weighed-down again. Or I am alone, so far from the earth that I can watch it spin, so far from my body that one hand meets the other like a total stranger, and I greet myself with a new and giddy pleasure, shaking hands.

A creature burrowed up through the earth, pushed into the Lodge through a loose floorboard in the closet, and walked down the hall into the living room breathing balls of fire that landed like tossed sunwheels on the couch, in the curtains. I was five and carrying my losses to date lightly, easily. Then something got Remy. A grey tabby dispersed like ash. That he had "wandered off" was the official word. I couldn't believe it. Not Remy. Not from me.

We were away that winter living north of the Island in a small French town, collectively chaperoning my wayward grandfather. He liked women, especially, for some reason, women named Ethel, and had cornered one in this zit of a place where Remy strangely took his leave. My parents resisted cross-examination on the subject, exchanging those knowing looks — to me damningly guilty — when I questioned them. I suspected other cats of being Remy in disguise, that cunning animal, and followed them around the neighbourhood. Marmalade or black as a bat, I missed his warm weight in my hands, his idling motor in my ear at night. I missed his claws, his stripes — he stepped out of them like a cage. Perhaps he disappeared into the language, the French none of us could speak.

My brother was having his own troubles in school because of this. Not fights, but academic disgrace. After a distinguished year in grade one on the Island, his star clearly rising, he was now in rapid descent, clutching a report card that bled red ink as he stumbled shamefaced through the door. His first real taste of failure. Mine of adult duplicity. Two kids sucking on aspirins was how we looked.

My grandfather had a mischievous giggle and like Elizabeth Taylor he believed in marriage. He must have been talked out of it this time though, as there were no nuptials to celebrate, no bride of fifty or sixty grinning down at me with large lipstick-flecked teeth. Celebration in general was muted that winter. In memory, deleted. Christmas is completely gone, though I do remember going to Midnight Mass at Easter, slipping out into the dark, sleep-deprived and dressed like a piece of candy. It was freezing. The ground was stiff, an alien surface. The wind slapped my new frilly hat into the bushes. Out there, alone, I heard a distant plaintive pinprick of sound. Remy. Crying. I called to him, loudly, desperately playing on the twisted thread of his lost self. Until finally the wind shoved his sweet springing name down my throat and someone grabbed my hand, cold and clawed like a tiny branch, and pulled me into the truck.

A cat can be made to vanish in any number of foul ways: under the wheels of a car, a schoolyard hanging (monkey bars are useful for this), in a tied and weighted sack dropped in a lake, a dog chasing instinct into a dark corner, a human doing research, a drawing and quartering so secret you can't even find the bones and blood. I was five but I wasn't a fool — what the years add to knowledge of cruelty is only detail.

The lodge that stood on the hill with flames growing out of its roof like wild red hair was our home on the Island. We returned in the spring to watch it burn. An entertaining event for some, with stored boxes of fireworks going off and exploding ammunition singing through the air. My parents and I missed the raging part and caught the tail end, a few lazy tongues finishing off the black carcass.

My brother and grandfather, who had come back a week earlier to open up the Camp, saw the whole thing, *from A to izzard,* my grandfather said, pretending to be an old man. That morning they'd been driven out of bed, choking on smoke, yet managed to find their boots and throw on coats over their striped PJs before bolting out the door. My grandfather also stopped briefly to gaze at himself in the hallway mirror. This may have been out of habit, or more likely to assess the effect of fiery clouds billowing behind him. A striking figure. *The very devil himself,* he must have thought.

The ice was still in the bay. The ones who live below the ice, the green-haired women with blue bodies and flowing black dresses, would have been gazing up as through a thick distorting window at my brother. Determined to save the Lodge, he was hacking at the ice with his Roy Rogers pocket knife, an empty pail beside him. The volunteer fire department from town had taken the wrong road and when they eventually arrived were in a partying mood, wanting more to dally with the fire than quench it.

We lost everything. Even our clustered fingerprints were nibbled off before the furniture and walls were consumed. A detective snooping around would not have found much material evidence of our existence. My mother's documented past, her treasured life in the old country, highland-flinged itself right out of view wearing her Uncle Alec's Black Watch kilt and bearing away an armful of photographs, bedeviling memory. She covered her face with her empty hands, as adults do, and wept. I turned away, taking stock of my blazing tricycle and smouldering bed, my dolls nothing now but a scattered fistful of charred and cracked eyes.

We lost everything, but somehow were no less unburdened. Before leaving the Island that winter my father had transferred the insurance from the Lodge to the new cottage he was building above the ice house, not being able to afford both. The fire was attracted to the wrong place, so all we as got out of it were a few good stories and some crude hunks of metal and glass, my brother's former penny and marble collections melded together into a kind of collector's parody. The situation wasn't completely hopeless, of course; some things you can never lose no matter what. The Aelicks' boys from the neighbouring farm had rushed into the flames and, with an unerring eye for the peripheral and useless, had rescued a number of items: a waffle iron that produced black inedible objects, the box of tackle containing lures that made even the fish snort derisively, and the two yard-high yellow-eyed ceramic hawks my mother had inherited from the first Ethel and had been trying to get rid of for years.

I had always liked those birds, admiring their crafty demeanor, and was glad to have one in my arms, warm from the fire, as my brother and I carried them like resident gods down to our new home, the cottage with the insurance. Wonderment is their element, those in the water that is, and they would have watched us coming to them in a dream, half-bird we must have seemed through the ice. The cottage, fragrant with raw lumber, smelled like the inside of a tree. We claimed our rooms, planting a guardian hawk in each, then ran out the door and up branching paths to the other cottages — Pine Crest, Mayferg, Waubuno, Twin Elms, Americana, But N'Ben, Dewdrop Inn, Sunset — to search for bedding and dishes and whatever it is that a family needs.

Our lives had now shifted closer to the water where I'd get *their* insinuating music in my ears and never get it out.

We had something to see through the picture window in our living room, unlike most people who have them. Not tidy squares of grass and asphalt, but this great expanse, the bay opening into the lake. *Whadaview!* our guests the tourists said, blind to what we saw. What was really out there, shifting and gleaming, wearing scales of light, a mutable skin, a disturbing depth. Daily as prayer we had this in our eyes washing them clean, whetting them to a keen sharpness. We lived beside the water as beside an enormous and unpredictable parent that might buoy you up murmuring in your ear, or pull you under, plugging your nose and mouth with mud, binding you with slime-green weeds. In the evening the lake caught the sun's fire, which made everyone gasp *whadasight!* while the women swimming less visibly below helped us skip the stones we threw by reaching up with long blue fingers and keeping them alight on the surface.

Our first phone call in the new place came in the middle of the night. We'd been hanging around the kitchen all day, ready to pounce if the thing rang — it was also our first telephone — but were helplessly mired in sleep when it did. My father was the one who struggled up out of bed and answered with a boyish smile that sprang nimbly enough to his lips for three A.M. A minute later it was gone, like the silver flicker of a minnow darting into deep water. We didn't see it again for weeks until the tourists started arriving and it had to be coaxed back onto his face for the sake of business. The call was from my grandfather. He was honeymooning in Cleveland with his new bride, an Ethel Lafleur from Sheguiandah, a woman he'd met at the fire and someone he'd been courting secretly since then.

This Ethel, with her tightly permed calico hair and leathery tough hide, was a slightly bizarre version, though to me she came to epitomize Ethelness. She wore thick stockings held up by unreliable elastics, had a chipped front tooth angled like a fang, and a blue-black tongue from chewing endlessly on jawbreakers. My parents were horrified. By her and by her house which was layered with dust and mildew and was as densely packed with curious objects as a museum. I had never before seen hair wreaths and framed fish skin. And she had dolls, old scary ones, that she kept up an active relationship with—her "babies" that stared like the dead at my brother and me while adult conversation, which usually swished so briskly above our heads, stopped and started like a machine that just wouldn't work. At infrequent but unavoidable Sunday dinners, she served salmon cakes (*sucker*, my father claimed) and mashed potatoes with black lumps entombed in them like flies. My grandfather was the only one who could relax and apparently enjoy these get-togethers, his attraction to his wife solid and not to be fathomed.

Just wanted to let you know, he shouted over the phone from Cleveland, this chased by his characteristic chuckle that bubbled into my father's ear like frothing champagne.

Sibling rivalry in my grandfather's family was conducted on a theological battlefield. One brother was a Presbyterian, the other a Methodist. Of his sisters, May attended the United Church, Maude the Anglican, while Minnie met with her friends down at the Kingdom Hall. They had divided up Christianity like so many flavours of ice cream and fought among themselves about the merits of each. My grandfather, with the sheer delight of annoyance written like a signature into all his motives, was for a long time uncommitted to any faith, until one day he unexpectedly became a Catholic. A trump card that made everyone, even the Jehovah's Witness, howl.

So we were Catholics too, though not the kind I think the Church envisioned when it considered its flock. My father remained skeptical, giving the minimum of devotion, while my mother, who grew up in a place where Catholic meant street gangs and beatings, entered the Church like an infiltrator. It suited some aspects of my brother's character, as he enjoyed collecting the medals and holy cards and putting in flawless performances as an altar boy. As for me, it abetted my credulity. I have a talent for belief the way some people have a talent for embezzlement or shoplifting. It gave me license. If you're going to open the door to sundry saints and angels, then why not the *pah-eens*, those tiny Indian tricksters who lived in the rocks, or the women in the water who spoke a submerged patois that drifted through the windows at night while lichen-scabbed imps, round as owls, curled up in the branches outside?

Priests called on us, though not for the sake of our dodging souls. They came to the Camp to relax, to release their eccentricities like dogs that needed a good run in the country. They kept a respectful distance from the unholy water, crossing themselves against it, while at the same time dealing fearlessly with the other fluid elements my parents had on hand. Our hospitality was reciprocated by their own brand of generosity. Almost any spiritual perk could be ours for the asking. If they drank too much, they got reckless and would dispense blessings like pie-eyed fairy godmothers. Trigger-happy, they sanctified the toaster, the shot glasses, the Crest Hardware calendar — once Father Donnelly winged a fly in mid-air — on and on until our kitchen grew hazy and numinous with grace, more sacred than the Vatican itself.

I had trouble with sin. I just couldn't get the hang of it. Later on, after I'd received First Communion and was old enough to go to confession, I began inventing sins for myself. Diving into transgression as into a fictional dirt-pile, smudging my soul in imitation of a typically fallible child. Our teacher depicted the soul as a milk bottle, shaded in spots or completely black, with the spanking clean bottle being the ideal, full to the brim with grace. But we weren't expected to attain it. Who would believe me if I told them I never sinned? So I aimed for liveliness and variety within a venial range, the fine embroidery of small iniquities — untruths and petty thefts and impure thoughts — wanting to give the Confessor some entertainment without incurring an overly punishing and time-consuming penance. *Bless me father for I have sinned*, whispered in the dim confessional to the shadowy figure behind the screen, was my cue to improvise, to deliver the goods like a double agent spreading lies about lies.

I saved the truth, the real confessions, for the women in the lake. I knew this about them, that they wept and sang. That they prophesied. What I wanted was help. Perhaps sympathy. Speaking under water slowly like a record on the wrong speed, I asked them for Remy. I did, and they gave him to me in dreams, a cat with fire in its mouth and sparks flying from its tail. He stood on my chest lightly as a sparrow. Though at other times, with a suffocating pressure, sodden and unbearably heavy. They were midwives. They pulled him out of the water and placed him in my arms (a stink of death rising). He was their poetry; they delivered him in their devious tongue, translating him into something I couldn't understand. I learned this about them, that they exact tribute. They had dull eyes, not to be read. You might catch a glimpse of them, a trailing limb, the unnatural hue of their skin, a tendril of hair like floating crowfoot. I thought nothing of half-drowning myself just to speak. I asked them, I wanted to know what it was that Remy took of me when he left, what did I have then that was now missing?

As an antidote to nightmare, Junior Lee from West Virginia, who couldn't have been more than five feet high and resembled the buffalo on the back of the American nickel, suggested flying. Not jumping off the roof into the wind's mad hands, nor sailing like Junior's wife Kate, fuelled by Canadian Club, into the outer reaches of everyone's tolerance, but dreaming wings, unfurling them triumphantly as flags, soaring into the sky far above the reaching women and the stalking cat with its burnt-black paws expanding into the night

I called to Remy and what came to me I didn't want. It wasn't what I meant by his name.

I knew about the difficulties of flight, the cost of weightlessness, the afflictions of creatures careening out of the sky suffering stage fright, lost nerve, shedding their intentions in a sudden shower. When my brother and I tried to levitate we stuck to the earth heavy as anchors. We didn't have to swallow stones for ballast; it seemed that's all we were. My father told us about a man who had rivulets of scars running down his back from having been airborne as a baby. An eagle had swooped down and snatched him off the ground where he'd been playing. The eagle, an intelligent bird, should have known better, should have resisted the impulse, as the mother was a crack shot and blasted off its head with her handy Remington, while the baby's sisters ran into the field, into a gentle storm of birdflesh and feathers, to catch their brother like a tumbling-down cherub.

When Junior Lee was even smaller, a boy, he used to fly kites. He said his father warned him repeatedly to hold on tightly to the string, *Hold on Junior for God-sake!*, so that one day when the kite got caught in the propeller of a low-flying twin-engine airplane, he was lifted into the air, up over his father's head like a passing shadow. He landed in a tree about a mile away, stranded high in its branches, bruised and badly scratched, one arm dangling, but intending to stay put because he'd finally let go of the string and was afraid to come down.

When I was five, birds appeared to me as lightly dressed miracles. Though even they had bodies made real by accident or disease: lung worm, heart failure, broken wings, severed talons, slashed eyes. It makes you wonder. We have all this material wound around us, this long constructing scarf of skin. Taut across the belly, holding in a rushing red sea. And those women, those old grimalkins, how they enter through unknown channels — at some point in your life they'll speak only in madness. Don't be deceived about childhood. You can be five and know that something is about to be born, something scratching inside you, batting around your insides like a cat playing with your guts. All summer you can feel it growing, ripening in the heat. You will be delivered of yourself, you think, but this takes years.

Boats purr across the water, a blended hum of voices fills the Camp. In the fall it empties into silence until the hunters arrive with their arsenal of punctuation, bringing the lyric of the lives they track to a full stop. Their lust is such that, dissolving into the bush, they sometimes take each other for quarry. That year, Abel Pogue, a veteran hunter, died in his sleep in Americana. His young grandson slept beside the body all night and in the morning would say only this, *I want his guns and his hat*. Doc Baily, who went into the cabin to comfort the boy, came out shaking his head, disgusted, muttering, *That little bastard*.

Around this time I was taken to school, led by the hand to a place I didn't want to go, and left there. No amount of begging bought me my passage back home. No one came to rescue me, not even my grandfather who could usually be trusted in matters of rebellion and escape. I was powerless, as we all were. Even though our cheeks were still masked in baby fat, sorrow was plainly visible on them. Its damp imprint was unmistakable, and yet this was taken no more seriously than the clouds boiling black and murderous above our parents' unprotected heads.

've wanted to achieve things. I've wanted at one time or another to lose weight or increase my vocabulary or make a lot of money in a hurry, and when I was a boy I wanted most of all to stop masturbating. In short, I've wanted to change my life, I've always wanted that, and it's a hard thing to change your life, you think it's a matter of willpower, that the reason why your life has never changed significantly is because you've never really put your mind to it, you've never made the required sacrifices, but then you do put your mind to it, you become obsessed with changing your life and make a concerted effort, and your life doesn't change, not one bit, and that's not encouraging.

My father once told me a story about going into a public restroom and seeing a man with only one arm — he was standing at an adjacent sink — and my father realized that he'd seen this same man back at the urinal, only he hadn't noticed the missing arm, or he hadn't noticed that there *was* a missing arm, either because he'd seen only the man's "good" side or because he'd

been too busy minding his own penis. My father felt
sorry for the man and offered to help him wash his single
hand, because it's not easy to wash your hand when that
hand is your only hand, and the man was touched by my
father's gesture, or at least that's what my father said. I
can't remember my father ever describing the actual
washing of the hand, but he was always a very thorough
man, and I can imagine him sandwiching the man's hand
between the two of his own, and scrubbing it first with
soap, then rinsing it and carefully drying it with paper
towels, though it's also possible that my father used only
one of his hands and that he worked in conjunction with
the man in washing his hand, that together they made up
a set of hands, one squeezing the other or however it is
that hands get washed, and either this strategy failed in
its objective, because the man wasn't at all accustomed to
the idea of hands working in unison since he'd never had
two hands, or the strategy succeeded and yet reminded
the man of a time when he *had* had both hands intact,
which might've also led him to recall the way that the one
hand had once worked, however unconsciously, in part-
nership with the other, and in that case I suspect that the
man left the restroom not only with a clean hand but
with a deep sense of sorrow, having been reminded in
such a practical and sensual way of what was no longer
his. I'm mentioning the breadth of possibility, I'm wondering what actually did happen, because I really don't
know for sure, and because I think it's possible that my
father made up the whole story, or maybe it was that my
father did offer to help the one-armed man but was
rebuffed, or maybe my father washed the man's hand but
then couldn't help afterward washing his own two hands
with unusual care, contagion no less compelling an idea
than love. But in any case what now seems significant to
me is that I never could believe my father's account, even
at that age — I think I must've been twelve or thirteen —
even then I knew enough to wonder why my father was

telling me the story in the first place, and I knew the story threw my father in a favorable light and that what I wanted most of all—it kept coming back to this—I wanted a father who washed a one-armed man's hand and never told anyone about it and never gained any satisfaction from not telling anyone. But my father wasn't like that, maybe nobody's father is like that, and I've always thought of his story as the very beginning of doubt in me, the plight of never knowing for sure and never quite trusting what others say because there is always a story behind any story.

One time, ten or so years ago, I was sitting around with a group of people—it must've been at a dinner party—and one of them said that he had nothing in the least to hide, that he couldn't think of even one thing that would so embarrass him that it would stop him from telling us, from revealing the secret to us, and I remember immediately thinking of a number of possible revelations, things I knew about him that he didn't know I knew. In his mind he wasn't really capable of embarrassment, he was one of the lucky ones who can fool themselves into thinking of their lives as open to inspection, although it should also be said, it's only fair to say, that some people make up secrets and then act as though they've been burdened with them, and it seems foolhardy to think that so-called sensitive people have secret lives and that everyone else doesn't, both seem equally unlikely. Still, I've always suffered from this sense of having 371 secrets and no place to keep them all, I keep spouting one leak after another. So maybe it was resentment that I felt toward that fellow at the dinner party, maybe I had it in for him because I couldn't be as carefree as he could, having secrets was too important to me, it gave me a mysterious quality that I thought others didn't have, and I imagined them the lesser for not having their secrets, for not having *my* secrets. It's always struck me as extraordinary that you can tell someone that you have a secret, let's say this *one* secret, and it absolutely takes the wind out of them if you don't reveal it right there on the spot, people think it's the height of impropriety if you say you have a secret and then don't tell it, but my feeling's always been that if you tell it, then you don't have it any longer, that's the nature of secrets, so it seems reasonable to tell someone that you have a secret — how would they know if you didn't tell them? — and then refuse to reveal what the secret is, that's the best way of creating and maintaining power.

The one I'm thinking of, she taught me the meaning of satisfaction and together we lived in a sheltered world, it wasn't my world and it wasn't her world, and it certainly wasn't *the* world, which is where you're really supposed to go with a woman, the two of you presenting yourselves as a couple for the scrutiny of others, an approach that was clearly impossible with the woman I'm talking about, and our failure in that regard was eventually our downfall. Every time we went out into public — even into a restaurant by ourselves, though I'm thinking more of certain occasions when we'd see other people in twos or threes or fours — it was a disaster, for neither of us had much aptitude for public talk, we both resorted to masks and couldn't so much as recognize each other, let alone prove ourselves recognizable to others, or at least to those who actually knew us, but when we were alone, just this woman and I, we stayed *inside* and created a world of games and names, it was all a matter of *keeping up* (not with the Joneses but with one another), and it was impossible to describe this world to anyone else (I can remember trying), though I guess that's what I'm doing right now, or taking a stab at it, for my benefit and edification as much as for yours. Feminine allure had always been for me a form of escape, a way of entering another world, I realize now that it was a

way of gaining admission to the adult world, even after
my status as an adult was secure, a foregone conclusion,
even when I was an adult-and-a-half I'd still look at a
woman and think she held behind her the key and if I
could only wrestle it away from her I'd become something respectable, which was why those excursions into
the public were so frightening and fraught with anxiety,
they were supposed to show that I was an adult and that
this woman was the reason why. Women were always
coattails for me — I can see that now — and I always
managed to find and sleep with women who saw *men* as
coattails, I guess that was a little stupid of me, and
together we were stepping all over each other, this
woman and I, screaming at each other to grow up and
take the initiative. As a boy I thought of sex as the
quickest ticket out of the family, it was either fuck your
sister or fuck someone else's sister, excuse the bluntness,
and the latter strategy managed to get you the hell out of
the family, and the family was in my view — and I'm
referring now to my perspective as a child — a suffocating nest that offered only a mediocre form of privacy,
and so the first girl I ever had sex with was an *out*, I used
her in that sense, and I can still remember the thrill of
having sex with her, doing what I knew my mother (not to
mention *her* mother) would never condone, and this girl
was willing to do anything, and we did everything, we
even one time included her sister and a Siamese cat in the
venture — two years younger and all legs is how I remember her, the cat didn't figure prominently — and the thrill
of it was always to go on a kind of field trip unlike any
other pre-adult field trip, and possibly, always possibly,
to produce something new, something that belonged to a
new kind of family, which gave me a power, so that if I
was still under the authority of my father, I was also
sleeping with a girl whom he couldn't sleep with, and I
might just become a father myself. Of course I felt guilty
about all of this, I was hardly *free* in my sexuality, there

was always the guilt, always a parental figure to elude, or subvert, and my clearest memory is of being in the girl's bedroom, with the door open, in accordance with her mother's notions of modern chaperonage, engaging in cunnilingus and yet at the same time preoccupied with something else, and for that reason always staying alert, keenly listening for her mother's footsteps up the staircase, a kind of warning signal it was. No, not privacy by any stretch of the imagination but an idea of pleasure as coming from subversion, from doing what you weren't supposed to do, though of course there were church mice, and I would later become one for a spell, who saw it the other way, who couldn't understand it all as a game, as a way of creating excitement.

I visited his office twice a week for about five years, sitting in a chair — it was always the same chair, though the location of the office changed a couple of times — a chair that wasn't comfortable and it wasn't uncomfortable, and he sat across from me, his feet usually on an ottoman, legs crossed at the ankles, and a small white clock sat next to me on a table, it was facing Dr. Weiss, that was his name, and he'd look at the clock sometimes, I'd catch him, but he had to do that, there wasn't any other way to know that fifty minutes had elapsed, and for the first year I think I felt hurt almost every time he said, Well, our time's up, or whatever it was he said to end things, I can't remember exactly. Most often I'd leave the office in a depression, not so much from having brought to the surface certain facets of my life that I wished didn't exist, but from the embarrassment of having sat there and talked myself blue in the face for fifty minutes (as a rule, Dr. Weiss said almost nothing), talking about anything that came into my mind, or *almost* anything, and I worried most not about my own predicament, what had led me initially to seek psychiatric help, but about my performance in the office, as a patient, I worried whether my fifty-minute monologues had wowed the doctor or not, whether I'd come off as a fool or just what, and of course I had little indication one way or the other from Dr. Weiss, since he said so little, and if I asked, and in my weakest moments I did ask, he'd simply throw the question back at me, and he was right to do that, my doubts were at the heart of what needed investigation, and he'd say, Why would I think you're a fool? You'd think it, I'd say, because I'm squirming in this chair, I'm vomiting words and hoping against hope that the overall impression is favorable. I remember how I'd usually leave the office with a morbid sense that he was happy to be done with me, that after I left he'd open the door to another patient, a preferred patient, someone who talked eloquently for the fifty minutes, making sense and reaching significant conclusions, and I wasn't like that, I was always saying one thing and then immediately qualifying it with another, a zigzag that got nowhere, so that if you were to transcribe the whole thing and then whittle away the asides and qualifications, the prefatory comments and heartfelt vacillations, there wouldn't be enough left to fill even one lousy page. I can remember one time, with this failure in mind, deciding that I'd qualify nothing, that I'd be straightforward and that I wouldn't guess all the time at his secret reaction to what I was saying, and the next session took forever, more like fifty hours than fifty minutes, and I said almost nothing, I couldn't think of anything to say, it's a patient's nightmare, and Dr. Weiss simply sat and stared, and occasionally he smiled, I'm not sure why, either embarrassed for himself or feeling sorry for me.

I can't really remember any longer what it was like at the time, I'm forced to almost make it up as though it never happened, but it did happen, and at the time I was trying to put the pieces together, I know that, and most of all I wanted an anchor, I was in my early twenties and

I wanted something that was stable and that I could call my own, or something that would call me its own. I'd attended Sunday school as a child, the church was never really pushed on me but it was there, it was a convenient place to begin the search. I wanted something solid then and I still want that, but I can't find it anymore, and I've grown accustomed to not finding it, I look around and nothing seems especially transcendent, nothing really fits the bill. I can remember as a boy how I'd find these rocks and I'd keep them, two or three at a time, I'd set them on the nightstand next to my bed, and I thought of them as precious, but eventually I'd take them outside and toss them just about anywhere, it really didn't matter, they'd become ordinary again. Now I'm left with the normal expedients, such as sex, it's this huge container into which you can throw just about anything, and in that sense sex is not unlike religion, since one of the things people do with religion is assume it as a ubiquitous category, which means that everything from this morning's rainfall to Aunt Betty's cancerous tumor becomes religiously significant, and that's how I used to think, it's shameful now to admit it, there was a time when I believed in God and even went to church, though attending services finally proved too disheartening, there was always this feeling afterward in the pit of my stomach, I couldn't ever get over that, the feeling afterward, it was the same feeling I'd felt as a child after being dragged to a Sunday service. Someone I once knew, an assistant minister at a Presbyterian church in another town, we were in his office one day and he said he wanted to say something to me, he had something important on his mind, but first there was a bit of gossip, a story about a man who was coming in for counseling and whose wife was truly beautiful, the minister referred to her as *comely*, that seemed a strange way of putting it, and the man was impotent, that was the twist, because somehow his wife's beauty intimidated him, and they prayed together — the minister and this man — right there in his office, week after week, eyes closed and heads bowed toward each other, they prayed for an erection is what it must've been, not a typical prayer request, not the kind you stand up and make in church when the minister asks whether there's any *special* requests — no, those are always reserved for some poor asshole who's dying and doesn't think it's his turn — and I think about that man from time to time, I don't know what's become of his wife's beauty but I wonder whether God ever answered his prayers. After telling me about the impotent man, that was just a teaser, this minister spoke frankly and said that it was his opinion that my main weakness as a Christian was in not loving my fellow believers, and of course he was right, people usually are when they say things to me, and eventually I did leave the church because of that weak link, my intolerance of others, and after that it was just God and me, as Protestant a religious experience as you're likely to run into, and we fought it out, just the two of us, and then even that went away, I didn't believe in God anymore. It's a shameful thing to lose your faith. I can remember those first few days after I'd formally decided that I had nothing in me any longer, no belief whatsoever, I'd been drained of faith, it was like the end of a marriage, but it was also like being born all over again, it was somehow deeply religious I can't help but admit, and the world was completely new, and what before had seemed like too much confusion and chaos was now pure luster, not that things were necessarily better but the stage lights were shining a little more intensely on the surface of things, laying bare a new set of temptations, and I didn't feel myself so much drawn, I'd simply become a different kind of voyeur.

I felt no particular intimacy for any of the cus-tomers, except for this one, a man who always wore the

same threadbare brown suit, who walked into the book-
store every Sunday night at nine-thirty, his hair slicked
back with an oily substance or maybe it was just water,
his skin as white as skin gets, a middle-aged man of small
stature who suffered from a case of nerves, to say the
least, and when he spoke, and he never spoke freely, he
spoke as though he didn't want to speak, as though it
made him twice as anxious to open his mouth as it did to
keep it closed. He told me once, he whispered it as
though there might be others interested to know, he said
he worked for a gentleman's estate, that the gentleman
was a bibliophile, that the gentleman never went out into
public. That was the extent of what he said, but I felt
lucky to be told anything, I knew he'd never told any of
the other employees, he must've sensed their impatience
with all that he asked of them, their unwillingness to
cooperate with his vision of things, and it's my guess, I
might be wrong, but I think that that's why he eventually
came only on Sunday evenings, when I worked alone.
He'd spend an hour walking around the store, deciding
on the books he wanted to purchase, asking me occasionally to pull down a book that was beyond his reach,
selecting maybe fifteen or twenty, mostly out-of-print art
books — except for a few pocketbooks on spinning racks,
our stock was made up entirely of used titles — and when
he was ready he'd bring them to the front counter, just
before ten-thirty, that was when we'd close, and once at
the counter, I'd be on one side and he'd be on the other,
he'd insist, always with an economy of gesture, I never
remember there being any words, he'd insist that he
alone be allowed to touch the books, as though these used
books had suddenly become clean and pure as soon as
they'd been chosen, and so we came up with a procedure,
I indulged his conceit, or maybe I indulged *in* his conceit,
in any case he'd open each book to the first page and
show me the price as marked, and I'd enter the price in
the cash register, and then he'd place the book in a box

(I'd have gotten one from the back room), which he'd already lined with brown paper bags, unopened and laid flat, and then he'd open the next book, I'd enter its price — in no time we'd be working as a team, taking satisfaction in the coordination of our efforts — and he'd stack each book in the box, one atop the other, but always with an unopened bag laid flat between the books, so that no two books ever touched once they were rung up, once they were officially his, and that made a kind of sense. One time he had two boxes of books, he'd bought more than his typical share, and he asked me to help carry them to his car, and together we went outside, it was an old Pontiac parked around the corner, and after he opened the door, just as I was beginning to set the box on the front seat, he slipped a paper bag between the box and the seat, he did it as though he had to. What I didn't sense at the time was the extent of this man's problem, the scope of what he was undertaking, which is to say I never realized that there was no gentleman, no figure-head of the estate, I never realized that this man was himself the bibliophile, the one who never showed his face in public, and maybe that's what we had in common, because at the time I never showed my face in public, appearances to the contrary.

It was in Dr. Weiss's office that I first spoke of sex, before that I'd never had anyone with whom to talk about it, I think it safe to say that I was mostly young and naive at the time, a wealth of adolescent sexual experiences notwithstanding, but during the last year and a half of my treatment we rarely spoke of sex but almost exclusively of one another, what was going on or not going on between us, though I talk about this as though Dr. Weiss were talking too, telling me of his own life, confessing to me his innermost doubts and desires, and of course all of that was very much off-limits. I remember once seeing Dr. Weiss on the street with a little girl, it must've been his daughter — I don't remember the color of her dress but I can still see the tiny pair of pink socks — and yet afterward, at our next session, there wasn't anything much to say, after I'd mentioned seeing him there wasn't anywhere to go with the topic, he simply stared at me and waited for some elaboration, and I think what I wanted most was to know something further about him, frankly I liked him, there was a kind of nervous restraint to his demeanor that I identified with, with which I could sympathize, and I tried at points to tell him that, that I liked him, and he'd stare at me, and I'd say, You probably think I don't know the first thing about you, but I really do, I can see by the way you hold yourself, it's in your gestures and your facial expressions, and occasionally you say something that gives away how you think, a disposition toward sadness is how I think of it, and by this point I know every tie you own and all your shoes, of which you have only two pairs, remarkable as that seems.

At one time I couldn't stand the idea of having another person living on the other side of my apartment wall, or living above or below me, and when I wasn't living in an urban setting I never had enough money to benefit from the privacy of a house, a single-family dwelling is what I think they call it, so I'd sit in some apartment, when I was younger, and I'd listen, and I'd figure they were listening too, and I'd walk around all the time as though there was someone else there listening to me, as though there were really two of me, one watching and one being watched, and I realize now that I don't do that anymore. I also don't have as many secrets, and I could be wrong, I'm really only guessing here, but I tend to think that when you're on your deathbed with your thirty-odd secrets, or however many you're left with at that advanced age, I'll bet those secrets melt away right before your eyes, one by one, and you're forced to do without any secrets at all — that is, without any sense of self-importance. It's a good thing to be less paranoid, even if you have to relinquish some of your secrets to get to that point, you never get something for nothing, it's one trade-off after another as far as I'm concerned, and the psychotic who finally decides that he *isn't* the king of Prussia is making a decision about what's more important, and what's always seemed most important of all, and I'm deeply convinced of this, I lose all cynicism when I get to this, what's most important is to keep making those decisions — however unconscious they may be, I'm not sure where intention comes into this — to keep making those decisions about what is and isn't important, realizing that what's important has a way of changing. When I was a young man, I wouldn't have liked the man I am now, or who knows, I might've been amused by him, but probably not, he probably would've struck me as someone I wouldn't want to become, and of course now when I think back upon myself as a young man I'm glad I'm not like that anymore, all nerves and misplaced intensity, though of course I *am* that person, we're one and the same, I guess we just don't always see eye to eye.

She was unabashed, I liked that about her, and she had a large mouth, it was huge, and when she'd smile she wouldn't so much smile as pinch her lips together and curl the edges of her mouth, so that she smiled when she tried not to smile, and when she actually tried to smile, then her mouth opened wide, it became a big dark circle that let out a laugh that caught like a cough, and I can remember kissing her, I remember wanting to kiss her and then getting to kiss her, being lost somewhere in that mouth, my eyes closed and my mind swimming. But things changed, and it was the mouth that changed first, or I changed it, the way I thought about it, it became a receptacle of ill-feeling, I began to see that when eating she lacked the oral coordination necessary to get the

food into her mouth without smudging the edges, so that
invariably I'd see food, little wet bits of food, stuck on
her lips, and it bothered me to see food on the outside
and knowing it should be on the inside, it was a problem
of placement. I'd say, You've got food on your mouth, and
then I'd take a napkin to wipe away the fleck of food and
she'd react instantly, moving her mouth toward me, the
way children sometimes do, as though hands were of
limited usefulness, and it was that gesture — the mouth
moving toward me, the chin slightly lifted — I could find
no forgiveness for that gesture, and in my mind her
mouth had become unwieldy and even ugly, it's a terrible
thing to say.

I don't remember thinking about it until years after
I'd left college, and then suddenly, it wasn't really a
choice, or it didn't feel like a choice, I realized that I
wanted to do something with my life, I wanted to make a
difference, however corny and foolhardy that may sound
now, and I wanted to do it in the theater because that's
what I knew something about, an inheritance from my
grandfather, and it was in the theater that my talents lay,
if they lay anywhere — more often than not they seemed
strewn everywhere in insufficient measure — but there's
a difference between strongly desiring something and
actually getting there, and I never did get there, I never
got close. No one gets there without ambition, that's for
sure, but there are ambitious people who never do get
there, there are even ambitious people who never set one
foot in front of the other, they sleep ambitiously and
they'll die ambitiously, and that's sad but at least they
know what they're missing, there's a kind of knowledge
gained in wanting something and never getting it, it's
called disappointment, and the people who get it don't
always know what it's like not to get it and the people
who never wanted it, or somehow judged the object of
desire as beyond the realm of possibility, and therefore

took the healthy route and expelled it from their minds, those people don't know what disappointment is, they've never felt it. Disappointment is knowing what the jacket looks like and knowing what it would be like to wear it, but then you never do get your hands on the jacket, and that's a shame, that's enough to make you realize what life's really about, it's about wanting I think, and everyone wants at least one thing and would give up just about anything for that one thing, but no one gets to live longer than the designated period, I don't care what the preachers say, and some poor suckers don't even get that far — a friend of mine drowned in a river when he was twelve, asshole couldn't swim (isn't dog-paddling some kind of survival instinct?). But even those people who live to be a hundred years old don't get a hundredth of what they really want, and that's disappointment whether you're still around to feel it or not, and a person must sense it, or at least fear it, when you're lying in bed, it's your last day on earth, forgive the morbidity, and you want *more* and you aren't going to get it, and years before, alive and healthy, you'd spent your adult life reading magazines and newspapers and watching television and hearing about it, right and left you'd heard about the people who had their fingers on the pulse, hands on the ropes, you'd ended up worshipping those who got what you wanted, you'd been driven as much by envy as by anything else.

I was living in New York at the time, and I'd come home to my apartment, a sublet in Little Italy with wooden floors painted an institutional gray, it was a nice enough apartment, a few cockroaches but I'd seen so many terrible apartments and this one seemed a castle in comparison, and I went over to the sink to get a drink of water, it was the height of summer and oppressively hot, and I was at the sink, running the water, waiting for it to get sufficiently cold, it didn't always come out cold right away, and I looked out the window at an apartment building next door, and one floor down I saw into an apartment that had venetian blinds that were open and I could see a woman standing in what appeared to be a bedroom, she was wearing a teddy, I think that's what it's called, it was cream-colored and she was very pretty and I was watching and thinking that coincidence had somehow led to *this*, it wasn't the kind of thing that transforms your life but you take what you get. I was still holding the glass under the running water, or beside the running water, and watching this woman as she sat on the edge of a bed and she began rolling a pair of stockings up her legs and connecting them to the doodads at the top, attached to the teddy they must've been, and I stood by the window for a moment, then suddenly realized that I could also be seen, so I walked over and switched off the kitchen light and returned to the window, and by this time there was a man in the room as well, standing beside the woman and dressed only in a white T-shirt and darkly colored socks that were limp around his ankles, and he picked her up, right off the ground, and tossed her on the bed, and the act of tossing — she flew through the air and landed on the bed, she would've broken a bone if there'd been no bed — that act of tossing, it was both aggressive and spoke of something between them, and that *something* was reflected as well in the look on her face after he'd tossed her, after she'd landed she was smiling widely, her eyes spoke excitement, and then the man lay down on the bed, too, and it didn't take long before they were fucking, though to tell the truth there was something wild and confused about the entire session, I quickly noted the conspicuous absence of sound, that would've helped, and I felt — and maybe this always happens, maybe it's part of the price of admission — I felt *outside*, looking in, not knowing what was going on, and with the distinct impression that *this* was not how it would've looked if I'd been the man, and before long I was thinking another thought, I was thinking that maybe this thing had been set up for my benefit, or for someone else's, maybe it wasn't at all authentic, maybe they knew the blinds were open (as far as I could remember, they'd never been open before), and maybe they wanted to be seen, it was a show in some sense, and people have sex differently when they know they're being watched, or whether they know for sure or not they suspect or want to be watched, it's more like a pornographic movie, though of course it *would* look that way to me, since I was essentially looking at a screen, sitting in a theater, and how was I to doubt that this wasn't a true voyeuristic experience? But there are two kinds I think, two kinds of voyeurism I mean, one where you see something raw, pure, something not intended to be seen, and the other where someone is playing to you, giving you a wink of the eye the whole time, and I like the former and not the latter, because as I watched and eventually she began rubbing against him, that's really the only way I can describe what I saw, part of their bodies were by this time obscured by the edge of the window, at first I felt betrayed because it was made-up, it was almost an act of charity that I naturally resisted, but then everything changed, and the sex became something more private, it was a kind of rubbing for her, a secret way she achieved pleasure, and it was more pragmatic, not as pretty or picturesque, and at that moment I liked the woman, maybe I even loved her.

My grandmother used to talk to herself, she'd walk around her house and conduct elaborate conversations, and I grew up wanting to resist that impulse, I understood the desire and yet I was determined to conquer it, but all along I must've known there was a reason behind the impulse, a split in the mind I guess it's called. As a boy I sometimes had a habit, I couldn't control myself, I'd think about things I didn't want to think about, there'd be a voice inside that would say things I didn't want to hear, and I'd tell myself to stop thinking these things, but of course that didn't do a lot of good, and eventually I got so I didn't like the uncontrollable voice, I'd been fascinated but now I'd lost patience with it, I'd gotten scared is what it was, and so I began to say, Fuck you, I whispered those words to myself, a little snarl, and I can remember one summer—my sister and I were staying with our grandparents—I said this same thing, Fuck you, over and over, and after that things got easier, the other voice lost some of its authority and I became less afraid. Years later, after my mother died, I'd visit my father maybe once every two years, he was living then in a retirement community, and whenever I was around him I was nearly speechless, I could never think of what to say, it was a kind of power I had over him, he'd end up doing all the talking, an endless babble, and yet only a few hours later, after I'd left my father, someone would meet me at an airport and we'd be in a car on the way home and I'd be running at the mouth, rambling incessantly, there'd be this long string of words coming out, no hint of control, and I sounded just like my father, I was convinced of it—the same intonation, the same painstaking delivery.

PAULA HOROWITZ

Wheat Field Under Threatening Skies with Crows

from The Pennsylvania Review

Pete stays up all hours, stooped over his papers in the bright circle of light in the otherwise muted room. We sleep on a staggered schedule; my side of the studio couch is empty before he regains consciousness. We have no children but we have each other, and now Papa, who finally made the big journey to die among his own. We gave my father our room because of the private bath.

Really, he doesn't seem that sick, though he weighs only eighty pounds. I don't think of him as old. Pete calls him a crotchety old man, noting only his craggy face and his beard which is hardly distinguishable from the white sheet on which it rests.

Papa lies silk-pajamaed on our big bed and his presence is felt right through the ceiling of the kitchen where we silently eat our dinner, each with our own thoughts.

Though not demanding, my father needs his coffee on a tray because "in this country they hold your cup by the rim." I don't accept the possibility of his dying because he's always been there for me and he seems to have enough vitality to survive the frailty of his body.

Every morning he bathes carefully with the delicately scented soap I remember from my childhood, and while he's too weak to come downstairs, he stays interested in all that goes on in the house. Which isn't much, to tell the truth.

We lead a quiet life and I feel secure with Pete. We get along well and appreciate what we have. It's not all that it set out to be but courtesy and loyalty have to be worth something. My father is an artist and a romantic. He has tremendous authority, a kind of psychic strength. It's true that he's also vain and even silly.

When I was about six my father dragged me to art museums. We rode the blue and yellow streetcar to the heart of the city. It was sticky during the summer and wet the rest of the year, but my father made me feel it was always the best possible weather. We both fit under his big white umbrella, which, as far as I know, was the only big white umbrella in the country. He sang with the rhythm of the rain falling on our bright roof. On warm days he looked dashing in thin white cotton shirts with a touch of silk at his open collar.

The solemn art gallery with its huge statues and high white walls made me feel in need of my father. It was almost like a church, I thought, because of its formidable significance. People shuffled about gravely and spoke in hushed voices. Not my father. I held his hand tightly and listened to his comments but I rarely knew what they meant. I suspect he used me so it wouldn't look funny that he was talking to himself. As I grew older I stopped holding his hand and began to understand something of what he was trying to make me see. We looked at only a few pictures but examined each one for a long time. Sometimes we sat down on a velvet-covered bench in front of a large canvas, say *The Nightwatch*, and he would bring seventeenth-century Amsterdam magically into the present. His eyes would narrow, so that the

bristly brows almost hid them — somewhat like a sheep-
dog's. He was full of humor, sarcasm, and awe. For Van
Gogh there was something close to reverence, as when he
showed me *Wheat Field Under Threatening Skies with
Crows*. He said, "Ja, something terrible is going to happen. The wind is blowing and the sky is turning dark.
The painter is sucked into his madness. That yellow
exploded in his head. The crows are screeching that he
must die. He doesn't mind, you know, it's life that is so
unbearable for him." The painting frightened me. I felt
cold and kept staring at it with wide eyes. My father
made a telescope of his hand and disappeared into the
wheat, forgetting me. Then suddenly we would move on,
his mood changing with every painting he studied, while
he told me little anecdotes or fantastic stories about each
scene.

When I was thirteen he demanded participation:
"What do you think of that Ruysdaal in the corner?" —
and listened to my groping sentiments. Often there
appeared a mildly mocking expression around his sensitive mouth but one time he turned his head toward me,
startled, and said, "You have good intuition." After that
I was less afraid to search for the meaning behind the
artist's compositions.

Our visits to the museums were followed by dinner
at the "Club." The atmosphere there was heavy with
formality. I used to believe the frozen waiters could hear
me swallow. My father purposely made out-of-place
remarks.

"What do you call this, waiter?" holding a crystal
fingerbowl at arm's length.

"A fingerbowl, sir."

"Did you think we came to the table with dirty
hands?"

"No, sir. One might need it after the meal."

"You think I eat with my fingers because I'm an
artist."

"Indeed not, sir." When the dignified waiter discreetly reached for the bowl, my father said, "Just a minute," and calmly drank the water, taking deep enjoyment from the look of consternation on the man's face. I was impressed by these improprieties.

At age eighteen or so I felt that sometimes he went too far in his attempt to make a game out of life, or perhaps I began to assume responsibility for his actions. He was so very unpredictable. Again at the Club:

"The only thing that gets any younger here is the brandy, my man."

"I'm sorry, sir." My father's mobile face betrayed his mood to me.

"What do you think of my daughter?"

"Nothing, sir."

"You mean you don't find her pretty?"

"Yes, of course I do, sir."

"Aren't you a little old to look at young girls?"

"Well, I wasn't looking with the intention, that is I just observed."

"So you wouldn't like to take her to a dance."

"Of course not, sir." The unhappy man in penguin costume glanced nervously around the sedate room.

"You mean my daughter isn't good enough for you," and Papa dismissed the waiter with a small gesture, feigning affront.

Eventually we stopped going to museums together.

Now he's upstairs, thousands of miles from home, his eighty pounds filling the house, quietly but unmistakably. I wonder if he still thinks of women? He used to speak of the intelligence and sensitivity of women and their capacity for suffering. I think I don't altogether please him. Times change. We both work, Pete and I. God, when was the last time I was in a museum?

Sometimes, after work, when the day help has left and Pete is still at the college, my father asks me to provide him with a painting. I sit next to the bed and describe an imaginary canvas.

"Does it have a name?" he wants to know.

"*The Party*. A light and breezy setting. Very fluid. Early twentieth century. People talking."

"About what?"

"I have no idea. Not much, I think, judging from the expressions on their faces. It's an aquarelle, beautiful colors."

"What kind of a party is it?"

"How should I know? A party. Let's skip that one."

"I don't want to skip it. You seem to like the work and yet it's a boring party. It isn't easy to make an exciting painting out of a dull subject. Try harder." Sighing, I look past his pillow at the wall.

"They're academics. Probably mathematicians. Sweaters and ill-fitting trousers. Beards. There are five men and three women. The women are wives. Middle-aged, the whole bunch."

"I see what you mean, but how do you know they're mathematicians?"

"I saw the painting, remember? They're being sociable. On the coffee table are crackers and nuts."

"No brandy?"

"Papa, listen. I'm coming to that. Wine glasses on the table." My father closes his eyes contentedly.

"Logs are burning in the fireplace; the glow plays on the redwood beams of the ceiling and lights up their faces." He opens one eye.

"So it's winter then. Good. Go on."

"The guests are just talking, you know: 'almost every particle which ends in a set G returns to G infinitely often — at a tag sale — charming, absolutely charming — we had his tail docked when he was a baby — a delicious pastry, what's in it? — always go to London in December — the sojourn in G is positive — but their ears look really quite funny — a single point of positive measure — he charged me fifty dollars to tell me my spine is curved — do you still go to the same vet? — a set of positive measure with empty interior — " I was enthusiastically borrowing from one of our parties and getting into the game when my father commanded me to stop. "Wait," I said, "there is also a younger woman with glasses, sitting on the floor in front of the fire. She wears a rather wild dress, a jaunty beret, and tons of jewelry."

"Thank God," says my father.

"Yes. But she doesn't open her mouth. She looks bemused. The men feel threatened by her."

"Scientists are morons," declares my father. "What else do they talk about?"

"The weather, until one of them gets up with an awkward 'early class tomorrow.' They leave, end of painting, and time for your pills."

"I believe you underestimate the depth of scientists."

"You called them morons, I didn't."

"I didn't mean it. They keep my heart ticking, after all."

"Well, that doesn't necessarily make them the life of a party."

"As an artist and as a man," begins my father dramatically, "I regret deeply that people can't enjoy themselves anymore on a winter night by the fire. They said absolutely nothing of the slightest interest."

"You're making too much of it."

"Maybe they were philosophers."

"They were mathematicians," I insist, kissing his dry forehead before I quickly leave the room. I listen for a moment behind the closed door. He'll have the last word, I know.

"She sits in front of that computer all day. No wonder."

Downstairs I find Pete in front of a stack of blue books.

"Let's go to a movie, Pete."

"Now? I'm grading exams. You go." He doesn't even look up. It was a dumb idea. I kick his sneakers viciously under the table and go outside. In the dreary, gray, late winter afternoon I walk block after block, keeping my arms stiffly pressed against my body. I am disturbed by that cryptic "no wonder." Wondering. Wondrous. Wonderful words of my childhood — words that open the prisons of the mind. Would I think of farm subsidies if I could see Van Gogh's *Wheatfield* now? Papa hears the call of the crows and lives each day. Am I substituting contentment for magic? But who has time for play these days? Deep inside my pocket I grasp the house key in my gloved hand, relaxing my shoulders and slowing my pace. I'm going home.

My father is sleeping more, he eats very little. I sit by him quietly, reading. On Sunday he wants a smoke, inhales deeply, and says, "I've been thinking about a still life but I can't get it right. I need to get my mind on another work; that would help me clarify things. I feel unsettled." He looks at me with febrile intensity.

"All right. This painting is done on fine-grain snow-white canvas. It's bold, yet sensitive, with particular care given to detail. The colors are serene and at the same time sumptuous. There's a fairly dark attic studio with two small roof windows. The walls are lined with bookcases filled with leatherbound volumes of Wagner, Mahler, Strauss. Stacks of sheet music. There's a grand piano in one corner; the teacher leans against it. He's old and stooped, maybe seventy-five."

"That's not so old."

"No." I won't argue or the image will slip away.

"Go on with the piano lesson."

"It's a violin lesson." I can see my father getting excited about this unexpected piece of information. "The student is a young boy, tall and clad in blue jeans. He's in front of a music stand. The teacher looks at him with great affection. 'You know she played "The Lark" and made it sound like a buzzard.' The boy eats this joke up—he knows exactly what his teacher means. He starts playing a scale with perfect intonation and the buzzard joke is still lighting up his heart.

"'Enough of that. Let's hear some Brahms,' says the teacher. The sun pours dusty rays into the room while the two concentrate on music conceived long ago. The old man and the young boy need few words for their communication.

"'The down bow is too fast; the high Ds are under-developed. It should be more lyric.' The boy nods and adjusts his bow speed.

"'Fine, fine.' Their physical distance doesn't prevent the student from sensing the slightest gesture of disapproval from the master. He stops and points with the bow at the score in front of him.

"'Is the shift up worth it or should I stay in first position?' The silver-haired man moves the fingers on his left hand up and down an imaginary fingerboard.

"'Would you prefer third finger on the high A, three, two, one, one? Why do you lift the bow at the D#? It's a difficult piece to find a common denominator tempo for. The way you are to think of it is this: Tah tah tah, pam pampam pam.' The violinist searches for the exact tempo required with the emphasis on the right note.

"'No. You're overworking. Don't press down.' Another try of the phrase.

"'Now split the difference,' the teacher smiles. 'Right! Very beautiful. Pick it up at three seventy-seven?' The blue-jeaned boy knows he pleases his teacher. There's harmony in the room and their close-ness is palpable. He sings a clear arpeggio and continues to pour out music until the master sighs, 'I lose it at the last E,' rubbing his eyes luxuriously with both hands under his glasses. It is such a characteristic gesture that the student's mouth turns up slightly at the corners. His mirth comes out in the cadenza, his right at free association. He plays it capriciously, with a daring for which he seems too young. Now it is the quiet smile of the teacher that warms the room.

"They work well over the allotted lesson time and while the bow is untightened the teacher warns, 'Be careful you don't tread water. Don't make too-rapid descents from the mountains to the plains.' The violinist understands. He's reminded of something he read about Brahms: 'Wagner says he's Schumann bound in leather,' he says, resting the violin lovingly in its case. Now the work is done and the teacher laughs heartily at this.

"'Quite so,' he says, and briefly touches the boy's shoulder when he leaves the studio."

It is peaceful in the bedroom. We look at each other, freely, like children. "That's the way it was," I say softly, breaking the silence. My father nods and I notice how relaxed he looks.

For several weeks I don't see much of him. He's asleep when I get home, but I've begun to take my after-dinner coffee upstairs. Pete is understanding; he cleans up the dinner dishes as a matter of course. The bed looks enormous. My father's presence appears to have diminished. He doesn't really seem to need me anymore. But I have my needs. I hang up his robe and refresh the water in the vase of chrysanthemums. I turn off the light on his nightstand and the one on his dresser. Then I sit next to him, my feet on the edge of the bed.

"Landscape," I say. "No verbosity here, just elegant knife-heaped-up paint. It is very dark and still. The time is early spring. The tension of growth is in the air and the scent of fertility. It is night. A fine rain is falling softly. The grateful soil accepts the life-giving water. Under the surface of the earth is a stretching and a reaching toward the light that will come. Gently the slumbering hills are awakening; a blue light defines the horizon. The sun rises behind a thick blanket of clouds and rain caresses all life on the land. The earth's saturated belly is getting ready to bear fruit. There's a whispering in the bare trees whose saps are beginning to flow. The oaks are holding on to last year's memory and the sumac too, with red-brown soggy heads all pointing in the same direction, trained in the lessons of survival. And now the rain has stopped. The earth begins to steam under the afternoon sun, sending its water back to the heavens. The light is young, with a clarity unknown to summer. Chalky grace of silver birches and weeping willows wrapped in a vague aura of delicate yellow tremble with promise. A wispy phantom mist over the lake has cleared and the spectacle of the firmament is reflected in the still water, mare's tails, in fantastic patterns. When the light changes shadows begin to fall. A breeze distorts the wavy rhythm of the mare's tails, forms become softer, magical . . . time seems to stop. A crescent moon looks down coldly on the pale birches, the closed willow curtains, the craning necks of the sumac."

I am ten again and hold my father's painter's hand. He rests peacefully.

From forgotten places a voice chants, art can conquer death. And laughs. What do you think of my daughter?

My glass filled with dew is raised to you, to me! I lean against the moon and am transparent. Without plan or purpose. Life surges through me. Grabbing my white umbrella I sail down, scattering starlight in the room. I pick up my cold coffee and when I turn at the door I see my father smiling.

IVOR IRWIN

Twenty Clicks

from *The Indiana Review*

nominated by Peter Schneeman

Linda started shooting dope again. Two days after her thirty-first birthday. "It's me or it's H," Kenny had said, and she had cried, promised to quit and then gone on doing it. In the middle of berating her, he had looked into those eyes, beautiful and green as a chunk of her Daddy's lawn, and five-sensed a cul-de-sac; the old erotic thrill painted over by a brand-new shellac of inexorable gloom.

The laws of change are synchronous. They had been close for eleven years, four years on and off in college, living together for two and married for five. His job, the car, the condominium, and their relationship were braided together. If you change one thing, Kenny felt, you were forced to change everything.

That morning, on his third day alone, Kenny sits swilling coffee back and forth through his teeth. Looking out from the window of their apartment, he sees a perfect black cumulostratus blocking out all natural light. Yet, below, in the street, his car, a blue MG midget, glimmers — light from where? — and looks perfect; underneath she is rotten, victimized by the tons of rock salt city workers throw down.

"Why do you do this to yourself?" he had asked her. Code for his rage at the aggravation of his having to shop his sperm elsewhere.

"Because rust never sleeps," she had replied with a shrug. Well, Linda may have come across as scintillant and dry to her junkie friends, but he knew that her wit and wisdom came second-hand from Neil Young and Rimbaud. It is he who rusts. Listen hard and you can hear your arteries harden. Junkies, those who know what they're doing, live in a state of suspended animation.

Things have been taken from the apartment a few at a time. Most of the electrical appliances are gone. Empty spots show like bikini lines on tanned skin. And the thought of *that* leads him back to her. It is the first time he has been alone since he was fifteen and an island of belligerence at St. Charles Reformatory. Now he sings to himself or listens to the hum of the refrigerator. To escape this wasteland he has spent the last three nights at the movies, dosing himself with *weltschmerz* at a Fassbinder festival; alone amongst mostly gay couples, watching them hold hands, whisper, neck, and squeal with pleasure at things he found intensely sad.

Kenny drinks a whole pot of coffee but can't eat. He showers and then loses himself so in self-pity that he brushes his teeth until they are pink, blood and toothpaste bubbling on the bristles.

Five cigarettes later he is on Lakeshore Drive, weaving in and out of lanes and not using his signals, emerging from his daze to see a bullet-headed creature blowing the horn and giving him the finger from the cab of a Chevy truck with tires four feet tall. *Another Sportsman for Bush*, the bumper sticker says. All the way to Sheridan Drive Kenny plays dodgems, making the appropriate little boy "NNNYEEOW" noises; the odorless bitterness of Phisoderm on her clitoris nagging and following him extra-discreetly, the way secret policemen don't wear raincoats when they tail east-bloc diplomats, because they've seen all the right movies.

Barraclough is on the phone the very moment Kenny steps into his office, calling a meeting for fifteen minutes hence. He chugs down two more cups of coffee, smokes one of Angel's filterless Camels and commences giving orders: sweep the floors; be careful how you fill the batteries; empty the ashtrays; pile the skids up neatly — Bla! Bla! Big boss man.

Angel is hungover. He gives Kenny his dirty look, eyes all hooded menace. Instead of picking up the dirt with a dustpan, he brushes it into the corner when he thinks Kenny's head is turned. "Jesus, Angel, do a job right or don't do it at all." Kenny ends up doing the job himself.

"Wha's a matter wid you, cono Capitan Bligh?"

He and Angel are big on the original *Mutiny on the Bounty*. Charles Laughton stays with you. "Barraclough's coming," Kenny shouts, watching over McQueen, the crazy cracker's, shoulder as he pours water from a jug into the forklift batteries. McQueen is hungover too. His banana-bunch hands tremble as he struggles to aim water into the tiny maw of the cell, splashing drops down the side and onto his arms. He should wear rubber gloves but he won't because he doesn't *have* to. Kenny ends up doing that job too as Angel and McQueen stand smiling, their arms folded, chirruping into each other's ears.

"Joo loo' like asshole doctor, man."

L.C., Kenny realizes as he looks at his watch, is going to be late. It seems that he always picks the days that Barraclough randomly decides to come around on to be late. "Proctologist," Kenny says. "The word, Angel, is proctologist."

"Whadever," Angel sneers. "Joo hafraid of El Gordo, Kennee? Tha' fa' chicken chit."

"No, I ain't," says Kenny. "I just need my goddamn job." Actually, Barraclough is no longer a fat man. The insurance company said that obesity meant unreliability and uninsurability. Word came down from Mount Olympus (his father-in-law) that young execs must either get thin or say goodbye. Barraclough had dutifully crash-dieted and exercised it all off. Still, svelte or stout, he remained the same martinet bastard as ever, and the sobriquet stayed with him. "We all got bills to pay."

"If you didn't have that pretty mayonnaise wife, an' that pretty English sports car, you wouldn't have to fret and be in such bocoo financial shit," laughs McQueen.

Angel and McQueen each had ten years on him. Vietnam vets with wives who worked, neither of them gave a damn about anything. They were decent people but there was always either or both the war or his in-laws between them; not a wall but a scabbed-over sore that they, but never he, could pick at. Angel, who exaggerated his Puerto Rican accent to the max, and McQueen, thespian of Kentucky hillbilly dumber-than-thou — all bullshit.

Barraclough walks in with Catalina, his secretary, who follows a measured five steps behind. All the boys in the factory, the warehouse, and the office, have the hots for Catalina. She is a sensuous, hefty, fortyish Cuban woman who wobbles on high stiletto heels, wears miniskirts an inch or so below the crotch, and thick black Cleopatra eye makeup. She seems, to Kenny at least, to be a stock parody of femininity, like the wretched drag queens who reconnoiter Broadway at night. But the boys love her.

They gather in a circle of steel folding chairs under fluorescent light. Barraclough punches the air with his index finger as he lets loose his wisdom. His biceps show through the cloth of his suit, tailored deliberately too tight around the arms and thighs to show off all those new muscles. Catalina takes notes, holding her pen like a glass cutter to avoid breaking her long burgundy nails. Kenny flashes on his mother-in-law; valium-calm, yet deeply upset after a dishwashing accident. Words of wisdom to Linda: "There's nothing worse than uneven nails."

"We gotta be ready for the Christmas madness, guys," Barraclough says. "We gotta be set. We gotta run it like a well-oiled cog in a Cadillac."

"We gotta's" began every sentence and Kenny gets lost in the incantation, thinking of how happy he'd be to come home to find Linda nodding in front of the television. Anyway he could keep her, the inexplicable comfort of just having her there. ". . . and believe me. If you guys don't want this job, there's an army waiting in the unemployment line that I can hire for way less than the company pays you guys."

"You a bocoo number ten American, you know, Mister B," McQueen says, grinning that self-satisfied point-man grin, Cherokee cheeks showing like red golf-balls under the fluorescents.

"Yeah, bocoo number ten, boss," adds Angel, and Kenny wonders how they manage to keep their faces straight.

"Well, I'm glad you see things in a positive way," smiles Barraclough, relaxing for the first time, smiling at Kenny and Catalina.

L.C. walks in then. He's got his hair dreadlocked and he's walking *that* walk. Bad news because Barraclough is a rabid bigot and a half. Kenny nods for him to sit down and L.C. does his own dinner-theater thing of pulling out his chair, scratching the back legs against the waxed floor, and slouching every which way until he's comfortable.

"We gotta be punctual. You all know that, guys. Don't you know that, Mister Davis?" The hand that Barraclough isn't using tenses and twitches inside the pocket of his sports coat, keys chime together beneath the cloth.

"Yes, suh, Mister Bear-claw. But I was in a . . ."

"Barra-cluff."

"I can't say that," L.C. squeals. "Ain't no way I can say that." The big boss glares into an open palm but L.C. goes on. "I was in a accident an' I gots a cold."

"Oh." Barraclough's eyebrows move up and down in agitation and Kenny wonders if they move spontaneously or of their own will.

"I gots a serious-ass cold but I come in because I know Kenny need me bad." L.C. winks at Kenny and he reciprocates. "But then I got hit-an-motherfuckin-runned by a truck on Fullerton."

"Wha' kine o' truck was it, L.C.?" asks Angel. "We'll look for the guy after work an' fuck him up."

"Was a pharmacy truck."

Kenny manages to put a hand over his mouth and stifle a laugh while Angel and McQueen splutter through locked lips. It was funny: like Linda, *she* got hit by the pharmacy truck every day. And, you know, — get this — *junkies don't catch colds.* Opiates and the miracle of suspended animation.

"I don't see the joke," says Barraclough, not losing the beat. "We gotta be houseproud. . . ."

The patter goes on and on; like, Kenny thinks, when he was working his way through college, working at the meat market, working with Sicilian kids. At break they'd smoke pot and measure the length of a stomach intestine, all pink and mushy in their hands. Miles and miles of it. Pino DiPrizio, who claimed he was a part-time outfit "collector," said humans had tripes that could stretch from "heaya ta Milwaukee." Doubtless, Barraclough could lay out a cat's cradle of company jive that stretched as far as Duluth, given the opportunity. Art Barraclough is a breed of low-level apparatchik-executive carefully weaned and nurtured on measured doses of W. Clement Stone, EST conventions, handball, and way too much meat. Ayn Rand over football because, as he told Kenny at the company picnic, "football is the greatest game in the world but, darn it, dangerous." Easy to pigeon-hole, triter than any stereotype, but indefatigable and impossible to stop. Call a fellow like that a cockroach and he will stop a long minute and find the buried compliment: The cockroach will last forever — past Armageddon — will it not? All the right words communicated with the unctuous, yet truly zealous voice of a man who truly loves his job. The motto: *Festina lente*, baybay.

"We gotta be as proud of where we work and who we work with as we are in our own homes and families." Well, fair's fair, Barraclough's never been to McQueen's house.

"Any questions, fellas? I represent the company and, as they say in D.C., the buck stops here. We're a family here and you should not be afraid to speak up." There was, of course, as ever, no reply. "Just remember. We gotta be two hundred and one percent, seven to eleven, twelve till four. Work makes you free." He nods to Kenny and walks toward the office. Work makes you free, Kenny thinks. Wasn't that written on the wrought-iron gates of Dachau?

Barraclough seats himself on Kenny's desk and lights up a foul smelling White Owl. There is a *Newsweek* next to the in/out tray, and, instead of making eye-contact, Barraclough thumbs through it as he speaks.

"How many times has L.C. Davis been late lately?"

"Last time was a month ago." That *really* was the last time, but guys like Art Barraclough believe you prepare advanced contingency plans for the kismet factor.

"He was late last time we had a meeting."

"Coincidence," Kenny shrugs.

"Right," Barraclough says, digging his teeth into the cigar, hissing consonants. "Yess. Yeah, r-right, o-kay, *my* decision. Out of your hands. If he's late again I want to give him the bullet."

"The bullet?"

"The bullet."

"Okay doke, but, you know, you just said it was out of my hands." Barraclough examines the poster of Nastassia Kinski and a snake on his wall. About to get into sexism. "No offense, Art, but why don't *you* fire him?"

"He's a vet and . . . and all that stuff but . . ." Barraclough tries to stand up casually but a few sheets from the pile of papers he has sat down upon stick to his buttocks and fall off one by one. "You been here eight years, right?"

"Right." Tch. Tch. Ring the alarm, there's been a screw-up. L.C. Davis is not a vet and *somebody* has been neglecting his personnel files.

"We gotta agree, Kenny, that a lotta what success is about is about attitude. And yours, normally, is good. You have a college education, you work hard, and you got the right instincts. Eventually, you could go real far." He throws out that index finger again and points right at Kinski's beautiful tuchis. "Your paperwork is a mess though, man. Your Achilles heel. That and your sentimentality for those guys. And . . . and for what you make, good money and you know it, you gotta be your own secretary." He looks down into Kenny's carefully polished safety-shoe. "This sexist stuff has to go. I told you, if we hire a femme exec, and believe me the writing *is* on the wall, she's naturally gonna be offended by something like this. The way you prepare for the future is to be ready for it. Get rid."

"They work hard, Art. And nobody works harder than L.C."

"Attitude. Attitude. Attitude. Yours is good but that . . . that nigger's is bad."

"I don't like that word."

Barraclough looks at him, finally making eye-contact, and there's nothing but utter contempt. Kenny swallows his saliva in tiny gulps. He thinks of the insides of Linda's arms. Porcelain skin and collapsed veins. Permanent damage, even after she cleans up. Early on, when they were both just chippying at weekends, they had daubed Preparation H, the junkie's amulet, on their tracks and watched the wounds shrink. How had they missed their happiness after working at it so hard?

"I want him gone. He'll give you the excuse."

"We always get the work done."

Barraclough does some business with his grey gabardine suit. He kneads the cloth, fiddles with the chain on his vest, puts his hands in his trouser pockets, lifts, and takes a quick peek at his red socks. After all these years Kenny can finally put his finger on why the guy irritates him so. It's not the overt ambition or the canned wisdom; none of the easy stuff. It's the fact that Barraclough is only three or four years older than him, thirty-four or thirty-five, and works that whole fifties attitude he's learned from all the other execs. He's not the little old man he pretends to be; he's a kid who's learned everything through osmosis.

"A general is always responsible for his troops, Kenny, m'man." He re-lights his cigar and looks at his watch. "A general has to make a few gestures and examples every now and again, just to keep the pot simmering."

"Look, Art . . ."

"Who has time to read for pleasure during working hours?" Barraclough rolls up the *Newsweek* and taps it against an open palm. "I know you think I'm a complete asshole, Kenny, but, believe me, I wouldn't have it any other way."

"L.C. Davis *is* a good worker. He has the right attitude."

"Grow up, man. They invite you to their houses. You meet the wife and kids and you feel a certain responsibility, I know." Barraclough taps the magazine against a cufflink, "I'm human too."

"Let me . . ."

"Consider cleaning house."

"I will."

"I mean everybody but you. All new people."

"Art, I used to have a staff of seven. Now I've got three left and a bunch of students and part-timers. C'mon . . ."

Outside there is a commotion. Barraclough flings the magazine aside, wrestles the door open and charges out to the warehouse. A single order sheet still sticks to his ass and the sight is amusing enough for Kenny to forget his anger. He takes a deep breath and follows.

Angel and Catalina are arguing in rapid-fire Caribbean Spanish. The Cubans and the Puerto Ricans are always ranking on each other. Angel is lewd while Catalina is all dignified, ladylike contempt. If you don't speak any Spanish, things sound more wild than they actually are.

"What's going on here?" shouts Barraclough, thumping one of the bright yellow stock shelves with the meat of his fist. "What's this argument about?" From where Kenny stands, Art's skin, tinted by synthetic light and the shocking background, is the color of one of those Polynesian drinks at Trader Vic's, the kind that catch up with you later.

"It's nothing," says Angel.

"It's nothing," says Catalina. Her cheeks are red, despite the layers of makeup.

Barraclough shakes his head. "Is he harassing you, Catalina?" She says no. He walks briskly away. "Be at my office at four o'clock, Kenny." He walks fast enough for the piece of paper to finally fall away and float slowly down to the ground. Catalina follows her boss, swinging her bubble butt from side to side.

"It move jus' like guava jelly," laughs Angel.

"Ssssh!" hisses Kenny.

Angel, however, wants to crash and burn. "*Un dia te voy a jodar por detias*," he yells after her.

Catalina turns, spits on the floor and rattles off something in Angel's direction that refers to his tiny cock.

"What you say to her, Angel?" L.C. asks as she backs away, still spitting abuse, like the tail-gunner of a World War II bomber.

"I tell her I fuck her good," Angel winks.

"He told her," Kenny says, shaking his head, "that he was gonna go in through the out door."

They all laugh, except for McQueen, who sees something serious in the situation. "Y'all shouldn't talk to a lady in such a manner, Angel," he says.

"Kiss my ass," says Angel. Angel and McQueen go nose to nose, push each other in the chest and let loose a few ethnic slurs before Kenny and L.C. step in between them.

It's all too much for Kenny's mix-mastered, caffeine-soaked brain. "You fuckers are gonna get me fired," he shouts, "and if I get canned, you guys are coming with me."

"Take it easy, boss," Angel says, trying to soothe him, putting an arm around his shoulder. "I jus' flirt wid dc beetch. I know. She know. We know."

"That lady is a lady, Angel," says McQueen. "I'd walk a hunnerd clicks just to kiss them sweet lips."

"Maybe twenty clicks, ey *pendejo*?"

"I said a hunnerd."

"I would'n' walk tha' far for Vanessa Del Rio. Ain't no woman worth walkin' tha' far for, ey, Kennee?" Angel laughs and slaps L.C. five.

"Jeez, I wouldn't know," Kenny says with a shrug. He would have liked to say yes — the right woman: You'd cut off your arm for her: Walk a million miles — but right then he couldn't find the wherewithal.

"Ain't you ever been in love, Kenny?" says McQueen.

"Yes, I love my wife. Really." His empty stomach growls.

"You paid the price for marryin' rich and pretty, di . . ."

"Don't overstep the bounds of familiarity, man," Kenny snaps.

Their wives weren't even part of the equation anymore. Was that the way to be? They were just *there*, like mother. All *his* standards and bonds came from somewhere else, he realized; somewhere even more warped, where you translated everything through the prism of achievement.

Through the prefabricated fiberglass furred walls, Kenny hears the sound of a delivery truck arriving, like the cavalry. He pushes a button to open the loading dock door. "Show time, guys," he shouts.

"Show time," they say, one at a time, slapping each other five. All three walk away grinning. They start up their forklifts, do a slick 180 degree turn in synchronized unison, bring their forks up and down, in and out, bow in his direction — he, of course, reciprocates — and the day begins.

At twelve-thirty Kenny cannot bring himself to go into the cafeteria. He buys a pack of M&M's and a cup of evil-tasting chicken broth from vending machines and sits down in his office. The telephone rings.

"Hello, Catholic boy."

"Hi, Catholic girl." His heart plays semi-quavers.

"I had to call you," she says.

"It's all right."

"I know you don't like me to call you at work."

"They listen, that's all. I don't care." He lights a cigarette and draws a Van Dyck moustache on a glossy *Newsweek* photograph of Raisa Gorbachev.

"I'm at home," Linda says. "I'm taking some more shit." He is not sure if she's high or not. Her voice has that phlegmy quality. "I need to see you."

"Why don't you just stay home?" he says. "Really, it'll be okay."

"It won't," she says. "We're too old to go through this shit again and again."

"You're strung out, Linda. Let's talk when . . ."

"I don't want to get straight. Last time I cleaned up . . ."

"You stayed clean for four fucking years, girl."

"Listen to me," she screams, "and don't call me girl. The last time I got straight, it was for you. For the love of you."

"I still love you. We can do it again." There is a long, long silence. So silent, as McQueen would say, that you could hear a mouse piss on cotton.

"I've seen the needle and the damage done . . ." she sings.

"Don't."

"Can't avoid clichéd ole Neil, can I?" She starts to weep. Too high? Eight miles high? Twenty clicks high? "Do you remember what you said to me Tuesday morning?" Linda has always been able to cut from hysteria to indignation — without gears.

"No." He really doesn't.

"You said I'd never had an original thought in my life."

"I'm sorry," he says, the tears burning his cheeks. "You were shooting up at six o'clock in the morning. Doing wake-ups. You got strung out again so fast. I'm sorry. I got pissed."

"I made your breakfast first, Kenny." She cries again.

"Yes, you did, Linda. You sure did." If she can feel his contempt through the wires, can she feel his love? There is another protracted silence.

"I need to see you, Kenny. We need to talk."

"When?"

"Now."

He loves her so. "Where?"

"Home."

"Okay."

As he climbs the stairs, Kenny sees two men struggling as they carry segments of the bed down. White boys with lank hair. They are emaciated, wall-eyed with dope, and carry their light burden as if it's heavy.

Linda sits Indian-style on the floor, looking, save for tiny irises, almost healthy, immaculate and gorgeous in a blue worsted blazer-skirt ensemble. Her hair is coiffed, nails manicured. A smile locks into that firehouse garage mouth. He is so hungry that he feels lightheaded. If he eats he will be slow-witted; he takes another cup of coffee.

"Well, hi, you con artist you," he says. "I like your moving service. What do you call them — Opium Express?"

She ignores him. "Hi, Kenny. I'm absolutely cash poor. Can you give them a few bucks cash? Enough to get them some Ho-Ho's and doughnuts or whatever."

"Sure," he shrugs, taking two crumpled tens from his pocket. All he can do is stare at her, watch her look at her nails. "How do you do it? How do you pull it off?"

"Suspended animation, you know. I still take my vitamins and eat right. I don't eat shit, like them." She nods, reassuring herself, and lights a cigarette.

"Is there some particular reason for me coming home, or, umm, did you just want to rub my nose in . . ."

"Nostalgia, I suppose." She opens up a cellophane bag and takes delicate bites on Japanese seaweed between puffs of her cigarette. "The scene of the crime."

"Nostalgia isn't what it used to be," he says, "but let's get back together anyway."

"No, I'm going away." The cigarette sticks to her lower lip and tears her eyes. "See, I'm all dressed up."

Like a little girl going on a trip. "I love you." The two zombie men walk in, catch the conversation, and walk out. "I want you to come home. We can work it out."

"I'm going to Amsterdam," she says. "I called you because I need some road money."

"Jesus, Linda, I know you hocked everything. You can't have spent it all."

"A new life," she says. "I'm going to do what I always wanted to do."

"Dope?" he whispers.

"Yeah." She wipes her eyes. "China white is cheap and plentiful in the Netherlands. And they all speak English."

"Would it be too uncool of me to ask for an explanation?"

"Don't be coy. You really don't understand, Kenny," she says. "You used to do it with me, but you never really *liked* it."

"Hey, I quit that shit *because* I liked it."

"Got straight?"

"Right." She looks from his face to his chest; green eyes, green eye-liner: Cold? Ashamed? "I just finally made my mind up that I love skag and that's that."

"Look, I really love you, Linda. Stay with me and we'll work it out."

"I did that already." She sticks her tongue out at him and he realizes that the thing he had loved in her was not bravery after all, but a rich girl's armored arrogance. "You used to be so great, Kenny. I remember when you did burglaries so we could get off."

Soon she'll mention who turned her on to shooting dope the first time. It's easier for him to just head her off at the pass. "How much money do you *want*, Linda?"

"Two, three thou."

He takes the checkbook from his pocket. "There's twenty-three hundred in the account. I'll give you eighteen." He writes out a check. She folds it and puts in into her purse.

"It's not you, Kenny. It's the dope. I love dope."

"I'll put up with it. Stay."

"Kenny, I just want to shoot dope. I wasted years . . ."

"With me?"

"Jesus, stop taking it personally, Kenny."

"Ha!"

"I'm a junkie, Kenny." He shakes his head. "I love you but I'm a junkie. All the years I was straight, whether I worked or sat at home waiting for you, I craved it. I craved the shit, Kenny. It's like . . . it's like a polyp you can't cut away."

If a hunchback has his hump surgically removed, does he miss it? "I'll quit my job."

"I'll come and see you after I clean up. I love you."

"I love you too."

The two junkies re-enter. "This is Eric," she says, pointing, "and this is Nicholas. I've been staying at their place." He glares at them.

"Tell him. There's been no hanky panky."

"There's been no hanky panky, dude," Nicholas says.

"Hanky panky" is a euphemism she picked up from her father. Kenny thinks of Barraclough and osmosis.

"I'm going," Kenny says.

"Aren't you gonna kiss me goodbye?"

Kenny walks back to her, crouches and gives her a kiss. "You broke my heart," he says.

"You'll be okay," she says.

As Kenny opens the door one of the junkies touches him. "She really loves you, dude. She told me so."

"Leave the coffee machine and something for me to sleep on, will you, Linda?" he says, walking out.

When Kenny gets back to work, he empties the M&M's out onto his desk and arranges them into lines of color. The dominant color is red. Years ago, it seemed, they had been more even-handed. Today, he was sure they surveyed the kids.

Nastassia seems to be looking right at him. Like a good slippery fuck with some sweet young thing will cure all your ills, won't it? Pulling the tacks out with the tips of his fingers hurts. He rolls the poster up and puts a piece of scotch tape in the center. He lights a cigarette, fills his mouth with yellow M&M's, puts on his coat and decides that some physical work will do him good.

On the dock it is damp. Rain falls diagonally and soaks the concrete floor. The wind cuts through him and he feels as if he's ascending a waterfall sideways. McQueen zips by him, going way too fast.

"Are you crazy?" Kenny shouts. "Slow down."

"I been drivin' this damn machine for eighteen years, Kenny," McQueen barks. He takes away a pallet full of boxes and then reverses back out of the dark open mouth of a truck at an even more reckless pace. He drops a pile of skids an inch or so short of crushing Kenny's feet. "Where do you get the rocks to tell me how to do my damn job?"

"Do it my way or you're fired," Kenny barks back, candy mulch all over his tongue and teeth.

"Ain't nothin' bein' done different to the way I always done it," says McQueen. There's a quick glint of fear in his sad blue eyes: A quick one for the wife and kids?

"Well, things have changed."

Something hits Kenny in the chest and bounces off the concrete. A pair of safety glasses. He stomps on them but they don't break. "You're fired," he says, without looking up. "Have fun looking for work, you hillbilly shit, 'cos you ain't gonna get unemployment." It's easy if you just look away.

"What the fuck is wrong with you, boss boy?"

The next thing he's in McQueen's arms, tight up against his beer belly, smelling oil and sweat and booze on his breath, crying his eyes out as the wind and rain pummel them. The man holds his face up and rubs his head.

"You look like you in bocoo shit, boy," he says. "Your wife gone?" All Kenny can do is nod. McQueen's eyes are so close together that he resembles some kind of rodent, an alcoholic, red-faced rodent, *Rattus Kentuckyus.*

Kenny hears laughing. Angel and L.C. approach as Kenny steps away from McQueen and wipes his face with his sleeve.

"Somethin' wrong?" asks Angel.

"It's okay," McQueen says.

"You okay, Captain Bligh?"

"I'll hang you from the highest yardarm in the Puerto Rican navy, Mistah Guttierez," Kenny croaks. He puts his hand into his pockets and walks away.

Opening the dock door, he hears his name and stops to listen to what they're saying.

"Wha's up his asshole? Wha's the trayedy, man?"

"I done told you before," says McQueen. "The boy done married himself to a rich girl an' a lifetime o' heartache."

At four o'clock Kenny clocks out and goes to see Barraclough. Catalina sits at her desk outside his office, typing with a pair of gloves on. The sweet smell of Shalamar surrounds her. On the desk is a coffee cup emblazoned with the heads of John F. Kennedy and Ronald Reagan on either side of the stars and stripes. Behind the desk, on the wall, is a color photo of Fidel Castro; there is a dart right between his eyes.

"Viva Fidel!" Kenny says. Catalina just rolls her eyes and goes on typing.

Barraclough sits with his feet up on his desk. He gestures toward a seat and Kenny slides into it. The room is as clean as a hospital operating room. There are no photographs of his family, just framed diplomas from U of I, and an autographed picture of him in his fat-boy period with his arm around a dark man: "To Art," it says, "On To Victory!" There is a squiggly autograph which Kenny knows is the signature of Art's golden calf: Robert J. Ringer. Barraclough takes a long look at his Patek Philipe watch, which must have either cost a hefty chunk of change or be a counterfeit job.

"Have you made up your mind yet, Ken?" Now it's Ken.

"About what?"

Barraclough grins his predatory grin and offers a White Owl from a silver-plate case. He refuses. "We gotta knock off the bullshit, m'man." He lights up. "You're making what? Thirty-two five."

"Thirty-three five."

"Right. Okay. We gotta mutual Pontius Pilate thing here, I understand that. Angel and McQueen, the alky bros," he laughs at his own joke but looks upward for his cigar smoke when Kenny stares at him. "Angel and McQueen've got like almost twenty years, right?"

"Right. They both worked here *before* they went off to Vietnam too."

"Right. Yes. Anyway, we gotta call a spade a spade and a nigger a nigger." He chuckles again and holds up his hands. "I'm sorry, I forgot that *you* find that word an offense to your sensibilities. Anyway, the aah . . . L.C. Davis is gone if he's late again, right?"

"Right. I'll do it my own self. *If* he's ever late again." Kenny's chair has wheels on it and he rolls back and forth.

"Oh, he will be." Catalina pops her head in to say goodbye and he blows her a kiss. "Now, how about a raise to thirty-six seven?"

"Sure, but . . ."

"If I put in a whole new staff on the dock. Hungry Flip kids." He looks at his watch again. "We could give you one extra body to work with and save, I figure, nine thou off the budget. Makes us both look good."

Kenny feels a monster urge to beat the crap out of him. "I won't do it, Art," he says. "No way. No how."

"Yeah, I know, you think I'm an asshole. Think you could take me out?" Barraclough flexes his hand, showing off the callouses he's built up from plunging it into buckets of beans and sand. "I tell you, we'll be the Pontius Pilate brothers. We send 'em for physicals. Check their piss and . . . That's all she wrote . . . They'll be long gone. It'll put the fear of God into everyone here."

"Fuck you." Kenny stands up and rolls his chair into Barraclough's desk.

"Say it all you want, if it makes you feel better. It's good catharsis."

"Fuck you."

"No, fuck *you*," he says. He doesn't even do a double take. "Wise up, sucker. I speak for the big boys. This whole Machiavellian thing is too jive, even for me." Kenny digests what he's said slowly and doesn't know how to reply. "I'll tell you the truth. When I started this job I tried to have your ass fired and found out you were protected. *He* thinks you're smart." Kenny flings the chair to the floor. "Look, m'man, I like you. You got morals. But I'm the boss-man and I don't like being referred to as Mister Number Ten by a bunch of no-account fucks. Them Flip kids, you say 'Jump,' and they say, 'How fucking high, boss?'"

Kenny opens the door. "You can all go fuck yourselves."

"Don't take it so damned hard, Kenny. We're just a couple o' Polack kids from Kedzie Avenue. We got no power *yet*." Kenny spits on the floor. "I ain't so bad, you'll see. We're both street kids. The Pontius Pilate Brothers, think about it."

He walks out and hears Art Barraclough's voice echoing behind him as he traverses the corridor. "Sleep on it, Kenny. Sleep on it."

In Teddy's bar, across the street from the plant, the three of them are doing Jack Daniel's boilermakers. He buys them all a round, then another round. Then L.C. buys, only it's the cheap whiskey this time: Heaven Hill. On an empty stomach he gets drunk fast.

"They want me to fire you guys."

"Who do?" says L.C. "Bear Claw? I'll kick his monkey ass."

"No," Kenny says. "The big guys up top."

"Your daddy-in-low?" says McQueen, for all the world an Indian in the dark bar lit by nothing but a neon Old Style sign.

"Yeah," he laughs, "my daddy-in-low."

"Wha' joo goin' to do, man?"

"Quit, I guess," he says, throwing back his shot, wincing.

"You crazy," L.C. says.

"But, you're my *friends*," Kenny says. They all cackle and he goes off to puke.

When he comes back they hardly acknowledge him. Absorbed in trying not to be sick again, he concentrates on his gullet, where it feels like there's a brillo pad, rusty steel wool that grows with his every breath. They talk about Vietnam. Talk about the same old thing.

"Fuckin' Tet, man. Reporters fly into fuckin' Camp Evans like they own the goddamn place. Fuckin' Morley Safer in his white hunter leisure suit and ascot faggot shit," sneers McQueen.

"The guy from *60 Minutes*?" says L.C.

"Yeah, he's a pussy *maricon*," says Angel.

"Say to me, Morley Safer did: 'I need a jeep to take me to the Powder River.' So's him and his faggot crew can have night shots of rockets and tracer flyin' into Hue."

"Number ten *pendejo*."

"We heard this story before, L.C.," Kenny says, leaning on McQueen's chair. "Ain't we?"

"You respect my shit and I'll respect yours, boss boy." McQueen points a finger in Kenny's face. He can see elaborate Chinese dragon tattoos quite clearly in the neon light, all the way up McQueen's arm, them and eczema-like spots caused by battery acid burns. "I done listened to your boo-hooin' an' caterwaulin' this afternoon."

"I'm sorry, man." McQueen, a mean drunk, pushes Kenny away from his chair. He almost falls. Only Angel's hand, grabbing hold of his shirt until he rights himself, saves him from falling on his ass and embarrassing himself. "Shit, I told you, I'm sorry."

"Go home," McQueen says. "You can't drink."

"Fuck you all. I thought . . ." L.C. is looking at him, shaking his head. Linda has that look too: when she's tying off her arm with a belt, holding it in her teeth, slapping the shit out of her arm, trying to find a fresh vein and he *dares* to cringe. That same exact look. He picks up his coat and leaves.

When he gets home, Kenny finds that everything of value has been taken. Everything that's hockable. Even the ceiling fan is gone. Bare wires dangle from the ceiling and, directly below, lumps of plaster lay scattered and crushed on the hardwood floor like stepped-upon insects. It takes a while to register that the Persian rug, a wedding gift from her parents worth five thousand bucks at least, the old man had solemnly informed them, was gone too.

"Oh, Linda, Linda, Linda," he moans, and his voice echoes back off the emptiness.

He finds some thumbtacks in a drawer and takes out the Kinski poster he has kept rolled up in his coat pocket. He pins it up on the wall and stands with his arms folded, staring. It has been seven years since he's been with another woman.

Hunger hits him and he walks into the kitchen. All the appliances, aside from the drip coffee maker, have gone but there is at least some food in the refrigerator and comfort in its electro-Gregorian hum. Opening the door, he finds a one-pound chub of salami, some cheddar cheese and some eggs. "All that cholesterol will catch up with you sooner or later," she had said. Health-conscious Linda. It is a big sick joke. Attached to the door is a magnetized cast-iron pig with a bubble coming out of its mouth. The bubble says: "No!"

Kenny takes out the salami and begins to gnaw on it; it's Kosher Zion, his favorite kind. There are quite a few smashed pots and spice bottles. Obviously, she looked everywhere for the emergency cash and got a little pissed because he'd one-upped her.

He walks back into the living room, sucking and chewing on the salami like it's a lollipop. Looking out through the window, he sees, reflected in the brights of a car that quickly passes by, that a teenage kid in a Cubs cap is trying to break into his MG. He eases the window open slowly, slides up the storm window, and can see nothing at all below him.

"Freeze, or I'll . . ." he shouts, but, before he can get to "shoot your ass," the kid is off and running. Sneakers slap rubber weaker and weaker against the pavement until Kenny invents footstep noises in his own mind, for himself. He had been in a gang once: stole cars, mugged queers, burgled houses in Barrington and Kenilworth; carved people up for no real reason. As good as sex it had been. A million years ago, before he got sucked in by the silver tongues of social workers. Never at a loss for a hackneyed proverb, Linda had said: "What goes around, comes around," when he'd confessed the sins of his flaming youth after lovemaking. She had, in fact, made herself the instrument of the almighty, or whoever the bugger was who made it go around and come around.

He should have let the kid steal the car, he realized. The laws of change *are* synchronous. He has clung to and sucked at the teat of exact replication for too long. It was over with Linda and he didn't want the job any more. The condo was in her name. Daddy had insisted on that when he'd given them the deposit money; that and separate bank accounts. In nature, repetition can only be approximate; exact repetition causes cancer and death.

Outside there is only darkness interrupted by the slight scimitar curve of moonlight, as if someone has turned on a flashlight under the far edge of a trash can lid.

Kenny takes off his shirt and smells rancid booze and cigarettes. The bed, he hopes, will still be in the bedroom. In the morning, if the car is still there, he will go either south to New Orleans or west to Flagstaff. Places he's never been. He will toss a coin.

EUGENE KRAFT

We Gather Together

from New Mexico Humanities Review

And so I told my Father I would learn English and he said, No. And I did not say, Yes. But I thought, Yes. And that a Mennonite never does. Go gegen der Vater. But am I a Mennonite, I ask for the first time. To myself, silent, not spoken. Natürlich.

That time he did not say, I knew how to read German, but I know he thought it, when he looked. When my Father looks, everybody understands. He is a very big man, I think. By the way.

He is Our Leader. Mennonites here in Kansas and everyplace other, we have no pastors, only a Leader in the biggest house where we gather together for the Bible and praying services. He was always the Leader, my Father, even in Russia and in Liverpool and in Port of New York.

When we did not know where to go or what to say, in Port of New York. The people all pushing each other, dirty and the officials people. The officials people pushed the other old men and my Father also. They were afraid and made looks like they were not afraid. This made them look more afraid, still. But not my Father, his big body, his big beard, was not afraid, not at all. He was peace.

This I fight against. This is the same thing I fight against when I say to my Father, I will learn English.

I know I have a very big fight.

But it is all peace, this Mennonite life and we are always gathering together to pray for peace and the journey from Russia to Port of New York — the Brethern hated it, the dirt, no water to wash, dirty eats slopped in tin bowls. The Brethern are immer clean and full of peace and they hate it, sleeping next to Italianisch, Franzoizich, Katholica, dirty peoples. Even Jew. But for me, what joy. For the Brethern, for the other peoples, it is the journey, a place to go to. The end of the journey is the important thing. But for me, the journey is the end. The noise and the fighting and the dirtiness, the pictures, is the end. The Women Volken in their bright colors, not like the Mennonite women. Of course.

And so all of my journey comes from me, from inside me. And a help from the center of the earth.

And this is why, early in my journey, in my Father's house, in the cottonwoods, I begin to write this, even though I do not understand it then.

And this is why I learn English.

And this is what I write:

I

My Journey

And so I knew I must wait to learn English, wait a little. I will wait a month, I say to myself. My Father does not watch me in this time, but I know he watches me. Without looking. Then for the first time in my life it happens. I speak without thinking. In two weeks, not a month, I say at supper, I will learn English and the words have come out themselves.

And so I know I have a Power within me.

This is very excited, but I speak quiet and my mother is not so frightened. My Father answered, Why will you learn English? as asking, Why do you think it rains tomorrow?

See, I say, logisch. You will need someone to talk to the Kansas people about land, to the surveyor, about the buying new land, you will need Übersetzer. Which means, in English, interpreter, I learn later. I will be Übersetzer to the others, the Kansas people who buy our Turkish Red wheat, who will buy our cattle, who will buy our farm things, eggs, und so weiter.

Suddenly my Father is very angry and he shouts for the first time, NO, hitting the table. NO. By our God, the Bible and the words of the great Menno Simmons, auf Deutsch, that is ENOUGH FOR ANY MENNONITE. NO MORE. NO. MORE.

And I am always good at school, at remembering everything in words. And so two weeks later I go not to the Sabbath Praying in my Father's the Leader's house. And at the dinner table my Father, eating for half an hour says, Why are you not at Sabbath Praying today?

I go to Praying, I say, but at First Lutheran Church of Liberal, Kansas. Not inside the Church, I say, happy, like a child, but outside the Church, to listen. Just to learn the English, I say. I hear the First Lutherans sing a song, I say, Then I sing it, at my Father's table, on a Sabbath:

> We gather together to ask the
> Lord's blessing,
> Ordaining, maintaining His king-
> dom divine.
> The wicked oppressing now cease
> from distressing,

> Give praises to His name, He for-
> gets not His own.
>
> We all do extol Thee, Thou Leader
> triumphant,
> And pray that Thou still our
> Defender will be;
> Let Thy congregation escape
> tribulation,
> Thy Name be ever praised, O Lord
> make us free!

My Father and the table is very quiet. The next week I work very hard, much harder than the other sons, to fool them. We are harvesting the maize.

But I go not to the Sabbath Praying the next week, but to the First Lutherans.

Then at the dinner table I tell my Father I do so. The table is again very quiet. Then my Father says, You will learn English. Then he eats no more. I know he thinks, the son is lost. And I am very happy and very afraid.

II

And now I write this later, much later, after many things have happened. So if somebody finds it after. I take English lessons from this Mrs. Carpenter, a teacher on her man's farm, near Liberal, Kansas. When we Mennonites first came to Kansas she was very nett to us, giving us things we needed, the women tools for the Kücher, and needles and threads. I asked her for English lessons but I say, I cannot pay. And she laughs and says, Just bring me some of that good Mennonite bread every week and some of your Turkey Red wheat for my man. Mrs. Carpenter is First Lutheran and I think, now, that she helps our women because she wants us to become First Lutherans. Because: when we begin lessons she wants to teach me the Bible in English, but I say, No. I will learn newspaper.

And this because our Elders laugh at newspaper, say nothing new is in it. And I say I will learn song, We Gather Together to Ask the Lord's Blessing. But not Bible. Mennonites have this book already.

She makes her face hard, ready to anger, but I say, NO, with hardness, much hardness. I will learn newspaper for the Mennonites. But first the song, not like our songs at all.

We learn the song and then the newspaper.

And the newspaper is the best thing I had, better even than the journey on the boat from Liverpool. The newspaper is the world, Catholics, Jews, Chinese, Indians. Nothing is peaceful in the newspaper.

The Liberal Gazette: October 16, 1878. Liberal is in the middle of the state of Kansas. Kansas is in the Middle of North America. North America is in this time the middle of the world: where all wish to go. These are the first things I learn from the newspaper.

III

But it is very hard for me. Learning to read *The Liberal Gazette.* I go very fast, but there is nobody to explain the newspaper to. This makes me feel bursting, bursting all the time. And my Father does not use me for trading with the Kansas people, we did this before auf Deutsch. And I get more and more excited at the newspaper, the stories. Sometimes after the lessons I walk for a long time on the prairie. The Brethern say little.

Then: early in 1878:
I read the story in *The Liberal Gazette:*

> An uprising of Indians was
> reported a few days ago about sev-
> enty miles from the northern
> border of Kansas. The raid was
> concentrated along the Solomon
> River. A less severe raid has been
> said to have occurred along the
> Saline River in north central
> Kansas. Several families in both
> areas of the state have left their
> homes. One man is reported to have
> been killed. No more details are
> available, but the Governor's Office
> and the Army have issued a joint
> statement declaring that the
> Indians (primarily Kiowa) have
> been captured and that there is no
> reason for alarm.

I read this story very quiet, it is a very short story
on the bottom of page two. When I have finished the
story, Mrs. Carpenter says, You can bet that the government declares that. It always declares that. How could
they get people to settle out there if they told the truth? I
smell Little Wolf and Roman Nose again. And I see the
shadow of Crazy Horse.

Thus I first hear the names.

Then, it is night. I ride the horse home first, then I
walk the horse. I am all the time thinking, all the time
very quiet, but coming ready to burst.

So: the Mennonites do not say the truth, because it
is different from their thought.

So: the Kansas newspaper does not say the truth,
because it is different from their desire.

Then: Who does say the truth?

I think, riding my Father's brown mare: I WILL.

This thought makes me feel to bursting and I get off the mare and run very fast with the bridle, to quiet me. Because of a greater thought, no, feel, comes: it is all different. For many years, I think, it is in Kansas not like the Mennonites and not like the Kansas people, but like the Indians.

Because: Mrs. Carpenter says, For ten years there have been Indian troubles. Killing. Burning houses. Tormentings. But the politics do not say this and the newspapers say what the politics say. But the people in the towns, the people the Mennonites do not talk to, they say the truth. Whisper in quiet voices.

Then I think: It is not what it really is, Kansas is not what it really is. And Russia was not. And Germany was not. And then the world is not. Is like the big, dirty ship with the dirty eats, mixed up, fighting. Loud noises, the ship jumping up and down in a storm, the Italianisch dancing, like on the ship. The Jews whispering, like on the ship. But nobody says this: they say, we thank God for this peaceful life, we Mennonites, we build white wood houses in the towns, we Kansas people, we kill the rattlesnakes, there are so many rattlesnakes, we fight the Indians and conquer them forever.

But I will say what it really is. And that day I think: I will write it down, what I do.

And I know that this truth comes from in me and my witness is true. But I know also that I am twenty-four years old, no money, do not know anything but Mennonite life. I must have power like my Father. So I must learn English very well, read many things. Two or three times I go into Liberal to learn about the Indians, but see, I am different from the other men, my long beard, my long black coat, my big hat with the round top. So when I ask Kansas people, what happens with the Indians, always the Indians, they do not speak, but look at each other. So I think, I will learn to talk to Kansas people from reading, and I will talk to Mr. Carpenter.

So I study reading very hard and get better quickly. Mrs. Carpenter is very excited, she laughs a lot, nobody makes such progress as you, she says. When the lesson is over on one Wednesday I ask, can I speak with your husband? She answers, about what? I answer, the Indians.

So Mr. Carpenter and I speak after every lesson not to learn about the Indians, but how to speak to Kansans. I know he does not know about the Indians, he is too peaceful, he talks about progress, like the newspapers. There is much to learn in reading, then I start writing to write this, with much to learn. The two ( ) for when you speak quietly and " " for when you use real words.

And Mrs. Carpenter asks if I can come to her school in the day time so she can show me to the pupils, show them how good I can read. I say, "Yes." But then the next day I say, "Only if I have five lessons a week, five evenings. I want to learn English good." And she doesn't know the real reason, but she says, "Yes."

Then I stand in front of the children and she gives me *The Liberal Gazette,* and I read to the children. But I see the children laugh because I leave my hat on (she says quietly, "Take off your hat") and at my clothes.

And later I say to Mrs. Carpenter, "Now what can I learn besides the newspaper?"

And she says, "The Bible in English." I say, "No! The Bible I have read with my people. Something new." She says, "A history book my students study." But I say, "No. New! New this year!"

And she thinks.

And she gives me *Uncle Tom's Cabin* by Harriet Beecher Stowe. She says, "This is not new this year, but it isn't very old. It is very famous. It's a great book." And for the first time in Kansas somebody tells me the truth.

IV

Uncle Tom's Cabin

Uncle Tom's Cabin is a book about a Negro man, an old man. He is very brilliant, but he pretends all the time that he is stupid. But he is not. It is his master, Simon Legree, who is stupid. This book is a great book and fills up my nights and days for many months. First I read slow and then I read very fast. I do not tell you all that is in the book, not nearly all, but I say it is like the ship to Port of New York: the people are all very strange. And one part of the book that is most strange is the time when Little Eva dies.

Little Eva is very comisch, comical. Harriet Beecher Stowe was trying to make this part of the book comical because it is very serious, I think. When she dies, Little Eva, angels come down and she speaks very lying, very funny. I think.

But Uncle Tom is very smart and very black, full of evil, full of sin. I say this, excited, to Mrs. Carpenter and she is very surprised. "No, no, no," she says, again and again. "He is not. Uncle Tom is not brilliant, but he is very good, he is a saint."

Then I laugh, for I know she is lying. "Listen," I say, and I read from where Uncle Tom is ready to die.

> Tom looked up to his master and answered, "Mas'r, if you was sick, or in trouble, or dying, and I could save ye, I'd give ye my heart's blood; and if taking every drop of blood in this poor old body would save your precious soul, I'd give 'em freely, as the Lord gave His for me. O, Mas'r! don't bring this great sin on your soul! It will hurt you more than 'twill me!"

"You see," I say, "This beating and killing that he makes Simon Legree do. Now, when Uncle Tom dies, what does Simon Legree? Ho!" I say. "There is your answer. Simon Legree, he is stupid, but Uncle Tom is very strong and evil!"

Her face white.

"You are like the others," I say. "A baby can see Uncle Tom is full of sin, very black. *He makes Simon Legree kill him.* He is very, very interesting, this Uncle Tom, yes. But he is a devil from hell."

Then Mrs. Carpenter walks around the room and drops things and makes her dress smooth with her hands. Then she says, "I think I can't afford the time for any more lessons for you. With my pupils and my husband I just have too much."

Then I think, Liar, and I laugh. I need not that liar any more. Now I can read and write English.

V

I Live in the Trees

And so in mind I am completely separated from the Brethern. My mother is close, but she is very small and weak. I know that she is very stupid and I am sorry, but I have no time.

I think a lot of time, for the first time. The Brethern keep no clocks in Kansas, what use have they? They gather and garner by the sun. They sleep and breed by the moon. But I am twenty-four; the Brethern live a long time, ninety or a hundred years, longer than the Kansans, and they never talk about their age, because things are always the same. They gather in prayer peacefully, work, live and die peacefully.

But I think I will not live long and peace is not what I need.

So I do not work on my Father's farm any more. Now I see how stupid I was, how much time I wasted. I am very much hurried. What can those peaceful Mennonites do to me if I do not work? Sometimes the old people tell stories of how this one in Russia or that one many years ago in Germany was run out of the Mennonites because he would not abide by the Rule, but I am not afraid of this now. When there is something you must do, fear of old things go. Then there is fear from the new thing.

Perhaps I am not stronger than my Father, but I am different.

I go into the kitchen where the women are working and ask my mother for food. She give me food and cries, but I do not consider her tears, because I have no time. "Why do you not work?" she asks. "I am studying," I say, and leave the kitchen.

I think: when they stop giving me food I will go at night and steal. My need is greater than theirs and I do not care.

However, I do not study much because one day when I am reading under the cottonwood trees beside the river, suddenly I do not know what I am reading. The words are easy to read now, but the meaning is nothing, and the book falls from my hands and I know, I know, I will never read books and newspapers again. (What a joy! What a great joy! To know that you are called! To cut your life in two parts and throw away one half of it!) Words are like the Brethern's peace: real, but not serious enough: not real enough. And without thinking, then, I get up and walk into Liberal, seven miles.

The drunk ones:

The ones without money:

The ones without work:

The dirty ones:

And these are what I seek. These are what I need. And they say, "There is a great Indian rebellion up the

Saline and up the Arkansas and the greatest rebellion is up the Solomon. Many murders have happened, many houses have been burned. The Kiowa, the Cheyenne and the Sioux have gathered together. The Army has gathered together."

Then I feel such excitement that I almost come to bursting. (Especially for the Sioux; and I do not understand this.) And the drunk ones, without money, the Sinners, say, "This is the last one. We'll get the goddammed redskins now. After all, this is 1878. They're mad, those redskins, but they don't have a chance."

Then I know that I have one chance, perhaps: one last chance. And later I know that the sinners are very stupid, because they stay in Liberal and talk. They do not know that one time is enough, that one time is enough.

And so I walk to my Father's house and I go into the house and I get blankets and more food. And my mother cries and asks, "Why do you do this? Where are you going?" I answer, "I go to live in the trees." And I know I never will speak to my mother again.

And I think: in three or four days my clothes and my hairs will be dirty, very dirty. Good. Because it is the trees that give these ideas to me. This I tell you surely: the ideas come not from me, but from the trees. From the sounds of the leaves in the high trees, from the leaves in the very highest branches.

And I become wild.

VI

I Follow the River

And then I do not think for a long time, not for hours, not for days, and I do not know what happens. I am rolling in the leaves and running up and down in the dry river. I am doing this for days. For days I am running through the trees.

I am screaming, shouting. I am screaming and shouting for days.

Then I rest. Once the Brethern come down in groups, once with my Father, to take me back. They stand at the edge of the cottonwoods talking to me one after the other, to take me back. They call to me about love and peace and the teaching of Menno Simmons, but I stand and scream and run at them to make them go. Then once they bring sticks and ropes to catch me, but I see them coming and run away.

When you will do something, you know when something to hinder you comes.

Then after some days, some weeks, I am tired of this and I know it is time to go, to follow the Arkansas River. But I have sense and I go on a Sunday when the Brethern are at a dinner at one of their houses. Then I steal clothes and wash myself and cut my hairs and beard short. I think with care of what I need and take bread and meat and knives and matches. And money.

And when I leave the house I think: niemals, niemals, niemals, niemals, niemals mehr, meaning, NEVER, NEVER, NEVER, NEVER, NEVER MORE. Never more will I smell the clean Brethern smell, and I follow the river to find the Indians and the fighting.

Those days, those days, what joy, what joy! (I write this now and you will think, no more time for joy now, he will have not much more joy.) But for a time, I had, when I did what I was made to do. All alone, without even the cottonwoods overhead, following the river. The smells of the rotting leaves now fallen down, the smells of the river standing in pools, what joy!

But I still have sense and after a while I think: I must have a horse or the fighting will be all gone before I come. And I must talk to the Sinners to find exactly where the fighting is, and buy clothes like the other mens, so I do this in Great Bend. I go to the General Store and buy pants and a shirt and a hat. And then outside of Great Bend I burn my dirty Mennonite clothes and dress in the new clothes and return to where the Sinners are gathered together in front of the Saloon. I must go further, I learn, to the north, toward Nebraska. And I hear the great names for the first time: Dull Knife: and a greater name: Roman Nose. And I think before I die, I want to see them. And I hear, and it fills me to bursting, talk of the greatest: Crazy Horse. But I think it will never be good enough for me to see him.

And I am glad to get away from Great Bend, with the mud everyplace in the streets and the bad white houses, not built careful like the Mennonite farm houses, but to last for a week, and some with only one or two rooms. And the women too, dirty, and the men talking, talking all the time and spitting tobacco.

I will follow the Saline and the Smoky and the Arkansas to the Solomon and then—I follow what I find. Like Simon Legree in *Uncle Tom's Cabin*. I find Blackface.

VII

Blackface

This is how I find him:

One morning I am leading my horse through some short trees by the river and I come over this small hill covered with dry tumbleweeds to a very flat land. I am singing the hymn:

> We all do extol Thee, Thou Leader
>   Triumphant,
> And pray that Thou still Our
>   Defender will be.

> Since from the beginning the battle
>   we were winning,
> Thy name be ever praised, O Lord
>   make us free!

and then I see, some distance away, a tall Indian laying on the earth, flat.

I stop in the trees.

For a long time the tall Indian lays there flat, one side of his face on the earth, away from me. He is listening, I think to myself. He is listening to things deep in the earth: gophers and moles and snakes underground: and deep, black water, moving fast.

What else does he hear?

For a long time I wait on him. Then he gets up slow with his back to me and from his pack takes little leather sacks and paints his body and his face. Red stripes all over his face and body: and then he screams like me in the trees and makes fists, waving his hands in the air and jumping and running.

Then I am very, very surprised, for he turns suddenly and looks at me and his face is very black, almost like a Negro's. His body is dark like the Indians, but his face is black. And then he laughs at me very hard, with pointed teeth in his mouth, looking into my eyes.

Then I know: he felt me watching me all the time.

I think: he knows I am like him.

I will follow him.

VIII

Following Blackface to the Battle

But he never speaks and I do not know his name. But I call him Blackface, like the children say the Devil's face is black. And for days I follow him, while he does not look back at me. But he knows I am there. And we go north along the River.

It is very strange, for all the time I am thinking about Blackface and he is thinking about me, I know certainly. But we think very deep down. He does not think of me like, where does he come from and what is his name, but he has me in his blood. And I do not think, why is this Blackface alone and where is his Tribe?

He walks a hundred yards ahead of me, leading his horse or sometimes riding it and not looking, and for me he is only a dark shadow I do not look at. But there is a very strong rope between this Indian and me. Sometimes he stops and lays down flat on the earth again with his ear listening. Then he goes on and does not look back.

I do not know why, but I am thinking often of the dance I saw one night when I was with the Sinners: wild music and dancing such as the Brethern never think of. There is such excitement in me when I see and hear this.

Then it is late in the fall when we leave the River. Here there are small hills and trees and I think: we are no more in Kansas. This is another country. And then finally I have found the battle. I have no rifle, only a pistol, and I stand in the trees and watch. Blackface lays in the trees and shoots. And there are soldiers laying behind dead horses in the sand of the river. The battle is already maybe two, three days old and the soldiers, I think, are very brave and very tired, with nothing to eat. But the Indians fighting the soldiers do not see me, do not think of looking behind them for a white man.

And in two more days the Army comes and the soldiers are saved and the Sioux and the Comanches ride away. And I see two very strange things, which fill me with excitement: Blackface shoots not only to the soldiers, but also to the Indians. He does not shoot the Indians very much because (I think) they are comrades. Then later I think, no: because the Indians will find him and kill him. They will see that he is shooting the other Indians.

And the dirt, the dirt! Flying in the air when the Indians ride, and the screaming! Words cannot say what this great excitement causes in me. Words cannot say. The screaming is like dirty sounds too, in the autumn air. I am so excited I do not sleep for three days and nights, almost.

And the other thing: when I wake up Blackface is not far away, sleeping. And I lay there watching him. He wakes, and then I see a man, without clothes on, laying on the other side of Blackface. He is a white man, but very dirty. I walk around Blackface and look at him. He is dead, or sleeping very deep, with both hands and feet tied. And I go back and sit on the earth and watch Blackface.

Then, after hours, Blackface wakes up and sits and looks at me. Then he goes to the man laying on the earth. Then.

He makes fires with two stones close to the man and cooks food and eats it, all the time watching the man very close. Then he takes soup (I think) or something strong to drink and lifts up the man's head and feeds it to him, like a kind mother, and covers the man with a blanket.

And this later I understand in the days after. Blackface wants the man to grow better, but not for what I think. But after some time Blackface knows the man will die, he is too sick, so there is not much time left.

When the man is better, the hour just before death, Blackface takes a wooden stick from the fire and burns the bottom of the man's feet. Then Blackface looks at me, with his black face and red lips. Then he lifts the feet again and burns them again. The man screams very loud.

And the man screams very loud, again and again. And Blackface looks at me again.

Then Blackface takes off his soft shoes and burns his own feet and rolls on the earth with the pain. In the whole world I can see only his eyes. Then he takes another stick with fire and burns the man's body here and there. The man screams a long time. Then Blackface burns himself in several of the softest places and rolls on the earth a long time, from the pain. Then he faints. When he wakes to, he looks at me. His lips bleed from his teeth. I can stand close to Blackface now and look at him. There is very great fear and excitement, but Blackface faints again and in the night the man dies.

I do not understand how this is, but the whole time now I am feeling in my mind the way a boy thirteen or fourteen feels in his body when it begins to become fruitful: some new, terrible change has come that will always be in me.

And we continue on our journey beside the Solomon, and my heart is singing, singing, and it is the singing only that keeps my heart alive. We ride and walk through the cottonwoods:

> We gather together to ask the
> Lord's blessing,
> Ordaining, maintaining His king-
> dom divine.

And then we come to three very tall cottonwoods, equally separated apart and both Blackface and I know that this place is a very important place. We can feel it through the earth, and Blackface walks very soft on the earth. And we come to the Battle, or when the Battle is just over and I do not know it will be like this. And so I go back between the three trees and kneel down and vomit up. I do not know where Blackface is. I do not think of him.

But the next day the Indians clean away the dead men and the dead women with their dresses over their heads and at night they light the fires in a circle. And then Blackface comes. These are Comanches and Sioux, but Blackface is not one of them. But he sits near me on the earth and thinks very hard. He thinks (I know) they will tie him up like the other twelve white men who stand there tied to poles, waiting. Then they will kill him.

But when it is night and they are eating and drinking very much, their eyes sparking in the fire's lights, looking at the white men with sparking eyes, Blackface does this: he runs screaming and without any clothes into the middle of them. His big dark body is all covered with red paint and he runs into the fire and then through it. And then he screams and rolls on the ground from the pain. And then he gets up and dances, screaming and making terrible faces.

And then Blackface does a thing I know they will kill him for: he tears feathers from the heads of the Chief and the other Indians sitting on the ground and sticks them in his hair and dances and screams in front of the Chief, laughing at him.

This is a great man, I know then, Blackface, greater than my Father. I think then I have found my answer. My heart has for long panted and sighed for the courts and fountains of this Lord, as the Bible says it.

For the Indians then think he is crazy and then they respect him. I am wrong again, standing in the trees and watching, big pimples from excitement on my arms. The Indians do not kill him.

They sit with faces with no thought on them, looking at him.

They know then that the savage Blackface knows things that they do not: they respect the savage of Blackface.

This is why I write this long story, sitting in the trees, far away, by my own fire: to say also that Blackface is not crazy and I am not. Before tonight, the Great Night between the three tall trees, I write this:

We come out of the earth, Blackface and I, out of the hard earth, and nobody taught us what we know. It did not come to us from our Brethern, my Father, for an example. It came like a river's sound, or the river's sight at Great Bend, which I will never see again. It came like a river's sound, a long strong sound from the center of the earth.

It is true, true, like the dry weather in Kansas, year following year, like the tornado, like the grasshopper storm. It is true like the Rattlesnake, which is very quiet and does little, but is full of savage power from the hot sun and the hot earth. For I tell you, there is blood in this land of Kansas, and when I walk on this hard earth, bubbles of blood rise from the weight of my feet, like sweat on Jesus Christ's face. And from knowing this, we, Crazy Horse, Blackface and I are driven out east, west, north and south of Eden, like Cain, Ham and Hagar. Also, we tell our story with authority, because we choose to take the pain already there. We take the Great Turn, never going back, and we kill our own, telling not of the Last Battle of the Savages, but of the Battle now coming. The great war drum booms across the level land. Hear the sound of the war drum.

WALLY LAMB

Astronauts

from The Missouri Review

"**N**ext slide," the astronaut says. For a second, the auditorium is as void and dark as space itself. Then a curve of the earth's ulcerated surface flashes on the screen and the students' silhouettes return, bathed in tones of green. This is the third hour in a row Duncan Foley has seen this picture and heard the smiling public relations astronaut, sent, in the wake of the Challenger disaster, to the high school where Duncan teaches. It's September; attendance at the assembly is mandatory.

A hand goes up.

"Yes?" the astronaut says.

"What did it feel like out there from so far away?"

"Well, it was exhilarating. A whole different perspective. I felt privileged to be a part of a great program."

"But was it scary?"

"I'm not sure I know what you mean?"

"Could you sleep?"

The astronaut's smile, which has lasted for three periods, slackens. He squints outward; his hands are visors over his eyes. "Truthfully?" he says. "No one's ever asked me that one. I didn't sleep very well, no."

"What were you afraid of?" another voice asks. "Crashing?"

"No," the astronaut says. He has walked in front of the screen so that the earth's crust is his skin, his slacks and shirt. "It's hard to explain. Let's call it indifference. The absolute blackness of it. Life looks pretty far away from out there."

For five seconds longer than is comfortable, no one moves. Then ten seconds. "So, no," the astronaut repeats. "I didn't sleep well."

A student stands, his auditorium seat flapping up behind him, raising a welcome clatter. "How do you go to the bathroom in a space suit?"

There is laughter and applause. Relief. The astronaut grins, returning to his mission. He's had the same question in the first two sessions. "I knew *some*body was going to ask me that," he says.

Scanning his juniors in the middle rows, Duncan spots James Bocheko, his worst student. Jimmy's boots are wedged up against the back of the seat in front of him, his knees gaping out of twin rips in his jeans. There's a magazine in his lap, a wire to his ear. He's shut out the school and the astronaut's message from space. Duncan leans past two girls and taps Jimmy's shoulder.

"Let's have it," he says.

The boy looks up—a confused child being called out of a nap rather than a troublemaker. His red bangs are an awning over large, dark eyes. He remembers to scowl.

"What?"

"The Walkman. You know they're not allowed. Let's have it."

Jimmy shakes his head. Students around them are losing interest in the astronaut. Duncan snatches the recorder.

"Hey!" Jimmy says out loud. Other teachers are watching.

"Get out," Duncan whispers.

"Get laid," the boy says. Then he unfolds himself, standing and stretching. His boots clomp a racket up the aisle. He's swaggering, smiling. "Later, Space Cadets!" he shouts to all of them just before he gives the door a slam.

On stage, the astronaut has stopped to listen. Duncan feels the blood in his face. His hand is clamped around the Walkman, the thin wire rocking back and forth in front of him.

Stacie Vars can't stand this bus driver. She liked the one they had last year — that real skinny woman with braids who let them smoke. Linda something — she used to play all those Willie Nelson songs on her boombox. Stacie saw Willie Nelson in a cowboy movie on Cinemax last night. It was boring. He wears braids, too, come to think of it. This new bus driver thinks her shit don't flush.

Nobody at school knows Stacie is pregnant yet, not even the kids in Fire Queens. She's not sure if they'll let her stay in the drum corps or not. She doesn't really care about marching; maybe she could hold kids' jackets and purses or something. Ever since she got pregnant, she has to go to the bathroom all the time. Which is a pain, because whenever you ask those teachers for the lav pass, it's like a personal insult or something. She couldn't believe that geeky kid who asked the astronaut today about taking a crap. God. That whole assembly was boring. Except when Jimmy got kicked out by her homeroom teacher. She's not sure if Jimmy saw her or not when he passed her. He gets mad if she speaks to him at school. He's so moody. She doesn't want to take any chances.

The bus jerks and slows. Up ahead Stacie can see the blue winking lights of an accident. The kids all run over to that side of the bus, gawking. Not her; she doesn't like to look at that kind of thing. Jimmy says there's this movie at the video store where they show you actual deaths from real life. Firing squads and people getting knifed, shit like that. He hasn't seen it yet; it's always out. "Maybe it's fake," she told him. He laughed at her and said she was a retard—that if it was fake, then you could rent it whenever you wanted to. She hates when he calls her that. She's got feelings, too. Last week Mrs. Roberge called Stacie's whole science class "brain dead." Stacie doesn't think that's right. Somebody ought to report that bitch. Those police car lights are the same color of the shaving lotion her father used to keep on top of the toilet. Ice Blue Aqua Velva. She wonders if he still uses that stuff. Not that it's important. It's just something she'd like to know.

Duncan is eating a cheese omelet from the frying pan, not really tasting. He's worried what to do about Jimmy Bocheko's hatred; he wishes he didn't have all those essays to grade. Duncan replays the scene from two days ago when he'd had the class write on their strengths and weaknesses. Bocheko had done his best to disrupt the class. "Is this going to count? . . . What do we have to write on something stupid for? . . ."

"Just do it!" Duncan shouted.

The boy reddened, balled up the paper he'd just barely started and threw it on the floor. Then he walked out.

The other students, boisterous and itchy, were suddenly still, awaiting Duncan's move.

"Okay, now," he said in a shaky voice. "Let's get back to work." For the rest of the period, Duncan's eyes kept bouncing back to the paper ball on the floor. The astronaut's assembly today was *supposed* to have given them distance from that confrontation.

At the sink of his efficiency apartment, Duncan scrapes dried egg off the frying pan with his fingernails.

This past week when he did the grocery shopping (he uses one of those plastic baskets now, instead of a wheel-around cart), he forgot the S.O.S. Yesterday he forgot to go to a faculty meeting. He was halfway home before he remembered Mrs. Shefflot, his carpooler, whose husband was already there picking her up by the time Duncan got back to school. He knows three people his age whose parents have Alzheimer's. He wonders if it ever skips a generation — plays a double dirty trick on aging parents.

When the phone rings, Duncan tucks the receiver under his chin and continues his chores. The cord is ridiculously long; he can navigate his entire residence while tethered to the phone.

The caller is Rona, a hostess at the racquetball club Duncan joined as part of his divorce therapy. Rona is divorced, too, but twenty-three, eleven years younger than Duncan — young enough to have been his student, though she wasn't. She grew up near Chicago.

"What's worse than getting AIDS on a blind date?" Rona asks in her cheerful rasp. At the club, she is known as a hot shit. Kevin, Duncan's racquetball partner, thinks she's desperate, would screw anything.

Duncan doesn't know.

She is giggling; he has missed the punchline. This is the second AIDS joke he's heard this week. Duncan waters his plant and puts a bag of garbage on the back porch while Rona complains about her boss.

" . . . to get you and me over the mid-week slump," she is saying. She may have asked him out for a drink. There is a pause. Then she adds, "My treat."

Duncan has had one date with Rona. More or less at her insistence, he cooked dinner at his apartment. She arrived with two gifts: a bottle of Peachtree schnapps and a copy of *People* magazine. All evening she made jokes about his kitchen curtains being too short. Fingering through his record collection, she told him it was "real vintage." (Her favorite group is Whitesnake, plus she likes jazz.) After dinner they smoked dope, hers, and settled for James Taylor's Greatest Hits. She didn't leave until twelve-thirty, two hours after the sex. This struck Duncan as inconsiderate; it was a school night.

"I think I'd better beg off," Duncan says. "I've got essays to correct tonight." He holds them to the phone as if to prove it's the truth. Kevin is probably right about her. He's glad he used that rubber she had in her purse, embarrassing as that was.

"Oh wow," she says, "I'm being shot down for 'What I Did Over Summer Vacation.'" Duncan tells her he'll see her at the club.

Duncan's ex-wife used to love to read his students' work. She always argued there was a certain nobility amidst all the grammatical errors and inarticulateness. Kids being confessional, kids struggling for truth. After they separated, Duncan kept dropping by unannounced with half-gallons of ice cream and papers he thought might interest her. Then, when she had her brother change all the locks, Duncan would sit on the front porch step like Lassie, waiting for her to relent. Once she stood at the picture window with a sheet of notebook paper pressed against the glass. *Cut this shit out*, it said in Magic Marker capitals. *Grow up!* Duncan assumes he will love her forever.

Wearing underpants, sweatshirt, and gym socks, Duncan crawls between the chilly sheets. He snaps on his clock radio and fans out the essays before him. He'll do the worst ones first. The disc jockey has free movie tickets for the first person who can tell him who sang "If You're Going to San Francisco, Be Sure to Wear Some Flowers in Your Hair."

"Scott MacKenzie," Duncan says out loud. He owns the album.

Halfway through his third paper, he looks up at the radio. The announcer has just mentioned James Bocheko.

"Bocheko, a local youth, was dead on arrival at Twin Districts Hospital after the car he was driving . . ."

When the music starts again, Duncan turns off the radio and lies perfectly still, confused by his own giddy feeling. He leans over and picks up James Bocheko's paper which he took from the floor that afternoon and flattened with the palm of his hand. The wrinkled yellow paper is smudgy with fingerprints, the penmanship as large and deliberate as a young child's.

Strength's: I am HONEST. Not a wimp.

Weakness's: Not enouf upper body strength.

Duncan drinks bourbon from a jelly jar until the shivering stops. Then he dials his old telephone number. "Listen," he says to his ex-wife. "Can I talk to you for a minute? Something awful happened. One of my kids got killed."

At two, he awakens totally cold, knowing that's it for the night's sleep. When he rolls over, his students' papers crinkle in the folds of the quilt.

Stacie sits with her hands on the table, waiting for her mother to go to work.

"You ought to eat something besides this crap," her mother tells her, picking up the large box of Little Debbie cakes. She blows a cone of cigarette smoke at Stacie. "A fried egg or something."

It's the second morning since Stacie's felt like eating, but the thought of an egg puckering in a frying pan gives her a queasy feeling. She's eaten three of the cakes and torn the cellophane packaging into strips.

"Mrs. Faola's knitting a sweater and booties for the baby," she says, trying to change the subject. "Pale pink."

"Well that'll look pretty g.d. foolish if you end up with a boy, won't it?"

"Mrs. Faola says if I wear something pink every day for a month, it will be a girl."

Her mother takes a deep drag on her cigarette and exhales. "If that wasn't so pathetic, it'd be hilarious, Stacie. Real scientific. I don't suppose you told the mystery man the good news yet."

Stacie picks at a ball of lint on the sleeve of her pink sweater. "You better get going," she says. "You'll be late for work."

"Have you?"

"What?"

"Told him yet?"

Stacie's cuticles go white against the table top. "I *told* you I was telling him when the time is right, Mommy. Get off my fucking case."

Linda snatches up her car keys and gives her daughter a long hard stare. "Nice way for a new mother to talk," she says. Stacie stares back for as long as she can, then looks away. A ripple of nausea passes through her.

Her mother leaves without another word. Stacie watches the door's Venetian blind swing back and forth. God, she hates her mother. That woman is so intense.

If it's a girl, Stacie's decided to name her Desiree. Desiree Dawne Bocheko. Stacie's going to decorate her little room with Rainbow Brite stuff. Mrs. Faola says they sell scented wallpaper now. Scratch'n'sniff—she seen it in a magazine. Stacie might get that, too. She's not sure yet.

Everything is finally falling into place, in a way. At least she can eat again. This weekend, Stacie's going to tell him. "Jimmy," she'll say, "Guess what? I'm having your baby." She hopes they're both buzzed. She could very well be a married woman by Halloween; it could happen. God. She already feels older than the kids in Fire Queens. Maybe they'll give her a surprise baby shower. She imagines herself walking into a room filled with balloons, her hands over her face.

When the phone rings, it embarrasses her. "Oh, hi, Mrs. Faola. No, she left about ten minutes ago. Yeah, my pink sweater and pink underpants. No, I'm going to school today."

Mrs. Faola lives in Building J. She watches for Stacie's mother's car to leave, then calls and bribes Stacie to skip school and visit. Today she has cheese popcorn. Oprah Winfrey's guests are soap stars.

"Nah, I really think I should go today." Stacie repeats. She loves to see Jimmy in the hall, even though she can't talk to him. No one's supposed to know they're semi-going out. "When *can* I tell people," she asked him once. "When you lose about half a ton," he said. She's *going* to lose weight, right after the baby. Mrs. Faola says Stacie better get used to having her feelings hurt — that that's just the way men are. Stacie would die for Jimmy. Mrs. Faola had an unmarried sister that died having a baby. Stacie's seen her picture.

"Tomorrow I'm staying home," she promises Mrs. Faola. "Gym on Friday."

She guesses most people would find it weird, her friendship with Mrs. Faola, but she don't care. Last week they played slapjack and Mrs. Faola gave her a crocheting lesson. She's going to give her a home perm when Stacie gets a little farther along, too. In her mind, Stacie's got this picture of herself sitting up in a hospital bed wearing a French braid like Kayla Brady on *Days of Our Lives*. Desiree is holding on to her little finger. They're waiting for Jimmy to visit the hospital. He's bringing a teddy bear and roses for Stacie. The baby has made him wicked happy.

Mrs. Faola is right about abortion being a fancy name for murder. Stacie won't even say the word out loud. At least her mother's off her case about that.

She stands up quick and gets that queasy feeling again, but it passes. She coats her mouth with cherry lip gloss and picks up her notebook. On the cover she's drawn a marijuana leaf and surrounded it with names of rock groups in fancy letters. She keeps forgetting to erase BonJovi. Jimmy says they're a real suck group, and now that she thinks about it, they aren't that good.

On her way out, she looks at the cowgirl on the Little Debbie box. She's so cute. Maybe Desiree will look something like her.

Unable to sleep, Duncan has dressed and walked, ending not by design at an early morning mass at the church of his childhood. In the unlit back pew he sits like a one-man audience, watching uniformed workers and old people — variations on his parents — huddled together, making their peace. They seem further away than the length of the church. In his coat pocket Duncan fingers James Bocheko's list of strengths and weaknesses. The priest is no one he knows. His hair is an elaborate silver pompadour. From the lectern he smiles like a game-show host, coaxing parishioners to be ready for the moment of grace when it comes hurling toward them. Duncan thinks of spiraling missiles, whizzing meteors. He imagines the priest naked with a blow-dryer, vainly arranging that hair. He leaves before communion.

This early, the teachers' room is more quiet than Duncan is used to. He listens to the sputter of a flourescent light, the gurgle of the coffee maker. Jimmy Bocheko stares back at him indifferently, his eyes blank and wide-set. A grammar school picture. Duncan draws the newspaper close to his face and listens to his own breathing against the paper. The boy dissolves into a series of black dots.

At 8:15, Duncan is seated at his desk, eavesdropping. His homeroom students are wide-eyed, animated.

"My brother-in-law's on the rescue squad. The dude's head was ripped right off."

" . . . No, that red-haired kid in our health class last year, the one with the earring."

"Head-on collision, man. He bought it."

A girl in the front row asks Duncan if he knew a boy named Jim Bocheko.

"Yes," Duncan says. "Awful." The girl seems disappointed not to be the one breaking the news. Then she is looking at his reaction. He thinks foolishly of handing her Jimmy's list.

The restless liquor night has already settled in Duncan's stomach, behind the lids of his eyes. The PA hums on. "All right, quiet now," Duncan says, pointing half-heartedly toward the box on the wall.

" . . . a boy whose tragic death robs us just as his life enriched us." The principal's mouth is too close to the microphone; his words explode at them. "Would you all please rise and observe a moment of silence in memory of your fellow student and friend, James Bocheko?"

Chairs scrape along the floor. The students' heads are bowed uneasily. They wait out the PA's blank hum.

Duncan notices the fat girl, Stacie, the chronic absentee, still in her seat. Those around her give her quick, disapproving glances. Should he say something? Make her stand?

The girl's head begins to bob up and down, puppet-like; she is grunting rhythmically. "Gag reflex," Duncan thinks objectively.

Yellow liquid spills out of her mouth and onto the shiny desktop. "Oh, Christ, get the wastebasket!" someone calls. "Je-sus!" The vomit splatters onto the floor. Those nearby force themselves to look, then jerk their heads away. Two boys begin to laugh uncontrollably.

A gangly boy volunteers to run for the janitor and Duncan assigns the front row girl to walk Stacie to the nurse's office. "Come on," the girl says, pinching a little corner of the pink sweater, unwilling to get closer. Stacie obeys her, bland and sheep-dazed, her chin still dribbling.

Jimmy Bocheko's moment of silence has ended but nobody notices. The vomit's sweet vinegar has pervaded the classroom. Windows are thrown open to the cold. Everyone is giggling or complaining.

" . . . And to the republic for which it stands, one nation under God, indivisible . . . ," the PA announcer chants.

The first-period bell rings and they shove out loudly into the hall. Duncan listens to the random hoots and obscenities and details of the accident. "If he gives a quiz today, I'll kill myself," a girl says.

Duncan turns a piece of chalk end over end. He wonders if the decapitation is fact or some ghoulish embellishment.

A freshman thumps into the room, skids his gym bag across the floor toward his seat. "Hey, Mr. Foley, did you know that kid that got wasted yesterday? He lives next door to my cousin," he says proudly. "Whoa, what stinks in here?"

Stacie keeps pushing the remote control but everything on is boring. That Willie Nelson movie is on Cinemax for the one zillionth time. She wishes she could talk to someone like that last year's bus driver — someone who could make it clear. Only what's she supposed to do — call up every Linda in the stupid phone book? It's *weird*; he never even knew. Unless he's somewhere watching her. Like a spirit or something. Like one of those shoplifting cameras at Cumberland Farms. She lies down on the rug and covers herself with the afghan. Her stone-washed jeans are only three months old and they're already too tight. She undoes the top button and her fat flops out. She can feel it there, soft and dead against the scratchy carpet and she lets herself admit something: she didn't tell him because she was afraid to. Afraid to wreck that hospital picture she wanted. Her whole life sucks. She could care less about this stupid baby . . .

She wakes with the sound of footsteps on the porch, then the abrupt light. She clamps her eyes shut again. Her mother's shadow is by the light switch. The rug has made marks in her cheek.

"What time is it?"

"Five after seven. Get up. I'll make supper. You should eat."

Stacie begins quietly when the macaroni and cheese is on the table. "I got something to tell you," she says. "Don't get mad."

Her mother looks disgustedly at something—a gummy strand of hair hanging down in Stacie's plate. Stacie wipes her hair with a napkin.

"There's this kid I know, Jimmy Bocheko. He got killed yesterday. In an accident."

"I know. I saw it in the paper."

"He's the one."

"The one what?"

"The father."

Stacie's mother is chewing a forkful of food and thinking hard. "Are you telling me the truth?" she says.

Stacie nods and looks away. She hates it that she's crying.

"Well, Stacie, you sure know how to pick them, don't you," her mother says. "Jesus Christ, you're just a regular genius."

Stacie slams both fists on the table, surprising herself and her mother, who jumps. "You could at least be a little nice to me," she shouts. "I puked at school today when I found out. It's practically like I'm a widow."

This makes her mother hitting mad. She is on her feet, shoving her, slapping. Stacie covers her face. "Stop it, Mommy! Stop it!"

"Widow? I'll tell you what you are. You're just a stupid girl living in a big fat dream world. And now you've played with fire and got yourself good and burnt, didn't you?"

"Stop it!"

"Didn't you? Answer me! Didn't you?"

"The jade plant looks nice over there," Duncan says. His ex-wife has rearranged the living room. It looks more angular, less comfortable without his clutter.

"It's got aphids," she says.

He remembers the presents out on his backseat. "Be right back," he says. When he returns, he hands her a small bag of the raw cashews she loves, and a jazz album. His ex-wife looks at the album cover, her face forming a question. "I've been getting into jazz a little," he explains, shrugging.

Although he would have preferred the kitchen, she has set the dining room table. The meal is neutral; chicken, baked potatoes, salad.

After dinner, he wipes the dishes while she washes. She's bought a wok and hung it on the kitchen wall. Duncan's eyes keep landing on it. "What's the difference between oral sex and oral hygiene?" he asks abruptly after an uncomfortable silence. It's one Rona has told him.

"Oh, Duncan, how am I supposed to know? How's your family?"

"Okay, I guess. My sister is pregnant again."

"I know," she says. "I saw your father at Stop and Shop. Did he mention it?" She hands him the gleaming broiler pan. "He was wearing a jogging suit. Gee, he looked old. He was mad at your mother. She sent him to the store for yeast and birthday candles and he couldn't find the yeast. Then there I am, the ex-daughter-in-law. He was having trouble handling eye contact."

"Did you tell him where the yeast was?"

"Yeah, then he thanked a pile of apples over my left shoulder and walked up the aisle." She turns to Duncan with a worried look. "How come he's limping?"

"Arthritis. It's weird, Ruthie. He and my mother are turning into little cartoon senior citizens. They go out to lunch every day and find fault. Last week I got stuck in a line of traffic; there's some slowpoke holding everybody up. It turns out to be my father. They're, I don't know, shrinking or something. She has a jogging suit, too. They wear them because they're warm. I can't help seeing them from a distance. It's bizarre."

Two years ago, when the specialist confirmed that his wife had indeed finally conceived, Duncan drove to his parents' house to break the news. His mother was out, his father in the back yard pruning a bush. "See what a little prayer can get you, Mr. Big Deal Atheist?" his father said, jabbing Duncan in the stomach with the butt of the clippers, harping all the way back to an argument they'd had when Duncan was still in college. When he went to hug him, Duncan drew back, resentful of his father's claiming credit for himself and his god. They'd been putting up with those fertility treatments for two years.

Duncan's ex-wife begins to munch on the cashews. "These are stale," she says. "Good, Now I won't pig out."

"I'm going out with somebody. She's divorced. Somebody from racquetball."

There is a pause. She pops more nuts into her mouth and chews. "Well," she says, "that's allowed."

"So when did you take up Chinese cooking?" he asks, pointing to the wok. He means to be nonchalant but is sounding like Perry Mason grilling a guilty woman. The wok is a damning piece of evidence.

"I'm taking one of those night courses at the community college. With a friend of mine from work."

"Male or female?"

She clangs the broiler pan back into the bottom drawer of the stove. "An androgyn, okay?" A hermaphrodite. I thought you wanted to talk about this kid who got killed."

He takes Bocheko's paper out of his wallet and unfolds it for her. "Oh, Duncan," his ex-wife sighs. "Oh, shit."

"The kids were high on the death thing all day, exchanging gruesome rumors. Nobody wanted to talk about anything else. Do you think I should write them a letter or something?"

"Who?"

"His parents."

"I don't know," she says. "Do what you need to do."

On TV, James Taylor is singing "Don't Let Me Be Lonely Tonight." On their honeymoon, Duncan and his ex-wife sat near James Taylor at a Chinese restaurant in Soho. Duncan and he ordered the exact same meal. Duncan is dismayed to see James Taylor so bald.

"You know my record collection?" Duncan says to his ex-wife. "Do you think it's real 'vintage'?"

"Real what?" she asks in a nasal voice. He realizes suddenly that she's been crying. But when he presses her, she refuses to say why.

Yellow leaves are smashed against the sidewalk. Duncan collapses his black umbrella and feels the cold drizzle on the back of his neck. An undertaker holds open the door. Duncan nods a thank you and sees that the man is in his twenties. This has been happening more and more: people his father's age have retired, leaving in charge people younger than Duncan.

He signs a book on a lighted podium and takes a holy picture, a souvenir. On the front is a sad-eyed Jesus, his sacred heart exposed. On the back, James Bocheko's name is printed in elegant script. Duncan thinks of the boy's signature, those fat, loopy letters.

In the main room, it's that pompadour priest before the casket, leading a rosary. Duncan slips quietly past and sits in a cushioned folding chair, breathing in the aroma of carnations. Someone taps his arm and Duncan sees he has sat next to one of his students, a loud-mouthed boy in James' class.

"Hi, Mr. Foley," the boy whispers hoarsely. Duncan is surprised to see him fingering rosary beads.

James Bocheko's family is in a row of high-backed chairs at a right angle to the closed casket. They look ill at ease in their roles as the designated royalty of this occasion. A younger brother pumps his leg up and down and wanders the room. An older sister rhythmically squeezes a Kleenex. Their father, a scruffy man with a bristly crewcut and a loud plaid sports jacket, looks sadly out at nothing.

Only James Bocheko's mother seems to be concentrating on the rosary. Her prayer carries over the hushed responses of others. "Blessed art thou who art in heaven and blessed is the fruit of thy womb."

When the prayers are finished, the priest takes Mrs. Bocheko's wrists, whispers something to her. Others shuffle to the front, forming an obedient line. Duncan heads for the foyer. They will see his signature in the book. Mrs. Bocheko will remember him from the conference. "I know he's no angel," she said specifically to Duncan that afternoon, locking her face into a defense against the teachers and counselors around the table. Only now does he have the full impact of how alone she must have felt.

He sees that girl, Stacie, at the rear of the room. She is wearing a low-cut blouse and corduroy pants; her feet are hooked around the legs of the chair in front of her.

"How are you feeling?" Duncan whispers to her.

"Okay," she says, looking away.

"Were you a friend of his?"

"Kind of." She says it to her lap.

In the vestibule, the undertaker is helping the priest into his raincoat. "So who's your money on for the Series this year, Father?" he asks him over his shoulder.

Stacie walks past two other girls, representatives from the student council who stare after her and smirk.

The door is opened again for Duncan. The drizzle has turned to slanted rain.

Stacie is lying on her bed, wondering what happened to her notebook. She hasn't been back to school in over a month, since the day she found out about

Jimmy — that day she threw up. She's not going back, either, especially now that she's showing. Let the school send all the letters they want. She'll just burn them all up and flush the ashes down the toilet. She's quitting as soon as she turns sixteen anyways. What does she care?

That Mr. Foley probably has her notebook. She's pretty sure she left it in his room that morning. Of all the teachers, Jimmy hated Mr. Foley's guts the most. He was always trying to get them to write stuff, Jimmy said, stuff that wasn't any of his fucking business. What she can't figure out is why he was at Jimmy's wake — unless he was just snooping around. By now, he's probably looked through her notebook, seen the pages where she's written "Mrs. Stacie Bocheko" and "Property of Jimmy B." and the other private stuff.

Being pregnant is boring. There's nothing good on TV and nothing around to eat. She wishes she and Mrs. Faola didn't have that fight. She still wants to get that perm.

She reaches back for her pillow. Drawing it close to her face, she pokes her tongue out and gives it a shy lick. She remembers the feel of Jimmy's tongue flicking nervously all over the insides of her mouth. She remembers the part just before he finished — when he'd reach out for her like some little boy. She gives the pillow several more little cat licks. She likes doing it. It feels funny.

Then she's aware of something else funny, down there. It feels like a little butterfly bumping up against her stomach, trying to get out. It makes her laugh. She kisses the pillow and feels it again. She begins either to giggle or to cry. She can't tell which. She can't stop.

"Why don't you ever make us write *good* stuff?" they wanted to know.

Duncan turned from the chalkboard and faced them. "Like what?" he asked.

"Like stories and stuff. You know."

So he gave them what they wanted and on Friday every student had a story to hand in. He has read them over and over again, all weekend, but has not been able to grade them. Each of the stories ends in death; sentimentally tragic death, the death of a thousand bad television plots. Not knowing where to put the anxiety with which James Bocheko's death has left them, they have put it down on paper, locked it into decorous penmanship, self-conscious sentences they feel are works of art. How can he affix a grade?

The newspapers are full of fatal accidents. A bride has shot her husband. A girl has choked to death in a restaurant. On the hour, Duncan's clock radio warns parents against maniacs, purveyors of tainted Halloween candy.

His wife is not safe. She could die in a hundred random ways: a skidding truck, faulty wiring, some guy with AIDS.

It was in a Howard Johnson's ladies' room that she first noticed she was spotting. "It's as if her body's played a joke on itself," the gynecologist explained to Duncan the next afternoon while his wife stared angrily into her hospital sheets, tapping her fist against her lip. "The amniotic sac had begun to form itself, just *as if* fertilization had occurred. But there was no evidence of an egg inside." Duncan recalls how she spent the next several weeks slamming things, how he rushed up to the attic to cry. There was no death to mourn — only the absence of life, the joke.

When he hears the knocking, he is sure it's his ex-wife, wearing her jeans and her maroon sweater, answering his need for her. But it is Rona, shivering in a belly dancer's costume. "Trick or treat," she says, holding out a tiny vial of coke. "We deliver." Inside, she lifts her coat off her shoulders and her costume jangles. She runs her chilled fingers over the stubble of Duncan's jaw.

■

The janitors have taken over the school, rigging the country western station through the PA system and shouting back and forth from the opposite ends of the corridor as they repair the year's damages. It's the beginning of summer vacation. Duncan sits in his classroom, surrounded by the open drawers of his desk. He's in a throwing away mood.

What he should do is make plans — get to the beach more, visit someone far away. He should spend more time with his father, who is hurting so badly. Sick with grief: that phrase taking on new meaning. "You're not alone, I know what it's like," Duncan told him last week. The two of them were fumbling with supper preparations in Duncan's mother's kitchen, self-consciously intent on doing things the way she'd always done them. "When Ruthie got remarried this spring, it was like she died to me, too."

"Bullshit!" his father snapped. His grip tightened around a fistful of silverware. "That divorce was *your* doing, the two of you. Don't you *dare* compare your mother's death to that. Don't you *dare* say you know what it's like for me." That was six days ago. Duncan hasn't called since.

He's saved the bottom right desk drawer for last, avoiding it as if there's something in there — a homemade bomb or a snake. But it's the confiscated Walkman, buried under piles of notices and tests. Duncan sees again James Bocheko, crouched in the dark auditorium.

Tentatively, Duncan fixes the headphones to his ears and finds the button. He's expecting screaming guitars, a taunting vocal, but it's electronic music — waves of blips and notes that may or may not mean anything. After awhile the music lulls him, makes him feel removed and afloat. He closes he eyes and sees black.

The janitor makes him jump.

"What?" Duncan says. He yanks off the earphones to hear the sound that goes with the moving lips.

"I said, we're going now. We're locking up."

He drives to the mall for no good reason. It's becoming a pattern: tiptoeing in and out of the bright stores, making small purchases because he feels watched. At the K mart register, he places his lightbulbs and sale shampoo before the clerk like an offering.

Exiting, he passes the revolving pretzels, the rolling hot dogs, a snack bar customer and a baby amidst the empty orange tables.

"Hey!" she says. "Wait."

He moves toward them, questioning. Then he knows her.

"You're a teacher, ain't you?" She's flustered for having spoken. "I had you for homeroom this year. For a while."

Bocheko's wake. The one who vomited — Stacie something. It's her hair that's different — shorter, close cropped.

"Hello," he says. It scares her when he sits down.

The baby has glossy cheeks and fuzzy red hair that makes Duncan smile. He pushes the infant seat away from the edge of the table.

"Did you find a notebook in your class? It's green and it's got writing on the front."

The baby's arms are flailing like a conductor's. "What did you say?"

"My notebook. I lost it in your room and I kind of still want it."

There's a large soda on the table and a cardboard french fry container brimming with cigarette butts. Behind her, the unoccupied arcade games are registering small explosions. "I don't remember it. But I'll look."

"I thought maybe you were saving it or something."

Duncan shrugs. "Cute baby," he smiles. "Boy or girl?"

"Boy." She blushes, picks him up so abruptly that he begins to cry.

"How old?"

"Stop it," she tells the baby. She hooks a strand of hair behind her ear with her free hand.

"*How* old is he?"

"Almost three months. Shut up, will you? God." Her clutch is too tight. The crying has turned him red. "Could you hold him for a second?" she says.

Duncan receives the baby—tense and bucking—with a nervous laugh. "Like this?" he asks.

Stacie dunks her fingers into her soda and sticks it, dripping, into his mouth. "This sometime works," she says. The crying subsides. The baby begins to suck.

"Uh, what is it?" Duncan asks.

"Diet Pepsi. It's okay. He ain't really getting any. It's just to soothe him down." The baby's shoulders against Duncan's chest relax. "You have to trick them," she says. Then she smiles at the baby. "Don't you?" she asks him.

"What's his name?"

"Jesse," she says. "Jesse James Bocheko."

Her eyes are gray and marbled, noncommittal. He looks away from them, down. "I'm sorry," he says.

It's she who breaks the silence. "Could you do me a favor? Could you just watch him for a couple of seconds so's I can go to the ladies' room?"

He nods eagerly. "Yes," he says. "You go."

The soft spot on the baby's head indents with each breath. Duncan *sees* his own thighs against the plastic chair, his shoes on the floor, but can't *feel* them. He's weightless, connected only to this warm, small body.

"Baby . . . ," he whispers. He closes his eyes and puts two fingertips to the spot, feeling both the strength and the frailty, the gap and pulse together.

SCOTT LASSER

The Minor Leagues

from Wind

They always came back. Gil just had to wait for them, sometimes a few seasons, and then they'd return, athletic young men uncomfortable in street clothes, like colts getting used to reins and saddles, still agile in their movements, but older. Gil would offer beer to the players, who drank it from the can in nervous sips. Then they'd sit forward in their chairs, heads down, contemplating how to break the awkward silence. "Have any trouble finding the house?" Gil would ask, and soon the stories would begin. They had all traveled the same route, to teams in Bristol and Clearwater, or Glenn Falls. One player had even made it to Toledo, but he'd come back too. Just as they all did.

Sometimes one of them would ask to get back on Gil's team, but most said they were through with baseball, and Gil understood this. Gil had traveled in the farm system, a system which had turned him from a prospect to a spent quantity, all by the age of twenty-six. He too had come back and hung his head between his legs, unable to speak the unspeakable, mute with feelings of longing and a desire to start anew. He had pitched five summers for minor league teams and spent four winters playing in South America. Like his players he came back with a scrapbook full of clippings and photographs, some from exotic places like Caracas and Havana. On the inside cover of the book Gil pasted a letter from the mayor of Paterson, who had written to congratulate him for his Oak Leaf Cluster, won over Germany in daytime bombing raids. It stood there as an explanation of what followed, as if Gil believed he needed thirty-five missions as a ball turret gunner to justify a life of baseball.

A short life. When Gil returned, back from the minors in the fall of 1951, he knew he was through. No team wanted a twenty-six-year-old, and affluence was there for the taking, a car and a house and even an education were suddenly part of his — of everyone's future. Rather than school, he took a job as a textile salesman, and later his boss moved him to Ohio to handle the Midwest accounts.

By then he'd married Sherry and had a daughter, and coming home to the same address night after night appealed to Gil after his many years of travel. But baseball nagged after him, and he often found himself stopping at sandlot fields on his way home, even after trips to Dayton or Detroit. Where there was a diamond and a crowd there was an event, an unfolding drama that Gil could not pass up. He kept a folding chair in his trunk, in case he happened on a field without stands. Gil told Sherry in the summer he had to work late. Sherry sold cosmetics and thus understood the vague working hours of a salesperson. She never noticed that on rainy days Gil always came home before six.

In the summer of '58 Gil passed a field south of Columbus. Baseball seemed so appropriate on such a day, played in the middle of the crops, in a smooth landscape not completely flat but with a natural curve, as if God laid it down sidearm. Gil felt proud to have risked his life for a country that had such a game — a pastime. He pulled up and found that the players were young, seven or eight, and yet he had to stay, for despite the errors and the terrible hitting it was a contest, a drama among boys the same age as his daughter, boys who might someday call for her at his house, thinking not of baseball but going about their quests with the same uncynical enthusiasm they showed on this dusty field. They were boys who played now as he had twenty-five years before, and there was something timeless in this, like the sun and the farms, and he was part of it and buoyed by his joy.

The coach of one of the teams had been an Air Force mechanic and a drinking buddy of Gil's. "How did you find me?" he asked Gil, who had the good sense not to say that he had not been looking. That night Gil told Sherry that he had agreed to help his old Air Force friend Chuck coach his son's baseball team. Sherry said she didn't know how he'd manage it, with the late summer hours his job required.

Chuck and Gil coached for three seasons, till Chuck Jr. lost interest in baseball and passed the apathy along to his father. Gil put together a new team, an unlimited age team. His players were young men in their twenties, top-level amateurs who aspired to be pros. A few had once played in the minors, though Gil's league restricted the number of ex-pros he could carry. So every spring Gil would sneak away to local college campuses and scout for players, recruit the stars, put together a squad which always won the league and the district. Sometimes he would win the regional, after which came the nationals in Battle Creek. The pro scouts would come, some of them Gil's comrades from his minor league days. They liked to reminisce and get the lowdown on Gil's team. A few of his players would sign and take their bonuses and dreams off to minor league towns. And later, they'd come back.

One April Gil got a call from Alfredo Schuster, who had played with Gil in Cuba and now bird-dogged for

Detroit. "I got someone for you," Alfredo said. "An outfielder. Kid really swings the bat. A bona fide star."

"Why don't you want him?" Gil asked. He was used to warm-hearted scouts trying to dump players off on someone who would never owe them a paycheck. "We do, but he's a bit of a risk. An ex-con, if you want to know the truth. Been out of Jackson a year."

"Jesus, Fredo," said Gil, but he agreed to talk to the kid, still just twenty-one, with a record of armed robbery of a 7-Eleven in Saginaw. Tommy Jaspers said he was looking for a fresh start, and Gil wanted to believe him. "First saw him inside the walls. Couldn't believe it," Schuster had said, adding, "The rest of the team had killed or raped somebody," as if knocking off a convenience store were the moral equivalent of taking a called third strike.

The kid, so sincere on the phone, was hard to turn down. Gil had a winning program, and he was proud of his accomplishments and those of his players. He followed their careers in the minors just as they followed their old team with collect calls from the road. Gil's squad was an extended family, a basis of support, a unit which Gil believed did real good in the world, if only to make a group of young men live up to one side of their potential. So Gil reasoned that if Tommy Jaspers could hit like Schuster said he could, then Gil and baseball could set him right, make him take pride in his life like the team took pride in its play.

When Gil watched Tommy Jaspers hit he felt that God had meant for man to play baseball. Jaspers put the bat on the ball with the grace of an artist. Other players, even the good hitters, stood at the plate with uncertainty; they waited for a pitch they might hit and swatted at it when it came along. Jaspers stood there like a man with a vision. He hit .475 in the regular season, and on the strength of his hitting the team breezed through the tournaments. Suddenly the scouts were in the stands, pumping Gil and even Sherry for information on the ex-con. Gil looked forward to going to the field even more than when he himself had played, for Tommy Jaspers was a pleasure to watch, and the team was winning, and everything Gil believed in, the holiness of the context, of baseball, was unquestionably affirmed every time the ex-con stepped up to the plate. In Jaspers Gil saw redemption and reward for his life. Jaspers was so good that sometimes Gil thought he might cry.

At the national tournament in Battle Creek, Gil's team lost in the semi-finals, in spite of Jaspers's thirteen for twenty-one. As a diversion before their last game, Gil and his players had visited the Kellogg's factory. They were shown the different stages corn goes through to become Corn Flakes, and at the end each player was given a box fresh off the line. "Feel this," Jaspers said to Gil. "It's warm. Still warm from the oven." Gil grabbed his box and noticed that Jaspers was right. Jaspers told all his teammates about the warm boxes, amazed that Corn Flakes had to be prepared and cooked and that they came out of an oven with the same wholesomeness as a loaf of bread.

The White Sox picked Jaspers in the supplemental draft and asked him to report to their AA team in Knoxville. He stopped by to say bye to Gil, who entertained thoughts that Jaspers just might make it, that he might not come back or if he did it would be with a major league uniform in his locker and a name known in the newspapers and spoken on national TV. You just had to watch him, Gil thought, and you could see how he could go from a sandlot field to major league stadium as naturally as an ear of corn could turn into an international breakfast cereal. Sometimes things like that happened.

That was 1966. Gil knew that it had not happened, that Jaspers never got to Knoxville, that he had gone off to war rather than to jail. This Gil learned from a collect call following a fight and an arrest in Kentucky. Later,

Gil wondered what had happened to Jaspers. Gil thought that maybe he'd been wrong about him, that maybe some people had no destiny but to take bad hops.

■

In 1973 Tommy Jaspers came back. Gil saw him through the screen door, though he did not recognize the thin, almost sickly soldier and only knew him from the name tag and then the eyes. Gil invited him in and Jaspers accepted the beer and said that no, he had no trouble finding the house. And then he told Gil that he'd been a prisoner of war for six years. Gil noticed his collar, which was too big. and he thought of some of the skinny old farmers he'd seen around, wearing shirts from days when labor had thickened their necks. Jaspers's neck looked as if it might be insufficient to support his head were he to get caught in a strong wind.

Within minutes Jaspers had told Gil that he wanted to play on the team. The romantics — the ex-minor leaguers who still wanted to play pro ball — also asked Gil for a roster spot, but they usually needed a half-hour to beat around the bush. Jaspers got right to the point. He said that life could be cruel, that he had gone to war to avoid a year of jail and instead he had spent six years in conditions he could not describe, and now he was back and he wanted to play baseball. Gil was looking for a catcher and didn't really have a place for him. As good as Jaspers had been, Gil did not believe that Jaspers could contribute to the team, but Gil took him back anyway. Jaspers had said that the idea of stepping up to the plate on a sunny day was enough to see him through six years in a North Vietnamese prison. The team had made a difference to this man. Gil wanted to embrace Jaspers, but he got him a second beer instead. "Sure," Gil said, "Let's go get you a uniform."

Gil's basement came equipped with a bomb shelter, a feature the builder had decided to add in the year the

Russians exploded their first atomic bomb. Rather than a door, a set of fake shelves led to the room, a six-by-ten cell with a seven-foot ceiling. The assumptions behind the room baffled Gil. Were the shelves to hide the shelter's existence from a neighbor who happened to be passing through his basement? And how was a room six-by-ten — and without plumbing — to support a family that needed a living room, a dining room, and three bathrooms? Gil disliked the logic of the nuclear age, so he turned the bomb shelter into his equipment room. "I don't want to live in a world without baseball," he told Sherry.

Gil and Jaspers descended the stairs and pushed open the shelves and picked out a uniform and jacket and equipment bag, and they measured Jaspers's shoe size, for Gil believed in equipping his team from head to toe. "It's a bit like the army," said Jaspers, who had played for Gil before there was sponsorship for complete outfitting. "Can I take one?" Jaspers asked, pulling out an aluminum bat. "I've heard about these. I was walking by the high school and I kept hearing 'ping, ping,' and I couldn't figure out what it was. They didn't have these when I left."

Gil walked Jaspers back to the front door. They shook hands and Gil watched him tie the equipment bag on the back of a motorcycle that looked as if it should have been scrapped for parts. When Jaspers sputtered off Gil no longer regretted giving the roster spot to him. Indeed, Gil was happy to have done it. By 1973 he knew it was pretty damn hard to do any real good in the world.

Jaspers never returned to his old form. Once in a while he'd get a string of hits, but then it would go away and Gil would recognize it as just another streak that all hitters have. Mostly Jaspers pinch-hit and he was happy to get his cuts in at practice and be part of the team and sit in the dugout as the game transpired on the field. This took a load off Gil, whose bench-sitters had been stars on other teams and were forever complaining about their lack of playing time.

By July Jaspers had taken on the role of assistant coach. He looked older than the players (and he was). Furthermore, his observations were astute. The team batting average rose to its highest level in Gil's fifteen years as a coach. Eventually, Gil relinquished his third base coaching job to Jaspers, whose presence alone seemed to be worth three or four runs a game. Despite the steady victories Gil felt a twinge of jealousy and worried about losing his team to one of his players.

As groups go, a winning ball club must be among the happiest. Athletes tend not to look within themselves but upon the contest, and as long as they're winning they are content not to question. Luck is an accepted and wholly necessary part of success, and when it decides to board with a player he will do nothing to disrupt its stay. So despite the three jerseys issued to each player, the team chose to wear only the blue. Individual players would not change undershirts or socks, and one even refused to wash his jock, feeling, like so many do, that it held whatever luck he might find in the world.

In August Gil's team won the regional and prepared for the national tournament in Battle Creek. The players would still wear only the blue uniforms. The scouts were calling Gil day and night, and a few started coming to practices. They surveyed the scene, dreamily contemplating the merchandise like art dealers getting ready for an auction.

Gil roomed with Jaspers in Battle Creek, where they worked out a strategy for victory. Gil and Jaspers gained confidence from these discussions, as if the creation of a plan guaranteed its execution. Jaspers was disappointed that no one wanted to visit the Kellogg's plant, so Gil went with him. At the end of the tour when they received their warm Corn Flakes boxes, Jaspers had tears in his eyes. "Funny," he said. "I don't even like Corn Flakes."

Gil noticed that it was easier now, that he could just sit back and let Jaspers coach third base and the team won. He worried that maybe it was easier because he did not care as much. He knew that at work a degree of apathy was essential for his mental health, but he was concerned in Battle Creek, for if he couldn't be passionate about baseball it was hard to imagine being passionate about anything else.

He tried to tell this to Jaspers. They went for a beer in a Battle Creek bar, but they talked about the championship game instead. The lack of interest ball players showed in talking about anything but baseball was something Gil normally liked. Gil himself liked talking baseball. He felt differently now, but Jaspers had long since made it clear that he would not talk about himself, and both came to believe that the only subject left between them was baseball. It was something they were good at.

Gil left after one drink and walked back to the hotel worrying about his catcher. He thought maybe he could not help but think about baseball. In his room Gil found a game on TV. He undressed with the intention of falling asleep in the glow of the major leagues. His body would recognize the change in the broadcast rhythms when the game ended, and he would wake and turn off the set.

Gil realized later that if he were ever to have a vision, to understand something true and profound, it should have been then, half-in half-out of sleep, with the Royals playing the Indians, the night before the biggest game of his coaching career. He had read that men were meant to have visions the night before important events. There was Constantine, who'd had a vision the night before a battle, the night before he turned Rome Christian. And Gil had read that Patton had them all the time. And the preachers on TV. And so why was he lying there in a hotel just sleazy enough to inspire, in Battle Creek no less, without a thought in his mind? Even during the war, Gil had not dreamed. Not even the threat of his own

211

death could make his mind transcend the narrow circumstances of his body.

He woke in the bottom of the ninth. The Indians were about to lose to the Royals. Jaspers's bed was empty. Gil looked in the bathroom, but he saw only two blue jerseys hanging in the shower, still drying after he'd washed them by hand that afternoon. He checked his watch; it was just eleven-fifteen, but already it felt like the middle of the night.

Gil finally forced Jaspers from the bar at midnight, and then only because it was Sunday and the bar had to close anyway. Outside the air was warm and full of moisture, buoyant and charged like before a thunderstorm. Jaspers mumbled something about "the Army" and shook free from Gil, who had now repeated, "C'mon, Tommy, we've got the game tomorrow," over twenty times.

"So what?" said Jaspers. "So what? It's not like I matter."

Gil would have said it wasn't true, that a lot, maybe everything, rode on Jaspers. He would have said that he had dreamed of winning the next day's contest for years, that there may be other things, more important things, in their lives, but that this game was one thing they could each put their finger on.

Instead Gil said nothing, not even a warning, for like Jaspers he did not see the car. Gil hadn't been looking for it, had only been watching Jaspers, who wasn't looking at anything, who was just walking across the street, just walking away. Jaspers buckled beneath the vehicle. It was a Chevy, a muscle car; it bounced over the body the way a car pitches and heaves over a pot hole or a speed bump. Gil ran to the street, ran because he couldn't help but run, his legs not really his own, just crazy things that churned by reflex. In his mind he knew there was no reason to rush.

The rest of the night was what Gil imagined a dream would be like: the bystanders and police, a young kid, sixteen or seventeen, crying, so broken up that the police had to pull him from his car. There were paramedics, purposeful men, at home with disaster. And there was Jaspers, lying with the side of his shirt not so much torn as scraped away, his head to the side, his left arm straight across his eyes as if he were shielding them from the absent sun. He appeared to Gil as he did when he slept, except for the thick puddle beneath his head.

Gil waited, waited for the paramedics to make a quick check of his ball player, waited for the police to jot down the essentials, waited for them to outline the body and measure the skid marks. He waited till the crowd lost interest, till those who had been thrown from the bar and had no place to go went somewhere else. Then he knelt and took Jaspers's hand. It was cold, calloused at the base of the fingers and on the fingers themselves. A tough hand. The arm was stiffening. It still covered his eyes and stuck off the side of the stretcher. Gil watched as twice the paramedics hit Jaspers's hand into the frame of the ambulance door, once almost losing the body. Then they set the stretcher back to the pavement and bent the arm to Jaspers's side, the way one might move the arm of a clock, from nine o'clock back to six. The ambulance pulled away deliberately, its siren still, its emergency lights off. The next morning was Labor Day, sunny and quiet, the papers mentioned nothing. In fact, it seemed to Gil as if it had never happened, as if he'd dreamed the whole thing.

In a way, the wives and girlfriends and families of Gil's players were relieved when the team did not win the championship game. A loss meant that a variety of filthy clothing could be washed. Some of it, like tube socks and batting gloves, could be thrown away, to be bought again for the next season. And the team could go back to wearing their white and gray jerseys, now that luck had faded with the color from the blue.

Gil drove home alone, with his dirty uniform and the second-place trophy in the backseat. He chose to stay off the expressways, to drive deserted two-lane roads with faded lines and thin, dusty shoulders. He passed small-town parks where people gathered, where children danced around brick grills and wooden picnic tables. He saw fields of corn, some harvested, others green and harrowed in fine, ordered lines. He paid little attention to direction. He just drove, drove till the sky and the landscape began to change colors, and he spotted three children, playing ball in a field. He found himself drawn there, as if his whole life now added up to this moment, when he would stop and watch three young boys play baseball. He pulled out his folding chair and sat there, well into the night, long after the three boys had noticed him and run home.

KAREN LATUCHIE

The Nature of Some Things

from The Paris Review

In the late spring, at the end of a day that was marked by nothing in particular, something just under the surface of the ground changed. Some degree of warmth was reached, or some level of moisture. Something vague and ill-defined became essential and made its way like a signal along the lace of tree roots in the backyard. By the next afternoon, the ground was pocked with small holes and the trees were full of cicadas which had emerged from underground cocoons as nymphs, wrestled out of their fifth and last impermanent skins, and, with perfect and mature tenacity, attached themselves to branches. Late in the day, the cicadas got in a few good minutes of song. Echoing between four young trees my father had planted the year before, the rasping crescendos of this insect declaration suddenly filled the backyard with a great noise. We stood as a family at the kitchen window. There was nothing to see except the last wash of daylight giving over to night. When, all at once, it was black outside, the cicadas were silent.

They were screaming again when I woke the next morning. It was their first full day as adults. When I came out of my room, my father was walking resolutely down the stairs. Without breaking stride he lit his first cigarette of the day. The plume of smoke shifted in his wake and rolled up the stairs as he continued down to the back door. I joined my mother in the kitchen. She was at the window in a long cotton wrapper, her arms held tightly around her waist.

"What's Daddy doing?" I asked. I leaned on the windowsill and pressed my nose to the screen.

"Don't get too close," she said, releasing one of her arms to pull me back.

"Why?" I asked, trying to shrug off her hand.

"I just don't like those bugs."

"Mom, there's a screen."

"Just don't get too close," she said. But she let me be; my father had come into view.

He was wearing his pointy leather shoes and his tailored brown suit which had a sharp iridescence, like the back of a Japanese beetle. He looked strong and careless, and his suit shimmered as he walked. He looked out of place in our backyard which was new and unadorned. The four trees defined a box inside the box shape of the yard. Along the property line were shrubs which someday would be beautiful and give us privacy. They were green tufts now; one or two of them had a few flowers sticking out at angles. My father looked at them impatiently as he approached one of the trees.

"My God, they're awful looking," my mother said.

"Daddy said they don't bite or anything."

"Maybe not, but, my God, they're ugly." She pulled her arms more tightly around herself. "And they have a very funny smell. Do you smell it?" I took a deep breath but I didn't smell anything.

Outside, my father was standing under the pin oak whose branches usually had the delicacy of a pen and ink drawing. Now they looked gnarly, abraded. It was the cicadas, sucking sap and shrieking. My father stared up into the small canopy of the tree. His cigarette was clamped in his teeth and he was squinting against the smoke rising into his eyes.

"He'll go deaf, for God's sake," my mother said.

The trunk of the tree was studded with the abandoned skins of the cicadas. Even from the kitchen, through the screen, they looked ghostly: perfect replicas of the insects, but empty and silent. My father brushed some of the skins away. They shattered and floated to the ground glinting in the sunlight. He grasped the tree trunk, so narrow his fingertips almost touched, and shook. His body rocked with the force he unleashed against the tree. For a minute, the tree itself was still, but then it began to undulate: from the trunk under his hands to the uppermost leaves as if it were a piece of stiff cloth being unfurled. My father leaned into the task and made the branches dance.

I began to hear a different sound inside the cicadas' scream: a dull scratching that had silence in it as well. It was the insect-laden branches rattling against each other. Slowly, as one by one the insects put all their energy into hanging on, the rattle replaced the scream. In all the other trees the cicadas were singing, but in the pin oak they had been quieted. Now, they made an unwitting noise, a clumsy music. My father shook harder. Suddenly, as if the signal had come up from the roots into the sap, the cicadas burst from the tree. They rose like a fiery explosion and then converged into a sinuous plume, their wings crackling, as they followed each other to a different roost. My father shook the pin oak until it ran dry of the insects and settled back into its own green. Then he moved to the next tree and the next until each of the four young trees was unburdened. Each tree sent up its swarm in a huge burst and with each burst the air came to life and then stilled into the hot blue morning which went on being full of the cicadas' scream.

Day after day my father carried out his tree-shaking ritual: cigarette clamped between his teeth, brown suit on workdays, T-shirt and Bermudas on the weekend, one-handed and with an umbrella if it rained. Most mornings, my mother watched from the kitchen window. I could see the cicadas explode out of the pin oak from my seat at the kitchen table; I only had to crane my neck a bit. Then the shades came down. My mother had begun pulling them down every morning: to keep the house cool, she explained. But she eventually admitted to another reason. "I'd close the windows too, if it wasn't so hot," she said one morning. She blew on her coffee. "These bugs could drive a person crazy."

A year's time had always seemed to me to have an uneven oval shape: the winter spreading out dark and long on the bottom, the fall and spring taking up the short sides, the summer rising into the top, perfectly defined curve like a radiant crown. But in this year the cicadas turned the early edge of summer ragged. They appeared three weeks before the end of school but they seemed to bring a leaden heat that was comprehensible only in the dead middle of the season. In their scream, full of impatience and demand, I heard summer being ticked away.

We ate dinner in the early evenings when there was still light and cicada noise left to the day. "Why do they scream?" I asked one night.

My father looked at me and then at my mother. "You see?" he said, fixing his eyes on her, nodding his head slowly. "You've got her scared of them too."

"I'm not really scared of them," I said, the words disappearing the instant they left my mouth.

"I'm *not* scared of them," my mother said slowly. "I just don't like them."

I followed their volley of words with my eyes, one side of the table to the other.

"Oh. I see," my father said, his mouth forming a thin, rigid smile. "You just don't like them. That's why you keep the shades down all day long and only lift them when the noise stops? You don't think she can tell that you're scared?"

"I haven't done or said anything to scare her," my mother said, bristling. "Maybe she just doesn't like the sound of their screaming either."

"They don't *scream*. They vibrate their abdomens!"

"Don't shout at me!"

"I'm not shouting," my father said, his voice lower, but still strained. "I'm just trying to make a point. You can't barricade yourself inside the house until they're gone!"

"Don't be so sure," my mother said, her jaw held tight. She bolted up from her chair, swirled the bottom of her wrapper open and took long strides out of the kitchen. Her hair, long and deep red, streamed out behind her like flame blown from its source.

My father watched her go, nodded his head when she slammed the bedroom door, and lit a cigarette. I cut another piece of chicken and chewed it as quietly as I could. I gazed down at my plate, twirled my knife in one hand.

"They're not screaming, Marilyn," he finally said. His voice was more normal now and there was resignation in it. "They vibrate their abdomens. It's their mating call." I nodded my head though he wasn't looking at me. He turned sideways, crossed his legs and blew smoke toward the ceiling. His head, backlit by the window, flattened out. When he stopped bringing the cigarette to his lips, there seemed to be no dimension to his face at all. Outside, the cicadas suddenly grew louder: a final call before night. But inside, the house was filling up with silence.

I cleaned the kitchen after my father left the room. He disappeared down the stairs to the den and my mother stayed behind her closed door. The living room light wasn't turned on, the hallway to the bedrooms was dark: the kitchen was an island of light. I walked plates and silver and glasses from the table to the sink, turning deliberately as if I were swimming laps, trying to keep my breathing steady. The edges of the counter and the cabinets seemed to grow sharper, and the corners of the room looked deep and hidden. The hair on my arms stood straight up like antennae desperate to pick up some small sound outside the boundaries of the kitchen where I was making as little noise as I could. I washed every dish with care, wiped down the table, swept the floor, but still the time came when I was finished. I turned off the light and immediately felt lost, felt that if it were suddenly switched on again I would be somewhere that I didn't recognize and that would never come to feel familiar.

I found a wall and groped my way to my parents' room. The door was still closed, and outlined in thin rays of light. I put my mouth so close to the frame that I thought I could feel the light on my lips, and I could hear my mother filing her nails. I whispered "Mom," very low. I could hardly hear myself. Then I whispered it again, a little louder. And again and again, each time screwing up my courage to give the word a little more punch. It took me several minutes to get my voice to its normal plateau, and then to say the word with enough inflection so that it cut through the thick silence, penetrated the door, and rose above the soft rasp of the emery board. "MOM," almost like a question.

She stopped filing. "What is it, Marilyn?" I had wanted her voice to be more inviting, or yearning.

"Good night," I said, again almost like a question.

The filing started. "Good night, honey."

Lying in bed I heard a neighbor's phone ring. I heard my mother take a shower and my father come upstairs to the kitchen and pour himself a drink. I was up very late and then very early, but my eyes were closed when I heard the cicadas start in at daybreak. I put my questions about them to the encyclopedia during that day. I learned their life cycle: years and years of a blind, dark pubescence before roaring out of the ground and becoming adults in a matter of hours. It was a drastic way of life.

There were six kids around my own age living on my street. Keith was the oldest, a year into junior high. Mark and Randy were twins, easy to tell apart. Paula was short and loud. Isabel's straight black hair was so long she could sit on it. Rita could walk on her hands. We had all been together at the end of the last summer on the afternoon when a rusty nail had punctured the bottom of my foot. Our houses had been new, part of a development that had just been completed; we had known each other for only a few weeks. But when I got back from the doctor, they were all waiting to hear the details. And none of them turned away as I explained that when the wound had been cleaned, a small piece of the sole of my sneaker and a patch of my sock had come out with the rust.

Now, on the first morning of the new summer vacation, I headed to Keith's house. I walked quickly, keeping my head low, wary of cicadas flitting wildly from tree to tree. There seemed to be fewer in the branches than there were in flight. They looked bigger now, more armored and gruesome. They sounded frenzied in a way I hadn't noticed before. They filled the air with their bodies as well as with their rasp. The noise was like a thick liquid, parting just enough for me to get through.

When I arrived, the six others were already in Keith's basement. Nobody wanted to be outside. But sanctuary indoors was edgy. Keith's mother was on the phone; her voice filtered down to us sounding shrill with complaint and her laughter had an iciness in it. We left there and moved from house to house, but everywhere we were crowded by details of adult life. The twins' father had his dental office at home and his nurse came into Mark's room to tell us that our voices were disturbing the patients. She had hard, pale eyes and she held her mouth so tightly, her lips disappeared. We could hear her thighs rubbing together when she walked away. At Rita's we had just settled in to watch TV when her grandfather came down from his room, pushed Isabel out of "his" chair, and lit a cigar. His cough was loud and incessant. He kept spitting into a handkerchief. We could barely hear the TV. When we left he waved us out of the room impatiently as if it had been his idea that we should go. But it was worse at my house. Maybe my friends didn't see it, but when my mother came downstairs to do the laundry, she seemed to career toward the center of the room as if she thought the ugliness of the insects' sound had seeped into the outer wall and she was afraid to go near it.

Over the next few days the seven of us made the rounds of our houses many times, leaving and entering them on waves of noise and nerves. And then, five weeks after they arrived, and with the same hidden logic of their emergence, the cicadas were gone, all of them dead at once. One morning their buzzing didn't begin. That evening, my parents took their drinks outside on the deck. I was sitting in the yard, leaning against the pin oak, my back to the house. I listened to their conversation: the words were indistinct, but the tones were familiar and comfortably far away. The sound of the ice in their drinks was clear and high; the whine of the mosquitoes in my ears painfully sharp. There were cicada wings scattered on the ground around me: birds had consumed every other part of the dying insects. When I picked up a wing to examine it, it crumbled between my fingers.

The next morning, I left the house as if it were the first day of summer. I felt like a diver, springboarding myself out the front door, ready to reenter a familiar element. But I landed in a vast stillness I hardly recognized. The screen door shutting behind me sounded like rifle shot. The crack lingered in the air for an instant and then dissipated like a wisp of smoke. One by one my friends came out of their houses and with each one, a closing screen door shot its sound high into the immense quiet. I looked up and down the street: it was all identical houses, perfectly edged lawns, small foliage. The colors were lurid in the morning light. The street seemed blasted open into the stillness by the heat. The cicadas had left this behind. It was as if their presence had caused basic molecules to rearrange.

The woods seemed the only place to go. They rose up at the end of our block in a great tangle: a refuge and a dare. We crossed their threshold into air that had a velvety thickness. We lowered our voices and picked our way through the undergrowth. There were patches of ground so damp and unfounded that when I walked over them chills of fear came up through the soles of my feet. Everywhere I looked there was decay and possibility. And out of the corner of my eye, I saw Keith sneak up behind Isabel. I hung back and watched. He grabbed her black braid and pulled. Her head went back and her eyes closed. His hands climbed one over the other up the rope of her hair. The moment seemed to lengthen. Her back arched slowly.

"Look at this!" It was Paula, yelling from somewhere ahead of us. Her voice made time jump back to normal. Keith flipped Isabel's braid into her face and ran off. Isabel found her footing and followed him, and I followed her to where Paula stood. The others came up around us. The noise of our footsteps stopped.

Paula had spotted an old farmhouse set in a clearing surrounded by high trees. It was painted white and had a porch and gables. Storm doors led to a basement. There was a weather vane in the shape of a rooster, motionless on the roof. There was a garden planted in three rows, and a clothesline with wooden pins pushed to one end. I wondered if the plants in the garden were flowers or vegetables.

"Who lives there?" Isabel asked quietly. No one knew.

"Maybe they're the ones who owned the land our houses are built on," Mark said. His voice was dreamy.

"If they used to own the land, they'd be rich now from selling it," Keith said, turning to look at Mark. "And they wouldn't live in that house if they were rich."

"They might," I said quickly. "If they were aliens and they needed humans for food."

Keith turned toward me slowly. He was smiling. Mark shook his head. Paula's laugh came out loud and rowdy. She added tunnels and torture chambers to the house. Randy put mutants in locked rooms. We were all laughing now and the sound of it goaded us on. The people who lived in the house became ghosts, then white-slave traders, then evil spirits. They were invisible, watching us, coming up behind us. Our words grew more daunting and dramatic as the afternoon passed. There was nothing to undermine our determination to grow bold. I could feel the summer taking its natural shape again, arcing us high above the guarded world we reluctantly returned to in the early evening.

We went back to the woods the next day and climbed into a tree at the edge of the clearing. Each of us found a branch with a view of the farmhouse and settled in as if we had come to the generous lap of a storyteller. We had expected to see someone in the yard, or a car in the driveway, a curtain pulled aside, clothes on the line. But the scene was unchanged. It had the perfect stillness of a diorama. Rita climbed to the highest branch she could reach.

"It looks the same," she said, her voice falling down to us. "Maybe nobody lives there."

My eyes settled on the garden. I could tell it hadn't been planted too long ago. "Well it looks like no one's home now anyway," Keith said in a low, expressionless voice, as if he'd heard my thought, and then heard fear in it. No one argued with him. And no one took up the stories we'd been telling about the house the day before. The eeriness we'd concocted for it seemed silly now. Leaning back against the tree trunk, I felt the thudding of someone's leg swinging impatiently against a branch. Then I felt another join in and another until the tree was shuddering. I don't remember which one of us said "Let's go take a look," but it seemed so inevitable that we all might have said it at the same time.

We entered the yard and stood together, stiff-limbed and surprised. Up close the house looked large and normal. Any of us might have lived in a house like this one. My father could have come home from the office and opened this door just as easily as he did our own. The shades were all pulled down here too. Someone had planted a hedge of bushes years ago: they were tall and full. It was tomatoes that were growing in the garden.

We moved in on the house, each of us gravitating to a different window. I went to a door and could see, in the separation where the curtains almost met, a slice of the stove and of a spice rack above it. It looked airless and remote in there, but the longer I looked the easier it was for me to imagine myself part of what I was seeing. When I heard glass breaking, I knew that one of us had gotten in. The world behind me disappeared. The door opened from inside. I walked into the kitchen. I felt exhilarated and defiant. The other five were right behind me. We closed the door.

We stood in a cluster at the center of the room. Mark was the first to move. He opened a jar of peppercorns and sent them rolling across the floor. They gave off a delicate, nervous sound. Rita followed him. She dusted the stove with curry powder and made a comet trail of oregano flakes on the counter. No one said a word. Keith turned and swept the other spice jars off the rack. The noise they made hitting the floor was harsh and brilliant. Paula looked to each one of us as she swung her arm up and back and closed her hand on the rim of a bowl sitting on the counter. She lofted it in the air above our heads. It hung there for an instant. We scattered in time to watch it smash where we had just been standing. The shards slithered along the floor toward us. We scattered again.

We ran from room to room, banging into each other, knocking into furniture, gathering speed and energy. Our voices rose in a wave of sound. The house seemed more and more fragile as we raced through it, more and more our own.

I found myself in a bedroom. I saw everything in an instant. The plain white spread on a double bed, a table on either side, framed photographs, lamps, a chest of drawers. I felt the absence of people amid all the signs of their lives. And I felt myself reaching for the spread and yanking it back so that it billowed up and sank in a heap. When I tore the sheet, tiny threads floated up into the air and the rip of the cotton was like a bolt of electricity let loose in the room. I ran from it and into the living room. I could hear the others all around me. The house was loud, as if the noise we were making was coming from within the walls or up from the floor. The place shook. Keith came into the living room. I jumped up on the coffee table. He was watching me. I jumped again and again, flinging my arms up and down to add power to my weight. The table groaned and buckled. I leapt off as it collapsed. Keith grabbed one of the broken legs and dragged it across the seat of a sea-green chair: the stuffing came out in soft white wads. I scooped some up and threw them back at Keith as I ran from the room.

I sprinted around the house. There was evidence of us everywhere. I heard all the voices in the kitchen and ran toward them. Paula was leaning into the refrigerator throwing jams and relishes, mayonnaise and mustard out behind her. I had to dodge the flying bottles. I could hear the twins' voices on the second floor. I looked through the vent in the kitchen ceiling and saw them pounding on the grating from above. Keith was trying to move the stove. Rita and Isabel and I ran to his aid and we rocked it between us, tearing it from its connecting pipes, thundering it away from the wall and crashing it on to the floor. The sound was huge, but above it I heard Mark and Randy shouting. The grating was hanging by one hinge, and in the vent hole I could see their faces, red with effort and excitement. Looking at them, I felt the heat of my own skin.

I turned and picked up bottles from the floor, smashing them against the counter. Rita pulled dishes from the cabinets and dropped them around her. Isabel picked up the ones that didn't break and hurled them into the sink. Keith pulled up the unglued edges of the linoleum. I heard a tearing sound above us and then several more and suddenly there were pillow feathers coming down through the vent in the ceiling. Slowly at first, and then so furiously that they were in every breath we took. Paula yelled for the twins to stop and it was the first clear word any of us had said since we'd come into the house. We all yelled with her the second time. Our voices seemed muffled by the feathers. I swept the air with my hand to keep them out of my mouth. Randy and Mark finally heard. They looked down.

We were standing in food and broken pottery and glass. Somewhere in another room, something broken settled noisily into something else broken. Each of us looked around the kitchen, carefully avoiding the others' eyes. The last feathers came down slowly.

We ran from the farmhouse at the same time, but each of us was running alone. I felt as though something were following me, keeping pace with me effortlessly though I was running as hard as I ever had in my life. When Keith passed in front of me I saw his face briefly. He looked like he felt what I did. But I could see that nothing was following him, except me.

Neither of my parents was at home. I walked slowly from room to room and I began to imagine slashing the seat of my mother's deep blue sofa, dropping my father's bull-shaped paperweight onto the glass coffee table, breaking the rungs of a chair. Each image had a thrilling exactness. I could feel the heft of the paperweight and hear the report of splintering wood. I had to make myself look at the furniture and see its particular heaviness. In the kitchen I remarked out loud how smart it was to build the stove into the wall. I checked to make sure I was right in thinking that our pillows were made of single slabs of foam. I walked the length of the house again and again, taking the measure of its sturdiness. And still, I could see holes into it.

When I sat down to dinner that night everything appeared to go on as usual, but I perceived a world tilted at a precarious angle. My parents didn't even suspect how much they didn't know. The thought made me tremble. My fears had an unfamiliar strength. I ate huge mouthfuls of food so that I wouldn't be able to talk. I kept my eyes moving from my mother's face to my father's to my plate. If they never settled on one thing, perhaps they wouldn't have time to give me away.

My father was telling us about a small pile of cicada wings he had found in the backyard, describing their delicacy and the leaf-like veining that ran through them. It surprised me that he spoke about them as if he'd found a treasure. I was waiting for the moment when my mother would leave the room saying she wasn't going to listen to him talk about those horrible things. But she never did. She said "oh yeah?" and "how do you like that" a few times as he recounted the cicada's strange life cycle, but that was all. Mostly she watched him while he spoke and the more animated he became, the more amused and contented she looked. That surprised me too.

"So, these cicadas will be underground for seventeen years now," my father said with a flourish. "Isn't it amazing?"

I nodded my head. I didn't tell him I already knew that or that I knew everything else he had just told us about the insects. I kept chewing.

"So that means, honey, that you'll be twenty-nine the next time they come up," he said leaning toward me. He was watching me eat. "Twenty-nine. They'll still be juveniles after seventeen years, and you'll be twenty-nine."

I nodded my head again, and turned back to my food. Out of the corner of my eye I saw him look at my mother and shrug.

"Pretty hard to imagine," he said, and I managed to mumble "yeah" between mouthfuls. But it wasn't at all hard for me to imagine it now. I just didn't want to. I preferred trying to imagine the next day when, with any luck, I wouldn't know too much more, about anything, than I knew at that moment.

JOSEPH W. MOCKUS

Kenosha

from STORIES

In the spring of 1936 word circulated underwater that Paradise had settled on the surface of Lake Michigan, and the fish in the harbor began to bite. It was common for a fisherman to raise his bamboo pole and find two or three ascending the line.

Every afternoon Eva Grabowski could be seen on the pier, fishing in the shadow of the red lighthouse. Her mother's boarders were partial to perch and so were the boozers in the tavern. When old lady Grabowski fried fish for her customers, she put extra salt in the flour and her beer sales doubled.

Eva was tall and scrawny. Her eyes and mouth were too small for her nose, and her blond hair lacked luster. Although she was twenty-five, her indiscriminate enthusiasm made her seem much younger. She became feverish a week before a picnic. But she was popular at the tavern, where she tended bar, because she was friendly and she was always interested in what people had to say. She was a source of news about doings all over Kenosha. When people heard old man Puchenko yelling one morning, Eva was the first to tell them how old lady

Puchenko had got up while her husband was asleep and scattered thumbtacks outside their bedroom door. When a snapping turtle took off the tip of Whitey Stulgaitis's forefinger, people went to Eva for details.

"That's what I like about Kenosha," Eva would say. "There's always something interesting going on."

People were concerned when Eva showed an interest in Adam Michelewicz. They thought she was too immature to get involved with such a dubious character. Adam was a strutter with a challenging grin who came to the tavern to play pool for drinks. Old lady Grabowski claimed she never saw him stick his hand in his own pocket, but the men did not resent buying him beers, because he was a linguist. He spoke Russian with the Russkies, Lithuanian with the Lugans, and Yiddish with Mr. Izzerman when he stopped in for schnapps. He was unbeatable at dice.

Despite his good looks, Adam was not favored by the younger women who came to the tavern. They felt there was something unappetizing about a man of their own generation who came from the old country. Eva, who was so cheerful with every customer, seldom had a word for him. When it was ladies' choice, she never asked him to be her partner for the Polish hop.

Adam ate more fried fish than anyone else because it was free, but he did so with a look of disdain. After every mouthful he pointed at his throat, his eyes bulging as he stamped his foot on the bar rail. Old lady Grabowski always gave him a chunk of bread in case a bone got stuck going down. "There go my profits up the chimney," she would say.

One night Eva became annoyed at his antics. "It ain't hard, if you know how to eat them," she said in Polish. "You just pull out the backbone, and the little bones come with it."

"In Poland the fish don't have sneaky bones you can't find with your tongue."

"Then maybe you should go back to Poland, if everything's so perfect there."

Everyone shushed to overhear this unprecedented exchange. All the patrons agreed that these two were an unlikely match. Nevertheless, on the following Saturday, they went to a matinee at the Butterfly Theater.

They approached the box office together. Then Eva fell a few steps behind. Adam looked at her as if she had gone crazy.

"What are you standing back there for?" he demanded. "Do you think you can get in if you don't buy a ticket?"

"You're the man," Eva told him. "You're supposed to buy."

"Did I sign a contract that says this? Do you have it down in black and white?" Sighing loudly, he paid in pennies, counting them out one by one, then retrieving them before the cashier could sweep them into her drawer so that he could count them again. Beads of sweat appeared on his brow.

By the time he had finished, Eva was already inside the Butterfly, waiting by the popcorn machine.

"Don't tell me," Adam said. "I'm expected to be the sucker again. I didn't know I was escorting such a great lady who never has a penny in her purse."

As they took their seats he said, "I got the last laugh. You didn't get any butter."

When he saw her home Eva slammed the door in his face. Her mother was in the backyard, plucking stewing hens she had just slaughtered. Her forearms were matted with blood and pinfeathers. "Did your boyfriend sneak a feel in the movie?" she asked coyly.

Eva told her mother how Adam had behaved, expecting her to be outraged. The old woman narrowed her eyes and nodded, "You should set your cap for him," she said. "He knows the value of a dollar. When you get married, he won't be handing you an empty purse. Then you can buy yourself a bottle of toilet water or a box of candy."

"Honestly, Ma, the way you think! People in Kenosha got a different way of looking at things."

All the same she went out with him again. He took her to the Chinese restaurant on Main Street.

"What are you worried about?" Adam asked, as he watched her toy with her food.

"I was just wondering who's going to pay for this. I'll pay for my own, but I ain't paying for you."

"Don't worry. I don't want you slamming the door in my face again."

On the way back to the tavern they detoured to the lake and walked along the beach. Although the night was warm, the beach was deserted. Eva saw a bonfire far ahead, but when they reached it, the wood was charred and smoking, and no one was there. The moon lit their faces. Eva looked at Adam's and liked what she saw. Because he was stumbling in the sand, she took his arm.

"Now that I've been a big spender," he said, "maybe you appreciate my smile a little better."

"I would have settled for a hamburger," Eva relied. "But you could spend some money on yourself once in awhile. People judge a man by the way he dresses."

"So now I need a personal tailor to keep you from slamming the door in my face."

"That jacket's not too bad. I could sew it up so that nobody'll hardly notice."

Adam pulled a pint of schnapps from his jacket pocket. Eva guessed there had been a predecessor he had emptied before he picked her up. "I'd rather have a beer," she said, when he offered her the bottle. But she didn't want to seem snooty.

The liquor went straight to her head. "Ain't we lucky to be living on top of Lake Michigan like this?" she said. "Here's where I come to watch the fireworks on the Fourth of July. This is where you get the best view."

"I don't waste time on those fireworks."

"That's just dumb. You don't take advantage of the things you could do in Kenosha. Next week the Dagos are holding their festival in Columbus Park. I always go. The Dagos like it when the Polacks come."

Adam snatched a pebble off the sand and hurled it into the water. "You should see the festivals in Poland."

"That's your trouble, ain't it. You're always talking about how good things were in Poland. It puts people off. With your looks and personality, you could be real popular. Even Mr. Izzerman likes you, and the Jews are very clannish. But then you start arguing about Poland. You should be more positive about Kenosha. It's a beautiful place."

"It's a factory town, Eva. Half the air comes out of the smokestacks of Nash Motors."

"You're prejudiced. I remember reading once that Joan Crawford and Franchot Tone were riding on the Northwestern from Chicago to Milwaukee, and when they got to Kenosha, Joan Crawford said, 'This is the most beautiful town I ever saw, and this is where I want to live.' And Franchot Tone jumped off the train and went straight to a real estate agent. But the man who owned the house they wanted wouldn't sell. Once they get property in Kenosha, people don't give it up. And Joan Crawford offered him a lot of money, too."

"Joan Crawford should see Poland. She'd kiss Kenosha goodbye."

"Is that what you got planned?"

"Of course. Do I look like I got a screw loose?"

"Then you have a lot of nerve asking girls to go out. Thanks for the warning. I suppose that makes you a gentleman."

"Maybe I don't plan to go alone. What if I make you like me better than you like Kenosha?"

"You should be so lucky to snag a Kenosha girl."

They started home, but Adam was too drunk to take her back to the tavern.

"What street is this?" he kept asking. "It looks like Chicago to me. How'd we get to Chicago?"

"It's Seventh Avenue. I'm taking you home. You won't be the first drunk I put to bed. Just don't get ideas. Ma taught me where to kick."

Adam's room was above the office of Petronek's junkyard. There was no light in the hall. "Oh, Eva, it's too dark," he wailed, as she pushed him up the stairs. "I don't see anything, but it's all spinning. I made plans. Did I kiss your hand when I came to your mother's house? I paid for dinner in dollar bills. Now I'm afraid I'm going to wet my pants." When they reached his door, he said, "Don't look at me. Just leave me in the hall like a bottle of milk."

There was no electricity, but Eva found a candle, which she lit with a match from a matchbook she carried for customers who smoked. The walls were planks of untreated wood. The only piece of furniture was a rusted mattress spring covered with a threadbare blanket. A clothesline spanned the room, and on it Adam's meager wardrobe hung on misshapen wire hangers. There was no window. Eva never imagined such a dwelling could exist in Kenosha. By the time she had taken it all in, Adam was asleep in his clothes on the blanket-covered springs.

She sat beside him and touched, then stroked, his yellow hair. "To think of you living like this," she said, "like some old bum." There was a pump outside in the junkyard where she supposed he washed himself; there was an empty jar near the foot of the bed. "How can you live like this? What do you do with your money?"

She knew he had dozens of jobs. Every morning he swept out half the stores downtown. He dug graves at St. George's. He slaughtered poultry for squeamish housewives and made deliveries for drivers who were sick or hung over. One morning he'd be at the front door with dry cleaning, the next with bread.

Eva looked around the room, which seemed to offer more dark corners than its four walls should yield. In one of those corners Adam's money was hidden. She could feel its presence.

"You're saving to go back to Poland," she said. She smiled. "I'm surprised you didn't have a nervous breakdown, spending all that money tonight. Your hands were shaking when you paid the bill. Don't worry, honey. Ma's always got food in the house. The next time we go out, I'll fry up some chicken. You'll be surprised how much you like living in Kenosha. Just don't expect me to see you off when you go back to the old country. That's when I'll slam the door in your face for good. You got a lot of nerve, planning to kiss my hand. You can kiss my ass, Mister. That's what you can kiss."

Over the weekend Eva went through her mother's attic and found a mattress that had been partially burned by a boarder who had fallen asleep with a cigarette in his mouth. She collected a couple of kerosene lamps, two kitchen chairs that didn't match, a table, a picture of Niagara Falls, some sheets and blankets, and an encyclopedia volume which her brother Frank had dropped in the bathtub.

On Sunday afternoon Frank borrowed old man Puchenko's pickup truck, and they drove everything over to Adam's place. Adam was out on a job, but Mr. Petronek gave them a key. "What's he got to steal?" he said.

Frank left a note:

Dear Adam,

We got a dog at home who can always smell where Eva was. I will be bringing that dog over regular.

JOSEPH W. MOCKUS

If he smells Eva on the mattress, I
will beat the shit out of you.

Sincerely yours,
Eva's big brother,
Frank Grabowski

When Adam took Eva to the festival in Columbus
Park, he was sober as a Protestant. Eva was uncomfortable.

"What are you so moody about?" she said. "I know
priests who would give a girl a better time."

"I'm doing penance for being a drunk. Don't you
like me in sackcloth and ashes?"

"I like you better when you got a little pep."

The park was lit with oriental lanterns. Tarantella
music blasted from speakers that dangled from trees.
Italian girls with perfect posture walked arm and arm
from one stall to the next, while old women in black sat
on benches, watching for impropriety. Although the
crowd was large, Eva seemed to know almost everyone.
She stopped to chat with friends she had known in high
school before she stepped out to help her mother with the
tavern. People took her aside to tell her the latest gossip.
Adam had some red wine. Then he bought some beer.

After it was over, Eva and Adam sat on the concrete
steps of Mount Carmel. Adam was no longer sober, and
Eva was able to relax in his company. When she looked at
him, she saw that he was grinning again.

"You're looking at a man who's been corrupted,"
said Adam. "All of a sudden I'm living in a palace. I got a
mattress to sleep on, and every night I fuss for hours to
make sure my sheets are smooth. Adam Michelewicz
can't sleep any more if there's a wrinkle in his bed-
clothes.

"I thought you might enjoy a few comforts. There's
no reason for a person living like that in Kenosha."

"I'm thinking I should throw a party to impress the neighbors, but I don't have neighbors I want to impress. What do I care what the people in Kenosha think?"

"Does that include me?"

"You I haven't figured out yet. You're a special category. I want you to read me like a book, but I'm afraid for you to know my secrets."

"What kind of secrets you got?"

"Listen to her! I tell her I don't want her to know my secrets, and right away she asks what they are. Do you think you can know all about me from taking a look? I'm not just some good-time guy who spends money like it was water out of the lake. 'Let me pay for your ticket to the movies, Pana Grabowska. Let me buy you your dinner.'"

He jumped up and stood with his back to her. Eva reached out and touched his arm. "Sit down. What's got you so riled up?"

"No. I want to stand. I'm looking at the festival." But he turned to her. "A man needs someone who knows all about him," he said. "Otherwise he can't get satisfaction out of the things he's got to do. I got all these people back home who knew me when. I don't want to kill them or smash their faces. But I want them to fall down on their knees in front of me. I want to rub their noses in the dirt and lord it over them. But inside me there's a voice that says, 'What makes you think you're better than them? Your shit don't smell like roses either.' A man needs someone who says, 'Go on. You're right. They treated you like garbage, when all the time they should have kissed your hand.'"

"I like getting even as much as the next person" said Eva. "But for me it's a side dish. It ain't the main course. There was a girl at St. Casmir's who got a solo over me because I had a cold, and she was snotty about it. So when I got a solo, I acted snotty too. But it was the singing I loved the most. There's nothing like the music at St. Casmir's. It's better than anything on the radio."

"With you it's always something in Kenosha. What are you going to do when I take you to Poland?"

"I got no interest in Poland. Even if Gary Cooper asked me, I wouldn't leave Kenosha."

That night Eva prayed longer than usual. The breeze from the lake through her window was as warm as day. From the surrounding bedrooms she could hear the boarders' snores, which had lulled her to sleep ever since she could remember. "Dear Mother of God," she whispered, "please make him forget those grudges of his back in Poland. Make everyone be nice to him, so he has friends wherever he looks. Keep the weather good like it's been so far. Make him crazy about me."

By August they were spending all their free time together. They fished for bullheads in Pike's Creek. They ate hot fudge sundaes at the Old Dutch Kitchen and took a bus to Twenty-second Avenue for frozen custard. Sometimes Eva borrowed Frank's Nash, and they drove to the county line for rigatoni at The Center of the World, a roadhouse between Kenosha and Racine. "I don't cotton to the people in Racine," Eva said. "They don't know how to make conversation like the people in Kenosha do." On Friday afternoons they ate smoked pike on the steps to the statue of Lincoln in Library Park. On Mondays they played bingo at St. Casmir's. Adam always won, and the old ladies gave him dirty looks.

Eva was waiting for a sign. She daydreamed about Adam taking out his wallet and declaring, "Today everything's on me." But, more often than not, Eva paid for the hot fudge sundaes, for the bus rides and frozen custard, for the gas and the rigatoni. She even bought Adam his bingo cards, and he never paid her back out of his winnings.

One afternoon, as they sat beneath Lincoln's statue,

Adam said, "I'm heading back in three weeks. You're coming too."

Eva forced herself to pretend that nothing unusual had been said. "But I thought you were having such a good time. Just last night you won twenty bucks at bingo. You were walking on air. When we went to the Dago festival, everybody slapped you on the back and said they remembered you from last year, because you kept mixing beer with your wine and got so drunk."

Adam simply shrugged. He tried to put his arms around her, but Eva pushed him away. "All right," she said, "I'll go. Do I have to buy my own ticket, or are you treating for a change?"

All the next week Eva asked everyone she came across whether she should go to Poland. She even mentioned it to the boy who delivered the Kenosha *Evening News*, and he was dead set against it. "In Kenosha," he said, "you always got the lake to go swimming in when it's summer. In the Old Country they got sharks in the lakes. You go for a swim and come out with your legs eaten off." Mr. Izzerman said, "At least in Kenosha the political situation is stable. Believe what I tell you, that's no small matter." Fat Tekla, Whitey Stulgaitis's baby sister, flew into a rage when she heard Eva might leave for good. "You should have told me before I picked you to be my best friend," she ranted. "Now you stick a knife in my back. If you go to Poland, I hope the boat sinks." When she had calmed down, she added, "Who you going to tell about your honeymoon if you're living in Poland?"

Only Eva's mother urged her to go. "In Poland you'll live better than Catherine the Great. He'll buy a business with the money he saved from being a cheapskate. If you're smart, here's what you'll do. Every time he makes a decision about the business, you'll say, 'That's horseshit.' Even when he's right, you'll say, 'That's horseshit.' Pretty soon he won't know if he's coming or going, and you can take control."

"I don't hold with that way of thinking, Ma," Eva said.

When her decision was made, Adam did not take the news well. "It's not the end of the world when someone kicks you in the balls," he said.

On the Saturday he left there was a farewell party at the tavern. Everybody came. Adam flirted indecently with dozens of women, using words that were never heard in mixed company. Even milquetoasts talked of taking him out in the alley.

By six Eva had had enough. Without a word she went to her room and sat like a statue on the edge of her bed. From downstairs she heard a dozen arguments going on at once. Barstools were overturned. Beer glasses were smashed against walls. People called each other bastards and sons-of-bitches in five or six languages. At nine-thirty Adam pounded on her door. His nose was bleeding, and his left eye was swollen shut. Frank, standing behind him, said sheepishly, "I beat the shit out of the greenhorn."

Adam's open eye bulged like a crazy man's. "I'm staying," he said. "But your bastard brother is making me go. I told him, 'I'll marry the bitch and live in Kenosha.' But he says he's throwing me on the train like a piece of garbage. Tell him I'm staying, Eva. Make him listen to reason."

"Get out," Eva said quietly. "I don't want to see you again." She closed the door.

A month after his departure Adam wrote to Eva from Poland. The letter was so formal it was like hearing from a stranger. He could remember nothing of his last hours in Kenosha, he wrote, but in the back of his mind was the suspicion he had behaved badly. If so, he sent apologies.

Thereafter he wrote once a week. The autumn, Eva learned, had been the most beautiful in Poland's history. Everybody in his village had been amazed to see him. At

first they didn't recognize him, because he had turned
into such a classy dresser. Everything he wore was high
quality German merchandise. In conversations with the
villagers he never brought up his grievances, but he let
people know he wanted no favors. If someone bought him
a drink to get on his good side, he bought right back.
Mothers and fathers put their daughters on display for
him like poultry at a market. Everyone asked, "How did
such a young man get so prosperous on his own?"

On New Year's Eve he compiled a list of businesses
that interested him, but he was in no hurry to buy. Every
other day he went sleigh riding with this or that family.
"They used to hold their noses when they passed me on
the street. Now they force their handkerchiefs on me
when I sneeze."

In the spring he bought a match factory and became
the boss of men who, a few years before, had pretended
they were out of town when he appeared in their neighborhood. On paydays they waited for the axe to fall for
the sins of their past, but he fired no one, and they were
uneasy. "Their stomachs are always upset," Adam
wrote. "They have bags under their eyes." He added, "If
you used your head, you could be sharing this joy."

In turn Eva sent Adam news of Kenosha. There was
a new bell in the steeple at St. Casmir's When it rang,
everyone smiled, because the sound was so pretty. On
Christmas Eve the priest had interrupted Midnight
Mass to tell old man Puchenko to quit picking his nose in
the presence of the Lord. Old man Puchenko said he had
never been so insulted, and now he spent hours with Mr.
Izzerman and talked day and night about becoming a
Jew. Fat Tekla had had an abortion in Zion. Adam was
instructed to tell no one, because the Stulgaitises still
had family in Lithuania near the Polish border. The
fireworks on the Fourth had been spectacular. It snowed
on Easter. "Kenosha is like a kaleidoscope," Eva wrote.
"Every day there's something new you never expected.

But you can always count on the lake staying the same. And you can't beat the people for being friendly."

Then Eva stopped hearing from Adam. Fat Tekla said, "It looks like your boyfriend got writer's cramp."

"He's got a business to run," Eva replied. "Things are probably piling up. With the holidays coming it's the busy season for matches."

In the spring Eva took a job on the first shift at Nash Motors, which was hiring women to do war work. For a while she wore a pompadour. She imagined Adam surprising her one day. He'd say, "I come all the way back to Kenosha, and I don't even recognize you with your hair piled up on your head. But don't change it on my account. I'm starting to like it already."

Her mother became so fat she could not stand for more than five minutes, and Eva took over behind the bar every night. After a couple months she had Fat Tekla cut her hair short, which made her look older and thinner. She had an easy chair installed behind the bar and took to wearing houseslippers when she worked in the tavern. When the Fourth of July rolled around, she stayed in her room and put cotton in her ears to deaden the sound of the fireworks.

"To think of me, ending up like this," she complained to her mother. "The way I used to brag about Kenosha! Now I can't think what it was that made me rave so much."

"Learn from my example," said old lady Grabowski. "The first time I saw your father I lost my head. That same night I had dirty dreams about him. I said to my friend Olga, 'You should see what I saw,' and she said, 'I saw. He was scratching his ass when he thought no one was looking.' After that, when I dreamed about him, I saw him scratching his ass, and I didn't even want to go on living any more. Then I said to myself, 'Don't your ass ever itch?', and I stopped moping around. You're fed up with Kenosha, because the cheapskate didn't like it here.

You got to snap out of it and start acting peppy, otherwise I'll lose customers."

Eva always turned over part of her paycheck to her mother, who used this windfall to have the pipes cleaned behind the bar. The next year old lady Grabowski bought an upright piano from Petronek's junkyard, then regretted the purchase because it cut down on her take from the jukebox. When the men came back to reclaim their jobs on the assembly line, Eva was laid off. Her mother acted as if the enemy had surrendered for the sole purpose of diminishing her income. "I guess the good years can't last forever," she sighed, even though business was picking up at the tavern. Every day a dozen or more displaced persons from Eastern Europe stepped off the Northwestern from Chicago, carrying cardboard suitcases. Old women cooked free meals for them in the kitchen at St. Casmir's, hoping to fill out their sunken cheeks, and businessmen offered them menial jobs, which they did with a superior attitude. The men said, "Before the war I went to work in a coat and tie, but thank you very much for letting me mop your floors." The women painted their eyes like whores to come to the tavern, and the men, in threadbare suits, propositioned matrons, saying, "Let's go out in the alley and look at the stars. I can tell by your eyes you been waiting for a man like me."

The worst of the lot was one named Casey Dambowski, who worked as a sweeper on the third shift at Nash. He was dark for a Polack. His hair was black and curly, and his eyes had a cutting edge. The women who came to the tavern spoke of him with contempt, but some were less contemptuous than others. In the late afternoons he was often seen sneaking out of the houses of wives who should have had nothing on their minds but the meals they were preparing for their husbands.

Casey even made a play for Eva. He would sit at the bar near her easy chair, studying her out of the corner of his eye. One night he said in Polish, "I was wondering. You got some free time?"

"I'll serve you a drink, I'll ring up your money," said Eva. "Otherwise it's strictly business. There's still some people left in the world who have morals."

Casey strutted to the other end of the bar, where he made a pass at Fat Tekla. A few minutes later he was back near the easy chair. "I'm looking for someone to show me the sights," he said. "You got any suggestions?"

"Go to Chicago. There's more to see."

Old lady Grabowski, who had been eavesdropping, heaved an exaggerated sigh.

"What's the matter with you?" said Eva.

"All of a sudden I'm remembering the cheapskate right after he got off the boat. He was always giving people that smart mouth of his, but I saw through him because of his eyes. He put me in mind of a scared rabbit, looking for a friend. In those days you were too snooty to give him the time of day."

"If you think there's any comparison, I don't see it," Eva said. Switching to English, she said, "This one's a skirt chaser. Adam wasn't like that."

"He chased after your skirt, didn't he? Don't be so stuck up. Romeo wants to see the sights. Why hurt his feelings? I'm sick of you moping around in those house-slippers, scaring away customers. Whose fault is it any-way that you're down in the dumps? You had your chance to marry money, and you threw it away. Now you got a chance for a good time in the hay with a young bull. Second best ain't bad at your age."

"I don't want to spend an evening fighting him off. Besides, he's at least ten years younger than me. Tekla would tell everyone I'm robbing the cradle. She's always looking for things like that to embarrass people."

"Mention that married plumber she's sneaking around with. That'll shut her up."

Casey ordered a bag of salted herring. When she brought it to him, Eva said, "There's a festival coming up over the weekend. Do you like Dago music?"

"I'll go you one better," Casey replied. "I even like Dagos."

On Saturday night Casey sat at the bar downstairs, playing cribbage with old lady Grabowski, while Eva fretted in her room in front of the mirror. She was wearing an off-the-shoulder peasant blouse and dangling earrings, and every time she looked at herself she grew more uneasy. At last she went to her closet and chose a belted dress that buttoned up the front. She replaced her earrings with mother-of-pearl clip-ons and put on a hat she had bought for funerals. Nevertheless, when she glanced at her reflection, she thought she looked pretty. At the last minute she washed off the rouge, but her cheeks did not lose their color. "I can't help it I've got a good complexion," she thought.

"You forgot to powder your hair gray," Casey said when he saw her.

"I think you should know. I've got a touch of arthritis."

"I'm just taking you to a festival, lady. I'm not paying your medical expenses."

On the bus to Columbus Park Casey pressed his face against the glass like an ecstatic tourist.

"I don't know why you're getting so excited," Eva said. "They must have decent houses in the old country too."

"I wasn't living in Paris, lady. From the time I was sixteen until I got here, all I saw was wooden shacks and barbed wire. I'm not used to a place with so many streets."

It was nearly midnight when they returned to the North Side. They took lawn chairs and highballs into the moonlight behind the tavern and sat facing each other beside the chicken coop. The polkas on the jukebox seemed to come from miles away.

"I know all about you," Casey said. "Tekla told me."

"Tekla? She thinks she knows everything."

"She told me how you fell for a greenhorn who went back to Poland. How you're waiting for him to come back."

"That's all ancient history. The next time you see Tekla, tell her I'm not waiting for anybody."

"That's smart," Casey said. "Chances are he's gone for good."

"We were having such a nice time. Don't spoil it."

"Tell me, was your boyfriend a big shot?"

"He told me in a letter he owns a factory. He has twenty-three people working for him. He can speak four languages, not including Polish."

"Those were the ones that went first."

"You don't know what happened to Adam any more than I do. He probably has five kids by now."

"You think he was the only one? In my neighborhood there was a man who spent twenty years in New Jersey. In America his best friend was a tailor who made him an overcoat with places in the lining where he could hide his money. When the coat got so heavy he couldn't stand up, he went back to Poland and lived like Paderewski. One day the kid who sat next to me in school said, 'Did you hear about Paderewski? The Germans lined him up with the other big shots and mowed him down.'"

"It isn't fair," Eva said. "He probably lived in some terrible place in New Jersey, taking any dirty job that came his way, just so he could go back. That poor man."

Old lady Grabowski called repeatedly to Eva and Casey from the back door of the tavern. Her summons was ignored. "Shitheads," she muttered.

"Just a few more minutes," said Casey. "I don't feel right leaving you alone after what I just told you."

"You better finish that drink," said Eva. "Ma doesn't like people making noise near the chicken coop late at night. She says it cuts down on the eggs she gets."

After a few minutes Casey began to fidget. "How long does this quiet go on?" he asked. Eva did not respond. As if talking to himself, he said, "Am I so ugly she bawls in my face about some other guy?"

"I ain't bawling, so stop trying to act cute. I'm not in the mood for small talk."

"I know how you feel. I got dead people in my life too."

"Then you should know better than to make smart remarks. You're worse than some high school kid. Go back in the tavern and dance with a married woman."

"You're right," Casey said. "Tell me off. But give me some credit. I'm working to improve."

"I don't know how they live back in Poland, but people in Kenosha try to lead a decent life."

"You think you're so different? Until I was sixteen my life was, 'Yes, mama. Thank you, papa.' At night I prayed so long, it got on my parents' nerves. My father would call into my room, 'Are you still praying in there? Go to bed.' Then overnight I changed. Someone would sneak me some food, and even before I swallowed it, I'd think, 'Who's he trying to impress?' I'd even grab food out of other people's hands. Then I'd picture my mother and father and what they'd think of me. Now God gives me a second chance. Every morning I wake up and think, 'You lucky son of a bitch, you're living in Kenosha.' But old habits are hard to break. Already I've got a reputation."

"You should, the way you carry on."

"But what about the way I acted tonight? Did I go up or down in your opinion?"

"To tell the truth, I was kind of surprised."

"That's because I'm trying to reform. But I'm the kind who needs a helping hand. I try to get people's advice sometimes. Men I go bowling with, some of the older guys at work. But most of them say they wish they could act up like me. But I think a lady would understand me better, someone who's serious and wouldn't let me get away with the kind of things I've been pulling. We could meet once a week, if that was all right with her. Sometimes we'd stay in, and she'd help me learn English. Other times she could show me Kenosha. In return I'd take her out for a good time. And when she's out with me, she can leave her purse at home."

"A woman would be taking an awful chance."

"A lady I respect doesn't have to be afraid. When I'm falling for someone I get real shy. Even if I lose my head, all she has to do is slap me in the face."

Eva rose abruptly. "Ma must be having a fit. Come on. You can't sit there all night. Pick up that glass. Don't leave it standing on the ground. Ma counts them before she goes to bed. And watch how you're folding that chair. It's time you learned to show respect for other people's property."

"Does this mean you're washing your hands of me? Or will you keep on taking an interest?"

Following Eva, who already was far ahead of him, he stumbled on the cocker spaniel, which had fallen asleep on the grass, and dropped the chair and the glass. Eva turned and came back to him, laughing. He grasped for her hand, trying to get up, and she raised her arm. "Are you looking for a slap already?" she said.

Eva went up to her room, crawled beneath the blankets, and lay staring at the dark ceiling on which she saw Adam strutting in his shabby jacket. She got up to open the window for the breeze from the lake. The air didn't help. She lay on her back, staring at the ceiling. "Oh honey," she said out loud, "to think of you dying like that, after saving your money all those years just to go back."

She knelt at the window and looked over the roof-tops that obscured the lake three blocks away. "Dear Mother of God," she whispered, "thank you for making me keep my mouth shut. It used to get my goat that I had to pay for everything, but now I'm glad I did it. It made him feel appreciated. He never admitted it, but he was happy in Kenosha."

The plant whistles announced the change of shift. Soon smokestacks would begin anew to add texture to the clear sky. People would drive by the tavern in their Nashes with bamboo fishing poles tied to the roofs. As the fiery sun lit the lake, the perch in the harbor congregated at the pier to await the minnow-baited hooks that would transport them. They looked up toward the blinding frontier of their purgatory and murmured, "Oh Kenosha! Kenosha! You golden factory town."

LANCE OLSEN

Family

from *The Iowa Review*

Zach had been splitting wood most of the morning down by the shed when he first sniffed the familiar scent of his father who had died five years ago in a mining accident. It was early spring. Pale green buds fuzzed the birches along Amos Ridge and the ground was soggy and almost black with runoff. Zach straightened and let the axe swing down by his side. He sniffed the air again like a cat suddenly aware of chicken livers on the kitchen counter. The intimate aroma was hard to pin down. Some honey was in it. And some salt. Cinnamon was there. And maybe some sourdough and pine needles. Beyond that, precise words didn't work well. Something sweet. Something acrid. Something like rum and something gamy and musty and earthy and clean all at the same time. He hadn't smelled anything like it for half a decade but he knew it right away, down behind his stomach, down behind his knees. It didn't frighten him and it didn't gladden him. It was more interest that he felt.

He turned and squinted a little into the intense sunshine fanning through the branches around him and

saw his father standing with his hands in his pockets in a
misty golden nimbus of light near a wild dogwood. He
looked just as he had on the day he left the cabin for the
last time, wearing overalls and olive-green rubber tie-up
boots and a stained undershirt and yesterday's beard.
They stood there eyeing each other for several heart-
beats. The Zach nodded slightly in a gesture of acknowledgment and his father's ghost nodded back slightly in a
gesture of acknowledgment and Zach turned and picked
up his axe and picked up a foot-and-a-half pine log and
set it upright on the stump before him and started
splitting wood once more because there was still a good
part of an hour left until lunchtime.

Strip mining had peaked outside of Frenchburg,
Kentucky, in the late sixties and early seventies and then
it began falling off. Houses went up for sale. Ken's
Market, one of the two grocery stores in town, shut
down. The lone car dealership burned to the ground one
night and for nearly two years no one seemed to have
enough money to clean up the charred remains. But
Zach's father didn't have much else that he felt comfortable doing so he decided to stick with mining as long as
mining would stick with him. The company had brought
in a mechanical monster called Little Egypt to make the
job of digging more cost-efficient. Little Egypt was a
machine the size of a small hotel. It was several stories
tall and several stories wide and it was covered with
gears the size of most men and it looked more like
something people would use on Mars for space explora-
tion than it did like something people would use in
Menifee County for mining. Its sole purpose was to dig
into the earth, slowly, cumbersomely, relentlessly,
twenty-four hours a day, seven days a week, three-
hundred sixty-five days a year, processing coal as it
went, eating, gnawing, wheezing and clanking away
with a deafening sound. Zach's father, who was fifty-
seven at the time, was part of a team of men responsible

for keeping the huge gears of Little Egypt clear from crushed stone and grit and keeping them oiled and running smoothly. One day in late summer during his lunch break Zach's father sampled a swig too much of shine a buddy of his offered him, turned tipsy, and tripped as he was shinnying among the intricate workings of the behemoth. Instantly he was pulled into the innards of the creaking, banging, raucous colossus, kicking and screaming, and was never seen in one piece again. Until, of course, that spring day.

At noon Zach's wife, Amelia, called him for lunch. She had made bean soup and black bread and apple cobbler. He washed his hands at the spigot outside and walked around his dark blue Ford pickup truck and went in and sat at the table near the stove and began to eat. Amelia told him how she was going to Frenchburg to pick up some things and Zach told her how he was going to start patching the aluminum roof on the shed that had blown off during a big storm last November. Amelia told Zach how she had phoned Madge at the next farm over and how Madge and Opal's dog Mork had been bitten by the first copperhead of the season and how the dog's snout had grown a lump that made it appear as if it were raising a plum under the flesh. As Zach listened he became aware of another presence in the kitchen. He glanced up and saw his father standing by the refrigerator, hands in the pockets of his overalls, watching the couple talk and eat. Zach's father wasn't smiling and he wasn't frowning but his eyes seemed a little more yellowish than usual and they seemed infinitely sad. He didn't speak and he didn't move. He just looked on as Zach raised a forkful of apple cobbler to his mouth and then washed it down with a gulp of water. Amelia noticed Zach staring hard and long at the refrigerator and turned to see what he was looking at.

"Your father's here," she said after a moment.

"Yep," Zach said, cutting himself another bit of cobbler. "I reckon he is."

And that's how it started. Zach's father just appeared one beautiful spring day in a misty golden nimbus of light and Zach and Amelia acknowledged his appearance and then they didn't say a whole bunch else about it. After all, they had a lot of other things to think about. The field down the road needed plowing and planting. The shed needed mending. The winter wood needed tending to. And if they knew anything about Zach's father they knew he could take care of himself.

In the beginning Zach had the impression his father had come to tell him something he didn't already know. Maybe some secret about life that fathers come back from the dead to tell their sons because it's so important. Maybe some word of wisdom that would suddenly illuminate the world for him and release some vise that had been clamping his head so he could see things in a way he had never seen them before. But Zach's father never spoke. In fact he never made any sort of sound, not even when he walked across the wooden kitchen floor in his olive-green rubber tie-up boots. Zach waited two weeks, thinking his father might be trying to find the right words in which to stick his wisdom. And when at the end of that time Zach figured maybe his father could use some coaxing, he prompted him one rainy night by asking, "So what do you have to say for yourself?"

His father had nothing to say for himself. His facial expression didn't change. His eyes continued to look more yellowish than usual and infinitely sad and they focused on Zach's moving lips and then on Zach's blue eyes and then it occurred to Zach that the problem was that his father couldn't hear a word he was saying. There must have been some kind of interference between this world and the next. So he went and got a slip of paper and a pencil and he came back and wrote down his question and tried to give it to his father but the paper just passed through his father's extended hand as though it were no more than colored air and it fluttered to the floor.

When Zach told this to his wife, she told him she was convinced his father had come back to visit them because death was such a lonely place.

"Death isn't a lonely place at all," Zach said. "Lots of people are dead. He should have lots of company where he's at."

"That's all you know, Zach Ingram," she said.

Amelia smiled a considerate smile at Zach's father as you might at an infirm elderly parent or parent-in-law and let him accompany her from room to room and when she went outside to hang clothes and clean the outhouse. The ghost followed her at a respectful distance and took what seemed an exquisite interest in the simple chores of daily life: baking muffins, boiling pot roast, frying potatoes, scrubbing the skillet, folding down the quilt on the bed, hanging the winter coats in the back of the closet until next fall. She set a plate for him at dinner and even put scraps on his plate although he couldn't sit at the table without falling through the chair and although when he bent down and tried to pick up a crumb with his tongue the crumb passed right through his jaw. She lit a candle for him at night and put it on the kitchen table and brought a newspaper for him to read every Sunday when she headed into church even though she knew he wouldn't be able to hold it. Every night he stood in their bedroom door when they were ready to go to sleep until they said goodnight to him and turned off the lights and then he would wander into the living room and stand by the window and wait for the first gray glow of dawn. Sometimes Zach would come upon him standing at the end of Amos Ridge on Whippoorwill Point amid wild blueberry bushes and sassafras shrubs, looking out over the limestone cliffs and pines and cedars below, or kneeling by the thousands of large amazing jelly-bubble sacks of frog eggs in puddles that collected in ruts along the dirt road that led up to the cabin.

They had no idea how good his presence made them feel until one morning in July Amelia went into the kitchen at six o'clock to grind some coffee and discovered he was gone. She thought he must be in the living room at the window watching the orange sun roll up behind the trees but when she checked no one was there. She stuck her head into all the closets and then she went outside and searched the shed and the outhouse and the area around the woodpile. She woke Zach and told him what had happened and he immediately dressed and headed down to Whippoorwill Point and called out his father's name and when he didn't see him there he walked all the way to Madge and Opal's farm before understanding somewhere under his lungs that he had lost his father a second time. It hurt Zach terribly, like a hole in the heart hurts, like a hammer in the head hurts. He slowly walked back into the cabin and told Amelia what he hadn't found and then sat down in a foldup chair on the porch and didn't get up for three weeks.

He sat there with his left ankle on his right knee and his hands in his lap and he looked out over the ridge and waited for his father to return. The hot hazy sky purpled at twilight. Crickets chirruped. Stars blinked on in the sky. And after a while he put his chin on his chest and fell asleep. In the morning he didn't eat his breakfast. In the afternoon he didn't eat his lunch. In the evening he didn't eat his dinner. Gradually he became as quiet as his father had been. Amelia told him he was getting thinner and more pathetic every day and when he didn't respond to her she began to eat his meals in addition to her own. First it was simply a way not to let the food go to waste. Then it was a way to express her own grief, her own pain, her own sense of absence. She gained five pounds the first week. She gained eight pounds the second. She gained ten the third.

Late in August as Zach watched the burning ball of the sun dip behind the treeline he noticed two figures walking up the road toward him. Through half-closed eyes he took them to be Madge and Opal coming over to check on them. But the closer the couple came the easier it was to tell they couldn't be Madge and Opal: the man was too old and the woman too short. Zach squinted and then he cocked his head to one side and then he shut one eye and then the other and then he opened both of them and then it struck him that he was looking at his parents, both of his parents, walking arm in arm up the road as they often did after dinner. His father was still wearing the same clothes he had on the day he fell into Little Egypt. His mother was still wearing the nightshirt she wore the day she said living without her husband was a stupid foolish thing and crawled into her bed and pulled up the quilt and turned her face to the wall. The couple mounted the porch and walked by Zach and he rose and followed them and saw them halt in the bedroom door, watching Amelia, chubby, soft, round, and wide-eyed, watch them back from the bed.

Zach's parents were extremely considerate. They always stood in corners, out of the way, arm in arm, or, at night, by the window in the living room from which they could see the first gray glow of dawn. They never asked for anything, never offered advice, and never nagged. They took obvious delight in the woodgrain rippling through the kitchen table; the black-and-white patterns on the wings of the willet that magically appeared on the roof of the shed one cold autumn afternoon; the yellow-green leaves of tobacco ready for harvest in the field down the road; the five-inch-long acorn-brown lizard that perched every morning on the top step, head raised with dignity and alertness, reptilian grin frozen on its face; the short stubby ochre squiggle near the woodpile, looking at them with its black glassbead eyes. Sometimes at dusk they craned their heads slightly and closed their

eyes and sniffed at the cool evening air filled with hon-
eysuckle, jasmine, wet grass, endive, pine, moist soil,
leafy mulch, a hint of cantaloupe rinds. Sometimes in the
afternoon they bent over near a tall curl of wild grass
and studied the shiny blue body of the dragonfly arched
just above it.

Zach and Amelia barely noticed it when his mother
disappeared for two nights, returning with cousin Virgil
who had died at thirty-one when his sleek black Toyota
pickup skidded off Route 641 one rainy night in 1984
and smashed into a tree at eighty miles an hour. Or when
Zach's father disappeared for nearly twenty-four hours,
showing up cradling a baby in his arms, the Armstids'
little girl, who had died last year when she was two weeks
old because she had been born with some of her insides
backwards. Amelia was startled to see her uncle Ferrell,
who'd been killed in 1968 somewhere in Cambodia
although the government had always said it had been in
Vietnam, and her aunt Helen, who'd taken her own life in
1963 when she caught her husband Tom fooling around
with that cheap blond Bobbie Ann Stills. Zach tried to
shake hands with his nephew Billy, whose spine had
snapped during an accident on his Honda three-wheeler
RV in 1987, and he tried to hug his mother's friend,
Mildred, who'd been bitten by a rattler while picking
raspberries in 1956 on Madge and Opal's farm. Zeb,
whose tractor engine fell on him two years ago while he
was trying to tighten a bolt under it, showed up after all
the leaves had dropped off the trees on Amos Ridge, and
Abel, who choked on a chicken bone while watching a
1979 World Series game, appeared just as the skies
turned the color of a field mouse's neck and the first light
snow began to fall.

"House sure is gettin' mighty cramped," Zach said
when he stayed in on Thanksgiving to watch the Macy's
parade on television.

"Family's family," Amelia said.

Her voice was simple, kind, and firm.

Somewhere in his chest around where hope is kept Zach knew she was right and didn't say anything else. He felt good. He felt complete. He felt a system of networks, harmonies, symmetries forming around him and had a tremendous sense of being somewhere, and knowing where that place was, and knowing what he should be doing and why and how. Only he had to confess at the same time that it was hard to see the TV set, what with little Dinamarie playing tag with Hazel and Gladys and Grace and Gary Bob and Johnny Jim in front of it and Angie smooching with George over at the kitchen table and Susie and Flinn bopping each other over the heads because Flinn had decided to appropriate Susie's favorite rhinestone pinky ring which he wouldn't give back and Aunt Beryl was trying unsuccessfully to bake and Uncle Gus was trying unsuccessfully to clean his .38-gauge shotgun on the living room floor.

Sleeping was difficult too because the children wanted to be in bed between Zach and Amelia and many of the adults felt the need to stretch out on the floor nearby. Zach couldn't turn over or get up to visit the outhouse and he could never show his affection for Amelia who had never stopped eating two portions of each meal every day and was now the size of a large flaccid dolphin. Little Ainsley and Harlan and Jake and Remus wanted to help with all the chores but they continually got under foot. More than once Zach bruised an ankle or knocked a knee, tripping because he didn't see one of the children waiting right behind him like a shadow. Amelia fared no better in the kitchen where her mother-in-law and aunts supervised all her cooking, which she now performed nearly fourteen hours a day. Although no one except Zach and herself could eat, Amelia felt it only courteous to make enough for everyone. Sometimes at three in the morning she would rise and begin cooking breakfast and sometimes after midnight she would still be cleaning dishes. Over time she turned big as a baby elephant with wrinkled skin. She turned big as a bear whose stubby arms could no longer touch its sides. She turned big as a small whale which plowed through the cabin, shaking the foundation, moving ponderously yet carefully because she had lost sensation in her extremities and could no longer feel whether or not she might be bumping into things or people. Her neck disappeared and she forgot what it was like to bend from the waist and she only vaguely remembered what her once beautiful red-painted toenails had looked like.

By February the food supply had run down and Zach felt more tired than ever before in his life and Amelia could no longer walk. She could no longer fit through the bedroom door. Zach arranged pillows and blankets for her to lie in on the living room floor and he began feeding her through a funnel because she could no longer lift her hands to help herself. The voluminous flesh of her face tugged at her tiny miraculous brown eyes and made her look a little oriental. Fat from her arms and legs puddled near her on the rug and made it appear as though she were melting. All the ghosts were fascinated by her lying there gazing at the ceiling, unable to speak just as they were unable to speak, unable to partake of the world just as they were unable to partake of the world. They seemed to understand that Amelia was eating for all of them now, that her metabolism was lovingly digesting for the whole family. The adults solemnly kneeled by her. The children frolicked on her body as though it were an astonishingly soft playground. They burrowed under her breasts and they slid down the wonderful smoothness of her thighs and they curled by her massive head to nap.

Every day more relatives appeared: Samuella who had fallen down a well when she was three; Rachel who had cooked up some bad mushrooms when she was twenty-seven; Ferris who lived until he was ninety-four and would have lived until he was ninety-seven if he hadn't strained trying to pick up those logs in the autumn of 1934; Selby who shot Seaton because Seaton had knifed Seldon because Seldon had got Leanne with child when she was fourteen. More relatives than Zach could count. More relatives than he could squeeze into the space of his imagination. More relatives than he could squeeze into the space of his cabin. They spilled out onto the porch and they spilled out into the shed and by the middle of March they were sleeping in the woods all the way down to Whippoorwill Point and Zach couldn't go anywhere without stumbling over them, being surprised by their faces, finding them staring back at him from around the corner or under a bush or behind a birch. He gave up all chores except feeding Amelia and he gave up all food except Amelia's food and he went out of the cabin less and less and he stayed in his bed more and more. The hot weather settled down and he realized he should have planted months ago. The cool weather came and he realized he had nothing more for Amelia to eat and nothing more to grow next year and no more firewood for next fall and winter.

In September as the sky blanched Zach walked down to Madge and Opal's and borrowed some tools and supplies and began to construct a mobile pulley near his dark blue Ford pickup truck. At first the gizmo looked like an eight-foot-tall oil well. Then it looked like an eight-foot-tall oil well on a sturdy wooden base with wheels under it. When it was done Zach removed the skeletal braces and rolled the contraption over to the sliding doors that led off the living room. He padded the sturdy wooden base with pillows and blankets and then went to the shed and got his snow shovel. He returned to the living room and gingerly navigated among the ghosts until he reached Amelia sprawled in the middle of the floor. He shoved his snow shovel under a lump of fat that he took to be her flank and heaved. Haltingly, falteringly, agonizingly, he began to roll his gigantic doughy wife across the floor. She could not move herself and she could not speak but each time she found herself on her back she looked up at Zach with her exquisite brown oriental eyes which were infinitely sad. Zach avoided her gaze and put his back into the work. He rolled her through the sliding doors and rolled her onto the porch and, having removed the banisters there, he rolled her over the edge and onto the padded mobile pulley which groaned and wheezed and shook under Amelia's enormous weight. Then he struggled and pushed and heaved the mobile pulley around toward the front of the cabin.

Half an hour later Amelia flooded the back of his mud-spattered dark blue Ford pickup. Her rubbery arms and squelchy legs draped over the sides. Whitish flubber oozed all around her. She stared up at the trees above her. Zach climbed into the cab and turned on the engine and eased down the pedal. The shock absorbers creaked and swayed. The pickup lurched and began to crawl down the dirt road. When it tapped the first bump the metal belly scraped sand and gravel. But Zach didn't pay any attention to the bump and he didn't pay any attention to the sound. He already felt his heart expanding. He already felt a lightness entering his stomach. He blinked and smiled and looked up into the rearview mirror. All the dead people had collected outside the cabin behind him. They were watching the mud-spattered dark blue pickup creep down the driveway, winding its way toward Madge and Opal's and beyond. Zach saw them all raising their hands and waving goodbye. And, as he turned the corner, Zach caught a glimpse of them begin to follow.

SHARON SAKSON

The Girl from the Red Cross

from Nimrod

I have a fantasy about Jolene.

I imagine the day she went into the Red Cross office. I imagine the distracted look on her face. The personnel manager reviews her credentials.

"Well," he says, and Jolene looks at him intently, "we have a position in Beirut. Could you agree to that?"

Jolene is very solemn, as usual. "Yes," she says, "that will be okay." She leaves the office and walks down the street. And she wonders, where is Beirut?

Jolene. An American girl with brown hair. A girl of average height and average aspirations. A girl who liked to wake early every morning to press her white uniform and polish her comfortable shoes. A girl who once told me she never read the newspaper because it was "depressing."

Hundreds were being killed in El Salvador, Britain went to war with Argentina, Poles marched for freedom and the Israelis invaded Lebanon, and Jolene took as little notice as possible.

The story I have to tell about her is very different from the one you will have read in the *New York Times*.

I do not criticize the *New York Times*. They have their job to do. They gather the pertinent facts.

In their version: a young American nurse comes to Beirut, serves well, and dies. In their version, Jolene is a heroine. In their version, she achieves a sense of purpose. In their version, she acquires a place in history. Can any of us ask for more?

But I cannot settle for their version. I knew Jolene too well. And I am too much a seeker of the truth.

A seeker of the truth. Well. I am Raymond Ferrar, an old man of Lebanon. An engineer by profession. An English-speaking man. A man who has traveled widely and come back home to Beirut with one firmly held belief.

One cannot trust the facts to reveal the truth. This is why I prefer to tell her story, my way. In fact I can find only two points on which the *New York Times* and I agree.

Her name was Jolene Allen. She had brown hair.

She came to Beirut the way the Israelis came to Beirut, up along the coast road from Tel Aviv. She traveled with a Red Cross doctor and another nurse. When Jolene spoke of that trip, her eyes looked inward, and her voice took on that low, hushed tone which she also used to speak of her mother and anything to do with the Catholic religion.

She had never known scenery like that. She was a child of New Jersey, a child of weary, smog-filled cities and busy people in busy cars. She was not accustomed to the quiet hills of Lebanon. She described the ancient olive trees and steep cliffs, and how Arab peasants were hurrying along with their donkeys.

"Jolene," I said, "they were running from the war." But that was one of the many things that Jolene did not want to hear.

They rode in the morning, and she described the

sunrise as being "like a painting, only changing color all the time."

I said that paintings never change color. That real sunrises always do.

Our Lebanon sun rises over mountains. It is spectacular but does not compare in beauty to our sunsets, which are over the sea. I mentioned this to Jolene. She said she had never noticed the sunset in Lebanon. Since the sun sets every night, this is hard to avoid.

Awareness of nature was not one of Jolene's strong points.

At the time, I found it curious that she did not mention the tanks and armored personnel carriers and jeeps and troop trucks the group had surely encountered along the way.

"Maybe just one or two trucks," said Jolene lightly. She took off her earring and played with it in the palm of her hand.

Gerard brought Jolene to me, as he has brought me so many things in my life. Gerard, my oldest son. A doctor. A man of conscience. Himself the father of three sons.

He had stopped at the hospital near Shattilla and suddenly bombs had landed someplace quite nearby. Patients were screaming and crying and running in all directions. He had seen this girl, this nurse, standing in a window, clutching the sill, sobbing uncontrollably. He had pulled her away from the window and calmed her. He brought her to dinner at our house.

We had lamb, French wine, and canned petit pois from a neighbor who was leaving the war by boat, to Cyprus. A good table. But Jolene ate very little. We took our coffee in the garden, and I noticed her staring at me. "What state do you come from, Jolene?" I asked.

"New Jersey," she said, and I thought she would fall silent again, but the words came pouring out, as if she'd waited for years for this night to tell her story.

She was twenty-two years old and Catholic, she said, looking at us nervously, as though she expected us to disapprove. From Trenton, New Jersey. Her parents were not rich but well-off, a family that had raised four sons and then, this one daughter. A family that was devout to the Roman Catholic religion and went to Mass on Sundays and all appropriate holy days, the reward for which was huge meals prepared by mother and grandmother and aunts and Sister Bonita, who also turned out to be an aunt. (At this point the conversation was halted to explain to my daughter-in-law Ijil what *Sisters* were.)

Jolene burst on; yes, and can you imagine, she still wears her habit, not like some modern nuns, and she even cooks in that habit, yes, she brings an apron on Sundays and rolls up her sleeves. She sweats terribly.

Jolene laughed.

Ijil looked confused.

Can you imagine, said Jolene, staring at Gerard as if she really expected him to imagine it, that her family had pushed her to become a nun like Sister Bonita? And that she had almost done it? (Here she giggled.) All that stopped her, when the time came to really decide, was the thought of spending her Sundays sweating like Sister Bonita.

So she had become a nurse. St. Jude's School of Nursing, she said as though we'd heard of it. At first her mother had been terribly opposed, but had eventually decided that it would be okay since Jolene could now marry a rich doctor.

She worked at Princeton Hospital—

"Princeton!" said my son Phillipe. "My friend Paul Hardie went to Princeton University."

Jolene listened without hearing and rushed on. Princeton Hospital, it turned out, was a wonderful place, full of wonderful doctors and wonderful nurses. Even the patients were wonderful. Jolene described it in such glowing terms, the flower gardens, the murals on the walls, the fun in the staff cafeteria — that it was hard to imagine anyone bursting a gall bladder or bleeding internally or dying from acute myliocarditis there.

My son Gerard was tapping his fingers against his water glass as the dialogue of Princeton Hospital rolled on. I think he felt an implied criticism of the less-than-perfect medical facilities of Beirut.

I don't think that was what Jolene intended. She was merely providing a counterpoint for her life. She was trying to get straight in her own mind why it was that she had left the wonderfulness of Princeton for the uncertainty of Beirut. On this particular day, she did not seem to understand it.

"Why did you come?" Gerard asked, and Jolene answered quickly, "To do good."

One more point from that night.

My youngest son, Aran, who drives an ambulance for the Red Cross, asked her, "Are you married?"

Jolene reached up to twist her earring, a little gold thing. "No," she said.

This later turned out to be a lie. But I will say in her defense that Jolene had never felt close, and therefore married, to anyone.

That night there was bombing, and the servants climbed to the roof of the house to watch. They were fascinated by the explosions. Small slices of West Beirut would light up suddenly, from tracer bullets, followed by the crash and light of the bombs. They were thrilled when a stray shellcasing or rocket landed in our neigh borhood. Their screams and yells sickened me. I lay on my bed, face to the wall, and thought of the people the bombs struck, and how their real cries would sound.

I could hear the servants' voices: "The port's been hit!" "That one hit Hamra Street!" "Look at that explosion. It must have been someplace where they were hiding ammunition."

The war the Israelis brought to us that summer was more like entertainment than any of our other crises.

The next day my youngest son, Aran, brought Jolene to tea. Aran is a very young man of twenty who likes to defy me and had beer. Jolene said that the morning had been very hard work. They had arrived at the hospital at 6:00 A.M. and there had been people everywhere, so many crowded in the hospital that you couldn't walk, so many outside it was like a camp.

She had been bandaging and stitching and setting broken bones. She said she did many things that were really against regulations (by this she meant the regulations of Princeton Hospital) but that her supervisor had not stopped her.

"I'm not an operating room nurse; in fact, I had only the minimum courses in it. But there was no one else. So I assisted Dr. Lamm. There was this woman who had been hit in the stomach with a piece of metal, and she was pregnant. The baby was destroyed. We had to take it all out. Anyway, the woman died."

Jolene twisted her earring, then sipped her tea.

"I saw the bombs fall last night. Did you? We went to the roof of our apartment building. It was like the Fourth of July, there were so many explosions."

I said that I hadn't slept, that the bombing had been too frightening.

"Oh, we don't have to be afraid," said Jolene matter-of-factly. "The doctors told me that this side of Beirut is safe. The Israelis will never hit us. They know exactly which targets of the P.L.O. to hit. Especially we may be sure that they know where the Red Cross workers sleep."

"Jolene," I said, "the Palestinians fire back."

She twisted her earring and looked away.

My servant's sister works at the apartment building of the Red Cross and reported that Jolene was very easy to look after. She spent every night in the room of a Swiss doctor. Her own bed was never touched. It was as though no one was there at all.

Trenton, New Jersey, Jolene said, was the most wonderful city in the United States.

Since none of the others had been to New Jersey, it was left to me to doubt the veracity of that statement.

It had colorful ethnic neighborhoods, including her own Irish-Catholic one. At first, around the turn of the century, she thought, there had been some fighting between various groups. Czechs arguing with Germans, Poles who didn't know their place, Slovak children raised up to throw stones at Jewish children in schoolyards.

"You know, they call America the 'melting pot?'" she told us. "Because eventually everyone melts. Melts together."

She was unclear as to what exactly ignited this process. In her mind it seemed to be a specific quality of the region, as if the ability to get along with each other was a chemical that could be found in the Trenton citizens' drinking water.

The men worked in paint factories and lumber yards and steel mills, and after work went to bars and had beer. The women worked in shops or daycare centers (daycare centers had to be explained to Ijil, who had never heard of such a thing), and at night they cooked and waited for the men.

The Jews, it turned out, had moved away. To the other side of town, where they prospered.

I think that I was the only one at the table who understood that implied in all this was the idea that since the parishioners of St. Peter's and Paul's had been able to get along without resorting to bombing or guerrilla war, we of Beirut surely should be able to do the same.

The naiveté of the comparison made me chuckle, and I felt the disapproval of both my daughters-in-law, Ijil and Marie.

"Why did the Jews move away?" Aran asked.

"Well," said Jolene, playing with a glass of water, "the reason was, there was no room in our neighborhood for the Temple."

Oh.

We rarely ventured beyond the walls of our house that summer. Lilacs and jacynths grew in the garden. My wife struggled to keep good meals on the table. We ran through various shortages of food and supplies. The phones did not work.

Jolene came on a Sunday. She ate her mezza with unusual relish, tearing the thin bread and scooping up hummus and tahini with appetite.

I remarked upon her appetite.

"I always eat well on Sunday," she said. "On Sunday, at my house, we have a roast and potatoes and gravy and everyone is happy. After church."

I asked if she missed going to church.

"Oh, yes, very much," she said. "I feel terribly guilty about it because it's a sin if you don't go. If you want to be in the club, you have to play by the rules and go every Sunday. Aran says there's a Catholic church but it's too dangerous to go. I can't possibly go. I feel very bad about that."

She twisted her little gold earring. She continued to eat.

"I hope God will forgive me because of all the good I'm doing in Beirut," she said.

Jolene had been in Beirut for one month. She came to our gate early one evening and did not wait as usual for the servant to announce her, but walked slowly to the garden, and, not finding me, let herself into my study. I was startled. Both her forearms were wrapped with bandages, and there were two small bandages on her cheek.

"Hello!" I said. "What happened?"

She dropped herself into a chair, wincing as she lowered her forearms. Her eyes were dull and colorless.

"Sometimes," she said. Her voice trailed off. I waited.

"Do you have a cup of tea?" she asked.

Tea was brought, and many moments of silence passed. To fill the void, I talked of my own project, the building of a country club for the bankers of Jordan. I don't think Jolene heard me. After awhile there was a loud explosion in the distance and the sounds of gunfire.

"It never stops, does it," she said.

"It will stop when the Israelis have chased out the P.L.O. Soon, I think."

"Not soon enough," said Jolene.

There'd been an accident, she said. A house was blown up. Just outside Shattilla, just beyond the hospital. She'd been walking there.

"But I wasn't able to do anything," she said in a low voice. "What could I do? I tried. But everyone died. They all died. I tried to help. I really did. I can never seem to help enough."

I made no comment. The idea that one American girl could feel responsible for people killed in a city of war appalled me.

"It just goes on and on," she said.

Maybe it was time to go back to Princeton Hospital, I suggested.

"You must be kidding," said Jolene. "Back there? What good could I do there?"

"Why do you have to do good at all? Just go."

"I have to do *something*," said Jolene.

We got the real story of Jolene's "accident" that night at dinner from Aran. The building was blazing, he said. As he watched, Jolene ran out with a child under each arm, ran back in, carried out a young woman, went back in again and got another. In all, eight people were carried from the building by Jolene. Two of those were dead. The rest were put in Aran's ambulance and taken to the hospital. Jolene herself, after scrubbing at the hospital, was found to be suffering from large cuts down both arms and a cut beneath her eye that required nine stitches.

Jolene could not remember how exactly she had been cut.

"Jolene," I said gently, "it seems they did not all die. Aran says that six of those people lived. You saved them."

"There were a lot more people in that building," said Jolene miserably. "I couldn't get back in. I tried, but there were too many flames. I couldn't see the door."

Another part of Aran's story: an American television crew had turned up and filmed the scene. They spoke to Jolene, but she responded to them only in French, as if she were not American and did not understand.

Je ne sais pas quoi. I don't know why.

An accident, she said. Everyone died, she said.

Jolene stood up. "Aran, take me to the hospital."

"No," said my son Phillipe. Phillipe is a lawyer with the Phalange Party. He is close to the Gemayels and close to the Israelis and he seemed to know a lot about what was going on in Beirut that summer.

"Not into West Beirut at night."

"I wouldn't go anyway," said Aran huffily.

"I didn't do much work today," said Jolene. She looked at her bandaged arms. That night she slept in the small guest room in the children's wing of our house. In the morning the Swiss doctor called for her and they drove to the hospital.

It was not long after this that Jolene met the Israelis and made the trip to Broumanna.

It was inevitable that she would meet them. We are all together here, in this neighborhood of Baabda. My house, the apartments of the Red Cross, the Israeli headquarters.

Jolene passed the headquarters on one of her walks. The soldiers spoke to her in English, which she liked, and she was quite well along in discussion with some of the officers before she realized that they were Israelis. She shrugged. Soldiers were soldiers. Jolene made no distinction. For instance, she was not sure which side were the Moslems and which were the Christians, nor who the Phalange were, nor how the Palestinians came to be living in our city. Rather basic, one would think, to the make-up of someone who wanted to help in Beirut.

She knew a lot about severed arteries and compound fractures and general anesthesia and various infections caused by poor hygiene. Beyond that, soldiers were soldiers.

Broumanna is a separate city from Beirut, high up a mountain road. It was sheltered from the war; its elegant buildings and neon lights stand proudly untouched. Music from discotheques blasts in the street, young men line up with their coins at pinball. The cars are Jaguars and Mercedes. Women wear silk dresses and have diamond straps on their high heels. Men with neat manicures and Italian suits sip champagne and discuss the price and shipment of poppies from Turkey.

Gerard went through a Broumanna period and Phillipe still goes. Aran does not go, but that is because Aran fancies himself a gambler and likes to go to the casino at Juniyeh and pretend he has money.

At any rate.

There is every kind of restaurant there. Italian pasta and linguini; German sausage and beer. Jolene and the Israelis were served on a flower-filled terrace overlooking Beirut by a tuxedoed waiter who brought shrimp and French champagne.

The restaurants of Broumanna were inconvenienced by the war that summer to the extent that their wine lists were sometimes limited and the supply of Iranian caviar was totally cut off.

I worried about Jolene being seen with the Israelis there, but Phillipe told me, no, she was perfectly safe. In fact the Israelis were bringing in lots of business, Phillipe said.

You may know that this is the bottom line in any Lebanese discussion.

Jolene went several times, danced at the discos, drank good wine. She went up with the Israelis in their jeeps, and they left their Uzis and M16s on the table when they danced. Once a gun had fallen across a waiter's foot, causing him to drop the *veaux l'orange* on the terrace. This was a hilarious moment. At one of the discos there was, for decoration, a Jaguar automobile, spliced in half, and one of the Israelis had suggested that all the automobiles spliced in half on the streets of Beirut should be used to open discos. This was also hilarious.

I continued to worry. Jolene's perception of how things were in Lebanon could not be helped by Broumanna. Already she thought of it as a sort of play war, full of toy soldiers, toy bombs, toy crumbling buildings. The injured and the dying were real, but that was her job. She did not perceive in Beirut that summer any real threat to herself.

They want me to take a day off, said Jolene miserably.

We sat in the garden on a hot July day. Jolene was drinking iced orange juice, or rather had a glass of iced orange juice in her hand. As my wife had pointed out, Jolene never really drank, or ate, anything, in the usual sense. She played with things. Today she was sucking the ice and spitting it back in the glass. One hand reached up to twist the gold earring.

I said a day off sounded like a good idea.

"But what will I do?"

"Sleep. Relax."

"I don't want to sleep and relax. I want to do something."

I thought. There was not much by way of sights that one could safely see in Lebanon that summer.

"Write letters. To your family."

"You sound like my mother," said Jolene. Since I do not sound at all like Jolene's mother, I could only conclude that she did not wish to write letters.

She had received letters, though. My servant's sister reported that three letters addressed to Mrs. John Allen sat on the night table in Jolene's room.

Moreover, the U.S. embassy courier had come by only that day, bringing me letters from Houston. He had shown me a postcard addressed to Mrs. John Allen. On the front was a rather sterile-looking white building titled Princeton Hospital. On the back was one sentence which read—"*Why didn't you tell me you were going to Beirut?*" and signed, *John.*

"Why don't you write to your husband?" I asked.

"I left my husband," said Jolene. "He doesn't understand me."

I inquired as to whether Jolene's husband knew he had been left.

"He'll get the message. I mean, I'm not there, am I."

In fact Jolene's husband did not know he had been left. In fact they had been married less than one year. Things had been going okay, Jolene guessed. She had left because she felt like leaving. Felt like doing something.

"You wanted to travel," I suggested.

"Not particularly." In fact Jolene had gotten the address of the International Red Cross from a friend, had stopped in one day and now found herself in Beirut.

Knowing as I did that there was also a National Office of the Red Cross in the United States, I wondered if a different address obtained from a different friend might not have landed her a job treating flood victims in Mississippi.

I mentioned this to her, but the possibility did not seem to interest her. Jolene was not a great believer in fate.

She was also not a great believer in marriage. She had tried it, seemed to be her attitude. Her mother had told her she would be happy if she married a rich doctor. Her mother had told her she would be happy if she went every Sunday to Mass. Her mother had told her she would be happy if only she would do good.

Well, here she was.

You must know that I am hypothesizing here. These are not the things Jolene said to me that afternoon in July. These are her thoughts as I think she would have put them together. Should have put them together.

And that time there was one major idea that Jolene had not yet grasped.

Her mother was wrong.

August was finally silent. The bombing stopped.

Aran spent two days in the mountains with friends. The phones began to work. Jolene reported fewer injured at the hospital. Gerard reported that he had seen Jolene playing soccer with the Palestinian children. An agreement was worked out whereby the P.L.O. fighters would leave Beirut.

All of this was good news.

In fact there was only one small flaw on the horizon and that was Jolene. She came by less frequently, and when she did come was quieter. One morning I heard my servant's sister grumble that Jolene was untidy; she had spent the night writing letters but had not mailed them, leaving the pages strewn about the floor.

That was a day when I was very busy with the Saudis. I was showing them the plans for that part of Beirut they could buy cheaply now, while the Israelis were here, and rebuild profitably later, when the Israelis left. If the Syrians left and the P.L.O. left, the profits would be even higher, and we were contemplating this when Ijil entered. She approached with her head bowed, like a proper Arab girl.

"Jolene is here," she whispered.

I was annoyed. Surely Ijil of all people had the sense not to interrupt my business for this announcement. I shook my head and waved her away.

When I saw my Saudi visitors out, many hours later, Jolene was sitting sullenly in the hall.

"Why wouldn't you see me?" she said angrily. I don't think she even saw the Saudis. "You ignored me, for hours! You left me sitting out here! You wouldn't talk to me!" She banged her fist on the bench.

"A minute, Jolene," I said sternly.

Jolene leaped up at me, grabbing my arm. "You wouldn't see me, and I depended on you! You wouldn't see me, and I have nowhere else to go!"

"Jolene!" I said, and shook off her hand. The Saudis were extremely embarrassed. In our Arab states, young women do not cry out at their elders. The Saudis moved towards the door, their long robes trailing. Jolene ran into the garden.

I made what apologies I could. I was furious. I went to the garden, where Jolene stood.

"What's the matter with you?" I yelled angrily, "interrupting me like that with my guests? You are a guest in this house too, and you have no right! I have extended the hospitality of this house to you for three months and I never expected it to be abused in such a manner! You have the manners of a goat!"

"I'm not a goat! I have nowhere else to go, and you wouldn't see me!"

"What is it then? What's so damned important?"

"You won't understand now. You won't understand."

"Jolene. I have always understood before. What is it? What's happened? Are you hurt? Are you in danger?"

Some possibilities along the lines of those last two questions began to occur to me. I grew worried that maybe I was wrong. Maybe she had needed immediate attention.

Jolene sat down and clutched at her stomach. Her voice quavered.

"Forty people died," she said. "I was there at the port and I saw it. They were celebrating. We had to fill up all the ambulances. The men were leaving. They were riding in trucks. They killed their own families. By accident. Because they were happy. Don't you understand?"

I understood only too well. Phillipe had called from his office hours before with the news. The Palestinian fighters, who felt themselves to be victors and to be leaving Beirut with dignity, had fired their guns constantly into the air all morning. One could have started another war with all the bullets they let off, Phillipe said.

Bullets shot into the air may have a certain energizing effect that denotes celebration and victory and possibly the release of tension. Bullets shot into the air also have to land someplace, sometimes ricocheting off buildings, sometimes piercing the soft flesh of real people. But the fools hadn't thought of that, that morning.

When Phillipe told me, I had been disgusted. I was doubly so now.

"Jolene," I began, "you are one American girl from the Red Cross. Just who is it that you think you are? Do you think you can change Beirut? Change us? Change the Palestinians? Yes, you do," I said, because she was shaking her head in objection. "You have some misguided sense of mission that makes you believe that your presence here is somehow going to change things for the better. Well, forget it."

"It's not that!" cried Jolene. "I treated those people, with my own hands, all summer! Because some enemy was trying to kill them! And now, this morning, they are killing each other!"

"How are you going to stop them? You are nobody. You are a nurse who works with blood and bones and that should be enough for you, but it's not. You can't change Beirut, you can't change the way things are, and you can't come screaming into my house as if you blame me for this situation!"

I went into my study and slammed the door. The house felt unusually silent.

Jolene's mother probably never yelled at her. Not in her whole life.

The next day we heard from Aran that Jolene had not come to work. She sent a message to the Red Cross saying she was sick. My wife made a gift of flowers and sweet rolls and some local cures and took them to the apartment. She reported that Jolene seemed more tired than ill, that she had lain in bed and held my wife's hand and cried when my wife left.

I was disturbed with myself and disturbed with Beirut. There was a tremor of uncertainty in the ground. The Palestinians were still evacuating in the West, and, having not learned their lesson, killing off more of their families every day in celebrations.

For two days, this went on. Then my servants reported two Israeli jeeps at the front gate, and Jolene came to see me for the last time.

I opened the door myself that day. A form of apology. I wanted to show her that she really was welcome here. Anytime.

"I'm leaving," she said. She said it in a soft voice, and took my hand in a gentle clasp.

I was startled. "Why?" I asked.

Jolene laughed. "Raymond, you've been telling me to leave for the past two months!"

"You never listened before!"

"I know." She laughed again. "I just decided."

"We'll miss you," I said.

She left so quickly. She got in one of the jeeps, and they rumbled off down the road. Only then did I realize that she would be riding all the way down the coast, all through Lebanon, with the Israelis. Only then did I wish she hadn't gone, had waited for the Red Cross or me to arrange a ride with a more neutral party.

Now you may think that I have brought you up to that point where I may hand my story over to the *New York Times*. Now you will remember what you read about the Israeli patrol, gunned down just outside the city limits, seven people killed, including one American nurse.

No. That is not how it was.

I reconstruct the story from what I was told by others and what Aran learned at the scene.

That the two jeeps were stopped first in my neighborhood by an American peacekeeping force of Marines. That they were technically not supposed to be there, and, in spite of Jolene's pleading, were detained for an hour while a superior officer was sought and permission granted to leave the neighborhood.

From there the group passed a Lebanese army checkpoint, which did not detain them.

After this, they were stopped by the Israelis, on the matter of Jolene's papers. It seemed that since she had come in with the Red Cross but was not leaving with the Red Cross, the Israeli officer thought she did not have the proper permission to pass back across the border.

They were detained another hour while the proper form and the proper officer to sign it were found.

At this station, Jolene was reported to be angry, to have met some officers she knew from her Broumanna days and screamed at them that they were all fucking up her life, that she had to get going, that time was running out.

It is not clear to me what she may have meant by this.

The small group started out again, back through the Lebanese army, back through the Israelis, were in fact only twenty minutes down the road when they were stopped by a roadblock of Arabs.

It must have appeared to the group to be a Lebanese Army checkpoint. But it was not. I think I know what group it was, but considering the number of factions in Lebanon, it is not worth mentioning. It would confuse Jolene's story.

They stopped. There was some business of asking for Jolene's passport, which she angrily threw out. The passport was studied carefully, most likely by an Arab who couldn't read.

Jolene repeated again and again that she was an American nurse with the Red Cross.

She held up her Red Cross papers.

There was a long delay. Jolene gestured to the Arabs to move the damn roadblock and let them get on the way. The Arab standing next to the jeep laughed at her. Jolene kicked him in the stomach.

Everyone opened fire on everyone else. The dead: three Arabs, three Israelis, one American nurse.

One American girl from the Red Cross. A single act of frustration in one entirely frustrated life. The *New York Times* didn't mention that.

A television crew had the pictures of Jolene carrying the people from the burning building. Jolene's husband told me they have seen this again and again on TV since her death.

Aran carried her body in his ambulance, back up the road to Beirut. He told me that he cried all the way.

Perhaps I have raised Aran so that he is not afraid of his own emotions. Perhaps this is something I have done right.

Beirut is trying to settle down. We have what passes here for peace. And Jolene's husband roams the city, trying to push an investigation into her death.

I have not been very kind to him. He mourns the brave nurse of the *New York Times*. Not my Jolene.

I mourn her, but then, who am I? Just an old man of Lebanon, who understood nothing, who was not able to help.

I cannot get her out of my mind.

Today I will go into West Beirut to check construction on the Saudis' buildings.

As always, Beirut has survived.

ROSE SCOLLARD

Kerby Dick Launches His Wife onto the International Art Sea

from The Fiddlehead

Lawrence, Mattie Dick's first, was born the thirty-first of March 1949, the day they joined up with the mainland. She'd gone the full nine months without a cramp or a missed heartbeat, but the little fellow had come out dead anyway. Her neighbour Erla Shapley stayed a day to help her over the worst but then went home to her own brood leaving Mattie as childless as before she'd come.

There was some politician in the poor little mite, Kerby said, sitting awkwardly on the edge of the bed, his hands, large and raw-knuckled, fitted warmly over Mattie's.

How's that? said Mattie. Not yet feeling the grief for her first, she was already planning the next.

I think it was a protest meself, against being born a foreigner, said Kerby. Only the poor little fellow carried it too far.

They'd giggled togther until Mattie didn't know what was worse, her own laughing or the pitching of bed where Kerby jiggled it. It wasn't until later that night, lonely for the armful that should have been cuddling up to her, that she cried.

We'll have another one, said Kerby fitting his knees into the backs of hers and threading his arms carefully about the ruins of her stomach. Don't you worry.

With Patrick, her second, they never even got word to Erla. He emerged without a pang of warning, as reposed in his expression as a marble cherub. And the third, Arlette, at about the middle of the seventh month pitched about suddenly — in her little death agony, Mattie later said — and leapt forth in a way that had Mattie laid up for six weeks in her bed.

The doctor ordered Mattie into the hospital in St. Johns two months before the fourth child was due, and six weeks later delivered her of Angus, a bouncing squalling boy with Kerby's nose and Mattie's carroty hair. Angus lived for all of three hours.

This was the way it went for fifteen years. For most of that time Mattie was pregnant with not a living child to show for it.

It was Kerby who buried them. Apart from Flora, who lived three days and was christened by the hospital chaplin, the children were all barred from Christian burial. Kerby, who felt this was too strict an interpretation of the Lord's wishes, slipped each of them into the family plot in the St. Ignatius and Simeon Cemetery in the dark of night with Lord Keep Me Safe and Our Father and such little fragments of the service for the burial of the dead as he knew — the ashes to ashes bit, and the Lord will preserve thy going out and thy coming in and may pity for your little soul cause his face to shine on you.

After Isaac their twelfth child and seventh son emerged blue and breathless one November morning, Mattie and Kerby, sipping tea at the kitchen table with their elbows on the oilcloth, made a pact to let that be the finish of it. The crib that had stood up to fourteen years of disappointment would be put in the attic and the family lace that only Flora had had the use of would be folded away in Mattie's hope chest.

Lawrence would have been fourteen years old last Tuesday, said Kerby, and Mattie had a sudden vision of Lawrence's face, pinched in at each temple like the top of a heart turned sideways, with Kerby's ears flaring out at the sides like fleshy cheerful cornets. This picture was in the manner of a small revelation to Mattie and it could have been then that, having abandoned medical science as a means of realizing her hopes, she made a resolution to turn to art.

In the spring, an evening course in painting was offered at the new central high school. Mattie enrolled and one Tuesday evening went off for the first lesson. Kerby never said a word about it and was there in his chair when she got home, sucking comfortably on his pipe. But out back, the overturned sods humping out the garden showed the extent of his loneliness.

It was like going to school all over again, said Mattie. There I was in a room that smelled of chalk and old lunchpails, squeezed into a desk three sizes too small for me.

Did they teach you anything?

We won't be learning much till we get the paints.

You must have learned something in the two hours.

Not a thing, said Mattie.

The instructor had in fact given some preliminary lessons in drawing. He'd spent at least half an hour demonstrating the way to draw a head, sketching an oval and dividing it down the centre with a line from top to bottom and then crossing it with another a third of the way down. But the face when he was finished with it was nothing at all like Lawrence.

Mattie said nothing of her reservations to Kerby. She went into town with him the next Saturday and bought the brushes she was told, the palette and two kinds of paint—an assortment of tin tubes and a little box of round cakes of tempera in it. They lay unwrapped on the hall table till the next Tuesday rolled around.

This lesson was on the proper mixing of colours. Mattie sat absorbed before her palette squeezing daubs of colour all over it and, after she'd got over the glory of them, mixing up new ones even more compelling. The second hour, the instructor had them paint a small scene from a model he pinned on the board. Mattie threw it out when she got home and put the paints away in the drawer. She liked the colours but the act of painting felt foreign to her and, besides, the instructor's examples were nothing at all like the pictures in her head. She didn't think he'd make a painter of her.

That might have been the end of it, but that Sunday, with Kerby out digging aimlessly in the yard, the sun falling on the flowered oilcloth reminded her of Lawrence. She took out the paints, squeezing out what she wanted on the palette and, working on a bare patch of wall between the back door and the window, made a bold pinched in circle. Looking out the window at Kerby to see the way they went, she attached the ears. From there it was the easiest thing in the world to add the rosy cheeks and the smile, dimpled, saucy, yet somehow grave as befitted an eldest child. Kerby came in as she was working on the suit.

I'm putting long pants on him, she told him. He's the age to be embarrassed by short ones.

Kerby nodded and looked with respect at the developing portrait. It took her several hours to finish the suit properly and to attend to the problem of hands. She solved it with a walking cane that had belonged to her grandfather. She hadn't seen it in years. Now it popped into her mind as the appropriate thing for her son to be wielding, though for what purpose it wasn't clear.

Kerby heated some soup so she could keep working and they had supper in front of the wall where they could study this freshly risen apparition of their eldest.

It's a fine piece of work, Kerby said, chewing ruggedly on his bread. It fills an empty corner of the heart.

The next morning over her porridge Mattie studied the stick, a gentle sort of stick in spite of the two snakes twining up it, and decided that what it needed was a dog jumping over it.

After the breakfast dishes were put away and things put to order in the house she went to work on the dog. At first she had no idea how it would be and let her hand wander with the brush but by the time Kerby came back from the plant for lunch its eager little body was established in mid leap over the stick.

It's Kip! cried Kerby. Good old Kippy. Wasn't that little black and white devil the bane of my mother's life?

The next Tuesday, Mattie might possibly have gone to her class, but that afternoon they were going by Presley's farm and she had Kerby stop the car.

Now what's that old horse got to do with anything? grumbled Kerby, following her across the ditch to the fence.

I was thinking he's just the kind of horse the children would like to ride. She poked some grass through to the elderly, chestnut drawhorse that browsed by the fence but it stood there, too tired or too dull to take the offering.

Wouldn't they go for something with more spirit? said Kerby.

Mattie knew he was right, something like Anson's Sailor was more what they'd like in a horse. But seeing them in her imagination bucked and tossed about, her mother's fear got in the way of reason. She settled for this placid saw-backed creature in Presley's field.

He's a nice colour, she argued, a good rich chestnut. All the way back to the house she was wondering how she'd manage the glossy shine of its flanks.

By supper time she had it figured out and then was too engrossed to think of going to class. She worked all evening on the horse, making it shaggier and bulkier than life, increasing its centre of gravity till she felt it was ready for the children.

The children went on the next day. She put Gerald at the back, a sober, smooth-haired little boy. As his dependability became more and more evident, Mattie felt justified in making him the anchor for the group.

Jean went on next and was almost finished by the time Kerby came home for his lunch. Eight-year-old Jean was an amazement to Kerby who hadn't imagined they could turn out such a beauty.

She kept on all that afternoon. In front of Jean went Casey, Marie, and then Suzette who held on to two-year-old Arnold. Arnold was the chubbiest and most daring of the riders. He looked, when Mattie put the final touch to him, about to make a boisterous summersault head first to the ground. She couldn't help feeling a pang of fear for Arnold's adventurous ways and was glad to see that Suzette had a good grip on him.

Mattie had done this painting in their bedroom so it would be the first thing she and Kerby saw when they woke up. But the horse and its riders took up only a small bit of the wall. In the days that followed she extended the field behind the children with lots of flowers for them to pick, forget-me-nots, daisies, celandine, paintbrush and golden rod, never minding about the seasons, just putting what she knew they'd like. Then, cautiously, not wishing to deprive them entirely of adventure, she painted Sailor, bucking and snorting like anything but safely fenced in, with the older boys Lawrence, Patrick and Angus looking on. Arlette was with them, a madcap, tomboy sort of girl that made Mattie's heart leap with fear and hope as she emerged under the brush, carroty haired and wickedly skinny, already climbing the fence.

Even with these additions, only half the wall was used up and Mattie worried that the room seemed to tip to one side. Then, a day or two later, they were speeding alongside the Bay and she knew what the rest of the wall would be. She spent an entire week painting the sea, choppy and slate coloured, with whitecaps that caught the sunlight and two masted ships that tossed about on it. And because it looked a little dangerous for them, she put in the Bell Island lighthouse to keep them safe.

What about Flora, said Kerby. You don't want to be leaving her out. And little Isaac? But even before he asked Mattie had planned their inclusion, the baby among the daisies and forgetmenots, spreadeagled like little Jesus in the creche, with his sister beside him making daisy chains.

Now that's something worth having, said Kerby coming in for a break from the garden, on whose rocky soil his spade seemed to be imposing an ever more orderly arrangement. A fine way of filling up an empty wall.

The day after she finished the children, the two of them, by way of celebration, slept an hour later than usual and then had breakfast in bed. Kerby made the tea, hot and strong the way they liked it, and with the cups dangling from his fingers and the cream jug balanced in the hollow of his hand, brought the pot into the bedroom. Mattie was close behind him with the sugar and the plate of buttered toast and the cabbageleaf jampot that her mother had bought in Halifax. They sat there under the blue eiderdown half the morning sipping tea with buttery fingers and discussing the family.

She's a cheeky little piece, that Arlette.

She's going to break her neck one of these days and that's no lie, said Mattie.

Arnold's another one.

He'll need watching, she agreed.

After that there was no stopping Mattie. Inch by inch the walls of their small home filled up. There was nothing she wouldn't paint. Fires on bonfire night. The neighbours' houses, their maids and lads, and even their pets.

Every animal in the area had its alter-existence on the walls of the Dick home. A pleasant existence it was, with permanent blue sky and sunshine, plenty of green grass to munch, big meaty bones to gnaw, and balls of bright wool to get tangled in. Even Doris Malott's parrot was there, right in the hallway as you came in the door, looking with tight-beaked cunning on its owner who was trying, with the aid of a large water biscuit, to induce it to speak.

She did the boats too, inshore and offshore, the pitching dories, the nets, the lobster pots, the men in their oilskins and thigh high boots, the drying flakes and the fish plant where Kerby worked. It all took life under Mattie's brush.

The little chapel of St. Ignatius and St. Simeon went on the wall of the parlour. Mattie took special pleasure in its white-painted boards and thought that they shed some of their daisy brightness into the dingy little room.

She left out the cemetery, but she did the people, Father Martin first, plumper than he would have ever admitted to being, his neck overflowing a bit at the collar. To compensate Mattie put him in a crisp, new gown with shoes peeping out beneath the skirt of it as black and shiny as a dance hall man's. She had him talking to Mrs. McCall. Mattie, who was amazed and a little ashamed to see how well she had caught Mrs. McCall's forbidding presence, gave her a blue dress painted over the daffodils to offset the sternness of her legs. Besides these two she put the Presley boys tumbling down the church steps; Jesse Minter's new baby in its pram, swaddled from top to toe in pink knitting; and Arthur and Ethel Paskill gossiping with Mrs. Delisle.

There came a day at last when there simply was no more wall for Mattie to paint, not so much as a thumbnail's width of space where she could set her brush. She moped about looking out on the neat rows of Kerby's garden, her fingers itching to paint their orderly patterns. The sworls of the cabbage and the frondy gaiety of the carrot tops were allurements worse than anything Father Martin ever scolded against.

She tried walking out, down the road by the Bay and along the sea shore, but the birds running along the beach made her heart ache. Every shell, every worn bit of crockery glinting up at her added its own pain.

It went on like that for some time. Everything she saw became a picture in her mind and her head filled with pictures till she though it would burst.

I heard about this lady in Fogo Bay who painted pictures on the outside of her house, Kerby said one day. But for Mattie the idea of any painting of hers out in the wind and weather was a thought too painful to entertain. It would be like putting your children out, she told Kerby.

One day Kerby went off to town without her. Except for going to the plant each morning he had never done such a thing and Mattie couldn't keep a little loneliness from mixing in with the general misery she was feeling. Returning an hour or two later with a number of white-wrapped parcels, he came into the house, set down the packages, and cleared his throat. Impressed with the formality of his manner, Mattie stopped filling the kettle and sat on the kitchen bench to listen.

When he spoke, Kerby's voice was louder than usual and somewhat ringing, the way he might have spoken at a public meeting if he'd been inclined to such a thing.

Seeing how the pictures are building up inside you there, and seeing as putting on a twenty-room addition would take care of the painting for a while but would totally squeeze out the gardening. . . . He was joking she knew. All the same, for a moment Mattie had a vision of those twenty rooms, corridor after corridor of them, filled with children and dogs and scurrying shore birds.

Considering all that, it seems to me there should be a change of thinking about your technique. He blushed a moment over the unfamiliar word. Well what I'm trying to say is I heard of this International Art Sea on the radio and I don't see why you shouldn't get yourself out on it.

Carefully he unwrapped the biggest of the parcels. It contained an easel of polished pine with fine brass hinges. On it, after rustling about in one of the other packages, he set a canvas which gleamed, to Mattie's hungry eye, as white and tempting as a wedding cake.

I got you ten of these to start with, said Kerby. And I got some tinned ham and cake so you don't have to waste time with lunch.

She started right after they cleared away the lunch table. At first the canvas intimidated her.

It seems such a small bit of space after the walls, doesn't it?

But she started with something easy — a fine big picture of Kerby, standing the way he did, with his pirate grin and his ears all aflap. In his hands she put a little blue ship with white sails and herself sitting in it, looking out solemnly at the International Sea that was about to receive her.

I managed to get on board ahead of the old people, hurrying with the rest of the young up to the sun deck, where I claimed one man-sized rectangle by rolling out my sleeping bag. More were coming up every minute, finding their spot on this topmost, open air deck of the M/V Northern Sea, bound for Alaska. Most of my deck-mates looked seasoned, scruffy, their hair in long strings more through neglect than any politics. They were famil-iars of the truck stop, bus station, roadside, endless motion America of 1975. The dirtier they were, the more nonchalant, dumping down their greasy packs and look-ing around them as if getting on a ferry from Seattle to Alaska was a trip to the store for cigarettes. They would be headed for the canneries, like me. But this was my first trip away from home, and as much as I wanted to, I couldn't make it look easy. I had spent my first year after high school driving a produce truck for my father, and was glad to get away. Before me was the prospect of a season in the canneries: twelve-hour shifts, cold seawater and fish-slime, barracks life, and money that I needed badly, as I had some hopes of going to college. I stood next to my cheap nylon pack, checked to see that the straps were tight, the zippers zipped. I was trying to be ready for almost anything.

Beside the cannery rats, there were rock climbers and mountaineers on board, with their bright tubular backpacks and special clothes. Most of their hands and arms were scabbed and scraped up to the elbows, but more than anyone they seemed intensely happy, talking all at once, ferocious good health around them like a kind of aura. Then there were the young couples on their outdoor vacations: they moved in efficient tandem, talked quietly or used hand signals as they staked out extra-large spaces for themselves, spreading out new and expensive-looking gear.

I decided to risk leaving my pack so that I could walk to the rail. The old people were still shuffling up the boarding ramp.

"Look at those geezers," said the guy next to me, whom I later learned to call Jocko. "Must be a hundred of 'em." Jocko looked to be maybe nineteen, nape-length hair gleaming blue-black, dark intense eyes, soft, wispy first growth on his chin and upper lip. "Senile citizens," he said, smiling. He wore denim from ankles to neck, and had an eight-inch hunting knife on his belt. He gripped the rail, pulled himself back and forth in nervous motion, eyes gleaming. "You see that?" he said. "They got their own nurse." Jocko seemed to thrive on small excitements.

"Doctor, too," I said, "Guy with the bag."

I couldn't help feeling a trace of disgust, like thick saliva at the back of my mouth, watching the old people herding into the boat. My boat. *Our* boat. They would bring medications, bad smells, illnesses I couldn't pronounce. I had never had anything to do with old people. My grandparents all died before I knew them. There was a great-uncle Jimmy I used to be forced to visit sometimes: I remember him scuffing his slippers over the cracked linoleum in his kitchen; tufts of white hair sprouted above his ankle bones, exposed between the lamb's ruff of the slipper and the ragged cuff of the pajama leg. He would tell incomprehensible stories with great emotion, sometimes having to stop suddenly, he was so choked up. After meals he shuffled into the bathroom, just off the kitchen, and there he would gargle loudly, so that I had to set aside the last few bites of my bologna and cheese. In the car headed home after, my anger embarrassed my parents: "Couldn't he at least shut the door?" I yelled.

This was a Catholic senior citizen's group out of Tacoma. There were the spry and wiry among them, but most moving slowly, hunched, propped on canes, legs spindly in support hose. This was no cruise ship, just Alaska's ferry line running the Marine Highway from Seattle up to Sagway. They would make a holiday out of the eight-day trip there and back. In the waiting area on the dock they had stood all together making a lot of good-natured noise, chattering promises of clean air, the calm seas of the inside passage, a more than usual amount to drink, glaciers, mountains, a glimpse of a whale.

"Man, you see when they get on board?" Jocko was saying. "Move like fucking commandos. They grabbed all the window seats in the bow, got half the booths in the snack bar. Plus they got beds downstairs, you know."

"Berths, you mean," I said. "And it's 'below.'"

"Man, your own room on a boat!" He seemed happy to think about this.

"You mean cabin," I said. "It's called a cabin."

I could see Jocko tense, size me up. Then he relaxed. "Whatever the fuck," he said. "Cabin." He gave me a sly look, a smile hiding in there somewhere. "You got your port, you got your starboard, right?"

"The kitchen's called a galley," I said.

"They bust your ass, you land in the brig," Jocko said.

"Look," I pointed. "They brought their own priest." The man had his hand under an old woman's elbow. I saw the white chink of collar over his Adam's apple—always thought that looked sharp.

"In case somebody kicks off," Jocko said.

Behind us, somebody started to blow on a flute, and a kid with a guitar strummed the first few chords of a Neil Young song over and over. The deck was filling up, so I went back to defend my turf and scan the deck for unattached women. There were a few possibles: long hair unbrushed and clipped behind, comfortable in T-shirts and army pants. I chose to see them as being aglow with health and adventure. Reckless, even. My heart beat like a rabbit's. As it turned out, one of these had set up pretty near me, and sat leaning against her pack, busy changing her socks. She had thick black hair pinned up haphazardly, a big-boned kind of beauty, long eyelashes. Her thick brows were almost joined with a delicate thatching that I decided was an outward sign of passion.

"Deck's going to fill up," I said.

She shrugged. "That's okay, isn't it?" As if I were being selfish.

I made myself comfy on my sleeping bag, settling in for some relaxed conversation leading to who knows what. She had her old socks off; there was dirt between her toes and under the nails; her soles were yellow with callous except for the clean pink-white of the arch.

"Sure," I said. "The more the merrier. One big party."

"That may be the case." She offered her words like small polished stones. She would have me know, apparently, that she was a college girl, a year or two older than me, and disposed to disapprove of a raw youth such as myself. She didn't speak again, just worked at tugging on clean white socks. Then she straightened up and threw her shoulders back with a quick breath. She was about to get up.

"I'm Todd," I said.

Through a small hole in her t-shirt a nipple winked in and out of sight.

"Todd," I said again. Maybe I smiled too much.

"Lori." We shook, her hand big, firm. Before I could come up with anything else she was on her feet and walking away toward the rail, her t-shirt shaking down to cover her rear.

Jocko, as it turned out, had a greater talent for appealing to women's tender parts. The following afternoon I had been for some hours entranced at the stern rail, watching the water boil up from the screws that pushed us every minute further north, when Jocko shook me by the shoulder.

"Man, you know that Lori girl?"

"Shut me down in a hurry," I said.

"Wow, man, we just did some depraved things in the Men's."

I studied Jocko: he was, I suppose, in what is called the bloom of youth. There was rose in his cheeks, and his eyes were hard and bright with something that I imagined could pass for love. I had seen him with Lori earlier, at whisper distance, his lips moving, his hand slipped casually beneath her shirt to fondle her lumbar. Lori nodded, smiled, blushed. What could he have been saying to her? This to me was the endless mystery: what did people like Jocko say to people like Lori? Perhaps not words at all, but gurgles or coos, or something like the sound snakes make before they tangle and braid like rope.

Jocko was eager to narrate: "There was some serious ambidextrous shit, and then something she said they did in Senegal or someplace. Had to hold my breath for almost a minute! Like this—" Jocko made some incomprehensible hand motions. "I'm telling you, man, it's an unsafe world."

How much of Jocko's exploits were fairy tale or truth, I couldn't say, but my own efforts along these lines were of a more ordinary result. For despite some brief and fairly confusing experience with Mona Pfister in the bed of a pickup truck the previous summer, and some nights of smooch and fondle with Letty MacDougal parked by the reservoir, I still suffered from all the anxieties and false starts of the novice.

My only other prospect was Bernice, who wore a kimono and did modern dance on the deck, her blonde braids whipping. But we didn't get beyond comparing feet; hers were strong and homely, tools that every day she beat and flexed into shape. When she pointed her toes, her instep became a hump of muscle hard as tree root. Beside them mine looked flabby, somehow virginal. Other than her feet, Bernice's only topic of conversation was the person who owned them. "Dance is a way of being with myself," she said. I eventually took this as a hint, and was only a little chafed when later she fell into company with the rock-climbers, hang-gliders and other muscular sorts.

Jocko decided I needed coaching.

"You got to start out light, man. Be funny."

"I can never remember jokes," I said.

"Not jokes. Banter. Jive. They'll laugh at anything. The point is, get those giggles coming, you're halfway home."

"Got it," I said. "Go on."

Jocko gave me a sideways look. "Man, you crack me up. This ain't no fuckin' chemistry class. Listen: you hang with the giggle mode, you play it out, depends on the girl, maybe four minutes, maybe ten —"

"Four minutes?"

"Could be eight, you know. Whatever. Believe me, you'll know when it's time. There'll be this pause, this silence. Oh, man, that's when it's righteous: she looks at you, you look at her, the whole bit." Here Jocko himself fell silent, stared off over the water. He was a romantic.

"Wow," I said. "Then?"

"That's when it happens."

I wanted to grab Jocko by the collar, but he was bigger.

"What?" I said.

Jocko gave me a dazed look. "Man, don't you know?"

I can now look back and dismiss all this — call it folly, hormonal excess, the awkwardness of youth — but the fact is that the confused wants I had then added up to a kind of loneliness I cannot recall without a sort of tender pang. It seemed a sure thing that whatever coaching Jocko might give me, and whatever muddled plans I might have had for myself, this boat was one party I wasn't going to join.

My steadiest companion was the view. The M/V Northern Sea was cruising the narrow inside passage between the islands and the coast. Spruce-forested slopes rose steeply out of the water, their dark green threaded at intervals with waterfalls. The mountains rose up a thousand miles. A flock of seagulls hovered in our wake, now drifting forward over the deck, now falling back. And once, a bald eagle appeared above our heads, hung there a minute, then slipped away toward shore.

By the end of the second day I had pretty much exhausted whatever means of killing time the boat had to offer. There is only so long you can look at a boat wake, and only so many cups of coffee you can drink in the cafeteria with its rearward view of that same wake. The view of the green slopes to shoreward was beautiful, as was the water changing color throughout the day, but after a while even this got to be all the same. A few times a day I would trade in the view for the claustrophobia of the Voyager Lounge, which had no view at all, and with its clean formica booths could have been a cheaper version of almost any bar, anywhere.

Late on the second night, with everyone bedded down, I lay propped on an elbow and watched islands slip by in the seam between the water and the sky. The steady drone of the engines covered everyone's breathing. A few couples had pitched tents for privacy, away from the rest, their nylon domes colonizing the open deck space out beyond the protection of the roof. More than one glowed from a flashlight inside; I could see shadows move against the nylon. I counted: there were probably at least six people making love within twenty feet of where I lay. Not to mention what was going on below decks. I had seen them during the day, the old couples, coming up to our deck for the air and sun, strolling hand in hand. A whole cargo of love, I figured. As I began to drowse, I couldn't help but think of fair Bernice, Lori, and the other women bedded down around me, their features softened in sleep, lips drawn into the hint of a smile, the warm weight of their flesh holding them to the earth with something like the force of love. It was this weight of women asleep, drawn down into depths I couldn't reach — it was this weight that I wanted to get under, to draw over me like a warm blanket, and so find my night's shelter in their pure breath, their dreams like snow.

It was during that night that the old man died. The story went around: it was sudden, probably a heart attack, hit him during a cribbage game. Early the next morning, I saw him unloaded while we were docked at Sitka. I leaned over the rail and watched the pink casket carried down the ramp. They slid it into the back of the ambulance like gunners loading a gigantic shell. I realized that they must have had the casket on board, just in case. How many more? Somewhere deep in the hold, a storeroom stuffed with caskets. Pale pink. I had once before seen a pink casket: it was used to carry away the Russian Orthodox malacologist who lived (and died) across the street from us. He was to be cremated, and from these two cases I figured that pink meant temporary. The Russian died in his sleep when I was ten years old. He was an old man, and slept sitting upright so that his lungs would not fill with fluid. I knelt by our living room window and prayed as four men carried the casket across the steeply sloped lawn. I do not remember what I prayed for: that the men would not slip on the grass, that the coffin was securely latched. As a young man he had been sentenced to death by the Bolsheviks; his books on mollusks had been translated into thirty-two languages; he once yelled at me for throwing my frisbee in his azaleas.

Later that day, the priest surfaced on our deck to round up recruits for a memorial mass. Apparently he already had the Neil Young enthusiast lined up to do a song.

"I was hoping some of you people would come down," he said, ambushing me at the starboard rail. "Liven things up a little." This priest was maybe ten, fifteen years older than me. Still a young man. He liked his work. "It might be a good time," he said.

I had quit church before I got to high school, and now resented my urge to obey him. At the opposite rail from where I stood, Neil Young strummed langorously: "Yeah, yeah, hey, hey. Rock and roll is here to stay." Somebody else fooled with a mandolin. A group played cards quietly on the green indoor/outdoor carpet, all around them the jumbled stuff of our encampment: sleeping bags twisted like fitful sleepers, the contents of backpacks disgorged in heaps, rough-napped wool, denim, down jackets, aluminum cookware, clever camping stoves, bottles of cheap wine, food in Ziploc bags. From a huddled group of my deck-mates sweet clouds of marijuana smoke rose and drifted out over the stern. It seemed an odd sort of crowd to be inviting to an old man's funeral. But the priest was waiting for an answer.

"I've never been to a funeral," I said.

The priest just chuckled, a babyish sound.

"I figured you people were adventuresome types."

There was no mistaking the bullish force of his intent. A man under those robes. The only way I could get him to leave was to ask him what time.

In the Panorama Room of the Northern Sea were the eighty smiling faces of the Tacoma Catholic Seniors, pale, wrinkled, tilted up a little too high, the winking disks of their eyeglasses all trained on me. I was late and the priest, who had just stepped up to the altar, was waiting for me to take a seat. I felt thirteen again, standing idiotically beside the altar, the bungling altar boy. I tried not to look anyone in the eye, scanning quickly the few rows of folding chairs, then behind them the hard-backed swivel chairs around the card tables, and beyond that the ranks of big-backed easy chairs going back to where blazing windows gave out onto the ocean. The windows blinded me for a moment so that I had to shade my eyes with one hand while I looked again at the front rows. Every seat was taken. The priest sniffed, chairs creaked; I saw mouth-to-ear whispers, heard the crackling cellophane of lozenges, cleared throats, sighs.

"Psst."

She was sitting close by on a padded bench, a woman in a lime-green pants suit, her V-neck blouse white with small black polka dots. She was smiling at me. Next to her another old woman dabbed her eyes with a handkerchief. The first woman crooked a finger at me and made scrunching movements to one side to clear a space between her and her crying friend. I had no choice but to squeeze in. I tried to make myself feel thin, and breathed through my mouth to keep from smelling their perfume. We all watched the priest. He worked behind a folding altar covered with a white cloth. On a separate stand behind were the two gold chalices of the Sacrament; the cone-shaped cup for wine, the shallow bowl-shaped one for the communion hosts. He wore a white vestment, green stripe running down the middle. Added some zip, I figured.

Without much introduction he signaled for the music. Neil Young made his way to the altar. Neil wore his hair sort of nouveau-biker: clean and long, with a well-combed bush of a beard. He was paunchy, so that his guitar rode well out in front. He was dressed head to foot in camouflage. I expected nothing short of disaster: Neil slamming through "A Man Needs a Maid" in bad falsetto while the old folks stared in baffled silence. The priest would be embarrassed, and we would all be happy to have this over with.

I was wrong. Neil knew his business, and with a few brisk chord changes he swung into "Michael, Row Your Boat Ashore," as if this was something he did every day. And the crowd didn't just join in: they *pounced* on it. Everybody. Eighty voices: sweet, cracked, hoarse, strong, loud. These people took to singing like geese to formation.

"Sister help to trim the sails. Ah-lay-loo. Ya."

All around the room heads bobbed, toes tapped. The woman on my left held the soggy handkerchief to her nose and sang through it, her voice breathy as a cracked flute, wandering in search of the notes, but singing just the same. The woman in the lime-green suit was pressed against my right side, and I could feel the notes rise inside her as she sang. I felt her take breath and push it out again like bagpipes. Her face was flushed with the effort, but happy, as though singing was some of her best work. I joined in, softly at first, then louder so I could hear myself.

"River Jordan, deep and wide. Ah-lay-loo. Ya."

It came from the back: a line of harmony above the melody, slowly swelling and filling out, high and clear. Others throughout the crowd picked this up, and then some of the men dropped into a bass line. The sudden expansion into three-part harmony made the room seem dense, as if the number of people had tripled. I craned around to see who had started it; it was Lori, Bernice and some of the others, standing back by the windows, where the light made them almost silhouettes, swaying, singing. Jocko was there, too, singing as intently as if he had grown up in a church choir. Here and there throughout the crowd women were moved to scat a few lines. One table improvised some call-and-response. A group of white-haired men — old glee-club buddies, maybe — started fooling with a basso continuo. Neil Young went through ten verses, fifteen, and seemed to be making up more as he went along. The priest sang with his hands clasped, in his face a hint of the smugness to be expected of one who performs miracles daily.

"This old boat is a music boat. Ah-lay-loo. Ya."

Finally it seemed time for an ending, and somehow we knew just what to do: the tempo slowed, and we sang the long "A — " and held it for a few beats while voices filled in the harmonies. There was hope in it, and defiance and a little rage. And at last: " — MEN!" In this last note there was something like pure joy, and what sounded to me like all the satisfaction you will ever find in a room full of mortal beings.

Neil Young walked stiffly back to his seat, the last vibrations still ringing in his guitar. As he went past, I could see his underarms soaked with sweat.

The priest moved into that big silence with palms turned up to heaven.

"Dearly beloved."

His calm, full voice made it seem as if everything had been summed up. I saw what priests get paid for.

"We are gathered here today to celebrate a mass in memory of Frank Kinnealy."

The woman in lime nudged me with her elbow, bent her head near my shoulder. "Beautiful," she whispered.

The woman on my left nudged me in turn, and managed to produce a thin smile as she nodded her head, agreeing that yes, the singing had been lovely indeed. I straightened up and took a deep breath. I wasn't the only one breathing hard; I saw flushed faces, chests rising and falling. Our expended effort hung in the air with its own smell, like the warm, moist breath of some great animal.

The mass moved quickly, without embellishments. I still knew most of the responses, felt them come bubbling up out of my chest without trying. But as the heat of the singing wore off, I soon found myself bored as ever, trying not to fidget between the hips of the old ladies pressed against me on either side. When it came time for the eulogy, people edged out of the way of a man who made it to the altar from the back of the room. He was big, with broad shoulders and large hands. At one time he had been bigger. He faced us in a green plaid shirt and string tie, his jaws square, strong-muscled, eyes vague behind very thick glasses.

"A bag of wind," whispered the woman with the soggy handkerchief, close to my left ear.

Suddenly I feared for the man, watching him clasp and unclasp his big hands. He looked as though he wished he had written something down.

"I didn't know Frank Kinnealy real good," he began. I was surprised by the authority in his voice. Church Deacon? Union organizer? "But I did know him to be an exceptional human being."

"Kinnealy hated his guts, is the real truth," whispered the woman on my left.

"Don't you listen to my sister." This in my right ear from the woman in the lime green pants suit.

"... Elks lodge, benefits for the Children's Hospital, Friends of Seattle-Tacoma Airport, we all knew Frank to be the most warm-hearted ..."

"Spencer," said the soggy woman. "They say he killed a man in the army, but got off."

"... three undefeated seasons as a Little League coach ..."

"Shot him in the back."

"Don't believe a word of it," said Lime. "She was sweet on him, once. And now he's a bee in her bustle."

"Tell my sister to hush," said Soggy.

Spencer was now moving his hands impressively, the string tie swinging a bit as he turned to face first one side of the room, then the other.

"... a few more men like Frank Kinnealy, and the world would be a better place. And if I dare say," — Spencer's voice suddenly lowered, conspiratorial — "heaven in all her glory became a little bit better place last night."

Spencer nodded, confident that he had won the crowd. He made his way back to his seat, walking with an awkwardness that in a younger man would have been a swagger.

"The sin of pride," whispered the soggy woman.

The priest, not missing a beat, rose from his chair, stepped toward the congregation, lifted his arms.

"Let us pray."

We bowed our heads, the priest once more shifting the mass smoothly through the gears. He flourished the chalices, poured the wine, performed the miracles, sang us through the Great Amen, and bid the people come forward for Communion. I declined — though I almost did out of a nostalgic urge to feel again the papery host on my tongue, and maybe this time defy the nuns' old admonition not to chew. Finally, the priest blessed us and bid us go in peace to love and serve the Lord.

"The singing was beautiful," said the lime woman, right off the bat. "It's wonderful, so many young people on board, and so talented."

Her sister, on my left, slid long blue-veined hands along her thighs. "My husband would have loved that. He was a real music lover."

Just then a man stopped in front of her, making yukelele-sized strumming gestures and bouncing a little in one hip.

"These kids are pretty good, eh?" He gave me a wink. He offered an arm to the soggy woman. She placed a hand on my forearm, patted once, then allowed herself to be hoisted away.

Lime leaned close and whispered, "He's been after her this whole trip."

I watched them join the flow of people moving out of the room. The old man was laughing; he bent down to whisper something in her ear.

"Did you know him?" said the lime woman.

"The guy who, you mean the—"

"Kinnealy. I didn't either. And my sister—" she made a dismissing gesture toward the door where they had gone out—"she didn't really either. She just likes to cry over men."

The room was emptying out, except for those who were settling down to play cards, or taking their knitting to the big chairs by the windows. All my deck-mates had cleared out. The priest was wiping the chalices before putting them back in a plush-lined case of the sort you might put a trumpet in. I wondered if it was time for me to leave.

"I'm Roberta Grainge," said the lime woman.

Her skin was surprisingly smooth, though spotted with age. She had rubbed rouge into her cheeks, though I could see that there was a little natural color there, too. Her lips were thin, without lipstick.

"I'm Todd. Bannister."

Roberta returned a quick smile. She did not wear glasses, and her eyes were sharp, bright, pale blue with flecks of green. She turned them away, sighing. "Ah, well, they say it was his heart."

I nodded.

"Same as took my husband. But this was a nice, a nice service." She looked down at her lap, where she rubbed one forearm, the muscles stringy there under the loose skin.

"You usually sing at funerals?" I asked.

Roberta looked up, surprised. "Sure. Why not?" She laughed. "You act as if there's something wrong."

"I've never been to one before, that's all. I didn't know they did singing."

"Never been? You're lucky, I guess. That's all I do, go to funerals. Rehearsals, my husband called them. Always the joker. Why not sing? People should sing more often." She laughed, girlish now. "I sing in the street. I'm not embarrassed. *La-la-la.*"

"I bet you're not," I said.

Her laughter was easy, ready as breath.

"We had lots of music at Robert's—that's my husband. He loved singing."

"That's nice. I mean, I'm sorry."

Roberta looked up at me sharply. "Are you married?"

I shook my head. "You think it's a good idea?"

"Of course!" she said, in almost a shriek. "It's a wonderful relationship. Of course now, today, a lot of people just fool around."

"Do you?"

She gave me a dark look, but seemed pleased nonetheless. "That's an impertinent question."

I found myself just looking at Roberta. The skin from her cheekbones back to her ears was tight, polished. Her hair still had some steel color mixed in with the white; strands of hair curled behind her delicate ears, stray wisps floated free. I guessed that it had once been long and straight.

"You should come down here more often, you people, come and see us."

I had two opposing urges: to excuse myself and head back up to the sundeck in a hurry, and to step forward here toward who knows what. It was the last that won out, and I went ahead, embarrassed to find myself speaking words that have been said so many times on television by men with expensive-looking hair: "How about dinner?"

"Hoo! You don't waste any time."

"Does that mean yes?"

"No." She was suddenly prim. "I have a previous engagement." Then her sly smile came back. "There have been men seeking my attentions."

We agreed on lunch for the following day. She gave me her cabin number and a time.

The next day, I was below decks early. I had put on my good flannel shirt and my newer pair of jeans. I ducked into the Men's to check my hair, and to make sure the zits I had popped that morning weren't oozing. My hair was clean, but stiff-looking, I thought. Needs body. I had washed it that morning, standing goosepimpled in the dribble of cold water that passed for a shower, rubbing up lather on a bar of soap to use as shampoo. I used the same lather to shave what little beard I had, stooping before the dim, warped mirror. I now regarded myself: clean — glowing, even — a man of the wider world.

I was still fifteen minutes early when I found her cabin door and knocked. There was a sound something like her voice that I thought said, "Come in." I knocked again, and heard the same sound, so I opened the door. What I saw was a woman stepping out of a shower. She seemed smaller than the day before, and was wearing only her hair. Roberta stooped awkwardly and reached for a towel, but not before I saw too much: her spine curved into a hunch, her skin like cream of wheat spotted with raisins. Her skin sagged where her breasts had been, and again where it made a flap over her belly. Between the sharp points of her hip bones, pubic hair hid like a mouse.

"You there. Todd. I'm not ready. Get out."

I was backing out as she said these words, and I shut the door as quietly as I could, trying to feel as though I had not been there at all. I then spent a very long time sitting on the floor in the hallway, my knees drawn up, head in my hands, resisting the urge to bolt. What killed me was that I was on a boat: there was no place to go.

At last Roberta came out. I couldn't look above her knees. Her pants suit was brown this time.

"You startled me," she said. Her voice was steady.

"I thought you said come in."

"I was singing. I couldn't hear a thing. I thought it was locked."

I made a sound something like a cow does, only shorter. "I'm so sorry," I said.

"I should have locked the door. I'm—sometimes I forget things."

I hugged my knees, trying to be small.

"Well, come on," Roberta said. "Aren't you going to get up?"

I got to my feet, feeling like the schoolboy being lectured. I hung my head. "We don't have to have lunch," I said.

"You." Roberta tugged my arm. "Listen to me. Look at me."

Roberta had put on make-up. After I barged in on her, she had calmly powdered and rouged, carefully darkened her brows.

She was stern, then eager. "Listen. You think catching me out of my drawers was a big deal. Well, it's not. There was a time, maybe—there was some excitement, then — but those days — do you know what this body is now?"

She laid a hand on her chest, fingers spread.

"No, ma'am," I said.

"This is a medical specimen. Doctors handle me now, Todd. And they handle me plenty. There isn't a part of me hasn't had them feeling it. They talk about dignity! My body is rags, and I'll be glad to put them off when my day comes. They're only borrowed to begin with, anyway. The body's a loaner, my husband used to say. You've got a lifetime lease, and then *pftf*!"

Roberta wasn't finished, but at some point during the rest of what she had to say I offered her my arm, and we made our way slowly down the hall toward the cafeteria. What followed was something that I would understand many years later to have been a perfectly ordinary lunch with an ordinary old woman. It involved tuna sandwiches and chicken noodle soup, I think, and much talk of Roberta's children and grandchildren. In the course of things I gave a modest account of myself, my doings and my dreams, many of which I now like to think of as having come true. For I did go to college, my wages from the cannery covering almost two years tuition at a state school, and there I managed to find the wife that I daily strive to be worthy of, and launched myself into the suit-and-tie career that makes it possible for me to own property and buy a new car every Presidential election year. At the time though, the recital of these hopes of mine — sitting across a table from a woman who had what I took to be a supernatural ability to listen to what I wanted to say, sitting by a window with its view of the most beautiful part of this great earth — this ordinary recital, I say, took on a sort of drama, an elegance, even. It was as though my life had been thrown at last on the big screen, where my voice was full and speaking in a larger world.

After we were done, and after I had annoyed Roberta a little by insisting that I pay, it seemed only a logical extension of events that the voice of the ship's captain crackled over the loudspeaker, announcing that a whale had been sighted off the port bow.

We were in the hallway leading to the Panorama Room. Roberta had a hand on my arm, rocking side to side with short steps. The hunch between her shoulder-blades made her head push forward, her face down. She stopped, so that she could look up at me, bright with excitement.

"I've never seen one," she said.

"Neither have I."

It took a little while for us to make our way to the Panorama Room, where there were already a few dozen people pressed to the line of windows to port. We made a space for ourselves, Roberta pressed against my right side, one hand holding onto my arm. We had drawn near to Juneau. The mountains back of Juneau are draped with glaciers and rise several million miles more or less straight out of the sea.

It was hard to see into the glare. I scanned the wrinkled surface of the water, but saw nothing.

"I can't see so well," Roberta said. "Where?"

"He's down now," somebody said.

"He was about two hundred yards out," said another voice, which I recognized as Jocko's. I leaned back to look: the row of gray and white heads was interrupted by those of Jocko, Lori and Neil Young, who stood together, squinting out with everyone else.

Just then most of the people gasped.

"There!" Fingers pointed. "There he is."

I saw it: a smooth black shape humping out of the water, about 150 yards out. There was a spray of white.

"Thar she blows," said one of the men, and every-one laughed.

"Finback."

"Minke. Look at those ridges."

"Harold. Harold has the book."

"He's gone down to get it."

"I still say finback. Look how long."

The whale was swimming on the surface now; you couldn't see either the head or the tail, just the smooth black mound rising and falling.

"Just look at that," Roberta said.

The whale continued to swim on the surface, until suddenly the mound rose higher than usual, slowly burgeoning into the light so that its flanks gleamed and you could almost make out a lighter shade on the underbelly, and then up it came — I had seen too many photographs to believe that it really happened this way — the great black tail up in the air, water streaming from the flukes, and then down it went out of sight.

"It's sounding now."

"He'll be down thirty seconds."

"No. Forty-five."

We counted, everyone in the room trying to hold their breaths in longer than usual. I thought of swimming in the greenish dark, deeper than I wanted to imagine, blubber warming the slick length of my body, smooth strokes of the tail, mouth shoveling shrimp. I felt Roberta move beside me, as if in agreement.

"There!"

"Oooh!"

"So close," Roberta said.

The whale was only fifty yards away now, swimming alongside the boat, its tail plunging out of sight, then rising to the surface, churning the sea to white froth. You could see its blow hole open and close like a mouth, releasing sharp blasts of air that carried water up with them in a mist. Then the whale rolled part way onto its side, its side fin waving like a hand. You could see its eye, tucked at the corner of the giant mouth. Sad? Sanguine?

"Look at that," I said.

Roberta looked, and I watched her face, bright with the light from the water, smiling. Then I looked at the others, bodies leaned toward the glass, faces lit with the glare of the sea, happy as if come into some sudden bounty, though without surprise, as if it were something that, though not seen before, they had all along imagined to be theirs.

MICHAEL LEE WEST

Obstetrics

from The Kennesaw Review

Here it is in a pecan shell: there is something wrong with the landscape in middle Tennessee. It refuses to change, especially in summer—limestone piercing the ground like broken bones, cowboys driving pickup trucks with Pabst bottles anchored between their Levi-darkened thighs, and miles of shapeless green branches. Those are cedar trees, guardians of this state which, toward the west, slides right into the Mississippi River. I have always heard—though it is not a proven scientific fact—that ticks live in the cedars, spending their whole lives waiting for people to walk beneath them. And it's true. I've picked off many a tick after strolling around the edge of the woods. They say cedars are the only trees that survive in limestone, and middle Tennessee is built on a shelf of rock.

Anyway, you can imagine my mental state. Here I am, Thelma Faye Jones, a widow-woman living in the midst of all these cedars. You wouldn't believe the things I have seen all these years. I know that Little Buster Purdy's brain would not have been damaged if Dr. Lane had delivered the boy by Caesarean section, and Fred

Hall is suing Dr. Burke just to get money for a swimming pool. I'll tell you one thing, I know plenty. Now you probably think Thelma Faye Jones isn't my real name, but it is. How I ended up in a town called Cumberland is another story, but I have something else on my mind.

I'm a nurse at Cumberland General Hospital. Obstetrics is my specialty; I have worked the night shift for twenty-seven years. Don't get me wrong—I can work days if I wanted. I have my connections. However, there is something almost holy about being awake when the town is shuttered and sleeping. And, being a widow, I would rather work all night and get paid for it than sit home, scared to death, a shotgun propped on my knees. I live in the country, down a curved gravel road with no neighbors for miles. Cumberland might be small, but it has its share of rednecks and good old boys who have turned into savage criminals.

The obstetrics wing—or OB as the nurses call it— has the reputation of being the most cheerful wing at Cumberland General. The rooms are painted yellow, and cheerful gingham curtains hang on windows with southern exposures, even if they do face a scrubby cedar forest. In the daytime, rooms are flooded with light, washing onto the mechanical beds and the smiling mothers, nursing their newborns. That is one reason I like working in obstetrics. Intensive care, for example, depresses me, with its peculiar smell of death and unwashed skin. I can't tell you the other reason I work in OB. Anyway, there is something else you need to know.

At 1:27A.M. the emergency room calls, informing us a woman in labor just checked in—after midnight all patients must be admitted through our emergency department. I volunteer because it is boring to watch Dottie, the charge nurse, file her nails. When I reach the emergency room, I am shocked to discover the patient is Lynnie Clampitt! Even if you don't know her personally, you might know someone like her. There are rumors she was a cocktail waitress in Nashville—in a bar with bouncers, where the waitresses took turns swinging over the audience in big wooden hoops.

Oh, I know all about Lynnie Clampitt. She has deep auburn hair hanging in frizzy curls around her shoulders, green eyes rimmed in dark lashes, and a sharp little nose; she reminds me of an attractive fox. It is obvious she has watched her weight during her pregnancy. Lynnie is wearing an expensive maternity sundress, white lace threaded with pale blue ribbon, and she appears sunburned on the front half of her body. Every summer, the labor patients sport one-sided tans, for obvious reasons. It always seems to me that those women ought to find something more productive than working on one-sided suntans. And it is common knowledge that high temperatures are contraindicated in pregnancy (now there's a word with a ring to it, *contraindicated*). It literally cooks fetal brain cells. I look at Lynnie Clampitt and smile. "Well, you sure do have a nice tan," I say, watching the emergency room aide guide Lynnie into the wheelchair.

"You should see the back of my legs," Lynnie says. Her voice is real country, like she has been raised up in the hollers and came to the city for refinement. "They're just as white as flour sacks." She rubs her abdomen and sits down. I hold my breath, almost expecting to see powdery flour waft upward from her limbs as she arranges herself in the wheelchair. "This belly of mine got in the way."

I want to say "do tell," or at least inform her that "belly" is an undignified word for a *gravid* abdomen. I am a real stickler for proper obstetrical terms. When you have been in the medical world as long as I have, you develop an intolerance for lay words; it begins to sound like baby talk after a while. And it's not just me, either; I know plenty of nurses and doctors who feel the same way. In fact, the Chief of Obstetrics and Gynecology, Dr.

319

Robert Whitcomb, always jokes about his society-wife, Mary Jane, who creates euphemisms for every body part. That Mary Jane is something else, wearing dresses from Nashville and all that jewelry and still can't stop drinking. She's had a face-lift, too. But I've nearly said too much. As I push Lynnie's wheelchair down the hall, I suddenly realize her husband is not with her. "Is your husband here, honey?" I ask and immediately wish I hadn't.

"He's out of town." Lynnie wipes her eyes. "I had to drive myself to the hospital. And I forgot my suitcase. Left it in the bedroom."

I am so shocked, I squeeze the plastic handles of the wheelchair. I suppose you are wondering why I am all worked up over Lynnie. Well, it's because of her husband Claude. He was my son-in-law until he left my daughter Bobbie Ruth, left her for Lynnie. My daughter thinks all women who chase married men are lowdown you-know-whats. I consider this as I push the wheelchair across the green floor, listening to my shoes squeak on the tile.

"Oh, no." She grips the wheelchair. "Not another one."

"A contraction?" I say, just to let her know I am not ignorant. It is a matter of honor after what she did to Bobbie Ruth. I think: *May your labor be long and complicated.* Then I quickly think of a prayer for Lynnie and her baby, to cancel the other thought. I am ashamed of myself — me, Thelma Faye, a licensed nurse. "Breathe in and out," I tell her. "That's right, honey. You've got the hang of it."

Dottie and I settle Lynnie into a labor room. We administer an enema, examine her cervix, attach a fetal monitor. "Can you please reach my husband?" Lynnie asks, shifting in the mechanical bed. "He doesn't know I'm in labor. His name is Claude Clampitt."

As if I didn't know. Dottie glances at me sideways — she knows all about Claude and Bobbie Ruth, of course—and nods at Lynnie. "Sure, dear," she says. "We'll call him." Claude is vice-president of Kountry Vittles, a restaurant chain in Tennessee, Mississippi, Alabama, and Georgia which started right here in Cumberland. He makes a fortune now, but when he was married to Bobbie Ruth, he never had a dollar in his wallet. Five months before Lynnie entered their lives, Claude was promoted to vice-president. "Honey," I told her when he left, "you were almost a Yuppie." Bobbie Ruth laughed. "No, Mama. Claude isn't a Yuppie," she said. "He's more than a Yuppie. According to *Money* magazine, he's a high incomer."

Lynnie shifts in the bed and looks up at me. "If you can call the Kountry Vittles on Battlefield Road," she says, "I'd sure appreciate it. And if he's not there, could you just leave a message with the night manager?" As she presses her head into the pillow, her cheeks shine in the lamplight. For a moment, I feel no mercy as I picture her beautiful Victorian house, the one that should have been Bobbie Ruth's. Sometimes on my way to work, I drive by it, admiring the little widow's walks, gingerbread trim, stained glass windows. And that isn't all—Lynnie drives all over town in a gray Seville, wearing dark sunglasses, diamond earbobs, and ruffled pastel dresses. I glance at the fetal monitor. Another contraction is beginning, and I am unsure of my ability to conceal petty feelings for the duration of her labor. Lynnie chased Claude for months. From the beginning, she set out to win him from Bobbie Ruth, and she did, cracking up that little family. Before the divorce, Bobbie Ruth stayed home in their red-brick duplex with their two-year-old son Beau, worrying about toilet training and wallpaper patterns and perfecting recipes for lemonade. All that time, Claude and Lynnie were drinking piña coladas at the Hyatt Regency Nashville.

After Lynnie's contraction ends, I examine her. Her cervix is only three centimeters dilated, and the contractions are four minutes apart—not severe, not yet. I pull up the sheet and hand her the call button. "If you need me, just push this buzzer." Dottie and I walk to the nurses' station—just a little yellow Formica counter, with swivel chairs and a metal chart wheel. Dottie hooks a chair with her foot, sits down, and opens Lynnie's chart. Now, Dottie is just about the sweetest woman you will ever meet; she is a dedicated R.N., too. I watch her pick up a pen, writing nurses' notes. Lynnie is our only labor patient.

"Well, Dottie." I pull out a chair and sit down. "I can't call Claude, and you know why."

"I already figured that." She looks up from the chart. "I thought they were lovebirds. Shouldn't he be here? I mean, this *is* their first child."

"But not Claude's first," I remind her, picking up the Cumberland phone book—it's as tiny as a *TV Guide*. "Don't forget about Beau."

"You know what I mean. It makes me wonder if they're having problems." Dottie leans across the counter and grabs the phone book. "I can't get over how she talks, can you? So *country*. It's a wonder Claude can understand a word she says."

"I'm sure he can," I say. "But you never know." The truth is, you never know the truth about a person's private life, and most of the time it is useless to speculate. Still, before Lynnie's baby is born, I expect to learn more about her life than I care to know. That's the nature of obstetrics. I know too much already.

Before the divorce, Claude swore on a Bible, *Bible*, mind you, that he was not involved with another woman. Of course, by then he had moved Lynnie to Cumberland, set her up at the Colonial Inn. When Bobbie Ruth found a motel key in the glove compartment of his car, Claude told her *he* hadn't put it there. (I'm leaving a lot out—like the time Bobbie Ruth bundled up Beau and drove around the parking lot of the Colonial Inn, searching for Claude's car. She found it, too.)

After Claude left, Bobbie Ruth rented the other side of the duplex and enrolled in the local secretarial school. I helped out as much as I could, watching Beau of an evening or inviting her over for supper when I wasn't working. We usually ate on the screened porch, which was built the year before my husband Royce was killed. It happened so long ago, I can't remember everything, but I do know if Royce hadn't been killed, I would have divorced him. When he drank, which was often, he hit me up side of the head. One night his car stalled on the railroad track, and while he was tinkering under the hood, a train slammed into him. I ended up with double indemnity, which did not, I assure you, make up for living with him. Bobbie Ruth was only two years old, so she doesn't remember Royce. I was already working the night shift at Cumberland General; in those days, I brought little Bobbie Ruth right to work with me. She slept in the doctors' lounge. Dr. Robert and the nurses made her airplanes out of tongue blades.

Anyway, Royce and I had terrible fights about cutting down trees to make room for the porch. Royce was stubborn. Knowing how I felt about cedars, he uprooted a large one from the woods and planted it right in front of the new porch. That tree grew sideways, as if deliberately blocking my view of the mountains. After Royce's funeral, I chopped down that tree, and everyone said it was the best view in Cumberland. It always cheered Bobbie Ruth to watch the sun drop behind the hills, listening to the bull frogs, waiting for the lightning-bugs to rise up from the weeds.

One afternoon, I invited Bobbie Ruth over for blackberry cobbler. As we ate on the screened porch, on the little wicker table, it nearly broke my heart to see how much weight she had lost. When she lifted the spoon, her wrist bones almost punctured the skin. I knew she still loved Claude, awful as he treated her. Bobbie Ruth was an attractive girl, but during her marriage, she had allowed herself to grow soft around the edges; she stopped wearing make-up or perfume. She was a good wife and mother, but the truth was, she didn't know how to handle men. Of course, I have always believed that by the time a woman learned how to handle a man, she no longer wanted one. I also suspected marriage did not work for everyone, but I knew what did. When I tried to explain my ideas to Bobbie Ruth, she slapped her napkin against the table and stared at me. "Well, you're really one to talk, Mama," she said, scooping up Beau, carrying him on one hip to her car, that pitiful old Volvo Claude bought the year he finished graduate school.

You are probably wondering what happened to make Claude fall out of love with Bobbie Ruth, who was, after all, senior class beauty. Beauty has nothing to do with holding onto a man — believe me, it doesn't. Some men — not all, mind you — fall in love, get married, and turn their wives into mothers. They start in subtle ways, they'll say, "Honey, would you mind putting pimentos in the potato salad? My mother always fixed it that way." And before you know it, you are putting hospital corners on the dishcloths because you-know-who did, too. You gradually stop cooking things you love — like hot chicken salad casserole and praline cheesecake — because *he* refuses to eat it. Then, before you know it, he says you remind him of his mother; and the funny thing is, you realize you *are* his mother, and when that happens, you might as well take a lover or get a divorce or join every woman's club that will not blackball you.

And Cumberland is snooty. It is a town full of magnolias and old money. When Bobbie Ruth announced she was moving to Nashville, I understood why. Still, I tried to talk her out of it. Just thinking about her and little Beau leaving made me lonesome. Bobbie Ruth wouldn't listen. She told me to mind my own business, or she might start meddling with mine. She sold her duplex, moved to Nashville, and landed a job with an attorney. And she refused to answer, as usual, when I asked if her new boss was single.

Of course, I am receptive to gossip, even though I have too much dignity to spread it. I believe in the Holy Bible. I believe life keeps circling until you almost know the patterns by heart. I have never been the topic of anyone's bridge party, even though I live with the possibility. I have my ways of finding things out — all nurses do. If you want to know who is sleeping with the undertaker or who has cancer of the prostate or who is a pervert, just spend some time in a hospital!

It wasn't too long after Bobbie Ruth and little Beau moved to Nashville when I heard Claude was running around on Lynnie — with a waitress at the local Kountry Vittles. Well, the girl had an emergency appendectomy right here in Cumberland General. Claude never darkened her door, and she was in the hospital five whole days.

One year later, I was in Memphis for a continuing-education course in fetal distress, and I saw Claude Clampitt drive in front of the Peabody Hotel. A blond with a frizzed-out permanent was wrapped around him. I don't see how he was able to drive. Anyway, there was no mistaking his car, a navy Jaguar, with custom license plates which said FOOD. That Jaguar had a cellular phone and a bar. I knew because he called Bobbie Ruth all the time from his car, arranging visits with his son. He casually referred to his luxuries. "I'm in my car, on the way to Birmingham," he would say. When he called Bobbie Ruth, he would begin each conversation by pinpointing his geography, as if she was still his wife, as if she still cared.

Lynnie was six months pregnant when I saw her in Kroger, pushing a cart down the frozen food aisle. I thought to myself, *she's hoping that baby will be a boy, to replace Beau.* You see, Claude never cared one tinker's damn about his son; he loved him, no doubt, but he did not begin to show it until after the divorce. All at once, he seemed to realize he had a little boy. It was as if the divorce seemed to improve his vision. He picked up Beau every weekend, returning him to Bobbie Ruth with stuffed animals, Fisher-Price toys, expensive suits with miniature bow ties. It wasn't long before Bobbie Ruth's duplex looked like a Sears catalogue. And that wasn't all—Claude and Lynnie took the boy to Disney World Gulf Shores; zoos in New Orleans, Knoxville, and Memphis. One blistering summer, they rented a house on the Maine coast. When Beau returned, Bobbie Ruth found a travel brochure in his little suitcase, and she read it until the paper became thin and wrinkled from so much handling.

You know how some folks are—once they taste adultery, they cannot stop. I tried to explain my ideas to Bobbie Ruth, but she refused to listen. She was ready to start a new life, but all I could think of was Lynnie swimming in her new heated pool. I always pictured maids carrying piña coladas and margaritas on silver trays. I couldn't stop thinking about her because she drove all over town in her Seville, with the astro-roof wide open, blowing and blowing her auburn hair. I wanted to cry when I considered Bobbie Ruth's situation in Nashville, waiting for clothes to go on sale with money she earned from typing all those long legal documents for her attorney, who, it turns out, is divorced too.

Since her move to Nashville, the situation has actually improved. Distance helps the mind distort the past, it really does. Now, Beau is four, and he is the happiest little boy you've ever seen. He loves his daddy, of course. All I have to do is mention Claude's name, and I can almost see the child's ears growing toward my voice. Bobbie Ruth tries real hard. She rents a townhouse apartment in southwest Nashville, where the crime isn't so bad, with a little brick patio. It is always filled with bicycles, roller skates, baseball equipment. Beau's room is snaked with black wires—Atari games, record player with tape deck, color television, and a complex gerbil cage with yellow plastic mazes running every which way.

From what my daughter tells me, Lynnie has not adjusted to Claude spending time with his son. Why, last July Claude wanted to take the boy to Cape Cod, just the two of them for the weekend—father and son. According to Beau, Lynnie pitched a fit. In the end, she got her way and went with them. So you can see why she probably wants a son of her own, to get Claude's mind off Bobbie Ruth. Everyone says Beau is the spitting image of his mother—except for his nose, which is slightly turned up, a typical Clampitt feature.

Now I see I haven't been completely honest with you. Shortly after Bobbie Ruth moved to Nashville, Claude drove up on weekends. It started out innocent enough, the two of them taking Beau out to dinner, trying to give him a sense of family. Although it hurts me to admit it, she took him to her bed. It was like pulling jaw teeth to get her to tell me about it, too. She said it was just for spite, but I didn't believe her for one minute. I know a love-sick woman when I see one. Then, all of a sudden, Lynnie started driving to Nashville with Claude, ending the dinners and Lord knows what else.

I look at Dottie, she is hanging up the phone. "The manager says they haven't seen Claude." She hands me Lynnie's chart. "Messages have been left at all Kountry Vittles between here and Memphis." She grips the counter and pushes out the chair. "I almost feel sorry for her."

"Don't feel *too* sorry for her," I say, tucking my feet about the base of the chair.

"Well, she didn't steal much when she took Claude away from Bobbie Ruth. Most men stay close to home when their wives are this close to delivery."

"I'm sure he'll be here." As I pick up Lynnie's chart, Dottie walks into the labor room. Now a patient's medical chart is a most interesting record, especially a woman's obstetrical/gynecological history. It is sometimes more than revealing, it can be downright incriminating. Lynnie's due date was July first, two weeks ago. As I turn pages in Lynnie's chart, I notice Dr. Robert Whitcomb is her doctor, which irritates me just a bit; he *could* have warned me to expect Lynnie, after delivering my grandson and who knows what all. When I first met Dr. Robert, years and years ago, he said obstetrics meant, in Latin, "to stand by." And it's true.

I turn through the chart and read Lynnie's birth history: Lynette Sue Birdwell Clampitt, age 28, *Gravida* II, *Para* O, *AB* I. Most women do not realize their doctors categorize pregnancies with Latin names. No matter where you travel, anywhere in the world, these obstetrical terms never change. In case you are curious, *Gravida* means how many times a woman has been pregnant, including her current pregnancy; *Para* represents how many live births she has already had — not including her current pregnancy; *AB* stands for abortions, which in medical jargon means miscarriages (a lay term, by the way) and therapeutic abortions. What I see astonishes me. My mouth opens, closes. My lips feel dry. I blink at the chart, wondering about the pregnancy Lynnie somehow lost, knowing nothing will surprise me. I picture her working as a cocktail waitress, swinging in that wooden hoop. I cannot imagine a baby fitting into her old life. Why, she was too busy chasing Claude! I look up as Dottie walks out of the labor room and sits down. "Lynnie is already dilated seven centimeters," she says. "And she's real upset about Claude. I asked her if she had any relatives I could call like her mother. And do you know what she said?"

"What?" I look at her sideways.

"She said, 'Ma is dead. An L&N train hit her car over in Wilson County.'" Dottie's eyes widen. "What do you think of *that*?"

"Why, an L&N hit Royce Jones, too," I say, remembering when the police called the night he was killed. They asked me to identify the remains; I wanted to refuse, I wanted to say, "You'll just have to find someone else." Of course, Royce had no kin, and I was a nurse; I had a pretty good idea what the police meant by remains. I pictured them spreading out in the darkness with flashlights, searching in the tall weeds, with all those katydids listening.

"Looks like you and Lynnie have something in common." Dottie reaches for Lynnie's chart. "Her mama got killed by a train, *and* she married your son-in-law."

"I'll say this for Claude," I rub my neck, "He was with Bobbie Ruth all through her labor. He not only drove her to the hospital, he came by my house and picked me up. He gave Dr. Robert a whole box of cigars."

"I remember," says Dottie, bending over the chart. "I was on duty."

"That's right," I fold my hands on my lap. "When they brought Beau out of the delivery room, Claude said, 'He's beautiful. I'm in love with him already.'" Then he ordered two dozen red roses for Bobbie Ruth.

"And look how he treated her." Dottie shakes her head. "That ought to tell you something."

"It tells me he's not fit to be married." She stops writing and stares at the chart rack. "Listen, Thelma Faye, if Claude does show up, why don't you pass the medications tonight? I'll stay with Lynnie. At least you'll be spared having to see him."

I do not have time to answer, as the emergency room calls—a patient has arrived in premature labor, and since Dottie is the charge nurse, she stays with the new patient. Lynnie is my patient, and she presses the call button whenever I leave her bedside. She clutches my hand all through the transition phase; she even calls me Ma. "Ma?" she calls out, leaning forward, clutching my arm. "*Ma?*" Is that you, Ma?"

"Now, now." I wipe her forehead with a cloth. "You take it easy."

"I want Claude." She turns her face to the wall. Her shoulders move up and down beneath the thin hospital-issue gown. "He promised me he'd be here," she says to the wall. "He *promised*."

It is not professional for me to speak the truth about Claude's promises. Instead, I lie. "He's on his way right now." I pat her arm. "He'll be here any minute."

"Really?" She faces me, her cheeks are lined with mascara and perspiration. "I was worried. You see, he has mixed feelings about this baby. He already has a little boy, you see." Her face twists as another contraction begins. It is pitiful watching her twist and moan, struggling to give birth to Claude's child. For some reason, Lord help me, she puts me in mind of Bobbie Ruth, all those years ago when she was Claude's wife. Lynnie ruined my child's life, flat out ruined it, yet I am helping her baby into the world. "That was a bad one," Lynnie says when the contraction ends.

I examine her. "Well, it won't be long now," I say, pulling off the sterile gloves. "You're crowning."

"Oh?" She pulls up on her elbows. "Can you see his little head? What color is his hair?"

His, his, his. I check and report the baby appears to have dark hair. "But, of course, all hair looks dark when it's wet," I say.

"Oh, I hope Claude loves this baby." She holds up her hands and blinks at the wedding band. Earlier I had taken off her jewelry, which included a two-carat soli-taire, and locked it in the hospital safe — standard procedure.

"Of course he'll love the baby." I adjust the rate of

her intravenous medication. "It'll be his own flesh and blood."

"You don't understand." She licks her lips. "Claude's son, Beau? Well, he just adores his daddy. And Claude loves him. Whenever he gets mad at me, he throws it up that I was the reason he lost his son." I am not sure how much longer I can listen. It occurs to me that I am getting too old to work the night shift. "Honey," I say before I can stop myself. "I know all about it. I'm Bobbie Ruth's mother."

"Bobbie Ruth?" Lynnie's eyes open, her throat moves as she swallows. *"Claude's* Bobbie Ruth?"

"Well, she's not Claude's anymore." I pretend to examine the intravenous tubing. It is strange to hear her say my daughter's name.

"I'm so sorry." Her eyes are full of tears. "I didn't mean to hurt Bobbie Ruth. Or Beau. I really didn't."

"Honey, I don't hold you responsible." I pat her arm and smile. She looks helpless with her damp hair sticking to the starched white sheets. There are little half-moon circles beneath her eyes. "Please don't cry."

"But you don't understand," Lynnie says, blinking, wiping her cheeks. "I *am* responsible — " She grimaces as another contraction begins. I study the fetal monitor, making sure the baby's heart rate is within the normal range. Satisfied, I bend over Lynnie, and she grasps my hands, clamping down against my bones. When the contraction ends, she settles her head against the pillow. I lean forward and smooth the sheets. "I'm going to call Dr. Robert right now. You're almost ready to deliver. You try to relax between contractions, all right?"

"Wait." She pulls me forward. "I want to tell you something." She swallows, her throat clicks. "I wanted to make sure Claude married me when his divorce was final. I was afraid he might go back to Bobbie Ruth. So I got pregnant. I lost the baby, but I got Claude." She starts crying again.

For a moment, I am unable to speak. I look at my hands, they are trembling in the pale light. "Now listen here, Lynnie," I say. "None of that matters now. Nothing matters but you and your baby."

"You've been so kind to me," she says, reaching for my hand. "I never would've looked at Claude if I'd known you were his mother-in-law." Another contraction begins, and I fix an ice pack, for the pain in her lower spine. In the nurses' station, I phone Dr. Robert. Mary Jane Whitcomb answers in that slippery voice I have learned to hate over the years. "And just who did you say is calling?" she asks.

"OB," I say. We go through this almost every night. It seems to me that Mary Jane ought to have better telephone manners; after all, she has been a doctor's wife for thirty years.

"Are you Miss or Mrs. OB?" Mary Jane asks. "Or would that be Ms. OB?"

"You know who this is, Mary Jane." As I grip the phone, I swear I can smell gin fumes through the receiver. "This is Thelma Faye Jones."

"You!" Mary Jane slams down the phone. Minutes later Dr. Robert walks into the nurses' station.

"I just tried to reach you at home," I say. Of course, I do not mention Mary Jane; it isn't as if he has any control over the woman.

"I wasn't at home," he says. "I was in the doctors' lounge."

"You've got a patient in labor," I say. "Lynnie Clampitt? She's almost ready to deliver. And you *could* have warned me"

"Well, Thelma, I didn't want to upset you." Dr. Robert adjusts his glasses and picks up Lynnie's chart. "Where's Dottie?"

"She's helping Dr. Tucker with a premature delivery."

He glances down the darkened hall. "I'm sorry about not telling you about Lynnie Clampitt," he says, pulling down the chart. "But you won't hold that against me, will you?" He steps forward, grabs my shoulders and kisses me right on the lips. I kiss him back, of course, and now, Lord help me, you know almost everything.

Lynnie's baby is a girl, seven pounds and ten ounces, with plenty of curly dark hair, born shortly before sunrise. She looks just like Claude, who does not make it to the hospital until seven A.M. I have already clocked out and am standing in the nurses' station unpinning my white cap when I see him standing in front of the glass nursery windows. I pick up my purse, hook it over my shoulder, and walk toward him. "Well, Claude," I say. I even smile. "You've got yourself a daughter. She was born at four A.M."

"Now I've got a rich man's family. A boy and a girl." His breath is a blend of alcohol, Lifesavers, and something else I cannot identify. I almost expect to see lipstick stains on his shirt. He grins, and I blink.

"Too bad you missed the delivery," I say. All night I rehearsed this sentence. I think about raising one eyebrow but decide against it.

"It was unavoidable." He turns toward the babies, spreading his palms against the glass. The plastic bassinets are lined up in an uneven row. "She looks like me, doesn't she?" he asks.

I lean forward and look at the baby. She certainly does look like her father, but I have no plans to reinforce the idea. Bobbie Ruth always says Claude would never have left her if Beau had resembled his daddy.

"I'm in love with her already," Claude says. I have heard those words before. "She's beautiful." The baby's eyes are open now, floating around like frog eyes in creek water. "What's wrong with her eyes?" Claude presses his cheek against the glass. "I sure hope she won't be cross-eyed."

I sigh. Most babies have strabismus, but I am not going to tell Claude. "Well, I'm sure she'll outgrow it," I finally say.

Claude's head swivels around. He stares for several seconds, then turns back to the window. "How is Bobbie Ruth?"

"She's fine." I lift my shoulders, watching him. "Some big-shot lawyer in Nashville has fallen in love with her.

"Is that a fact?" Claude's forehead wrinkles, and he faces me, leaning one shoulder against the window. "Is she going to marry him?"

"I reckon you'll have to ask her yourself." I look at him sideways.

He does not speak for several seconds, staring at the tile floor; a muscle twitches in his cheek. "Well," he finally says, "I'd better go in and see Lynnie. What room is she in?"

"Last on your right."

"It was good to see you, Thelma Faye." He pauses. "Does Lynnie know you're Bobbie Ruth's mother?"

"Yes. We got along right well, too."

"That's my Thelma Faye. You haven't changed a bit." He smiles and thumps my shoulder, the way he always used to. Then he walks down the hall and turns into Lynnie's room. She cried two hours after the baby was born. She said, "I'm going to name the baby after my ma. I'm going to name her Elmie." I tried not to look surprised, my own name being Thelma, which practically sounded like Elmie. When I come on duty tonight, I will bring her flowers from my garden: tea roses, cannas, zinnias. I might even buy a little present, maybe a bottle of that perfume, or one of those hand-made baby bibs a woman over in Lebanon sells.

After breakfast in the cafeteria — a scrambled egg and bacon sandwich, along with two cups of the best coffee in town — I walk out of the hospital, down the long sidewalk, toward the parking lot, enjoying the breeze which, I am sorry to say, smells of cedars. I pause in front of the obstetrical wing, blinking as the sun throws polished light into the rooms. I know which window is Lynnie's. The yellow gingham curtains are parted, sucking against the screens. She sits in the mechanical bed, backlit by the morning sun; her shoulders are framed by two pillows.

Claude talks on the phone, holding it to his ear as he paces around the bed. He is wearing a yellow paper gown over his clothes — hospital policy for handling newborns. As he throws his head back and laughs, Lynnie looks sideways, her chin eclipses a corner of light. Even in the thin hospital gown she is attractive. She turns and faces the window, staring beyond me, at the woods across the road. I notice a shape of light, a certain quality, that borrows from the cedars. It reflects against the panes, spilling across the tile floor, toward Claude, toward Lynnie, toward the clear plastic bassinet the nurse wheels into the room.

Although it is still morning, the sun pushes against my head like something hard as I walk to the parking lot. By the time I reach my car, I am perspiring. Summers in Tennessee seem hotter each year, even though it remains green, with the sound of cicadas rising up against the heat like carbonation. The insects are deep-throated in the country, congregating beneath my bedroom windows. I picture Dr. Robert, no doubt waiting on my screen porch, sitting in the white wicker rocker, listening for the echo of my car biting through the gravel.

For some reason — maybe it's the heat, I just don't know — I remember driving recklessly down that gray-gravel road after Royce's funeral. The car stirred up so much white dust, it wafted through the air for hours. Little Bobbie Ruth slept on the front seat; the ruffles on her dress vibrated as the wheels tunneled through the rocks. I parked the car in the shade and strode out to the tool shed, still wearing my widow-black dress.

Dr. Robert, who had left the funeral early, was sitting on the porch swing. He called out as I picked up the ax, but his voice was lost as I chopped into the cedar tree. It had grown into the mesh of my screen porch, blocking the view, depositing thousands of sharp brown needles on the gray wooden floor. The ax started the trees singing, the voice of cedarwood lifted straight up through dark-forest branches.

GARY D. WILSON

Up

from City Paper

nominated by Stephen Dixon

A n eye gazes back at her from the big mirror across the hall. Her eye. A slice of face too through the slit she's made between the doors. But mainly the eye. Staring. An empty hall.

She backs up to the fold-out stool next to the control panel and sits. She doesn't need to look or feel behind her to know where it is. The distance is as unconscious a part of her as breathing. She never thinks about it. She simply does it. Stands up, holds the door while people get on and off, sticks her head out to see that everyone has cleared, says "going up," or "down," whichever it happens to be, pulls her head back in, releases the door and sits until the next stop. Seven floors up, seven down. A round trip takes ten minutes, more or less, depending on traffic. In eight hours she makes forty-eight trips. She figured out once that she stands up and sits down 672 times a day, 250 days a year. And that times nearly twenty years on the job, and she doesn't need to turn around to see where she is.

Nearly twenty years.

It's been her life, the reason she's always gotten up,

same as a banker, a preacher, a doctor, whoever. The reason she's eaten, gotten dressed and walked out the door. God knows she has little else to show for it. No family, no friends to speak of, no real home — an apartment, yes, the same one she's rented since she started working here, filled with her things, yes, but still only an apartment. A place to sleep rather than to live in.

When she added it all up, she couldn't stand it. She knew then why a preacher suddenly runs off with a parishioner, a banker steals money from his own bank, a doctor starts selling drugs. She wants to say something inside you just snaps, but that's not quite true. Tears is more like it. A little hole at first. One in your pocket you can barely put the tip of your finger through. You know it's there and you should do something to fix it, but don't get around to it for one reason or another, and then suddenly one day it rips, gaping wide open, everything spilling out all over the place before you can stop it. "Go on, get out!" she was saying to the people on her elevator. "I mean it. Now! Get out! You! Yes, you. Everybody. That's right. Watch your step." Until the car was empty and the whole bunch of them stood in the hall, lined up and quiet, like a crowd waiting for a speech. So she gave one. Short and to the point, saying she was sorry but as of now she was shutting down her elevator. They'd just have to find some other way to get around. From the looks on their faces, you'd have thought she'd shot somebody. Finally a man laughed and glanced at the floor. Severals others did then too. Throats cleared, feet shuffled. Someone started to get back on, as if the joke were over. She held her arm across the doorway and said she was serious, no more rides. "But—" a woman said without finishing, as they all seemed to realize, everybody at once, that with her elevator down now too, like the automatic ones on either side of hers, there was no way up but the stairs or going clear over to B-wing. "Wait a minute!" a man shouted. "You can't just—" As they surged toward her, she stepped into the elevator and closed the doors. "Come on, open up!" A fist pounded. "Open up in there!" A rumble, like thunder. "You got no right, goddamnit! People have to be able to—"

There are voices now, from somewhere out of sight down the hall. One, she thinks Maxwell's, coming over a walkie-talkie, harsh and scratchy as an old phonograph record. The other low and indistinct, barely audible.

"What? She *what?*"

Mumble.

"Well get her the hell off."

Mumble, mumble.

"What do you mean you can't, Leonard? We have a hospital to run here, you know, not a baby-sitting service for nutskies. Do something!"

Silence.

"For Christ's sake, Leonard!" A pause, the voice then taking on a tone of resignation she could hear even over the walkie-talkie. "Oh, all right. Hang on, I'll be over as soon as I can."

It's about time, although she doesn't know exactly how long it's been, since she always depends on the clock at the end of the hall and now can't see it. Fifteen minutes? Twenty? An hour? She read once that if you put five people in a room one by one, without any way to measure time, and ask them to indicate by raising a hand when they think a minute has passed, you'll get five completely different guesses, and none of them even close to correct. Not that it makes that much difference. Except it *has* been long enough for a couple of people to come by and try to get on, and when the doors wouldn't open, leave without much of a fuss. Which surprised her, particularly after that first go round. In fact, it's been overall a lot quieter than she'd expected. Too quiet. Eerie. Like somebody's died. She shivers, wishing she'd gone to the bathroom first. But there really wasn't time, and how would it have looked anyway if she'd said,

"Excuse me, I'll be right back" in the middle of her speech or when that man was beating on the doors? It would have ruined everything. For starters, she wouldn't be the one in control now, the one who'd just forced Maxwell's hand. She isn't sure what she would have done if he'd decided not to come after all, because he's the one she has to see. Only she doesn't like being called a nutskie. She isn't any more than he is, or any of the rest of them. She did what she did because it had to be done. Which is simple enough for anybody to understand, if they care to in the first place. But they don't. And that's one of the things she's going to change when she has it to do over again. That and a lot else. Next time what she thinks, says, and does will mean something because she'll be somebody.

"Seen anything, Leonard?"

"Nope."

"Heard anything?"

"Nope."

"Know anything then?"

"Not much."

She's just able to catch them in the mirror. A full view of Maxwell, tall and lean in his khaki work uniform, bushy brows flicking like cats' tails, shoulders hunching, eyes roving from the hall to the walkie-talkie he carries in his left hand like a badge of authority. Half of Leonard next to him, which is plenty. Skinny, with stringy blond hair and an earring in his ear, she'd bet right now he wishes more than anything he could stick his finger in his nose.

"Well, I guess we better see what's going on," Maxwell says, starting toward the elevator.

The slit between the doors is perfect. It isn't big enough he can get his hand through, but they'll be able to talk without having to yell to each other. It's a trick only she can do, from having been there as long as she has. But then the elevator *is* hers, after all. She knows every square inch of it, inside and out. Every rivet, every nut and bolt, every wire, every screw. She knows every hum, every tick and rattle. The ones that should be there and the ones that shouldn't. Everything. It's all as familiar to her as the lines on a lover's face might be to another woman. And Maxwell understands that. It's the one thing about her he respects.

"That you in there, Woodson?" he asks.

"It's me."

"You alone?"

"Yes."

"That's good. Keeps it nice and simple. Just the way I like things."

"Me too."

"So, Woodson, I suppose you had something in mind when you, um, did this."

"Yes."

"Well I'd be real curious to know—"

"I want it back."

"Something missing?"

"Twenty years. Almost. The twenty years I been here."

"I see. And, uh, you say you want it back?"

"That's right."

"I'm not sure I—"

"You have it, don't you? Over there in your office somewhere in a file?"

"That's just paper, an employment record. It's not—"

"You figure it out then. It was mine and you took it. I want it back"

"I didn't take it. Nobody forced you."

"Then say I changed my mind. It's still mine and I want it."

"You can't give years back, Woodson. Time's not like bread."

"So everybody says."

"And for good reason."

"But that's a lie and you know it. You *can* give it back and I *can* use it over again, and I'm planning to do just that. I got it all figured out."

"That right?"

"Yes, sir, it is. What are you waiting for?"

"Just thinking, I guess, how to go about it."

"It's really not that hard"

He manages a quick smile. "Yeah, I suppose not. Let me see what I can do, okay? You sit tight right there until I get back now."

"I'm not going anywhere."

"Good. That's real good."

He edges away from the door, as if afraid to turn his back.

"What'd you find out?" Leonard asks. "What's she want anyway?"

"Her life."

"Huh?"

"Her life, Leonard. She wants her goddamn life back."

She may have dozed. Someone else is talking now.

"Miss Woodson? Hello. You in there?"

A face is pressed against the crack, trying to see in, like a dog looking down a rabbit hole. She could snap those doors together and pinch that nose right off, if she had a mind to.

"It's Dr. Blakely, Miss Woodson. I'd like to talk to you."

"Got nothing to say. No more than what I already told Maxwell. If you want to talk, talk to him."

"I already have."

"And?"

"He said you were upset."

"I'm not. I feel fine. And I'm going to feel even better pretty soon now."

"That's great. That's what I like to hear." He clears his throat. "Do you want to tell me about the trouble you're having with time?"

"Didn't know I was."

"Something about wanting it back?"

"That's not trouble, is it?"

"It might be if a certain person can't get it for you."

"He'd better."

"I'm not sure it's possible, Miss Woodson. After all, time's not—"

"Yeah I know, bread."

"What?"

"Bread."

"I see."

"No you don't. Everybody goes around saying I see, I see all the time and nobody does. If you saw, I wouldn't have to do this, would I?"

"Go on."

"I could just get it back and go on my way, couldn't I? But no. Everybody's acting like I'm nuts or something for even bringing it up. Well you tell me — what happens to it?"

"Time?"

"Yeah time. When you use it, where does it go?"

"I don't think it *goes* anywhere."

"Where is it then?"

"I'm not sure anybody knows. That's the whole problem."

"But it's probably still around?"

"I suppose so, in one form or another. That's what we—"

"Mine too?"

"I—I can't answer that."

"*Won't*, you mean?"

"Can't, I'm afraid."

"So am I. When I started looking around, I got real scared and I said to myself, you can't end it like this. You can't let this be all you have to show for your life. And I got to thinking I didn't need to. There was no reason I couldn't do it over. Fresh, right from the start, make it over exactly the way I wanted it. What's so crazy about that? People say all the time they wouldn't want it to live over again, and I say they're liars. I say they're the ones who're crazy. Give it to me and I'll show you. First off, I'll get an education. College now, not just high school. And maybe even beyond that. Maybe even medical school. Doctors are pretty well looked up to, aren't they? Except I know it takes a lot of work and time. But one thing I'll have starting over is time, all the time I need for whatever I want, huh? That's the beauty of it, isn't it? If more people realized that, they wouldn't be so unhappy. They wouldn't be so stodgy either. They'd be freer — you know, take more chances. And they wouldn't worry so much, looking back every day to see how much they've gotten done. So I'll be a doctor, maybe. Or a painter. I've always thought I'd be kind of good at that too. I have a good eye and a good sense of color. So a painter then. A doctor *and* a painter. Maybe an actress too, while I'm at it. Be nice to hear people applauding, wouldn't it, have roses all over the place, mobs of fans waiting at the door I leave by? I'll have to change my looks though, I know that. Been planning to anyway. I'll be thin. Not too thin. Just right. And pretty. You wanted to know, and I'm telling you. A face that's more striking the *second* time you look at it. A good smile too that has the eyes with it and not just the teeth and makes people smile right back, wins them over on the spot because it's so warm and friendly. And my daughter'll look just like me, the way mothers and daughters do on soap commercials. Her name'll be Grace. My son's name'll be Philip. He'll be handsome like his father. We'll have such a wonderful, close-knit family all our friends'll be jealous. And between what I make and my husband, we won't ever have to worry about money again. And I'll bring my parents back to life. And this time they'll be up and about and doing so much I'll never be able to keep track of them. And I'll have my sister love me again and laugh with me when we're together — which'll be as often as we can make it — about those silly, goofy things we did as kids. And everybody'll be happy, and they'll all look up to me as the one who made them that way. And I won't let them down either. I won't let anything ever be wrong with anything. Not for a long time to come. A long, long time."

His back as he walks off. The long white coat, shoulders hunched the way doctors do when they're deep in thought.

There's nothing left now but the wait. She'd say things are pretty much at a stand-off. Have been ever since the doctor left and told Maxwell and Leonard that she was completely out of her head and he doubted she would ever leave the elevator on her own.

They asked anyway, and when she said her conditions hadn't changed, they brought in a wrecking bar and tried to pry the doors open. But she was able to get the slit closed before they could, and she heard a lot of swearing, Maxwell saying he wished he'd never left the navy where they at least knew what to do with people like her. She was a little disappointed they didn't have any more imagination than a wrecking bar. She'd expected better, and their next attempt was — somewhat — but still not great. They decided to override her controls from the outside. But with a well-placed nail file and a shower of sparks, that idea came to a quick end too.

It's dark now that the power's off. Totally dark. But she can hear them — someone — coming down for her. It's the only thing they had left, short of ripping the elevator apart, which Maxwell would never do because it would look too much like he was admitting defeat.

The shaft goes seven floors straight up to a bright blue square at the end, weak yellow lights showing the way. She's only ever seen it, not climbed it. She'd be terrified to do that.

The sounds are coming closer now, tools chinking, boots scuffing the metal rungs. A short jump to the top of the elevator. Footsteps. A clank, the screech of hinges as the trap door opens, a flashlight poking in, casting about.

"Boo!" she says.

The light nearly drops.

"You're a real brave one, aren't you, Leonard?"

The beam down, up, holding on her face like a spotlight.

"It's okay, I won't bite."

He reaches in, hands her a leather harness. "Put this on."

"Well now, this is classy," she says, holding it up to herself like a gown.

"Just put it on."

She straps herself in, feels the lift as Leonard yanks on the rope and yells up to Maxwell. Her feet leave the floor. She settles. An elegant rise, like at the end of one of those forties movies where the star, decked out in feathers and lace, soars on a slow swell of music high over the heads of her admirers.

Clear of the trap door, she leans back, lifting a leg, a show queen in her own right now. A show stopper. Past one light, two, rungs like dashes between, Maxwell's voice telling Leonard, who's not far below, climbing the ladder behind her, how she reminds him of the heifers they used to hoist from the holds of ships when he worked at the docks, Leonard laughing.

But she isn't listening and hardly even notices the tiny black holes in the wall of the shaft with all kinds of creepy-crawly things inside, concentrating instead on the bright blue square above her and the rope leading straight up to it, and for all she knows, beyond.

CONTRIBUTORS' NOTES

A native of Toronto, Ontario, **Glen Allen** worked in the construction trades in various parts of the U.S. and Canada before becoming a newspaper reporter, magazine writer, and radio producer. He has been a correspondent in Chile and other parts of South America and has also taught English in southern China. He is currently the correspondent in Atlantic Canada for *Maclean's,* a weekly newsmagazine.

Tom Bailey, twenty-eight, was born in his mother's hometown of Indianola, Mississippi, and grew up trailing his father — a Marine Corps aviator — throughout the South. He is a graduate of Marshall University and the University of Iowa Writers' Workshop. He currently lives in New York and is working toward the completion of a novel that will also serve as the creative dissertation for his PhD at SUNY-Binghamton.

Louis Berney, a native of Oklahoma, is pursuing an MFA degree in English at the University of Massachusetts at Amherst. His fiction has appeared in *The New Yorker* and *New England Review and Bread Loaf Quarterly.* He is currently at work on a collection of stories, to be published by Ticknor and Fields in 1991.

Will Evans recently finished an MFA at Cornell and is currently a lecturer there. He has published stories in *Yankee* and the *New England Review and Bread Loaf Quarterly,* and his work has been featured in *The Best of Yankee Magazine* and *New Fiction from New England.* A collection of his stories won the Andrews Award at Cornell, and in 1987 he won the *Yankee* Prize for Fiction. He grew up in Haddonfield, New Jersey.

Elizabeth Graver grew up in a small town in western Massachusetts and attended Wesleyan University in Connecticut. After college she worked as a journalist and taught English to high-school students in France. She is currently completing her MFA in fiction at Washington University in St. Louis. "Square Dance" is her first published story. Other stories or essays have appeared or are forthcoming in *River Styx, Southern Review, Southwest Review, Stanford Humanities Review,* and *Symposium.*

Terry Griggs was born in Little Current, Manitoulin Island, and now lives in London, Ontario. Her stories have appeared in *The Malahat Review, Room of One's Own, The Canadian Forum, The New Quarterly, The New Press Anthology: Best Canadian Short Fiction #1,* and *The Macmillan Anthology.*

CONTRIBUTORS' NOTES

A collection of her stories will be published by The Porcupine's Quill in 1990.

A resident of Los Angeles, **Daniel Hayes** has recently completed a collection of stories, some of which have appeared or are forthcoming in *Massachusetts Review, The Quarterly, The Malahat Review, Epoch, Western Humanities Review,* and *Ambit.*

Born and educated in Holland, with a concentration on languages, **Paula Horowitz** is the mother of three children. In addition to writing short stories, she is interested in photography, backpacking, and mountaineering, which she has done, with her sons, in India, Nepal, South America, and Europe. When she's not traveling, she lives in Amherst, Massachusetts.

Ivor S. Irwin is a native of Manchester, England. He has worked as an assembly-man, clothing salesman, forklift driver, copywriter, and waiter in England, Canada, and the U.S. He received a BA in film from Columbia College, Chicago, and an MFA from the writing program at Penn State. His work has appeared in the *Review of Contemporary Fiction, The Long Story, Indiana Review, Ripples, Stuffed Pike, Hair Trigger,* and other magazines. He currently teaches at Roosevelt University in Chicago.

Eugene Kraft has been published in *Prairie Schooner, Cottonwood,* and *English Literature in Transition,* as well as in *New Mexico Humanities Review.* He lives in Washington, DC, and teaches at Montgomery College in Montgomery, Maryland.

Wally Lamb writes and teaches in Connecticut. He is currently completing his first novel, *Whales.*

Scott Lasser was born in Detroit and educated at Dartmouth College and the University of Michigan. His fiction has appeared or is forthcoming in *Missouri Review, Hawaii Review,* the *Detroit News,* and *Wind.* He lives in Milan, Michigan.

One of **Karen Latuchie**'s stories has been nominated for the 1990 Pushcart Prize. Her work has appeared in the *Paris Review* and *Southwest Review.* She lives and works in New York City, where she is a member of The Writer's Room.

Born in Kenosha, Wisconsin, the setting of his story, **Joseph W. Mockus** has also lived in Chicago and Washington, DC. He has worked as an editor for the National Safety Council and as a writer for Democratic political campaigns. He is a journalism graduate of Marquette University.

Contributors' Notes

A fiction writer and critic, **Lance Olsen** has published numerous short stories in journals such as *Bomb, Mississippi Review,* and *Cimarron Review.* He is also the author of two critical books on postmodern fiction. His first novel, *Live from Earth,* will be published in the fall of 1990 by Available Press. He teaches writing and contemporary fiction at the University of Idaho.

Sharon Sakson is an award-winning fiction writer, newspaper reporter, and television news producer. She gathered the background information for "The Girl from the Red Cross" while working in Beirut for ABC News in 1982. She is currently at work on a collection of short stories about Beirut and a novel set in Paris and Poland during the start of the Solidarity Movement in 1980. She is the author of *Miami 1990,* a guide to that city.

A resident of Calgary, Alberta, **Rose Scollard** is a founding member of Maenad Productions, a theatre devoted to the encouragement of the feminine imagination. Her work has been produced in Calgary, Edmonton, Vancouver, Montreal, and Seattle. She has also written many scripts for CBC radio. Her most recent play is *Firebird,* an adventure story about a mythical creature with creative and regenerative power.

Philip Simmons received an MFA from Washington University in St. Louis, a PhD in English literature from the University of Michigan, and is currently teaching at Lake Forest College in Lake Forest, Illinois.

A resident of Lebanon, Tennessee, **Michael Lee West** is a registered nurse, as well as a poet and fiction writer whose work has appeared in numerous magazines, including *Wind, Southern, First for Women,* and *Kennesaw Review.* Her first novel, *Crazy Ladies,* will be published by Longstreet Press in the fall of 1990.

Gary D. Wilson, a native of Kansas, holds an MA in English from Wichita State University and an MFA in fiction writing from Bowling Green State University in Ohio. He has taught at several colleges and universities, and spent two years as a high-school English teacher in Swaziland, Africa. He now lives in Baltimore and teaches at the Johns Hopkins University School of Continuing Studies. His work has appeared in numerous magazines, including *Kansas Quarterly, Witness, Wind,* and *Nimrod.*

APPENDIX

The magazines listed below participated in *Street Songs 1* by providing complimentary subscriptions. Any magazine may have its fiction considered for *Street Songs 2* by sending complimentary copies of its 1990 issues to the editor at Longstreet Press, 2150 Newmarket Parkway, Suite 102, Marietta, GA 30067.

Agni Review
Boston University
236 Bay State Road
Boston, MA 02215

Alfred Hitchcock's Mystery Magazine
380 Lexington Avenue
New York, NY 10017

American Voice
332 West Broadway
Suite 1215
Louisville, KY 40202

Beloit Fiction Journal
Box 11
Beloit College
Beloit, WI 53511

Black Mountain Review
Lorein House
P.O. Box 1112
Black Mountain, NC 28711

Black Warrior Review
P.O. Box 2936
Tuscaloosa, AL 35486-2936

The Capilano Review
2055 Purcell Way
North Vancouver, BC
Canada V7J 3H5

Carolina Quarterly
Greenlaw Hall #3520
University of North Carolina
Chapel Hill, NC 27599

Chariton Review
Northeast Missouri State University
Kirksville, MO 63501

City Lights Review
261 Columbus Avenue
San Francisco, CA 94133

Concho River Review
% English Department
Angelo State University
San Angelo, TX 76909

Confrontation
Department of English
Long Island University
Brookville, NY 11548

Crosscurrents
2200 Glastonbury Road
Westlake Village, CA 91361

Event
Douglas College
P.O. Box 2503
New Westminster, BC
Canada V3L 5B2

Fantasy & Science Fiction
Box 56
Cornwall, CT 06753

Farmer's Market
P.O. Box 1272
Galesburg, IL 61402

The Fiddlehead
P.O. Box 4400
Fredericton, NB
Canada E3P 5A3

Folio
Department of Literature
The American University
Washington, DC 20016

The Gamut
1216 Rhodes Tower
Cleveland State University
Euclid Avenue at East 24th Street
Cleveland, OH 44115

Gargoyle
Paycock Press
P.O. Box 30906
Bethesda, MD 20824

Georgia Review
University of Georgia
Athens, GA 30605

Grain
Box 1154
Regina, SK
Canada S4P 3B4

Great River Review
211 West Seventh Street
Winona, MN 55987

Green Mountains Review
Box A58
Johnson State College
Johnson, VT 05656

Greensboro Review
Department of English
University of North Carolina-Greensboro
Greensboro, NC 27412

Helicon Nine
P.O. Box 22412
Kansas City, MO 64113

Hibiscus
P.O. Box 22248
Sacramento, CA 95822

High Plains Literary Review
180 Adams Street
Suite 250
Denver, CO 80206

Hudson Review
684 Park Avenue
New York, NY 10021

Iowa Review
308 EPB
The University of Iowa
Iowa City, IA 52242

Jam To-day
372 Dunstable Road
Tyngsboro, MA 01879

Kennesaw Review
Department of English
Kennesaw State College
P.O. Box 444
Marietta, GA 30061

Malahat Review
P.O. Box 1700
Victoria, BC
Canada V8W 2Y2

Massachusetts Review
Memorial Hall
University of Massachusetts
Amherst, MA 01003

McCall's
230 Park Avenue
New York, NY 10169

Mikrokosmos
Box 14
Wichita State University
Wichita, KS 67208

Mildred
P.O. Box 9252
Schenectady, NY 12309

Missouri Review
Department of English
107 Tate Hall
University of Missouri
Columbia, MO 65211

MSS / New Myths
SUNY-Binghamton
Binghamton, NY 13901

New England Review and Bread Loaf Quarter
Middlebury College
Middlebury, VT 05733

New Mexico Humanities Review
Humanities Department
New Mexico Tech
Socorro, NM 87801

the new renaissance
9 Heath Road
Arlington, MA 02174

APPENDIX

Nimrod
Arts and Humanities Council of Tulsa
2210 South Main Street
Tulsa, OK 74114

North Atlantic Review
15 Arbutus Lane
Stony Brook, NY 11790-1408

Northwest Review
369 PLC
University of Oregon
Eugene, OR 97403

The Ohio Review
Ellis Hall
Ohio University
Athens, OH 45701-2979

Omni
1965 Broadway
New York, NY 10023-5965

Other Voices
820 Ridge Road
Highland Park, IL 60035

Paris Review
541 East 72nd Street
New York, NY 10021

Passages North
William Bonifas Art Center
700 First Avenue
Escanaba, MI 49829

Pennsylvania Review
English Department
University of Pittsburgh
526 CL
Pittsburgh, PA 15260

Plainswoman
P.O. Box 8027
Grand Forks, ND 58202

Playboy
747 Third Avenue
New York, NY 10017

Ploughshares
Box 529
Cambridge, MA 02139

Prairie Schooner
201 Andrews Hall
University of Nebraska
Lincoln, NE 68588-0334

Puerto Del Sol
Box 3E
New Mexico State University
Las Cruces, NM 88003

Quarry
P.O. Box 1061
Kingston, ON
Canada K71 4Y5
Queen's Quarterly
Queen's University
Kingston, ON
Canada K7L 3N6

RE:AL
Department of Philosophy and English
P.O. Box 13007, SFA Station
Stephen F. Austin State University
Nacogdoches, TX 75962-3007

Review
Department of English
University of Windsor
Windsor, ON
Canada N9B 3P4

Room of One's Own
P.O. Box 46160
Station G
Vancouver, BC
Canada V6R 4G5

Seventeen
850 Third Avenue
New York, NY 10022

Shenandoah
Box 722
Lexington, VA 24450

Sonora Review
Department of English
University of Arizona
Tucson, AZ 85721

South Carolina Review
Department of English
Strode Tower
Clemson University
Clemson, SC 29634-1503

South Dakota Review
Box 111
University Exchange
Vermillion, SD 57069

Southern Review
43 Allen Hall
Louisiana State University
Baton Rouge, LA 70803

Sou'Wester
Department of English Language
    and Literature
Southern Illinois Unviersity
Edwardsville, IL 62026-1438

Stories
14 Beacon Street
Boston, MA 02108

Story
F&W Publications
1507 Dana Avenue
Cincinnati, OH 45207

Story Quarterly
P.O. Box 1416
Northbrook, IL 60065

Webster Review
Webster University
470 East Lockwood
Webster Groves, MO 63119

West Branch
Department of English
Bucknell University
Lewisburg, PA 17837

West Coast Review
Department of English
Simon Fraser University
Burnaby, BC
Canada V5A 1S6

Western Humanities Review
University of Utah
Salt Lake City, UT 84112

William and Mary Review
Campus Center
College of William and Mary
Williamsburg, VA 23185

Wind
Route 1, Box 809K
Pikeville, KY 41501

Witness
31000 Northwestern Highway
Suite 200
Farmington Hills, MI 48018

Yankee
Main Street
Dublin, NH 03444